A TEAM OF ONE

AN UNSANCTIONED ASSET THRILLER

BRAD LEE

1

DIRECT ACTION

The whole op felt wrong from the start.

Alex's night vision goggles made the door—and everything else in his vision—appear green, but after fifteen years of almost nightly use, he barely noticed. He stood next to the entrance of the house made of hardened mud and straw. The wooden door looked old and warped from the sun. It didn't look strong enough for them to worry about blowing. A powerful kick would do it.

He shook his head slowly in resigned annoyance. No way would the man they were to capture or kill be here. Why would he hide in such a small town in this hot, poor country?

Rule number one: the intelligence is always wrong.

Not that it mattered. They were sent in, so they would get the job done. If he was here, they would find him.

It's what they did.

Lincoln—aka "Link"—silently moved his bulk in front of the door, close to the dented round knob. The equipment vest filled with extra mags and everything else he needed for the night made him look even bigger. Next to him, Alex's six-foot muscular frame seemed puny.

Ron and Hector stayed lined up behind Alex—call sign "Axe," covering the rooftops of the buildings across the street.

Over the past years, they'd done countless operations like this. Creep into an enemy area, so smooth and silent even the sleeping dogs didn't stir. Knock down or blow the door, clear the rooms, and kill those who kept them from completing their mission.

Just another day at the office.

Link looked at Axe. Despite the NVGs, they knew what the other was thinking.

This is a complete bust—or an ambush. Or both.

The brass had a hard-on for the guy a young analyst had dubbed "the Boomer"—a play on "boom," the sound his creations made when they exploded, and his supposed age. Rumors swirled, but the only things known for sure about the guy were that he'd been around for years, was highly educated, and a maestro with bomb making—he was the damn Michelangelo of explosives.

Even worse: he excelled at teaching others the art of blowing shit up.

His devices, and the ones made by his students, were killing people in regional conflicts all over the world. It was long past time for him to die.

The analysts argued about his origins: he was European. Or Middle Eastern. Or an American Green Beret gone rogue. The only description they could agree on came from an informant: fit, "older," and his eyes were spellbinding. "They see right through you. They pierce your soul."

Basically, the intel nerds knew just enough to track rumors and send warriors on wild goose chases after the guy.

Dangerous wild goose chases.

Now it was their turn to be tasked with finding him. The team had joked about the intel geeks' apparent plan: for them to gaze deeply into the eyes of everyone in the village until they found their guy. Whether those people were shooting at them or not.

Brilliant.

So here they were, in a poor village of narrow, sun-baked dirt roads separating rows of one-story buildings. Most were connected on each side. Some joined to form small clumps of buildings. The town sprawled, with seemingly no plan where new buildings had been constructed. It looked random. Want a home? Pick a bare piece of dirt and build there—no matter if it's in the middle of a street or up against the neighbor's wall.

The rotten smell of garbage mingled with the stench of open sewers. But every house had a satellite dish.

Axe shifted his weight, ready to enter first as soon as the door opened. Hector's hand grabbed his shoulder, the signal everyone was ready to go.

Link considered the door before he glanced at Axe.

Again, they were on the same wavelength.

I bet it's unlocked.

They had ceased marveling at how often bad guys didn't bother to secure their doors. Of course, bad guys never feared the locals. But if you messed with the USA, you'd better at least lock the door.

Axe nodded and took a half step forward, his M4 up and ready.

Behind him, Hector—"Thor"—and Ron followed silently. It was time.

Link's gloved hand grasped the knob and tested it. It turned easily and, thankfully, with no noise. Link held his shotgun, chambered with a breaching round, ready in one hand. It would make quick work of any deadbolt, hinges, or bar that might prevent the door from opening.

Axe held up his fingers, counting down. 3. 2. 1.

Link turned the knob fully and pushed the door. He moved out of the way as it swung open, allowing Axe to enter the large room.

One quick glance cleared behind the door and he turned to cover the left side of the room, knowing Hector would follow and clear right.

The green glow of the NVGs picked up the man in the corner, sitting on the floor, AK-47 across his knees. Awake, on watch... but not alert enough. This was why they attacked at zero-dark-thirty. Why they slept all day: to be wide awake all night. Ready to fight.

The enemy? Not so much.

The man's eyes widened in surprise and he tried to point the AK at Axe.

Wrong move. Axe shot him in the chest twice, followed by another between the eyes, the back of his head splattering against the wall, black in the view of the goggles. He toppled sideways, his dead weight knocking over a low, flimsy table draped with fabric.

As Axe's eyes looked for another target, he noted the doorway along the left wall, opening into another room. His brain also automatically registered the dark hole in the wall next to the dead guy that had been hidden by the table.

Another man stepped into the doorway to his left, but Axe was ready. His finger squeezed the trigger instinctively at the threat, relying on thousands of hours of training and experience to aim and shoot. He was an elite warrior, the best the USA could produce.

Which made the shock of the bullet's impact on his chest more of a surprise. The bastard had been faster than him.

The pain threatened to distract him.

He didn't let it. He focused his mind, using the pain to his advantage.

It wasn't the first time he'd been shot, after all.

He fired a second time, milliseconds after his first shot. Both bullets hit his enemy, a perfectly tight grouping at the man's heart.

Step one: push them back.

He fired again, putting a third bullet into the man, blowing off his face even as the lifeless body fell backwards.

Step two: a shot to the head in case the target is wearing body armor, like the plate that had just saved Axe's own life.

He took one step towards the open doorway, prepared to step over the dead combatant and clear the next room, before he stopped cold.

The hole in the wall.

He subconsciously understood the situation, his gut telling him what to do before his brain had processed the information.

He glanced at the hole again, trying to both cover the doorway and gather the intel his mind demanded. His sense of danger, honed to a fine edge over the past years, screamed at him.

"Trap," he announced, his voice not betraying the fear that seized his heart. His mind had noted the wire running along the floor to other parts of the room. It had figured out the hole was filled with explosives. The whole room was rigged to blow.

Still, one of the many mantras learned over the years came to his mind: *Calm is contagious.*

"Out. Now."

He stepped backwards, gun still on the open doorway.

"Moving," Hector called from behind him.

"Moving," Ron echoed from near the door.

"Covering," Link added from outside, heard more through the radio in Alex's ear than over the quiet night.

"Bombs," Axe added as he continued backwards. "Get away from this house."

They'd been inside five seconds and killed two enemy.

Axe cleared the door and hurried to the side, transitioning from covering the room to focusing on the dusty street and sleeping village.

Hector would have moved to the opposite side of the doorway and up the street. He saw Link across the street and several steps down the block, covering the rooftops above their heads.

Only Ron remained in front of the house, though across the street, moving away while covering the roof above Hector's head.

It was almost far enough.

The house exploded, bits of mud and rock flying outward. Dust flew up, hanging in the still air, clouding the area.

Then the firing started.

The staccato sound of the AK-47s came first, followed immediately by the noise of Link's M4, his shotgun shouldered for the moment.

Axe had no targets, though he shot the man who fell off the roof above him and landed with a splat at his feet, in case Link's bullets hadn't done the trick.

He heard Hector shooting behind him, then had his own targets on the roof of the houses above Link's head.

Tap, tap. Tap, tap. His bullets hit home, dropping the two enemy.

"We need to move. West. Go." Axe fired as the enemy popped above the roof line like whack-a-moles.

"Moving," Hector added in his calm voice, tinted with a slight Hispanic accent.

Link provided cover fire.

With the night vision goggles, they had the advantage. Cover and move. Fire while your buddies moved, then move while they covered you.

They would advance up the road and link up with the other four SEALS, waiting in a defensive position outside the town. As team lead, Ron would call them as he moved under Link and Axe's covering fire. He'd decide whether to hole up and wait for their reinforcement or continue to assault to the rendezvous.

"I'm down." Ron's voice was tight, trying to hold in the pain. "My legs got hit with shrapnel."

Damn, Axe thought. *That's not good.*

"I can't walk."

"I got him," Axe said. He turned and ran the few steps to Ron, propped against the wall, already bandaging his lower legs. "How bad?"

"Still in the fight, but I'm not walking out. You're going to have to carry me."

"Good thing I've been working out, I guess." He eyed the shredded legs in the NVGs. It looked bad—but survivable, if they could get him to a hospital soon.

They looked at each other in the dark as Hector and Link shot bad guys around them. The pace of fire picked up. It had been a trap, but they'd beaten the two guys who must have volunteered to martyr themselves by staying in the house rigged to blow... or had believed they could take out the SEALS without resorting to the explosives.

"Have Echo One meet us halfway?"

The gunfire lessened.

Ron nodded. "I'll call it in. We'll assault west as long as we can. Hole up if necessary. But we still have the advantage—"

Both closed their eyes in pain as the world lit up around them, as if the sun suddenly rose hours early.

"Flare!" Hector said, as the AK fire started up, twice as much as before.

The second part of the enemy's trap.

The flare drifted downward, bathing the town in light, and destroying the tremendous advantage provided by the night vision goggles.

"I'm hit." Link's rate of fire increased as he spoke. "Only my side. Missed anything important."

"Echo One, Echo Two, over?" Ron's voice was all business on the radio.

"Go Echo Two."

"In contact. I'm down, both legs. One other wounded. Heading to you. Can you advance and cover?"

Alex listened while kneeling next to Ron, protecting him as he added his gun to the escalating fight, his useless NVGs flipped up.

Enemy fighters flooded the street and rooftops.

"Negative. We're pinned down. They knew we were coming."

"No shit."

Axe fired at a tango on the roof, killing him. They might have a small window before more enemy got near them. He leaned close to his team lead. "Ronbo, hold on." Ron had hated the parody of the movie warrior's name at first, then grew to love it. "We've got to move." Axe let his weapon dangle on its sling as he crouched over the wounded man, grabbed him by the straps on his equipment harness, and heaved him over his shoulders with a grunt. He had to weigh upwards of 250 pounds with his gear.

Axe pushed himself up, staggering under the weight, then focused on a spot in front of him and breathed.

The only easy day was yesterday.

He grabbed his weapon, changed magazines again while noting his remaining ammo supply, and started putting one foot in front of the other. "Moving, plus one," he called out to Link and Hector. "Let's get the hell out of here."

The door to his right opened a crack and the muzzle of a rifle poked out. Axe fired and heard screaming—which halted after he fired two more bullets.

Ron held on with one hand while he worked his radio. "Air support?"

"They're working on it. Sudden cold feet from the host nation. We're on our own while they work it out," replied Eric—Echo One— who led the mission.

"Head west. We're on our own for now," Ron called.

Hector covered them while Axe advanced with Ron, then Axe covered Hector as he leapfrogged their position.

The hours of training paid off.

The weight lifting. The cardio. The thousands of dollars in ammo expended at the range.

The communication. The tactics.

The trust.

They were killing machines.

The tiny village overflowed with fighters. How had the intel nerds missed the massing of a huge force? They must have come from hundreds of miles around.

Communicate. Move. Shoot. Repeat. Down the road, around corners. Always working west towards the other team and the extraction point. Taking enough time to be safe, but moving as quickly as possible.

The night stretched on and on.

They left countless bodies in their wake.

"That was my last mag," Axe announced, much more calmly than he felt as he pulled his pistol. His legs trembled. He'd already gone through his ammo, plus all of Ron's.

"Me too," Thor said.

The sound of Link's pistol joined theirs a few seconds later.

They were near the outskirts of the village. Only about a few hundred yards to go… but almost out of ammunition.

They were in trouble.

A small alley appeared ahead, a narrow path between two buildings. They ducked into the space, so tight their shoulders touched both sides.

The firing died to the occasional potshot at the alley's opening while the enemy regrouped and advanced. They had taken a lot of losses, which might make at least a few hold back from charging forward to die like their friends had.

Hector stood near the street, shooting anything that moved, conserving ammo while keeping the enemy at bay.

Axe checked on Ron. He looked horrible. In pain and fading. He had just enough energy to check in with the other team. "Echo One, sitrep?"

"Holding our own. We're pinned down and running low on ammo. But we've killed a shit-ton of bad guys. There can't be all that many left, but there's enough to hold us here. You?"

"We're near the edge of the village. Down to pistols only."

"No go on the air support. Doesn't look good. At this point we're praying for an evac bird, but they're not even sure they can get that. Politics," Eric spat, his voice laced with disgust.

Ron slumped back, his eyes closed.

Axe looked at his brothers as the enemy's latest flare sank lower. "Anyone want to quit?"

He knew the answer. They'd rather die. Which, he had to admit, might happen soon.

"Still in the fight," Link said, checking the bloody bandage he'd slapped on the wound at his side. Ron nodded, his eyes still closed. Hector kept shooting bad guys.

"Okay, new plan. Thor, you and Link are going to carry Ron together. That should make it possible to run, or at least speed walk."

"And you?"

"I'm going to kill everyone."

Link barked a laugh at the joke, then saw Axe's face. "You're serious."

"You get close to Echo One, quietly. It's not that far. Stash Ron somewhere safe and attack the enemy near them from the rear. I'll be right behind you." Even as he said it, he understood the odds of him making it out were slim.

The latest flare sank below the edge of a building. The light faded. Time to hunt.

Axe flipped his NVGs down. The flares had come less frequently, so they hoped the enemy was running low, conserving them by sending each up later and later after the previous one. He'd have a minute or two of darkness.

"Give me a minute to clear a path and draw fire."

"Good luck, brother," Link said with a fist bump. "Don't fall behind or I'll have to come back for you."

"I'm not giving up. I'm getting out of this, too." The odds might be bad, but he'd never, ever give up.

Hector stepped into the street as the last light of the flare vanished, giving Axe space to get by in the close confines of the alley, then moved back to help Link with Ron.

With the advantage of the night vision goggles, Axe ran toward a cross street a hundred meters back in the direction they'd come.

He ignored the occasional shots directed at the alleyway. They were shooting blind. With any luck, the enemy's night vision hadn't returned yet, and he was invisible.

His legs ached from carrying Ron. It felt like he was running through mud, but once again his training paid off. The ability to focus and fight through the tiredness led him to a side street in the area where he guessed they had launched the flares.

He scanned the area and saw three men near the edge of a roof, arguing.

That's your last flare, isn't it, you assholes? You're trying to decide whether you should wait, or fire it now.

He accelerated straight for the building, holstering his pistol.

I hope this works.

He vaulted onto the hood of an ancient, beat-up car, stepped onto its roof, then threw himself forward and up, his hands grabbing for the edge of the building.

His fingers grasped at air and he thought he had misjudged the distance. Then his hands caught the edge of the roof and his body thudded against the wall.

The men above him fell silent.

With shaking arms, Axe pulled himself upwards, legs scrambling for purchase as he mantled onto the roof, like a swimmer emerging from the pool.

In a smooth motion, he pulled his knife from its upside down scabbard on his vest. The three men stared at him, still unable to see well in the dark. He stabbed the man nearest him, who held the flare. The knife slid into the stomach, under the rib cage, and up, piercing the heart.

A firm pull backwards freed the knife in time to thrust at the next man's throat, stabbing him in the larynx.

The last man ran, trying to flee from the demon in the dark. He tripped at the edge of the roof and fell. The thud of his head hitting the car was easy to hear over the sound of the sporadic gunfire a few blocks away.

Axe picked up the flare and stashed it in his leg pocket. He calmly picked up the nearest man's AK-47s and stripped the ammo from both the dead men. Then he jogged to the edge of the building and lowered himself down to the roof of the car, avoiding the dead fighter with blood oozing from his head.

When in doubt, sew confusion.

"Flares taken care of," he sent over the radio as he advanced down back streets to the edge of the village. "You guys ready? I'm going to create a diversion."

"Ready, but Ron's not doing so good."

"Copy. Give me a few more seconds. I'll tell you when."

He worked his way down a few small side roads. He climbed onto another beat-up car and used it to pull himself onto the roof of a building. Spread out on the roof, he saw about a dozen enemy, some resting with their backs to the wall around the edge roof facing the street, others on watch, peering over. A few took shots at the alleyway where Hector, Ron, and Link were pinned down. He'd been lucky to get out of the safety of their small alley when he had. The bad guys' night vision had partly returned, but not as well as his with the NVGs.

He looked down to the street as he heard many feet running a few blocks away. A group of fighters jogged up the road.

Axe guessed their plan: they would use the covering fire of the men on the roof to get to the alley.

His brothers were a minute from certain death.

He turned back to see a man on the roof look his way.

How well could he see in the moonless night?

He whispered one of the words he'd learned in his language: "Help!" He gestured for the man to come to him, wondering if the distinctive outline of his helmet and goggles would give him away. But it was so dark the enemy either couldn't tell, or felt reassured by hearing his own language. Stooped low, he came to Axe.

Axe stabbed him in the throat and caught him as he collapsed.

Axe staggered towards the next group of men, three of them, whispering, "Help! Help!" He kept his head down to hopefully hide the distinct silhouette of his helmet and NVGs.

He gently passed the dying man to the closest two, slit the last one's throat, then stabbed the first two before either could raise an alarm.

The noise of the bodies as they hit the ground, however, attracted attention.

No more stealth.

He aimed at the nearest group of fighters and fired the AK. They dropped, and he continued killing the enemy lining the roof. He felt no qualms about shooting many of them in the back.

With a glance over the edge, he checked the position of the assault group running up the road, smiled, and got to work.

Surprise, assholes. Axe hefted the bloody body of the nearest dead enemy and took aim as the group of fighters raced along the road under him. He timed it perfectly, dropping the dead guy onto the head of the man in front of the group, who tumbled to the ground with a cry of surprise and pain.

The rest stopped abruptly, trying to figure out the situation, two of them comically running into the backs of the fighters in front of them.

They all died as Axe shot them from above, leaning over the edge of the roof and hosing them with AK fire.

"Go now," he called over the radio as he ducked, taking fire from the enemy on the roofs across the street, who finally figured out they had an enemy in their midst.

Axe moved, popped up to shoot—and kill—before dropping and moving to a new firing position.

Repeat. Grab ammo from the dead enemy. Fire.

"We're at the hill," Axe heard over the radio. On the way in, they'd used a mound of dirt and trash on the outskirts of the village for one last observation before the final approach.

"Copy. Keep moving. I think you made it without them noticing."

"Come to us. We'll cover."

A valid plan. Usually. "How's Ronbo?"

A long pause from Link. "Not good."

"Keep moving. I'm good. We've killed so many I think they're having second thoughts."

"Can't leave you behind," Link argued.

"So don't leave. Keep moving. Just 'cause I'm behind you doesn't mean I'm staying behind! Go."

"Moving," came the terse reply.

The fight seemed to go out of the remaining enemy on the roof across the street. But it could merely be a lull while they regrouped or tried to flank him. Could there also be more fighters massing on a nearby street, planning an assault on his roof? Or worse—going after the team?

All warfare is based on deception.

Axe crawled to the nearest dead guy and pocketed his ammo. Then he hooked one arm around the fighter, holding the body in front of him, his right arm pointing the AK along the dead guy's side.

He prepared himself for the lift. There was a reason it was called dead weight.

Axe pushed, his exhausted legs straining, and raised the man up with him. He stood, aimed at the far roof, and fired.

Return fire immediately slammed into the man's body.

Axe cried out in exaggerated pain and pushed the body forward over the edge of the roof, ducking below cover before the dead man fell.

The rate of gunfire increased as the fighters emptied their clips into the body laying in the dirt of the street.

Suckers. Axe low crawled away, leaving behind the cries of victory from the fooled enemy.

Off the roof. Down an alley. In the darkness, he moved like a shadow across the open ground at the edge of town.

Slow is smooth. Smooth is fast.

He caught up to where he thought the guys would be.

"Friendly approaching from behind."

Axe got the acknowledgment from Link, then approached the group. They were a short distance from Echo One, concealed behind a pile of rocks. Even in the green glow of the night vision, Ronbo looked bad.

"Echo One is pinned down. Not by many, but enough. Evac is on the way. But we're going to die getting Ron on the bird if we don't neutralize those guys near Echo One."

"Good thing I brought you presents."

He handed an AK and ammo to both Link and Hector.

"Aw man, we didn't get you anything, sorry." Hector didn't talk much, but when he did, he could be pretty funny.

"Best guess to the enemy positions?"

Link drew a quick diagram of the situation in the dirt.

They worked out a plan. "Tell Echo One to aim high. And don't let the bird leave without me."

"Not a chance."

Once again, attacking from the rear proved successful. Axe killed the first two with his knife simply by crawling up behind them and slitting their throats as they focused their attention on shooting at Echo One's position.

The second group was well situated and impossible to approach stealthily. He shot them in the head, a part of his brain noting the aim of the stolen weapon was off a touch to the right.

As soon as he fired, he heard two other AKs. Link and Hector each handling their targets.

The night was quiet except for the *beat beat beat* of the helicopter as he worked his way back to the team.

Minutes later, safe in the bird, he felt where the enemy had shot him. His chest hurt, but it wasn't serious. The armor plate had caught the bullet.

Good aim. Well trained. He shot first. He was faster than me.

Axe slumped against the wall of the helicopter, fighting exhaustion. Tough night.

The corpsman working on Ron gave him a thumbs up and a nod. "He'll be OK," he yelled over the noise of the wind and rotors.

Link and Thor caught Axe's eye, giving him a nod and sharing everything with a glance. Their gratitude. Their respect. He shared a tired nod back. All part of the job. And they'd saved his ass plenty of times before.

It's what they did.

2

THE EXIT

The gym at the base only had free weights, but they didn't need fancy machines.

After debriefing the op, being reassured Ron would be fine, and seeing Link fixed up, Axe cleaned his weapons and took care of his equipment. Then he showered, ate, and finally slept.

When he woke, he hit the gym.

Axe strained under the weights, squatting down, then pushing up. Again and again. Who cared that less than twelve hours earlier he'd carried Ron around the village, jumped onto roofs, and walked miles? Strength mattered. Every day was an op day or a training day. Warriors didn't take days off.

He grunted as he straightened, racked the barbell, and turned to Hector, working out next to him in the small room. "The tango got the drop on me. Let's face it: I'm slowing down."

"No way. You're fine," Thor grunted as he bench pressed far more weight than seemed possible for his slight frame. "It was an ambush."

"Yes, but he moved faster. And it's not the first time. It happened last month. I was too slow and nearly got shot." Eye opening, but not as scary as his first op, when the goat stepped on a land mine. That had been a bloody mess. But at least it alerted them to the danger ahead. Still, he had to admit the truth to himself and his Teammate. Last night had been his last operation.

"Face it. I'm getting old." He was by far the oldest guy in the Teams doing direct action. After a certain age, people either got out or moved up.

He didn't want to rise up the ranks. He didn't want to be command. How could he leave the camaraderie of the small unit? How could he sit behind a desk—or worse: create slide presentations for the brass?

No way.

He kicked in doors and killed the enemy.

Sure, he picked up the lead when Ron got shot, but any of them could have done it. He came up with the plan, so he took point. No big deal.

Axe wiped his thick beard and long hair with a fresh white towel from a stack in the corner of the work-out room. He avoided looking in the small mirror on the near wall. He didn't need to be reminded of the gray hairs that seemed to multiply every day, especially on the beard.

Hector placed the weights on the rack and sat up. He was thirteen years younger than Axe and had no idea how much harder Axe had to work to stay in shape.

"I don't care how old you are, Grandpa. Happy for you to have my back any day."

Axe looked at his friend. The two of them had clicked from the start, despite their age difference. He wanted to get it off his chest. "I'm done. I told command today."

Hector choked on the water he was chugging. "Wait. What?"

"I'm out. End of this deployment. I'm not re-upping."

He shook his head before Axe could finish. "You'll change your mind."

Axe shrugged. "Paperwork's already done. They'll have me stay behind for the next few weeks, or act as backup. If we get any ops, that is." Things had been slow lately. Peace was breaking out all over.

Aside from hunting down the asshole bomb maker, it had been boring. Another reason to call it.

In previous years, life had been fun. Ops every night. Flying around different countries, taking down a compound or otherwise ruining the night of the bad guys. The politicians had gotten involved lately, winding down the various wars. In many places they let years of progress wither away, progress his warrior brothers and sisters had fought and died for. All because of a lack of a goal, strategy, or the will to win.

Hector watched him like a hawk, a half smile on his lips, waiting for Axe to laugh and admit to yanking his chain. It didn't come. "You serious?"

Axe nodded.

"And after this? What's the plan? And please don't tell me you're going to write a book."

It seemed like all anyone did these days. Leave the Teams and tell all, either by becoming an author or a motivational speaker.

"My dad left me his cabin in the woods and a small chunk of change. I'm going to settle down and—" He stopped. He'd barely admitted it to himself, and he wasn't about to say anything to Hector. How could he mention his desire to meet a woman, start a family, and give peace a chance? He'd sound crazy.

"And what?"

"Figure out what to do," he lied. He felt bad, being dishonest to his friend. His brother. But there was no way he could admit the truth. No, if it worked, great. If not… well, better to not have people asking him what happened.

3

THE WOODS

Three Months Later

The darkness protected him. If he couldn't use the ocean to approach a target's position, the woods at night were the next best thing.

Axe placed his steps with care, lightly weighting each foot, ensuring no leaves would rustle or twigs break before he completed the step.

He struggled to get his breathing under control. The run up the backside of the mountain had left him gasping for air. The fast pace required to arrive in time to take the shot had been brutal.

He stopped, putting all his senses on alert, but he felt no danger. Yet.

He edged forward to the spot he'd reconned over the past several days.

Dropping as he approached the slight rise, he slowed more, moving inch by inch. Silently.

The sky lightened by the minute. The sun would be up in moments.

Perfect timing. The target would be well lit and Axe would be hard to see with the sun directly behind him.

He sensed the target now. Whether from subconsciously hearing movement or some kind of ESP from years of practice, he knew his planning and work would pay off.

Axe slowed further, the smell of the loamy ground and pine needles filling his nose.

The sun hadn't hit the downward slope on the other side of the rise in front of him.

He moved a few inches to better see where he hoped the target would arrive at any moment.

Nothing.

Shifting aim, he looked further down the slope. There. At the edge of the clearing, way in back.

Damn.

Twenty-five yards further away than planned.

Too far. Definitely at the outer edge of his range.

Wait for the target to approach and take the shot? Or move closer, risking exposure?

He barely considered the options. The mission came first. Always.

The sun's glow illuminated the western-facing slope and clearing ahead of him

He used every trick from sniper training and years of real-world practice to make his way closer while staying hidden. But time wasn't on his side. The target would move off shortly. The light would change. He could be spotted. But hurrying would be counterproductive. And get him killed.

He stopped to gauge the distance. Yes. Close enough.

The target remained obscured by a few trees to the left of the large opening in the woods.

Come on. A few yards. Give me a shot.

He slowly flicked the switch. Ready to shoot.

The target advanced, left to right across his vision, and fully entered the clearing.

Almost. Almost...

Pressure on his finger…

Wait.

The target looked back at the two kids trailing behind.

Every muscle in Axe's body tensed.

He didn't take his eye off the target as he forced himself to relax. He had a job to do.

He repositioned, shifting silently.

Or so he thought.

His target turned towards him.

No way could he be seen. Right?

The kids looked too.

The sun shone on all three.

Pressure on his finger.

The high-tech camera shutter clicked quietly, capturing twenty frames per second. Mama bear and her two cubs stood facing him, alert but unafraid. Curious more than anything else. They sensed something but didn't know if he was a threat or not. Yet. If mama bear caught sight or smell of him, she'd charge to protect her cubs.

Axe's fingers expertly turned dials, changing settings, bracketing the shots.

He didn't claim to be a gifted photographer. The key—aside from getting into position without alerting his subjects—was to take so many pictures with different settings that at least a few would turn out.

The risk was high. If mama bear felt threatened, she would attack. He was close enough for her to be on him before he could rise and run. The small zoom lens allowed him some protection as long as he wasn't spotted, but he didn't have thousands of dollars for a pro lens which would allow him to shoot from further away.

If he wanted the pictures, he had to pay the price. In effort, stealth… and risk.

He watched and shot frame after frame as the black bears dropped to all fours, apparently convinced of their safety, and meandered out of the sunlit forest clearing and further into the woods, out of sight.

Axe relaxed, letting out his breath. He'd nailed another mission. He could now work his way backwards to the other side of the rise and return to his cabin. A quick bite to eat while downloading the photos onto his computer, then he could catch some sleep. He'd edit the shots in the afternoon when he woke up.

Months after retiring, he still couldn't sleep at night. He didn't have nightmares, exactly. But after so many years of sleeping during the day —and seeing so much violence, death, and destruction—going to bed at night didn't work for him.

Better to fall back on old patterns. Sleep during the day. Active all night. Take photos at dusk and dawn when the golden light was perfect for capturing the magnificent wildlife.

As he reversed course and made his way back to safety, he yet again reflected on his choice. Had he made a huge mistake leaving behind his life, his brothers, his Team? He crawled through the forest, taking pictures of wild animals to sell to city folk. Alone.

His team crawled through mud, dirt, or water, killing bad guys, making the world safe. Together.

Dumbass. You could be leading men now instead of taking pictures to sell to the one percent.

Safely over the rise, he stood, nestled the camera and long lens into his pack, and started jogging down the game trail for the eight-mile run to the cabin. The rising sun shone brightly on him and the area, lighting up the trees and making the forest practically glow.

About an hour later, his cell phone vibrated against his hip as he came into range of the tower across the valley. Still a mile from home, he stopped for a drink and checked the message.

Going crazy yet? Meet me at the range this afternoon. 4 sharp. Important. BYOGs. Red.

Red, aka Eric, his old platoon chief, wanted to meet him at the range?

A social call? Brother wellness check? Or an offer to be an instructor…

The chance to train the next generation hadn't appealed to him a few months ago. Now, he might jump at it.

It took him a second to decipher the rest, but it brought an enormous smile to his face when he figured it out. *"Bring your own guns."*

4

THE OFFICE

She hadn't been invited to sit. A bad sign.

Haley stood in her sensible, low-heeled shoes—at five foot ten she was tall enough and didn't want to tower over the men—and black pantsuit, tailored to hide her curves, trying to decide where to put her hands. Clasped in front? No. Arms down at her sides? It felt awkward. Then again, it always felt awkward when she got called in.

She settled on standing tall with her hands crossed behind her back, like a soldier at parade rest. It didn't feel any better than the other options she'd tried, but at least it conveyed the proper look: alert and ready for her chewing out.

Gregory Addison, director of Central Analysis Group, an elite, relatively new intelligence gathering and analysis division of the US government, sat at his desk. He pushed his fashionable glasses up onto the top of his head and rubbed his eyes in exasperation, then leaned back in his chair with a heavy sigh.

"You think you're special, don't you?"

Don't answer that.

He didn't mean her looks. She'd turned down offers to be a model from an early age. Thankfully, Gregory was one of few people, men or women, who didn't seem to notice her beauty. He focused on her mind... and her inexperience in the ways of the job. She brushed a stray strand of long blond hair back behind her ear, then returned to her parade rest position.

Haley fixed on his longish gray hair instead of looking him in the eye. It took quite an effort to hold herself back. *Of course I'm special!* she wanted to scream. *I'm the best and brightest here and you know it or you wouldn't have hired me.*

Gregory shook his head. Despite the long, stressful hours of the job, he had the youthful vigor of a man much younger than his sixty years. The crows feet at his eyes crinkled as he watched her. "Look at you. It's all you can do to stay quiet. Never play poker, Haley. You couldn't hide a full house if your life depended on it."

Damn it, not now. Her normally pale face flushed bright red from the truth of Gregory's statement. She couldn't hold back any longer. She had to defend herself.

"I—"

He interrupted immediately. "You got lucky."

She pressed her lips together, infuriated but committed to staying silent this time. His ability to know her argument before she spoke made her face flush redder, this time from anger instead of embarrassment.

He nodded at her silence. "Better already. At least your self-control is improving. Slightly."

Slow, deep breaths. Breathe and keep quiet.

People dreamed of working for Central Analyst Group—CAG—and for Gregory. He was brilliant. An exceptional manager, former super-star intelligence analyst, and her self-appointed mentor. She grasped how much extra effort he put into her.

She'd gotten the job on her own merits. Her skills at intelligence gathering and analysis were off the charts. But even she could acknowledge her youth and inexperience. Graduating college at eighteen, Masters at twenty, and CAG at twenty-one left her without many of the social graces most people develop. She spoke her mind and refused to hide her brilliance. Which made people dislike her. She didn't mind, as long as she could do her job, and do it well.

"Don't ever let your ego take over in this job, Haley. Don't discount confirmation bias. It messes with the best of us." His eyes switched over to a thousand-yard stare, and Haley wondered about his past successes… and failures.

"Earlier this year, you nailed it. The rest of the team was wrong— the bomber's location in the village was a trap. We should have listened to you and passed your theory along to the SEALs. But it's so much easier to be the naysayer and poke holes than it is to put the pieces together."

"That's—"

"Yes, now you have found a grand conspiracy." He rolled his eyes. "A diabolical plan to do… what? 'Something,' you wrote, correct?" He picked up her two-page report. "When? Oh, here it is, 'In the near future.' This isn't the CIA, Haley. We do better here."

It had been a mistake to write the report. She understood it now. To her, it made sense to raise the alert as soon as she had a picture, no matter how incomplete. The pieces were glaringly obvious. Why couldn't anyone besides her see?

Suddenly the truth hit her.

This isn't my little world. This is the big leagues and the rules are different.

"Finally," Gregory muttered.

She hated how he could read her mind. She understood he read her face and body language. Combined with his own history as one of the youngest analysts ever, back in the day, it wasn't magic. He merely followed the clues and analyzed the data.

This is another lesson. A big one.

Even as she thought it, she relaxed her face and body, denying him clues to her thoughts.

Gregory nodded approvingly. "Much better. Tell me what you decided. I admit I couldn't see it."

She eyed him suspiciously, wondering if he would just interrupt her when she started speaking, before realizing how much her look gave away. Again.

This is harder than I thought it would be. Do I want to spend my life learning how to hide my thoughts, feelings, and emotions?

Easy answer.

For this career—and for my country? Absolutely.

She cleared her face and spoke. "I realized you're right."

His bark of laughter surprised her... and it showed, which caused her to blush again.

"You were better at hiding your emotions, but you're not a liar yet, kid. Now tell me the rest."

"This is an important lesson, on many levels."

"Go on."

"It doesn't matter so much what I believe as what I can prove."

"Continue."

"There are always threats."

"Yes. And?"

"We're not like stock market analysts who can announce, 'The sky is falling,' every month until eventually the market drops and they claim they were right all along. We have to back it up."

"Right. Anyone can say, 'Watch out, something is going to happen!'" He pushed her stapled report with one finger, deliberately hard enough for it to slide across his spotless desk to fall onto the floor in front of her.

"Which is fine. It's unfortunately what many people do, if they're just putting in time before moving up, or moving out..." he tilted his head to his left, eyebrow raised.

Her turn to read him. She knew what the gesture meant. Outside his office, the building, and the ultra-secure grounds, miles in the distance, lay the Capitol building... and the White House. The implication that the job served as merely a stepping stone filled her with fiery rage.

In an instant, clarity struck. *Don't fall for it. He's playing you like a fiddle. He wants to see your reaction.*

She breathed again, calming herself, but not hiding her anger.

Let him see.

"Interesting," Gregory nodded with a smile. "This is the real deal for you. For now," he added, almost too soft to hear.

They stared at each other for a moment, teacher and student, comfortable with the exchange and the lessons learned. She appreciated how he didn't treat her any differently because of her beauty or connections.

If he treats me differently, it's only because I'm basically him forty years ago.

The idea both thrilled and terrified her. Would she be as respected, as knowledgeable, as good at her job, someday? Or would she move up and out as Gregory had insinuated, despite her current desire to stay and master intelligence gathering?

He gestured dismissively at her report laying on the floor at her feet. "Don't be the girl who cries wolf." He turned to his computer monitor.

Meeting adjourned.

She remained standing for another second, then picked her report up and turned, walking to the door. Back to her cubicle to sift through data, pull threads, and figure out the threat.

It wasn't just in her mind. Something was out there, coming for them.

Confirmation bias, my ass.

Gregory spoke as her hand turned the doorknob. "But Haley— don't let the sheep get attacked, either."

She nodded, mostly to herself, and left, already considering how to piece the puzzle together and save the world.

5

THE RANGE

Clang-clang. Clang-clang.

The double taps rang out from the bullets hitting the metal plates at the range. His magazine expended, Axe smoothly executed a reload and engaged the next targets.

Dead center every time.

With his last mag emptied, he cleared his pistol. He nodded, pleased with himself. He'd kept up his skills over the last months, visiting various ranges around the state.

"Not bad… for a has-been." The trash talk had been non-stop from Eric, his former platoon leader.

Ouch. He'd expected some good-natured ribbing, but that one stung.

They'd always be brothers. But once a man left the Teams, a subtle yet noticeable shift occurred. You were in or out. No middle ground.

"Not as sharp as you." He'd nailed every target—but took more time than Eric. He was slower than ever.

Good thing I got out before I got myself or one of my brothers killed.

"I have the US government paying for both the ammo and my time to shoot it." Eric gathered up his magazines on the table stretching behind the firing line at the outdoor gun range. His shaggy hair and beard, both dark red, the color of arterial blood, made him look like a vagrant. A very tough, mean, strong homeless guy who stood six-foot one and had two-hundred-twenty pounds of pure muscle.

Axe rubbed his own face, smooth these days to hide the gray that continued to creep in. He'd cut his hair, too, into some semblance of a short, corporate look. It just made it easier to maintain than the longer hair sported by nearly everyone on the Teams to blend in all over the world, where men didn't get haircuts every three weeks. "Things slow lately? Lots of time on the range?"

Stupid question. He can't answer that.

Eric smiled and reloaded his empty clips. "Here." He pushed the box of ammo towards Axe. "Reload. On me."

"Only if I buy the beer."

Eric glanced up at him, then looked away as if embarrassed.

What the hell was that look? We're not going out for dinner? Damn it, this whole deal really was a wellness check.

"Seriously, how are you handling transition to civilian life?" Eric's voice had a careful nonchalance, but backed by a partly hidden tone that showed it to be a serious question.

There it is. Where's this going?

He reloaded his magazines. He wasn't one to turn down free ammo. "Doing great. Selling nature photos to rich people who don't want to get their expensive hiking boots dirty."

"Or get lost in the woods."

"Yeah, that too."

"Dating? Settling down?"

He shook his head sadly with a wry grin. "It's not exactly a target-rich environment where I am. Small town." He hoped the disappointment he felt didn't come through in his tone.

"You're too picky, my friend."

"Probably. But there's an unfavorable tooth to tattoo ratio in my area."

"What the hell is that?"

"My initial screening procedure. Any potential date must have more teeth than bad tattoos. Count both, calculate the ratio."

Eric finished a mag and started another, considering the concept. "What's the cutoff?"

"Two to one. Four to one is better, but last month I lowered the bar."

Eric—aka "Red," from Erik the Red, a 10th century Viking warrior —did the math. "Average adult without wisdom teeth has twenty-eight remaining, so no more than fourteen crappy tattoos? Doesn't seem too hard."

Axe raised his eyebrows and pursed his lips. "Depends on the actual number of teeth, for one. I know it doesn't seem insurmountable, but these days…"

Red laughed. "I'll keep my eyes open for you." The SEAL base was only a couple hours away from his cabin.

You never know. I'd drive two hours a few times a week for the right woman.

"Any other criteria?"

"Well, female would be nice."

"See, I told you. Too picky."

They laughed. It felt great to be around a fellow warrior. He missed the camaraderie.

Hell, let's be honest. I miss it all.

A barrage of shots came from a few lanes down. Over the constant firing came the sound of the metal targets being nailed.

Impressive shooting.

Axe looked at Red with raised eyebrows, but, curiously, couldn't catch his eye.

His senses tingled. Something wasn't right.

"Anyway, nice shooting, Axe. I knew you'd stay sharp." Red holstered his pistol and added the refilled magazines to their spots on his mag carrier, then pulled his loose t-shirt down to cover everything. He checked his watch and reached for the box of ammo.

"What the hell? Aren't we were going out?"

Red grabbed him in a tight bear hug, then let go.

"Sorry, brother. Orders."

He turned and hurried back to his truck, leaving Axe stunned, disappointed, and pissed.

Orders?

As Red drove off, Axe noted the man who had successfully nailed his targets change magazines, then holster his weapon. He couldn't see him well because of the lane divider hiding part of his body, but he looked older, with military-short gray hair.

"You'll have to forgive him."

Eyes narrowing, Axe turned to fully face the man as he approached. Civilian clothes—jeans and a quality white t-shirt. Narrow face, strong chin. A serious man.

"And why will I have to do that?"

"I made sure he got a direct order."

Axe's anger flared at the idea of his friend being ordered to keep something from him. "And who the hell are—"

His mouth shut at the same time he instinctively snapped to attention. Out of uniform, he was hard to place, but Axe suddenly recognized the face.

"Sorry, Admiral." How had he not recognized a retired four-star admiral? A former SEAL, at that?

"Stand down, son."

Years of training made him react without thinking, moving into an at-ease position. SEALs weren't big on saluting or coming to attention normally, but in the presence of this level of brass, rules were rules. Retired or not. Especially in front of a man he respected so much.

Admiral William "Hammer" Nalen had been there and done that long before Axe had been born. He'd led men in battle and embraced the suck at every level, finally retiring a few years ago. They'd never met personally, but Axe had been under his overall command—at some level—for nearly his entire time in the Teams.

"Nice shooting, sir."

No harm trying to dig my way out of this with flattery.

Nalen chuckled. "Nice save, but you're not in trouble. Neither is Red. Actually, I owe you an apology."

"Sir?"

"I needed to speak with you. Completely off the record. So I called in a favor with his CO, who 'suggested' Red reach out to you, with the direct order not to alert you to the setup. Sorry."

Orders or not, he still could have given me a sign.

"I'd be pissed too, but when he got here, I reassured him I just needed a word with you."

"Why would you need to speak with me, sir? I'm retired."

"And spending your days counting teeth and bad tattoos, it sounds like. Seems like a waste of talent to me."

He'd been listening the whole time? Stealthy bastard. I didn't notice him until he started shooting.

"Here's the deal, son. I need you."

Axe couldn't hold back a sharp laugh.

Here it comes.

"Thank you, sir. Not interested."

Or am I? No, this is the bullshit I don't miss. What was this, a recruitment for a job at one of the private security firms?

He'd already turned down the biggest one. He wasn't interested in being a mercenary.

Someone must be paying a hell of a lot of money to send a four-star on a recruitment mission.

"I thought you were a patriot."

Axe held his tongue, not saying what he wanted to. Instead, he added, as mildly as he could, "You have a lot of guys who do what I do. Better, even."

"I don't have anyone like you. Hear me out. Not because of my rank, or your service. From one warrior to another. Let me lay it out for you?"

Well, hell. Put it that way, how can I refuse?

He nodded. "Let's hear your pitch. But I'm not a merc. I'm not going to guard convoys in some hell-hole, defend a compound, or play bodyguard to prima donnas. No thanks. But go for it, sir. Show me what you got." The challenge in his voice came out harsher than he meant, but Nalen didn't seem bothered.

"Let's get one thing clear first. You don't mention this to anyone. No one on your old Team, no cute woman with a nice smile and a tattoo on her ass. Nobody. We never had this conversation, no matter what you decide."

"Fine."

"I need more. I need your word. This isn't some crappy private security recruitment." He stuck out his hand and waited for Axe.

What has Red gotten me into?

"You have my word, sir. This conversation never happened." He grasped the admiral's hand and shook it firmly, looking him square in the eye.

A line from the SEAL ethos came to him. *My word is my bond.*

Nalen looked around at the deserted range and nodded to himself. The sun was setting, but they had a few minutes before the staff came around to clean up.

"I'll be brief. The president and I go way back. You know that?"

"Yes, sir. You were on a Team together."

The country had finally elected a warrior as president. Three years into his first term, some thought he seemed softer than the military community hoped he'd be. But the liberals tolerated him because of his 'Diplomacy first' mantra. The conservatives supported him because of his willingness to cry 'Bullshit,' and unleash the full might of the country when necessary. He used it rarely, but brought overwhelming violence of action when it was needed. Just like the former SEAL he was.

From what Axe read in the newspaper, it looked like he'd win a second term, despite not being able to please everyone.

"He and the First Lady had me and the wife stay the night. Lincoln bedroom, white house residence. Cool experience."

Axe waited. In the absence of a question from a superior of Nalen's rank, silence was expected.

"So the president and I are having a drink, watching a game on TV.

Volume way up. 'I don't hear as well anymore,' he says. 'Too many rounds sent downrange.'"

Axe nodded. *Same here.*

"Then he leans over to me and whispers that he suspects his conversations, in the residence, the Oval Office, everywhere, might be bugged. And-or he's got a traitor in his inner circle."

Axe's eyes widened.

He's paranoid. Too old, too much time on the front lines. PTSD?

Nalen nodded, seeming to know Axe's mind. "I thought he was joking or losing it. But he was dead serious. And my next thought…"

"What if it's true?"

"You see what I see?"

"Yes, sir. Who could he turn to? The Secret Service? It's the safe play. They're straight-laced. Hard to sway. But you never know."

Nalen nodded thoughtfully. "You never know."

"The CIA? NSA? FBI? The vice president? All probably safe, but if he's right and there is a problem, he'd be giving away the only advantage he has: knowledge of the enemy."

"'Appear weak when you are strong, and strong when you are weak.'"

"Sun Tzu."

"Yes."

He didn't even need to think about it. *Given the situation, there's no way I can refuse to help.*

"I'm in. Whatever you need. Does the president want to replace his body man?"

A president's 'body man' is a close aid, part entourage, part gopher, part fixer extraordinaire. Usually a younger man than Axe worked the job, someone with more polish and political experience, but Axe could see himself filling in temporarily while President Heringten's current guy got an unexpected but much-needed vacation.

"Good man, thank you. The president is working things out on his end."

"So what do you need me for?"

Nalen sighed. "You might not be so eager when you hear the

details, but it's better than it sounds. Pay attention. The First Lady's best friend is named Sarah. They're like sisters. They go way back to grade school together. Anyway, her youngest daughter is named Haley. She's a junior analyst at the CAG. Know what that is?"

"No, sir."

Oh, no. This is going to be a babysitting gig. I can tell already.

"A small, elite intelligence unit. Relatively new. Some of the best and brightest. Haley's going places. Smarter than most of the other people there added together. Made it on her own merits. There are people aware of her connection to the president but she is making her own way."

Nalen frowned with concern. "She's uncovered what she thinks is a plot against the country and president. Or rather, she has one loose thread she's been pulling but doesn't have any actionable intelligence. Just guesswork and a feeling. People above her aren't taking her seriously, but she's convinced there's something to it. She mentioned it in passing to mommy, just venting, understand, not asking for help. Mommy mentions it to the First Lady, who mentions it to the president. You see where this is going?"

"'Happy wife, happy life?'"

"Yes. He'd normally have someone look into it anyway—quietly, of course. But now he also has this sense himself that things aren't right. You know the feeling."

They shared a look. Every warrior with as much combat experience as they had knew the feeling. Call it gut instinct or a sixth sense, but it existed. Knowing when things were... off, somehow. Like he'd felt—and discounted—earlier with Red.

"Always trust your instincts."

"Exactly the president's attitude. Things have happened lately. Select people don't seem as surprised as they should be about a new trade agreement. He's kneecapped in negotiations with Congress. And very worried it could eventually extend to our military being at greater risk, depending on how deep it goes."

"Damn."

"Definitely. So he's stuck. He wants to help this young woman who is like a niece to him, keep the situation at home good. He wants to find out if he has a mole or traitor. And of course he needs to protect the country. But he doesn't know who he can trust."

"Sir, nothing against the president, but are you sure he's not seeing conspiracy theories?"

"No, I'm not. Honestly, he isn't either. But again…"

"What if?"

"Yes. Basically, neither of us is sure of anything. But I'm willing to do a favor for a friend."

"Your friend being the President of the United States."

Nalen shrugged with a grin.

"The favor being?"

"Providing some off-the-books help."

"Sounds illegal as hell, sir."

Another shrug.

"The President of the United States needs help. You're saying your heart doesn't still stir at the thought of answering the call?"

He knows what makes me tick because it's the same with him… and the president.

"Why me?"

"You have the needed skill set and maturity. You're retired. And you have absolutely no connection to the president, the First Lady, her best friend, Haley, or me. You can look around, then deal with it if necessary."

"It's likely nothing, right?"

Nalen nodded. "In which case, no harm, no foul. First Lady's happy, which makes the president happy. Haley learns an important lesson. No traitor, only the normal threats to our country, which we can handle through regular channels."

Axe considered the angles. "But I'm not a spook."

"No secret agent bullshit necessary. You'll meet with the young lady, listen to her pitch. Pick her brain. Help where needed, eyes-on stuff if absolutely necessary. She's the spook. You're the warrior. You've been there and done it all. If it's nothing, you'll know."

"If not? If there is a plot against the country? If there's an indication there's a traitor? What then?"

He shook his head through Axe's questions. "The odds that a junior analyst has somehow uncovered a huge plot against the country when no one else has a clue is minuscule."

He waited him out.

"Okay. If there's something there, handle it if you can. If you can't, you contact me as a last resort. But then I'll be stuck with it. Unless you have some major proof, physical evidence, the only place I can go is back to the president..."

"And we're all back to where we started. Not knowing who to trust."

Axe tried to think of a way out, but his conscience wouldn't let him. Unless... "Why not tell local police? Or some kind of secret agents? There has to be someone besides me."

"One, we don't want to ruin the woman's life. She gets known as the girl who cries wolf, a promising career is over. Two, politics. The president doesn't want to be seen as jumping at shadows. And three— we're back to 'What if it's true?'"

I might regret this. But if I walk away, I end up back at the cabin. Alone. Editing photos taken for rich people.

"Rules of engagement?"

"You're a private citizen. Don't do anything you wouldn't normally do."

"Come on, sir."

"Okay, how's this? Don't get caught. Because if things go tits up..."

"You hang me out to dry."

"Absolutely." He nodded grimly, eyes hard. "Tragic story. Veteran, a hero, goes off the rails due to PTSD. He's delusional. Horrible." He glared at Axe. "If you get caught, don't implicate the president, me, or Haley. You take one for the team."

Axe nodded. "Understood."

"Besides that, do what you need to do. Your reputation precedes you, Axe. If there's something going on, I have complete faith you will uncover it, figure out what's going on, who's behind it, and deal with it. Get in, get it done, get out."

Nalen offered his hand again. Axe didn't hesitate. He took it and shook, trying hard to hold back his grin.

Hell, yes! I'm back.

6

THE MEMO

Haley sat back in her tiny cubicle, her mind in overdrive. Most of the rest of the day-shift analysts had gone home already, but she stayed late both to work and to avoid the worst of the long commute. The large room of similar cubicles, which looked more like it housed a call center or HR department than the nation's elite intelligence analysts, was quiet.

She tried to relax and allow the connections to form.

After the dressing down from Gregory, she'd spent the day like every other day: head down, focused on the huge, multi-departmental database containing all the information from America's vast intelligence gathering apparatus. Every branch of the government, diplomatic to military, local police to FBI, all contributed their tidbits to the database.

The problem most often came not from too little information, but too much.

Despite the promise of artificial intelligence, it took a human to read the data and attempt to make sense of it.

It felt like drinking from a fire hose.

But she had the rare ability to pull together far-flung details and make sense of them. Most days it seemed like she had been born for this job.

The information at her disposal made her feel all-knowing. But she wasn't. The bad guys had gotten smarter over the years. America spied on the world and excelled at electronic surveillance. Only amateurs and idiots plotted openly enough to be easily caught.

It took a mind like hers to pull on the strands. Find the tiniest hints of plots, then shine light on them to determine the level of threat.

Unfortunately, her small role only involved searching, occasionally finding a clue, then writing a report about it.

She was not a god.

She was a cog in a vast machine.

Someday, though, she'd be in charge. Either here or... She indulged in a moment of fantasy. Senator Haley Cross. Or better yet: President Cross.

She'd reacted strongly to Gregory's hint that she was using her important role here as a stepping stone.

This is where I need to be. I'll be very happy as director here some day. But there's no harm dreaming of more. If it's meant to be.

In the meantime, what she thought would take a month started coming together by the end of the day.

The pieces fell into place.

A snippet from an intercepted cell phone call from the assistant of a prominent Wall Street hedge fund manager: "Mom, just trust me, okay? Have your adviser do what we discussed last weekend."

Multiple reports of strange buzzing sounds on Long Island.

Unusual activity in the stock market: big bets predicting the market and/or economy would collapse. And great lengths taken to disguise the bets — and who made them.

Up and down the eastern seaboard, criminal activity dropped 63% compared to the same months the previous year. It remained within normal parameters for the rest of the country.

Dozens more fragments competed for attention in Haley's mind.

Which ones had meaning? How were they connected? Could they

be random? Or did they fit together, an indication of an upcoming attack against America?

And if so, what kind of attack would it be?

That part eluded her.

Could it actually be confirmation bias? Do I want to save the country so much that I'm seeing threats where there aren't any?

She closed her eyes and relaxed, letting her mind go for a moment.

No fantasizing about the future. No dreaming of being in control and able to direct assets for further investigation of whatever she wanted.

She would never admit it to anyone, but she had a secret question she asked herself when she felt stuck.

What does my gut tell me?

The logical part of her had a tough time with trusting intuition. But she had never gone wrong when she trusted her intuition.

There's a threat. It's real.

And it involves the East coast—several locations.

But I don't have enough yet.

It's more than I had this morning, but Gregory will eat me alive if I go back to him with it.

I need more.

But I have to also cover my ass.

After this morning in Gregory's office, she realized she had to contend with another dimension of the job. She had to play the game.

Going to a superior without enough details threatened to get her a "Cry Wolf" reputation.

Not taking suspicions up the ladder would paint her as ineffective. Worse, if she suspected a problem and didn't at least mention it, explain her position—without being alarmist, like she had with her report last week—the possibility remained something bad could happen. People could die.

She wouldn't allow that.

She had to accept she wasn't a one-woman army. She existed in a team environment. Practicality and prudence demanded she summarize her concerns and share them. Perhaps other analysts would see a threat she'd uncovered, connect it with items on their desks, and together they'd solve the problem.

Or I'll have one more strike against me. Another opportunity to be known as, "The girl who cries wolf."

She opened a secure document and composed her thoughts. She'd walk the line, make her case, but not overreact. Maybe there would be enough to get someone to look deeper.

If not, at least you've gotten the ball rolling. Tiny steps.

It didn't turn out as measured as she'd planned, but the report sounded more like what the senior analysts wrote than her last one.

That one ended up on the floor at my feet in Gregory's office. This one won't.

Satisfied with the tone and scope, she finished the memo and sent it out to the other analysts, the managers, and copied Gregory.

It's enough to light a fire, but not enough to burn me down if I'm wrong. But it sure will make tomorrow interesting.

7

THE ASSISTANT

Todd Burkley stared at his face in the mirror of his office. Short, straight blond hair, fair complexion, nice teeth, blue eyes. A few inches shorter than he'd prefer, but fit. Mildly handsome, people had said.

"Not much longer now," he told himself. "Then you'll have your revenge. But first, time to practice."

He smiled, going for eager to please.

Hmm. Good, but not great. The eyes needed to be wider to continue to fool his boss of many years. He tried again. Yes. Nailed it.

From downstairs came the murmur of people talking and laughing, along with the smells of exquisite Italian food at the restaurant owned by his boss, Kelton Kellison. He also owned this second-story loft office space, half the buildings on this side of the street, and, if Todd was honest with himself, Kelton owned him, too.

For a few more days, at least.

Todd frowned at the expression of predatory greed which had clouded his face as he considered what would happen later this week. He had to be careful to not let it show, even in private.

He glanced at his watch. He had a few more minutes. Kelton had expressed doubts lately, and Todd didn't want cold feet stopping the plan he'd worked so hard on. All the time and effort, the years of hiding his growing hatred for Kelton, his long-time employer and supposed friend.

He controlled the anger trying to spill onto his face, smiling benignly instead.

Better.

More practice. The expressions had to be perfect.

Next: concern. He furrowed his brow and frowned.

Excellent.

Shock. Wide eyes with a hint of disbelief.

Very good.

He returned his face to neutral and tried again. He'd need this one when the killing started. Eyes wide and... he parted his lips and breathed in a tiny gasp.

There! Perfection.

Kelton would buy it hook, line, and sinker. He'd never suspect a thing.

As long as I can keep my hatred in check and not tell him off... which will be much more challenging than faking a few facial expressions.

He turned and walked back to his desk, looking out at the quaint street below through the tall office windows which were shut, as always. Had they been open, the food smells would have lessened, helping reduce the grumbling in his stomach. And he would have been able to smell the spring air, a welcome distraction from the stress of the last few weeks. But now was not the time for distractions. The next two days would be hard, but they were the culmination of years of dreaming, planning, scheming, and pretending.

Todd reread the concerning email on his laptop screen. Was it a distraction, problem, or opportunity?

The meddling troublemaker had made more connections. She could destroy his careful plans if she got lucky. If she pulled a few more threads, the whole endeavor would unravel.

He looked at his watch again, then closed his eyes, knowing what came next. He started counting down. After years of working for Kelton, he had developed a sense.

Five, four, three, two—

The cell phone on the expensive mahogany desk buzzed. One second off. Not bad.

The distinctive ring indicated the correct protocol was being followed. The call came over an app: voice over IP—VoIP—making it much harder for the NSA, FBI, or dozens of other organizations to eavesdrop. And this phone, the ultimate in secure communications, had only one use: for Todd and Kelton to communicate.

"I saw," Todd said with the perfect mix of concern and calm.

"How the hell is this happening?"

I have to talk him down. I will not let his fear ruin everything.

"Unknown, but I'll handle it."

"Personally, or professionally?" In other words, with his carefully recruited inner circle, or the hired help of AgaDefCo, a wholly owned subsidiary of one of Kelton's many companies.

"Professionally. Too far away to handle personally."

While technically Todd could fly a team to the D.C. area from the small airport serving eastern Long Island, it would have left a paper trail a mile long. Instead, he'd farm out the operation to one of AgaDefCo's managers who could be trusted for some dirty work.

"Do we have a leak? That's my big concern."

"Not likely. I think it's just that data is created. Right?"

Kelton made his first billion on data and analytics. In the early days of the internet, Todd had taken Kelton's original ideas and positioned the company to monitor the shopping, travel, and entertainment preferences of millions of people, selling the data to advertisers, political parties, and others worldwide. And with Todd's expert management skills, the company had taken off.

They both knew all too well how everything anyone did left a trail. Cell phones and cars tracked locations. ATMs, traffic cameras, and even people's doorbells recorded street scenes. Smart devices tracked everything from interests and preferences to how well couples got along, how often they were intimate, and the topics they discussed.

And everyone let it happen.

Americans had accepted a Big Brother state without complaint. All in the name of convenience and entertainment.

Todd looked at the beautiful calligraphy print, surrounded by an exquisite gold frame, hanging on the wall. A matching one hung in Kelton's office—both commissioned by Todd for Kelton's thirtieth birthday, back in the good old days, before Kelton's selfish manner had caused Todd to start questioning his life choices. "The evil was not in bread and circuses, per se, but in the willingness of the people to sell their rights as free men for full bellies and the excitement of the games which would serve to distract them from their human hungers which bread and circuses can never appease." ~ Marcus Tullius Cicero

The saying hung not as a warning, as most visitors thought, but as a reminder of the opportunities available to those who desired power. As an instruction manual of sorts. Content, distracted, entertained people were easy to control. In short, the quote was a guide to ruling the world.

And to making billions of dollars by knowing people and predicting their choices and habits.

Todd had been with Kelton from the beginning. College roommates. Employee number one. Always there, a constant adviser, guiding him to his biggest successes while Kelton played the role of genius businessman.

Todd had been responsible for everything except the original idea and the million dollars Kelton had inherited, which he used as seed money to form the company. It would have failed within six months if Kelton had been in charge. Instead, Todd's expertise had saved the day.

Kelton got extremely rich, becoming one of the top fifty wealthiest people in the world and cultivating a reputation as a brilliant man.

Todd got wealthy. But he received no credit, in public or private.

And he had no time to spend the money. Kelton expected Todd available 24/7. Hence the dedicated phone. Did he need a captive audience to make himself feel good? Or did he understand, at some level, that he couldn't manage without Todd?

"They'll hold her until this is done?" Kelton asked. Todd pictured him pacing in his spacious Brooklyn office. "We don't need any clever Karen interfering."

"Haley."

"What?"

"Her name is Haley, not Karen."

"You're so damn pedantic. Just find out what she knows, how she figured it out, and hold her until it's over."

"Perhaps she could have an accident? Just to be sure?" Todd didn't think he'd buy it. Despite all they'd done and planned, he still had a squeamish side when it came to physical interference. "Nothing permanent, understand. A slip and fall type thing. Out of pocket for a few days."

Todd heard Kelton stop pacing while he hesitated.

"We need this," he continued. "We need the time. Questioning her, holding her, would open us up to risk. Think of the things she'd see, the questions we'd need to ask."

Kelton sighed with displeasure. "Something small. Nothing permanent. The minimum necessary."

"Absolutely. You've got it, boss."

As he hung up after further assuring Kelton he would take care of everything, Todd shook his head and smiled.

He lacks the killer instinct. Which is why he has me. Not that he knows about all I've done. Boy, would he blow a fuse if he did.

In a few days, the tables would finally be turned. Kelton couldn't succeed without Todd, but Todd could easily succeed without him.

And, in fact, he greatly looked forward to it. He didn't need credit —publicly or from Kelton. The success would be satisfaction enough. But pulling the wool over Kelton's eyes—and those of the world— would be the cherry on top of the sundae.

And Todd's long-term plans made his heart race with delight.

In a few years, I'll be at the pinnacle of success. I'll be no one's right-hand man. And no one will look down on me ever again. The end justifies the means.

He switched phones and looked up a contact, then placed the call using another secure communications app.

"There's a situation I need you for. Tonight. Is that a problem?"

"I'm short a guy but can make it happen," the man said. "What do you have?"

"I'll send you the details. Snatch and grab, a woman who is causing us some problems. Followed by interrogation. I want you to handle that part personally." The man had been dishonorably discharged for doing what Todd had in mind for young miss Haley.

"Boundaries?"

"None."

"If it gets messy, or…"

"Then it gets messy. And as long as you get the results I need, you may use your preferred methods."

"Music to my ears."

"I'll send you details and questions. Find out what she knows, what she suspects, and who she's told about it. Report as soon as you can. Before morning."

"Then?"

"Make her disappear. And hey—do better than last time. Smaller pieces, and mind the fingerprints and teeth. She needs to be gone-gone. It's important."

"I told you, that wasn't on me. But yes, I'll take care of it."

"As you said, 'Music to my ears.'"

Todd hung up and checked his watch once more. Things were going well, aside from the situation with Haley. But she would soon be handled. Now he had time for a quick dinner.

He called downstairs and placed his order, then turned on the huge TV on the far wall. Using his tablet, he started the feed of security cams showing the interior of various warehouses around the area. He'd watch the final preparations for tomorrow while he ate.

Later, he would receive the last call of the night. This one from another man who thought he had Todd in his pocket when, in fact, it was soon to be the other way around.

8

THE BOMBER

The smell of dozens of sweating men filled his nostrils. Zeno, also known as "The Boomer" by the Americans, stood on the metal catwalk extending around the inside perimeter of the large warehouse.

He leaned his tall, muscular frame against the railing. The long hair he'd cultivated the last six months fell forward, requiring him to sweep back the straight brown hair, streaked with gray, so he could watch the men.

Below him, automatic pistols and rifles lay in front of each man on long tables. The men joked and laughed as they cleaned the weapons one last time. Others loaded ammo into countless magazines and slid them into pockets in the front of their plate carriers. Each had top-of-the-line equipment and the best armor plates available on the market.

They were his front-line warriors.

He and his team had taken these hard men and made them harder. Had transformed them from undisciplined, two- and three-strike losers into small units that trusted each other and—mostly—controlled their animal instincts. For a while longer, at least.

They'd be encouraged to unleash those instincts soon, and were looking forward to it, amazed at the turn of good fortune that found them trained, equipped, and well-prepared to kill.

One man, brawny with thick, dark eyebrows but a short, professional haircut and clean-shaved face, glanced up and saw him looking down. A nod of respect from the criminal followed, noticed by the man next to him, who glanced up as well. He nodded, and it quickly spread around the room until every man had met his eye and acknowledged him. He was their leader, their taskmaster, their teacher. He demanded perfection, loyalty, and—hardest for many of them—their self discipline. It hadn't been easy to win over these men, but he'd done it. Through tidbits of his history, told in supposed confidence by his lieutenants, they'd learned of his skill... and brutality. That alone had won over most. They respected violence and the dealers of it, and Zeno was ruthless to the core.

His leadership ability brought over most of the rest. Some merely wanted a person to follow, a man who commanded their respect without attempting to make them give up what they loved: destruction. Violence. Killing.

A few hadn't played along, which was to be expected. The data had suggested it, and the algorithm even successfully predicted which men would be problematic. They were promoted to supervise other teams, so the men were told. In reality, they were in charge of the crabs and lobster feeding on their bodies as they lay, gutted and chained, at the bottom of the ocean a mile off the coast.

He turned away before another round of respectful looks began. He had to visit several other locations and verify the preparations. His captains handled most everything well, but it never hurt to double check. Tomorrow would be a big day. A cold, evil grin spread across his face. While he didn't have a dog in this fight he'd been brought on to lead, it would be good to see America, so high and mighty, brought to her knees, and know he was responsible for much of it.

With one last glance back, he entered his office off the catwalk. He'd eat, then visit his favorite group, the bombers. Eventually, he'd end up back here to address the men in a few hours, prior to loading up and moving out.

Each group had been told Zeno had to lead a different team, one less well trained and needing his personal attention. Not like them, who would obviously exceed his expectations, even without his presence. Regretful, but necessary. All had understood. Of course they were better than the other teams.

His employer, too, believed he'd be leading from the front. But this wasn't his war, and he would be far away by morning. It would be too risky to stay in the area. No, he had a schedule to keep with a doctor he kept on the payroll as his personal plastic surgeon. By this day next week, he'd look very different. Should any of these men survive to talk to the authorities, which he doubted, the description of their magnetic leader would be completely wrong.

The only part that would possibly match would be of his remarkable, spellbinding blue eyes that pierced the soul.

9

THE MOTHER

Haley fumed as she read the text again, furious with her mother. The hidden meaning of the message was practical, given what she and her parents knew about the nation's intelligence-gathering capabilities—not to mention the abilities of other nations.

"Uncle believes in you but set up a blind date to help with your lonely streak. Tonight."

She must have told Barbara, also known as the First Lady, who told James. No, not 'James,' or even 'Uncle Jimmy.' President Heringten. He's taking pity on me and sending a babysitter. Or worse, some kind of super spy.

Why can't they leave well enough alone? If anyone finds out the president is helping me, I'll go from "The girl who cried wolf" to "The girl who cried to Daddy." Or, in this case, not "Daddy" but "Uncle," also known as "Mr. President," the most powerful man in the world.

She sighed and considered her alternatives.

I'll talk it out with whoever they send. Let him think I'm happy to have his help. Then convince him the team and I at the office are on top of it.

10

THE APARTMENT

As Axe got closer to his destination, he didn't need the phone's GPS to show him the way. The upscale two-story apartment complex sat off the road, brightly lit and nicely landscaped, surrounded by freshly plowed fields.

I thought I lived in the boonies. This is the middle of nowhere. A nicer apartment for less money, sure, I get that. But it must be an hour commute or more with traffic.

He turned right and drove down the two-lane blacktop road. He saw the appeal of the area: small rolling hills, peace and quiet. The immediate area wasn't even suburban yet, though it would be in a few years, he guessed. For now, it was farmland, farmhouses, and this incongruous apartment complex.

At the range, the admiral had given him more details, along with the request to meet Haley right away, tonight, after she returned from work.

Time was of the essence, but between Haley's work day and commute, he'd been told there would be time for dinner and a beer.

Red would meet him after all, at an out-of-the-way sports bar in the general direction of D.C.—and Haley's apartment in the sticks.

At dinner, he'd avoided beer and Red hadn't asked why, or anything about the events earlier. The setup at the range wasn't mentioned. They talked longer than Axe had planned, catching up. He'd hurried but, though no specific time had been set for him to drop by, he was later than he wanted to be. Driving first on the freeway, then these back rural roads, had taken time. He hoped nine o'clock wasn't too late.

With the lack of street lights out this far, and the night so dark—aside from the glow of the apartment complex approaching—he didn't notice the black panel van pulled only partly off the road until his high beams caught it. He moved into the oncoming lane, grateful for a lack of traffic this late in the evening.

Idiot. Turn your lights or flashers on.

He braked his truck as he passed, feeling guilty for not helping. He felt worse when in his rear-view mirror he saw the driver's side door open, the dome light illuminating a man in dark clothes holding a tire iron.

No, I've got a more important mission tonight than helping a stranded motorist. Even if the mission is babysitting a junior analyst who's seeing threats at every turn.

Axe accelerated the last quarter mile to the grand sign announcing the apartment complex: Occuquan Acres. Groups of two-story buildings that went on and on plopped in the middle of nowhere. Not civilization, but not quite nature, either. The worst of both worlds. Living here would drive him crazy. Four apartments to a side, eight apartments to a building, meandering in clumps back away from the main road.

Unsure of where #281 would be, Axe turned right and looked for a sign. Admiral Nalen had said building D, which should be along the right side of the complex, near the front, if the designers had any sense.

They didn't.

After driving a few seconds, he finally noticed the subtle letter, small and hard to see, on one building. 'R' Which meant he'd guessed wrong. The developer had lettered the buildings clockwise from the front, not counterclockwise. He was on the wrong side.

No big deal. It never hurt to get the lay of the land.

He continued to drive, slowing for the speed bumps, allowing the three-year-old pickup he'd bought a few months ago, his pride and joy, to ease over them. Just because he had a cool, full-size truck didn't mean he had to ram over every bump like he didn't care about the suspension.

Building M. Getting there.

Something tickled his mind. Was he supposed to call first? No, Nalen had been adamant about avoiding any electronic communication, including calls and emails, unless it was a dire emergency. "We don't know who's listening."

Building J. Now that he knew where to look, the letters were easier to spot.

It nagged at him.

What am I missing?

Such a quiet place. He supposed young professionals lived here, commuting to government or lobbying jobs in D.C. Either way, at this hour on a Monday night they'd be in, watching a popular TV show.

I should get a TV, and an HD antenna, if only for sports.

Building D ahead. Finally.

Strange. The black panel van sat at the curb nearest the entrance to building D. The tinted windows were dark but he could make out the shape of a man in the driver's seat.

How did he fix the tire so quickly?

Axe swung into one of the few non-numbered parking spots designated for guests, 25 yards from the entrance and facing away from the buildings.

Only paying customers get prime spots. And if you're delivering pizza or picking someone up, you get to double park wherever you want, I guess. Like the van.

He slammed the truck door and touched the handle to lock it automatically. Then he adjusted his black t-shirt, tucking it in better and adjusting the pistol, which felt odd tucked inside his waistband holster at his right side after so many years strapped to his leg. Thankfully, his short-sleeve button-down shirt covered it.

Can't walk around wearing my weapon for all to see, retired SEAL or not.

He made his way towards the doorway, moving closer to the front of the black van.

Where's #281? Front or back? Might as well try front first.

Five feet from the front of the van, the driver's side door opened.

No dome light.

His senses nagged at him.

The man stepped out, raising his hand in a friendly greeting. "Hey there!"

Dark, messy hair, full beard. Black pants. Black tactical boots. Tight black long-sleeve shirt. Right hand hidden by the door.

Hard eyes.

Shit.

His mind put it together in a flash. No way would Nalen send another operator and not tell him. The guy was a threat.

"Hey, is this building C? I'm looking for C, um…" he pretended to think as he closed the distance. "Number 302, I think. Adams? You know where it is?"

The man had been ready to strike, but Axe's subterfuge worked as intended, making him hesitate for a moment.

Axe had started out slow on the uptake from too many months off, but his skills hadn't deteriorated. At the last second, he changed his trajectory from angling in front of the van to directly at the man, closing the remaining feet in a second, slamming into the open van door as the operator realized his mistake and tried desperately to pull his arm around.

The guy almost made it, but the door slammed shut on his forearm, crushing it and causing the man to cry out.

He pulled his damaged arm from the door, the pistol he'd been hiding clattering to the ground.

But instead of cradling his wrist, he charged.

No matter how well trained or aggressive, he didn't stand a chance against Axe, even after months off.

Axe pivoted, using the man's energy against him, taking him down. The man hit the ground hard, his breath forced out, before his head bounced against the asphalt, knocking him out cold.

This has to be a snatch and grab for Haley. So one down, three to go.

He'd conducted enough similar operations to know. A driver, one guy providing security in the hallway or over watch, depending on the location. Two to enter and grab, assuming the element of surprise. It would take more if the target expected an assault.

I'm rusty. Have to get my head in the game and not mess this up. If someone wants to grab Haley, then Nalen, the president, and the woman are all onto something big.

He scooped up the man's 9mm pistol—the everyday weapon of warriors everywhere—and slid it into his cargo pants pocket.

I wish I had my Team. A sniper plus two other guys would make this doable. But me alone against three targets, with no backup, and not wanting to shoot everyone on sight? Bad odds.

But maybe…

Sorry, buddy, but you chose the wrong side.

Axe grabbed a handful of the guy's hair and slammed it against the ground, hard. Just to be sure.

That'll keep you out for a while, if not permanently.

He moved around and grabbed the target's upper body, dead lifting him the way he had Ron on the dusty street months ago. Staggering under the weight, he used his knee to swing the van door open, then stuffed the man back onto the driver's seat. Still out for the count, the man rested, his head back, seemingly asleep.

Perfect. Sleeping on watch. Happens all the time. Well, not to SEALS, but this guy is no SEAL. Well trained and aggressive, but not tier one.

Aware of the ticking clock and danger to Haley, he hurriedly closed the door, careful to minimize the sound.

The closing door jarred the body, the head falling forward. It no longer looked like he slept.

He couldn't take on three tangos by himself, especially without going in with guns blazing. He had to ambush them as they came out the door. When they were within sight of the van, believing their buddy had the lookout, they might be distracted. In a hurry to finish the job. Focused on getting to the van.

Easy enough to drop them from behind.

But who are they? Can I shoot them without fallout? They could be police, a CIA paramilitary group, or other good guys. Or at least, not the bad guys. No. No shooting unless I know exactly who they are... or they shoot at me.

He hustled around the van, checking the inside, aware there could be another tango waiting. The sliding door close to the apartment had been left open, as he suspected it would be. Easy out, easy in. Otherwise, the van was empty.

He ducked inside and knelt between the two front seats, fumbling across the knocked-out guy's body for the lever to tilt the seat back. He'd make it look like the guy had decided to take a nap. Improbable during an op, but the anger at their sleeping buddy might be the distraction that would buy Axe the few seconds he needed.

He found the lever and pulled, keeping the seat from falling too far backwards, then tilting the man's head back to rest serenely, facing away from the building.

Nighty-night. Now for your buddies.

He looked for the tire iron the guy had held minutes before getting out of the van along the road—a prop, he figured, to keep him from stopping to help—but didn't see it.

Maybe they took it along to pry the door.

He heard a thump and turned to see two men, dressed in black tactical gear, like their comrade, half dragging, half carrying the limp body of a woman between them.

He smoothly stepped to the rear of the van, staying in the shadows, careful to not move too fast and attract their eyes.

Too late for the surprise ambush from the rear as they exit the building. Shouldn't have lingered over dinner with Red. Speaking of whom, this would be so much easier—and better—with him and the rest of them. I went from a team of many to a team of one.

Could he ambush them from here? He visualized the process. They would be carrying dead weight between them. One would get in the van first, taking the weight of the woman's head and torso, the other man helping with her feet, then stepping in. They would close the door, then call to their driver to go.

This will work. But what about the fourth guy?

He'd only seen two. Did they actually come as a three-man team? Or is there a man on overwatch who had already called out a warning?

Adapt and overcome.

He crouched near the door, thankful for the lack of windows in the panel van. He considered drawing his gun, or at least the folding knife clipped inside his front pocket, but held back.

I'm not killing anyone unless it's them or me. Or Haley.

It happened as he imagined it. The first man backed into the van, holding Haley—or the woman he hoped was Haley, and not some random civilian whose abduction he was in the middle of thwarting.

The man never saw Axe or even knew he had been hit by a vicious elbow to his head. He just collapsed in a heap, dropping Haley. Thankfully, her head landed on the tango's body. He wasn't so lucky. His head bounced off the metal deck of the van with a thud.

The other man had good reflexes and kept his wits about him. He dropped Haley's feet and went for his gun on his leg in a drop holster.

Axe pushed himself out, the daily squats and trail running helping him fly to land on his enemy, defenseless with his arm at his side, his hand touching the butt of the pistol.

They rolled, grabbing at each other. Axe eventually landed face up with the man's neck held expertly in a rear naked choke hold.

The tango tapped frantically at Axe's leg.

No tapping out in combat, chief.

In seconds, the man went slack.

Axe pushed him off, then searched his pockets. If the guy had any experience, there would be…

Yes. Got 'em.

Flex cuffs.

With speed that comes with years of experience, the cuffs slid on smoothly as Axe looked around for the last man.

Not seeing anyone, but conscious of the potential for a sniper, he grabbed the man by the feet and dragged him, head bouncing as he backed into the van, avoiding the still form of the barefoot woman in jeans and a baggy gray sweatshirt, face hidden by her long blond hair. He dumped the third guy next to his buddy.

You assholes are going to regret this so much. Even more if she's dead, though. Do you have any idea who you've messed with?

He cuffed the second guy, who lay moaning in a heap, still mostly out of it, then bounced his face off the floor once, since he already had him on his stomach to do the cuffs.

The man reclining in the driver's seat seemed pretty out of it, so Axe didn't bother with cuffs for him, opting instead for a speedy escape.

We'll be long gone by the time he wakes up.

With the enemy secure, he moved the woman he hoped was Haley. He gently parted her hair, and stopped, staring at the face in the dim light from the building's nearby lights.

She was striking. Beautiful. More than that. Stunning.

Full lips, adorable dimples, strong jaw, and long, flowing, gorgeous blond hair.

She was breathing, and he didn't see any blood. "Hey, Haley? You okay? Wake up, you're safe now."

She groaned, barely aware of her surroundings, but coming to.

Tires squealed, and he sprang into action. Since the takedown of the driver, he'd gotten his head back in the game. Another vehicle only meant trouble for them.

Axe pulled Haley fully into the van as gently as he could while hurrying, then slammed the side door closed.

He was about the heave the driver out of the seat when he realized he had no time. Instead, he sat down on the guy's lap and threw the van into drive as his foot found the gas pedal.

They were facing the wrong direction for a quick escape.

To allow for the van's sliding door to face the building, the tangos had pointed the nose of the van towards the rear of the sprawling apartment complex, not towards the much shorter route to the street.

Which meant he'd have to execute a 180 while being chased by what was either the fourth guy in a backup vehicle or another full team. Which would be great if he could pull it off while sitting on this guy's lap in a cheap panel van. But it would open him up to weapons fire or a plain old blocking maneuver. Neither would be good.

Or... he could go all the way around, the long way.

He floored it and glanced in the mirror, seeing another black panel van closing fast. It all came together.

That's the one I passed on the road. A lookout and backup. But I fooled them when I drove the wrong way around. They figured I lived here. Fine. I'll take being lucky any day it keeps me alive.

The first speed bump surprised him. The thuds of heads bouncing off the van's floor made him smile until he realized Haley's head might be one of them.

"Haley? You okay? Hold on."

Her head throbbed.

Haley gasped in pain as her body lurched and head smashed against the metal floor she lay on.

Metal floor?

She used all her will to force her eyes open, but it didn't help. Her mind couldn't grasp the situation.

Where am I?

She struggled to sit up, her world moving underneath her.

I must have taken a blow to the head. How? Did I fall when I answered the door?

The door. The man outside with the handsome face. The man sent to help her.

He hit me, and I must have lost consciousness. The bastard.

She wasn't thinking straight, but realized she must be in a van. Driven by her abductor.

Not today.

Haley pushed herself up to her knees and crawled forward, years of warnings ringing in her mind. Never let them take you to a second location.

Whatever this is, it ends now. Stop the van, get out, run. Even dazed, I can run faster than anyone they could send after me.

The van lurched, the tires on the left side hitting a speed bump, and she lost her balance for a second, almost toppling over. Her eyes fluttered, and she felt herself slipping away.

Don't fall. If you black out, it's all over.

She forced herself slowly to her feet, crouched directly behind the driver's seat. Her mind played tricks on her: she saw two men on the seat before her, one laying back, asleep, the other driving.

Axe angled the van so the right side wheels missed the next speed bump, sending only his side of the van bouncing as his speed climbed. He risked a glance in the rear-view mirror to check the pursuers.

Haley struggled to focus on the situation. She had to get stop the van and escape.

The sleeping one isn't a threat. If he even exists. Get the driver.

She locked her fingers around the neck of the man driving and squeezed as if her life depended on it.

Because it did.

Instead of the van in the mirror, Axe saw the wild, desperate eyes of the amazingly beautiful woman directly behind him. Haley. Alive and awake.

Thank God.

Then her powerful hands lock around his throat and begin to choke the life out of him.

Haley squeezed for every catcall while walking along the street.

For every time a guy mansplained a topic she knew more about than he did.

For everyone who thought she was stupid because she also happened to be pretty.

And for every woman who had ever walked in fear.

Her fingers crushed Axe's windpipe, blocking his air. The sides of her hands put pressure on the carotid arteries in his neck, cutting off the flow of blood to his brain.

Axe let go of the steering wheel with both hands, clawing at her, driving the van with one knee to keep from losing control.

She must be confused and terrified.

But it didn't make his choices any easier.

He could slam on the brakes, which would propel her forward, breaking her grip... and likely her neck.

Leaving him alive, her dead or injured, and the pursuers in control of them both.

He could punch her face, injuring her further. And again, letting the bad guys following them get an advantage.

With everything happening, his mind struggled to recall the code phrase Nalen had told him.

Finally, on the edge of blacking out, it came to him.

"Knight to f3," he gasped, hoping she could hear him over the noise of the engine. And understand him after her ordeal.

"Knight to f3!"

The man was saying something, but her mind struggled to understand. Her head hurt so much. If she could take out her attacker, she could stop the van and make it all feel better.

She squeezed harder.

The man's head slumped forward while his hands clawed at hers.

Wait, what? Knight to f3—did he say that, or did I imagine it? King's knight opening—my favorite way to start a chess game, especially against... Uncle James.

Axe had been choked out in training enough to know he had less than a second left.

Desperate times call for desperate measures. Sorry, Haley.

He moved his foot off the gas pedal and to the brake...

And the hands let go.

Axe drew in a desperate breath and mashed the gas pedal back down, nearly throwing Haley off her feet.

She grabbed onto his shoulders and hung on.

"Thank you. You understand the chess reference? You know who sent me?"

"I... I guess. But, what the hell's going on?"

"Short story: I'm the good guy. These three are the bad guys. We're being chased by a van with at least one more bad guy. Sit down and hold on."

She slid into the passenger seat without question and buckled her seatbelt.

Her voice caught as she apologized. "Sorry I choked you. I'm... I'm kind of out of it. Somebody hit me."

"Look in the back. One of them clobbered you. Trust me, they're hurting even more than you right about now."

He hit the last speed bump head on, smiling at the double thump of men hitting the deck.

Damn, I'm having fun. Now that I'm not being choked out by the person I'm rescuing, that is.

Haley moaned next to him, holding her head.

Oops.

"Sorry."

"Are there two of you, or are you sitting on someone's lap?"

"No, you're fine. There wasn't time to move him."

Haley nodded. He forced himself not to stare at her face. She could be a supermodel.

"I'll trust you for now, because of what you said. But as soon as we're out of this situation, you have some explaining to do."

"We can talk now. Well, for a few more minutes, then things are going to get kind of wild."

"Don't you need to focus?"

"I've done this kind of stuff before. It doesn't take all my energy. Unless they shoot at us, then you have to drive while I shoot back. Do you think you can do that? Your head good enough to stay on the road if I need you?"

He heard her take a breath and make the effort to pull herself together. "Absolutely." It came out shaky, but he believed her.

11

THE PLAN

The van took the corner out of her apartment complex faster than any vehicle had before, she was sure.

For a moment the two passenger side tires floated off the ground, and the van tilted crazily.

That doesn't help my head.

Her focus started returning, though her head continued to throb.

Possible concussion. Don't fall asleep.

"What's the plan? There's a police station, but it's like five miles away, and in town."

"No police."

"Do you have a cell phone? I have an emergency number I can call."

"Not now."

After a minute, with the other van gaining on them, the man took the next turn, left, just as fast as the previous one. They were now on a dark, narrow country road, moving away from town. He glanced in the mirror every few seconds. She looked back too. The van fell behind at the turn but stuck with them.

"There's nothing down this road for miles. It's all hills and farms."

"Yes. It's the way I came in. Are you able to move fast? I mean, get out of the van quickly and move away, or is your head still messed up?"

"It'll hurt, but I'm functional."

"Perfect. Get ready."

They sped up a small hill, going airborne for a moment at the top.

Her stomach lurched.

When she was a kid, her dad would drive the back roads faster than he should have. They'd go over the hills yelling, "Weee!" together at the top of their lungs.

This wasn't as much fun.

"Um… the next hill's a lot bigger."

"Yep." The man's face, lit up by the dashboard lights, looked maniacal.

Oh my God. He's enjoying himself.

"Keep your seatbelt on, but get ready."

The van started up the hill, the engine straining.

"On the other side, I'm slamming on the brakes and turning sideways, across the road. Once we stop, or mostly stop, get out and run laterally. Like, to the side of the road. Don't run straight down the road or you'll die, okay?"

It was like a roller coaster, ratcheting to the top of the first enormous drop. Only she was actually racing up a hill in a van driven by a grinning psychopath sitting on the lap of a guy who might be dead.

"I'm not sure…"

He looked at her, the smile vanishing, his face serious. Severe. Commanding. "Can you do it or not?"

She only hesitated a second. She could do this. She had to. "Yes."

He nodded. "Excellent."

12

THE FLIGHT

One last check in the mirror. The other van was close.

I hope it's enough.

"Get ready."

I also hope she can handle this. Poor form to kill the hostage as I'm rescuing her.

He joked, "Don't worry, I'm turning the van to the left. If this doesn't work, they'll hit me first."

Haley didn't laugh. Didn't even smile.

Tough crowd.

The van crested the hill. All four tires left the road.

No way they'll risk it. They'll slow down... a little.

His foot left the accelerator and stamped onto the brake, not doing any good with the whole van in the air.

His fingers gripped the wheel firmly, but not overly tense. He had a good feeling about this.

The brakes screamed as the van returned to earth and the tires connected with the road.

Axe wrenched the wheel to the left, hard, but not hard enough to tip the van over. He hoped.

The rear fishtailed, and they skidded, slowing rapidly on the far side of the hill which blocked them from the view of the other van.

Then they were tipping, the van angling over onto Haley's side.

Axe expertly corrected the steering, his body recalling the two week tactical driving course he and the Team took. The best way to tip a vehicle—or keep it upright—not surprising, was to practice.

The difference between fear and excitement is experience.

As the van slowed, his eye caught the GPS temporarily attached to the grill of the van's air conditioner vent.

Awesome.

He snatched it from its cradle as he yelled to Haley. "Out! Now! Run to the side of the road!"

Her door opened as he spoke and she jumped out.

Impressive. She's handling the experience better than I'd have guessed.

He threw his door open as he saw the lights of the other van, bright in the dark night, shining into space as they neared the top of the hill.

Plenty of time.

The lights grew brighter. Any second now, the nose of the van would point downward. They would see the trap—too late to avoid it, though.

He had one leg out when the man he'd been sitting on came to with a moan, gasped, and grabbed his wrist.

13

THE SHINE

The goon's iron grip on Axe's wrist hurt like hell. Axe yanked his arm as he finished jumping out of the van, but only brought the man part way out with him.

The roar of the other van's engine filled his ears and the high beams hit him as it flew over the top of the hill and started down. The bumper scraped against the ground with a crash, nearly drowning out the engine noise as the front of the van landed hard.

He slammed the small GPS unit in his hand against the man's vulnerable wrist, once, twice, while pulling away, dragging the man out of the front seat and onto the road. Still groggy, the man refused to let go. At some instinctive level he must know his predicament had something to do with the person sitting on him as he came to.

Tires screamed as the driver of the second van finally realized the situation: the road blocked by the very van he'd been chasing, with no space or time to swerve out of the way.

Axe didn't have to look up. He was less than a second from being crushed when the two vans t-boned.

He didn't panic. SEALs are trained not to succumb to fear, no matter how dire the circumstances.

But as he struggled with the dazed man refusing to release his wrist, he had to acknowledge he wasn't having as much fun as earlier.

With one last huge heave, he used all his strength to lunge backwards, dragging the man with him.

Fine. You don't want to let go, I'll get us both out of danger and deal with you later.

Axe fell to the ground, his right arm stretched upwards, the man standing on unsteady legs, still dazed, leaning forward and holding stubbornly to him.

An instant later Axe was free as the van clipped the man, flinging his body into the air towards the side of the road, then crashing into the side of the other van.

Axe scrambled, backwards crab walking, desperate to get away from the ongoing crash. The sounds of breaking glass and crunching metal followed him, but in a moment he slid down the ditch of the narrow two-lane rural road.

He looked up in time to see the t-boned van flying sideways, before it caught an edge and began log rolling down the hill. The second van followed, mere feet behind, flipping end over end.

The crashing of both vans filled the still night air.

He stood up and checked himself over.

No harm, no foul... but that was a little close for comfort.

As the tumbling vans came to a stop down the hill, blocking the road, he focused on his two priorities: find Haley and continue the escape.

The headlights of the second van had died in the crash, leaving the night dark again.

It was as if nothing had happened.

Wonder if anyone survived? Airbags, anti-crumple zones... better hurry, just in case.

"Haley? You okay?" he called.

"I'm here." She rose from the side of the ditch, about ten feet from him, on his side of the road. The stars allowed him to see her vague outline. Her slumped body language, and trembling voice, told him the rest.

He pulled out his powerful mini flashlight and shone it on the ground as he hurried towards her.

"Hey, you did great. Are you hurt?"

He could see well enough to note the shake of her head, and, remarkably, the straightening of her body as she pulled herself together.

"I'm..." She took a deep breath, squaring her shoulders and looking at him. "I'm fine. But you are one crazy asshole." Her bark of laughter turned suddenly into tears, which she choked back. He reached for her, but stopped. Time for comforting later.

Pretty strong person. She'll be back to normal in a second, I bet.

"You're not the first person to say that, actually. But it got the job done. Bad guys are out of commission and I didn't kill anyone."

He considered the driver of the van who he had sat on, then tried to drag to safety with him, who had ended up a human hood ornament.

And the man—or men—in the second van. "Well, at least I didn't directly kill them," he muttered under his breath.

He shone the flashlight towards the wreckage, but something caught his eye at the edge of the beam. He directed the light to a tree on their side of the road, dozens of feet away.

Wow.

The man who had held onto his arm was in the tree. His obviously lifeless body hung disturbingly on a thick branch about eight feet off the ground, his head twisted 180 degrees the wrong way, looking at them.

He thought of Haley. "Don't look—"

Too late. She vomited repeatedly, bent over, fresh sobs interspersed with the heaves.

It was far from the most gruesome thing Axe had seen.

Not even in the top ten. But I bet it's the worst she's ever encountered. She's having a shitty night. Hope she doesn't lose it.

Axe hesitated, debating the merits of rubbing this stranger's back and offering comfort, or letting her deal with it on her own.

He decided to treat her like one of the guys. She worked in the business, right? She could handle it.

"Breathe through your nose. Try to lengthen your breaths. Don't think about what you saw. Put it away for now. Box it up. You can deal with it some other night. For now, we have stuff to do."

She breathed, spat, and raised herself up again. With another deep breath and a wipe of her mouth with the back of her hand, she focused again.

Very impressive. She should be a field asset instead of an analyst.

"I'm good. Sorry," she gestured at the remains of her dinner on the ground near them. "Caught me off guard."

"You handle yourself well. By the way, I'm Alex. Axe for short."

"Pleased to meet you," she said with a touch of black humor in her voice at the absurdity of social niceties given the situation. "I'm Haley. But you already knew that."

He laughed as he shone the flashlight at the wreckage, wondering how much time they had.

"I'm just glad to hear I'm helping the right person." Axe thought for a second, a plan forming in his mind. He directed the flashlight beam at Haley's gray sweatshirt, then at her feet. She had one slipper on and the other foot bare.

"New plan. We need to buy ourselves time to figure out the next step. Where's your other slipper? In the van?"

"I think so. I only had one when I jumped out. You know, before you set up a roadblock with our getaway vehicle."

Beautiful and sassy. Love it. Wonder if she's single... No. I have to keep my head in the game. Think about that later.

"So it's in the van or near your apartment. Perfect. Give me that one, please."

He eyed the sweatshirt again as she handed it to him, noting the college logo. "Your alma matter?"

"Yes, my favorite sweatshirt."

"That's too bad. Here's the idea: we cut it off you with my knife, make it look like... Well, you know."

She stood barefoot in the grass, stepping away from where she'd been sick. "Like they…"

He nodded. "Then we fling it into the trees over there on a low branch. Whoever stumbles upon this scene will call for help. It will take a while, but by morning the place will be crawling with police. Eventually they'll see your slipper in the van—hopefully, or at your apartment, which might work out even better. They'll find the second slipper alongside the road, and your sweatshirt in the branches. They'll spend hours looking for your body, thinking you're just like our friend up there." He gestured at the body but didn't move the flashlight.

Haley caught on instantly. "While we regroup, whoever set this up will think I'm dead."

"Yes. Or at least be confused about the situation. Giving us the advantage." Axe stripped off the casual shirt he wore, revealing the tight black t-shirt underneath. "You can wear this."

He handed it to her, turned his back and waited. "And hurry, if you—"

She gave him the sweatshirt, and he heard her slipping his shirt on. He used his knife to rip the thick material up the middle before jogging to the other side of the road and flinging it into a tree, then tossing the slipper on the edge of the road where it would be seen.

That should buy us some time.

14

THE RUN

The crickets had started chirping again.

Axe checked the vans while Haley waited nearby, not interested in helping with the job.

The two in his van were dead, or close to it, from being unsecured in the back during the impact and rolls that followed. Axe cut the zip ties on their wrists, pocketing the plastic pieces. "No need for the police to wonder why they were tied up in the back of a van," he reported to her as he moved to the other van.

"Three guys." He felt the pulse of the driver, hanging upside down by his seat belt. His head, like that of the man in the passenger seat, had taken the force of the airbags when they deployed. "Unconscious, but these two might live."

Careful of fingerprints, Axe craned his head to see into the cargo area, shining his flashlight on the face of the man in back. He lay on the ceiling of the upside down van, staring lifelessly at the floor above him through glassy eyes, his head bent at a sharp angle.

"The one in back is gone."

"Can we, I mean you... Shouldn't you..."

"We can get into it more in a minute, but the short version is I'm a civilian helping a friend. Rules of engagement are whatever they would be for a normal, everyday person. So, no, I can't kill them. Even if that's the smartest thing to do," he muttered to himself.

After the check of the vans, he was ready to head back.

"I can carry you," he said, shining the light at her bare feet.

She glared at him, giving him a drop dead look.

"No. Way."

Haley ran, pacing him as he lit the way with his flashlight pointed towards the ground. She kept as much as possible to the sloped, grassy side of the road, to save her feet, but often had to land several steps in a row on the asphalt. It wouldn't have been bad except for the pebbles and bits of glass that dug into her tender soles. He wondered how badly they were bleeding.

They talked while they ran.

"Just to be clear, the president sent me to help because he thinks you may have found something. He's concerned he's either being surveilled or betrayed by someone in his inner circle."

"Nothing I've found indicates that's the situation, but it's not what I have been looking for."

"Maybe his problem and whatever you've discovered are linked, maybe they're not. Either way, I'm here to help you."

She sucked in her breath and stopped.

"I need to walk for a minute. My feet…"

He knelt and held the flashlight to each of her feet. Blood flowed freely.

"Listen, you've done great, but if you keep going, you won't be one hundred percent when we most need it. Let me carry you."

She shook her head, gingerly taking a few steps. "I can handle it."

"Really, it's fine. Until a few months ago, I routinely walked and ran for miles with eighty to one hundred pounds of gear." He shone the light on her, top to bottom, then hesitated. "What are you, about… ninety-five pounds?"

15

THE HORSE

Haley knew her face betrayed her when she lied. She had to work on that. But she also knew when a man tried to play her. Being as attractive as a model, she'd had years of experience. He'd guessed her correct weight... then subtracted a bunch of pounds and lied about it.

"Nice try."

Axe paused, seeming to know he had been busted. "Fine. But I'd rather not leave you here, go get my truck, and come pick you up. Walking is too slow. Running barefoot is out because of the damage. It's not a knight in shining armor thing. It's logical, and I did it with a male teammate a while back." He turned his back to her. "A firefighter's carry is too hard and would be uncomfortable, so hop on. Let's go."

This can't be happening.

With a sigh, she wrapped her arms around his shoulders and hopped up on his back.

"Geez! Ninety-five, my ass," he mumbled as he grabbed her legs, which made her smile despite herself, glad he couldn't see.

16

THE UNCLE

Axe carried her down the road, making better time with Haley on his back.

Definitely not ninety-five pounds. Me and my bright ideas.

He could handle the carry for a while.

Glad I've stayed in shape since I got out. And it feels nice having her close like this. Much better than carrying Ron. Softer, warmer, lighter.

"How can you help?" Her breath tickled his ear, and he fought to block out the feeling. He had to keep his head in the game.

And she's much too young for me.

"I honestly don't know. They said you'd be the secret agent."

She readjusted her arms around him. So far, this babysitting gig was turning out fine. He'd gotten the better of three bad guys in a fight, had a car chase, set up an effective instant ambush, and had a stunningly beautiful woman clinging to him as he ran through the night.

Not bad for a Monday.

"I'm an analyst. Though…"

"What?"

She hesitated, and he got the impression she was deciding whether to trust him.

"I'd love to be a field agent. But with my connections, I'd be a liability."

"Because of the president being your…"

"He's my uncle. Not by blood, but Mom and Brenda are basically sisters, so the president is basically my Uncle Jimmy."

He grinned and shook his head.

Funny to hear James Heringten, highly decorated retired Navy SEAL and President of the United States, called Uncle Jimmy. But I guess he was Uncle Jimmy before he was the president. And the members of his Teams must have had a nickname or call sign for him. I'll have to ask the admiral.

"Yeah, even after he's done being the president, it would be risky for you to be in the field. And you'd never fit in."

She stiffened.

Uh oh, sore subject.

"What do you mean?" Her voice was frosty.

"Come on, don't play dumb with me. We've known each other," he checked his watch, "almost an hour. I know you're not naïve."

She sighed with exasperation. "So I'm pretty? Big deal. I can blend in."

He nodded, knowing she'd feel it, but said nothing, thinking it through. He ran on, his feet pounding on the cracked asphalt of the country road. Finally, he spoke again. "You're right."

There was a pause while she digested his words. "I am?" Her surprise came through loud and clear.

"If you want to be an asset in the field, go for it. There will be ops you're poorly suited for because of how you look. But there will be some no one else could pull off. They might not come along often, but they'll be there. Besides, you've handled yourself well tonight. I can see you in the field." He'd been shining her on earlier, downplaying her weight, but he hoped she understood he believed in her potential.

She was quiet for a moment, until she spoke, barely above a whisper in his ear, "Thank you."

"Now, though, I understand you have a theory something big is about to happen to the country, but you can't get any traction, right?"

"Yes, and I put more pieces together today. But I'm not sure how you can help, aside from saving me from being abducted. I'm the most junior analyst and I have no experience managing assets. All I do is write reports and dig through databases trying to figure puzzles. I don't even know where to start."

"If you could get anything you wanted, what would it be?"

Haley was quiet as he ran through the dark at a pace he could comfortably maintain. With Haley on his back, he'd turned off his flashlight after letting his eyes adjust to the night, not wanting anyone to see a light bobbing in the distance and remember it later when they heard about a car crash.

"A confession. A bad guy telling me what they had planned."

"Great. Let's go get us a bad guy."

"We just left them behind and now you want to run back?"

"No, they were too messed up. And with no way to escape quickly, we played it well to leave the scene."

He turned from the narrow country road onto the main road leading back to her apartment complex. They didn't have far, and cars might come along any minute. Axe stopped.

"Hop down. We're out for a walk. Less conspicuous.

Haley slid down his back, landing gingerly on her torn-up feet.

"So where are we going to get a bad guy to confess?"

Axe stretched his back, making an exaggerated showing of how good it felt to be free of her weight. He saw her fight back a smile.

"At their ultra-secret hideout, of course." He reached in his pants cargo pocket and pulled out the GPS unit he'd grabbed before exiting the van. "If they followed a trail to get here, there's a path back to their base of operations."

"But there's only two of us."

"True. But we work pretty well together." He paused and continued under his breath. "When you're not strangling me."

17

THE RESEARCH

Haley climbed into Axe's truck, careful of her beat-up feet, and looked longingly up at her apartment. The windows were dark. The guys who grabbed her must have turned them off before dragging her out.

Everything I need is right up those stairs, but I can't get it if we want to maintain the illusion that I've vanished. Still, a pair of shoes would be nice.

As they approached the apartment complex, she had explained to Axe how the abduction went down. When she looked out the peephole and saw a fit young man with a friendly face and military bearing, she opened the door, figuring him to be the operator sent because of her mother's meddling.

Before saying a word, she'd been hit on the head and knocked out.

She vaguely recalled being pulled into the van, but only became aware enough to act... just in time to attack the wrong man.

Could have happened to anyone.

Still, opening the door to the strange man had been stupid.

Won't make that mistake again. Assuming I get out of this alive.

She chuckled to herself, but Axe heard.

"What?"

"Sorry, but given the car chase, my torn-up feet, and the plan to go find, capture, and interrogate a bad guy, I wonder if I would have been safer with them."

She meant it as a joke, but regretted it the moment it came out.

"No," Axe said. "You'd be tortured until you gave them whatever they were looking for, then your body would be disappeared. Or mutilated and dumped somewhere public, depending on what statement they wanted to make to your managers, family… and the president."

The thought sobered her, and she lapsed into silence as Axe pulled his truck out of the quiet apartment parking lot onto the road, heading away from where they had recently walked—and the men who would have tortured her.

She held the GPS unit. It had been a simple matter to reverse the directions back to the starting point. The brand new device held only her apartment and the start of the journey. She guessed they used the cheap, dedicated GPS unit instead of their cell phones for operational security.

Onetime use. No way to trace them back any further than their base, which will be a temporary location.

If they suspected the abduction had failed, whoever remained at the building shown on the map would sanitize it and vanish.

The melodic female voice of the GPS told them they would reach their destination in 54 minutes. It looked like they were going to an industrial area in the suburbs on the other side of D.C. She'd never been there.

Haley reached for her phone in the pocket of her jeans out of habit but coming up empty. She could picture it on the small kitchen table, next to her mostly eaten dinner.

"Give me your phone. I'll research the area."

Axe unlocked it and gave it to her while he drove, checking his mirrors constantly.

"Industrial area." She zoomed in and checked the view of the streets on the phone's mapping app. "Run down. I doubt there's much activity this time of night."

"Good for us. But good for them, too."

Axe turned left onto a larger, busier road, as instructed by the GPS, then moved into the right lane.

"Quick stop. You stay here, I'll run in. What are your sizes? Shoes, sweatshirt?"

"We have time?"

"We make the time. I'm going to need you on overwatch for me, and you can't do it barefoot. Plus, it's going to get colder. I have a spare jacket in back," he gestured with his head to large silver toolbox set across the bed of the pickup truck. "But we need more."

As they pulled in to the 24-hour superstore, Axe looked at her carefully.

"What?"

"Even though you're an analyst, you took some field training, right? You can handle a weapon?"

"Yes, definitely."

They parked relatively close to the door but off to the side of the lot. Axe slid a switch to disable the auto dome light, then hopped out of the truck and unlocked the tool box. In a second he'd grabbed a black jacket, which he used to cover up the other items in his hands, and got back into the truck, shutting the door behind him.

He handed her a pistol, a tiny 9mm semi-automatic in a leather holster, along with two extra magazines. "Good?"

"Perfect." She checked it, then clipped it to her waist, thankful for the jeans and belt. "You have all this with you?"

"The guns and ammo aren't usually in the truck. I had them along because I met a buddy earlier at the gun range." He shrugged with a smile. "Happy it worked out this way." He nodded at the store. "I'll be back in a few minutes. Remember, for now we're in stealth mode. No one should know we're here. Don't overreact, but if anyone shows an interest…"

"I won't be taken again, don't worry."

He also handed her a black folding knife. She used the round hole to smoothly open it with her thumb. The perfectly balanced grip and black three-inch blade fit her hand well. The edge glinted in what little light shone in the front windshield. She had no doubt it was sharp enough to cut anything—or anyone. Combined with the gun on her hip, she felt dangerous.

"For less-than-lethal situations." He slid on the jacket and zipped it up, covering up his own, larger 9mm sticking out of its holster inside his pants. "Can you work your fancy analyst magic and find out more about where we're going?"

"Consider it done."

He smiled, the deep lines around his eyes crinkling, obviously enjoying the evening. He was a handsome man, but much too old for her.

I hope he realizes it. This is business, not a date.

18

THE RISK

Axe drove, following the directions of the GPS voice, pushing the speed limit to make up time. Haley tried on shoes from the six boxes he had bought. Three sizes of a cheap sneaker, three of decent hiking boots. She settled on the hiking boots while helping him navigate. Then she turned her back, taking off his shirt and replacing it with a new black t-shirt and a black sweatshirt he'd picked out.

They continued through suburbia, getting closer to downtown D.C. They'd pass the airport, then get to their location right on the edge of the D.C. and Maryland border.

He debated the best way to approach the warehouse. Haley had discovered an abundance of information about the building. A local commercial real estate company had it listed for rent with a full web page with several pictures of the interior and exterior. "Huge open drive-in space, separate office area, kitchenette, and two bathrooms (one with shower) included in lease."

They agreed it would have been easy for the bad guys to find information about the building being vacant and for rent, break in, and use it as a staging point.

It looked like a dump. The gray building had a lone loading dock for a semi or other large delivery vehicle, barred windows high along the back wall, and a front entrance with a solid-looking metal door. Six vehicles could park on one side, plus four in the front. Haley hadn't been able to find a view of one side, but from the interior photos, only one window could be accessed at the ground level, and it probably had bars covering it as well, like the others.

If I had the Team, this would be easy. Alone, a frontal assault is suicidal.

They were getting close to the airport, time to make the call. Recon only, which they didn't have time for? A frontal assault, with the inherent risks of being one man against an unknown number of enemy? Or stealth, going in through a window or skylight?

Or the craziest idea—a bluff.

"Can you shoot? I mean, really shoot?"

Haley looked at him and nodded. "The CIA's basic training, plus I hunted as a kid." At Axe's raised eyebrow, she explained further. "Dad wanted a boy," she shrugged. "And we lived on a farm a few years. I shot my first deer at 11, but hated it. Too beautiful of an animal to kill. After that I only shot vermin: groundhogs, skunk, or the odd fox that came to close to the henhouse."

"You've never killed a person, though, right?"

She shook her head.

"Well, here's hoping you don't have to. But are you alright as my overwatch? If I put you on a roof with a line of sight to the building, can you cover me with a rifle?"

Haley nodded with certainty. "No problem."

"Even if it means you might have to take a life?"

She didn't hesitate. "Of one of the assholes who knocked me out and were going to do who knows what to me? Definitely."

"Then we're going to bluff our way in."

Risk little, win little.

19

THE PREP

The rifle looked mean. Haley had fired guns before, even M4s exactly like this. But never in a real-life situation. No matter how realistic her instructors had made the simulations in training, tonight had a different feel.

Breathe.

Haley took a breath deep into her diaphragm, held it for a few seconds, then let it out, calming herself and focusing on the task at hand.

Axe would boost her up to the rungs of the fire escape ladder at the back of the building, a few buildings away and across the street from their target warehouse. She'd set up back from the edge, with a good view of the front door. From there, she could cover Axe as he implemented his crazy plan.

"Trust me, it will work. I look, move, and act like them," he whispered as he slipped on a heavy tactical vest, the pockets full of spare ammo magazines and other equipment.

Looking at him in the dim light from a far-off streetlight, she had to admit he could pass for the man she had opened the door for. Muscular, fit, and strong looking. Her guy hadn't worn a vest, though, and hadn't been as clean-cut looking.

"What about the vest?"

"Well, it's a risk, but I'm not going in without it. I'd rather risk getting made than not have it if I get shot." He tapped his chest. "This plate will catch anything up to a rifle round, depending on the distance."

They knelt in the bed of his truck at the rear of the building they'd picked from the satellite overview of the neighborhood. She would have an unobstructed view of the main entrance to the warehouse.

He passed her one of the new handheld radios he'd purchased less than an hour before, and they each slipped in an ear bud.

"Check?" Axe whispered, turning away from her. She heard him clearly in her ear.

"Check." She clipped the radio onto the rear of her jeans.

They'd set the radios to voice activated transmission, so they wouldn't have to take fingers off triggers to talk.

Axe continued the briefing. She heard him through the radio and right in front of her. "Only shoot if you have no other option. Then shoot to distract. Aim high, or to the side. We have no idea who these people are. Hell, they might be your agency, police, or some other friendly with a valid reason to question you. Maybe the goons back at your place went overboard. So let's not kill anyone unless it's absolutely, positively necessary. Right?"

"Got it." She kept the tremble out of her voice. She had dreamed of someday being in the field, but never thought it would happen suddenly like this. She always figured she'd have more training, then some easy ops with other, more experienced agents, getting her feet wet little by little.

I've been thrown into the deep end of the pool tonight and I need to learn to swim. Now.

"Right. Up you go." Axe cupped his hands together. With the pickup parked directly under the fire escape ladder, it wouldn't be difficult to access the lower rungs.

She slung the M4 over her shoulder after double checking the safety, then stepped her right foot up on his hands.

Then he lifted, sending her flying up to catch the lowest rung. She pulled up while Axe pushed, which helped her reach the next rung, then the next. Finally, her feet could make contact with the bottom rung. She looked up and continued to climb.

20

THE BOMBS

Axe taped the rodent smoke bombs to the inside of the radiator on the black cargo van they'd rented at the airport. Haley had taken Axe's idea and run with it, picking the van and booking it from his phone while he drove, maxing out the insurance coverage.

They would need it.

Axe had driven the van from the airport, following Haley driving his truck. They had parked side by side in the tiny back lot, facing the alley, ready for Haley to exfil quickly if necessary.

He smiled as he finished prepping the smoke bombs.

God bless America. A brief stop at a 24-hour big box store provides everything I needed to assault an enemy position. Well, except the guns, ammo, vest, and plan, but I have to earn my keep somehow, I guess.

He smashed two holes in the front windshield with a blanket-covered hammer from his tool chest, leaving a gap big enough for him to see and shattering the rest of the glass. No one looking in could see him in detail. He repeated the process on the passenger side window.

Finally, he lit the smoke bombs normally used to eradicate pests in their holes. As thick smoke billowed from the van's front grill, he lowered the hood but didn't latch it. More smoke poured out from the narrow gap.

Not sure how long the smoke would last, he hurried into the van and drove down the alley, away from the warehouse, before making two quick left hand turns, ending up pointing directly at the front door, three blocks away.

"Ready?"

"Eyes on. No movement."

The dense smoke was harsh, flowing into the van through the heating vents and the holes in the windshield, but the drive took only a few seconds.

"Here goes."

"Clear." Haley sounded tense but ready. "I'll have a good view of the door and the passenger side of the van, but won't have a view or shot of the driver's side."

"Understood."

I hope she doesn't shoot me in the head.

He swung in fast to the warehouse parking lot, the space nearest the door, slowed nearly to a stop, then coasted forward until the van's bumper hit the concrete wall with a thud.

Perfect. Too slow for the airbags, but hard enough so anyone inside heard and felt it.

Then he slumped forward, trying not to breathe in the smoke, his right arm pushing against the steering wheel making the horn blare, loud in the quiet of the deserted neighborhood.

I hope this works.

He felt vulnerable, sitting in front of an enemy structure, head down, waiting. Trusting his life to a partner who hadn't fired a rifle in months, and never at a human.

He tried to reassure himself.

A hundred yards away is an easy shot, despite the angle for the elevated position. If it even comes to that.

He'd been fortunate to have the best training the military could provide. But most of it centered on teamwork. None of it included being a one-man team with a person he had to both rely on and protect.

I wish I had Ron running this. He and Hector behind me. Link at the door, setting a breaching charge. And another unit surrounding the building, with a real sniper on overwatch.

They were called teams for a reason. They worked together, not alone.

Adapt and overcome. That's the real lesson I learned.

It took only a few seconds.

"Door's opening. Looks like two guys. They're confused and concerned."

She sounded like she would burst any second. "Calm down. Breathe. We've got the advantage," he whispered.

He heard her take a breath. When she spoke again, she sounded better.

"One guy looks young, mid-twenties. Red hair, pale skin, thin. The second guy is older, your age. Tall and muscular. Dark hair, cut military short. They're coming towards the side door."

Axe feebly raised his arm and moaned loudly.

One guy tried the passenger door handle, then the sliding cargo door, but Axe had locked them all.

"Young guy looks concerned. Old one is suspicious. Young guy going around to your side. Old guy is—"

He heard it before she could finish. The passenger window shook. The already-broken safety glass held for a moment, then crashed inward as the man hit it again.

"Young almost at your door. Old isn't buying it. Gun!"

His mind had already assessed the problem. Two targets, but the priority had to be the older guy at the window with a clear line on him. In the Team he'd let the sniper deal with him, but with Haley...

Axe leaned back and angled his gun towards the window. He opened his mouth to yell for the man to freeze, but the word hadn't come out when the man pitched forward, then fell to the ground.

The crack of his M4 followed an instant later, two shots ringing through the deserted streets.

He didn't hesitate, turning to push his door open, gun coming up into the face of the younger operator standing on his side of the van, recognition of the ambush registering on his face.

As he stepped out of the van, his foot slid behind the target's ankle. With his free hand he punched the man's sternum, tripping him. Axe followed him down, his knee going into the man's stomach, knocking out any wind left in him from the hard fall to the concrete.

He rolled the stunned, gasping man over, fishing a zip tie out of his cargo pant pocket, and secured the man's wrists tightly together. The ties available at the store weren't military grade, but they'd hold as long as the guy didn't have a knife.

"I shot your partner," Axe told the man tied and pinned beneath him. No need for him to know about Haley. "And I'm not feeling any remorse," he added for her benefit. "It was me or him." He hoped Haley understood the message directed at her.

"Who the hell are you?"

Axe grabbed the man by his short red hair, pulled back a few inches, and slammed his face into the ground.

"How many inside?"

The kid moaned.

Axe lifted his head again.

"Stop! Okay, dude, it's just him and me."

"Anyone else in there and you get parts of your body cut off when I make it out alive. You willing to risk it?"

"It's the truth. Honest. What's going on? Where's the guys and the other van?"

The deception fooled him, at least.

"Ran into a little trouble. Let's go inside and have a chat. You first, okay?"

No one had come out the door at the sound of the shots, so the kid might have told the truth.

He'd explained to Haley his theory: two vans of three men meant they'd been short staffed. The most likely way to take on the mission required eight guys—four to a van. The six men in the vans earlier meant the warehouse most likely held one or two guys: either junior, senior, or support personnel. Any experienced shooters would have gone in the vans to abduct her.

Axe crouched and helped the tango to his feet by lifting the man's bound wrists, making it impossible for him to move away without excruciating pain. "Name?" He lifted the wrists higher, putting more pressure on his shoulders.

"Ow! Cody."

Just a kid. Inexperienced, assigned to stay back.

"Cody, where did you serve, and how long?"

"The sandbox. Security for supply convoys."

Yep. Junior varsity.

"Play your cards right and you'll make it through tonight. Clear?"

"Yes, sir."

Compliant is good... as long as he's not faking.

He pushed the kid in front of him, around the rear of the van, his pistol pointing the way.

Time to make sure the suspicious guy is truly dead.

With his entire body, including feet and legs, hidden behind young Cody, Axe surveyed the damage to the man laying face down along-side the van. Without a vest, the bullets to the man's side and back had been instantly fatal. The vast pool of blood soaked his black shirt and spread out, dark in the weak light of the bulb over the front door to the warehouse.

Good shot. Glad she didn't miss and hit me.

He hoped Cody's lack of experience kept him from realizing his partner had been shot in the back, not from the front by Axe's weapon in the van.

"Inside. Move. Are you going to get shot by anyone as we walk in?"

"No, sir, I told you, it's just me and him."

Axe pushed him ahead and walked through the open door.

21

THE SHOTS

Haley watched through the rifle's scope, keeping her finger off the trigger as Axe pushed the bound prisoner through the door.

She did her best to not think of the man she'd shot.

People get away with murder all the time in America. Thirty to forty percent are never solved, she remembered.

But there's no going back from this. I took a life.

Her mind filled with the vision of the man's body falling sideways as her shots hit him.

Think of something else. Right now.

She scanned the area around the warehouse, forcibly drawing her attention away from what she'd done and to the matter at hand: protecting her partner.

The street remained still, with only industrial buildings for several blocks, all dark for the evening. Street lights were scattered far apart, providing little illumination. In the distance, she could hear traffic from a busier street, but nothing nearby.

How far does the sound of gunfire carry? And is there anyone close enough to care and report it?

Her mind drifted back to the shots.

The man had been suspicious from the start, coming out the door behind the younger man and looking around. She saw his eyes narrow as he scanned the street in each direction. For a moment she felt his gaze meet hers as she watched through the scope.

Did I cause him to suspect a setup and go for his gun?

Impossible. He couldn't have seen her. She lay a hundred yards away, a few feet back from the building's edge. The odds of the man noticing her were slim.

No. He had suspected something about the van, or acted out of instinct. After hitting the window enough to push it in, he'd gone for his gun so fast, she didn't even think. She pulled the trigger twice and watched him fall.

Focus.

Once again she scanned the street. Then the area around the building, avoiding the body and dark pool of blood.

She kept the rifle pointed at the door and turned her head to look to her right, down the street.

"All clear," she whispered into the microphone.

The next step in the plan had Axe clearing the building, as long as he didn't meet too much opposition. If he did, he would let her know, exfil, and she would cover him as he escaped in the van or towards her on foot.

They would worry about the van later, reporting it stolen if necessary.

If there were only a few people, as he suspected, he'd interrogate anyone left alive.

Anyone I didn't kill.

The voice in her head wouldn't let it go, no matter how hard she tried to distract it.

I did what I needed to do to protect Axe, myself, and the country.

She watched the door and felt a switch flip inside herself as she realized the truth.

I'd do it again.

"Thank you for telling me the truth about no one else being here," she heard Axe say to the remaining man over the radio. "Now, it's time for you to answer questions. Let's start here: you're going to talk. You understand that, right? So it's a matter of how long you intend to hold out."

"I'll tell you whatever you want," the young man said, clearly picked up by the microphone of Axe's radio.

"We already know parts of the plan. Lie to me and there are repercussions. Understand?"

"Yes, sir."

The kid sounded willing to help. She hoped it wasn't an act. They needed actionable intelligence and had suggested different questions to Axe, though could also whisper in his ear if she wanted more details about anything said.

Come on. Get me something good. Something to make it worth me taking a life.

22

THE TALK

The kid—Cody—held himself together, but he fought hard for control, his thin face red from the stress, making the small pimples on his forehead look angry.

He's scared. Good. That will make him more cooperative.

Axe had used the building's structural supports to maximum effect. He didn't want to torture the guy; it's not what he did. The key was to let the enemy think about the horrible ways they could be hurt if they didn't cooperate. So Axe had the kid lay on the ground, on his back, and redid the zip ties to bind the prisoner's wrists together around one of the vertical support beams.

With the tall, lanky kid stretched out on his back, Axe had found rope to tie one ankle to another beam. He cut it, then tied the other ankle and ran the rope to a pipe along the wall at the perfect angle for what he wanted to accomplish: spreading Cody's legs at a very unpleasant angle.

He wrapped the rope once around the pipe, then took in the slack.

The kid's legs spread wide.

Axe pulled more.

"Hey!" Cody struggled, trying to counter the discomfort of his the unnatural stretch of his groin and inner thighs.

Axe gave a sharp tug, and the kid screamed.

"Stop! I'll talk, I told you!"

Axe tied a knot, keeping the rope tight but easily undone for potential adjustment.

Cody watched from the floor, legs spread uncomfortably wide, close to hyperventilating.

Axe strolled towards him until he stood between his legs, then took one step back. He balanced on his left foot and took a short practice kick, pretending to line up for a football field goal.

"No, no, please, come on, dude! Ask your questions."

His terror looked—and felt—real.

If this is an act, the kid missed his calling. He should have gone to Hollywood.

"Who hired you?"

The answer came instantly. "AgaDefCo."

Shit.

One of the top three private military firms, Agasaya Defense Contractor Group—AgDefCo, or just Aga—hired veterans of all types, loaning them out to corporations, and even other governments, for security and fighting all over the world.

"Why?"

"I mustered out a month ago and applied. I've been begging them for work. This is the first gig I've done for them." It sounded like he couldn't believe how wrong his first job had gone.

"No, not why did they hire you, why did they hire everyone? Tell me the mission brief."

Cody's face reddened further when he realized he'd answered the wrong way. "They said everything was need to know. My role was to stay here and…" He trailed off, looking away.

"What?"

"Guard the building." He frowned and blushed a darker red, looking embarrassed at how much he had messed up his one job. "The other guys vetoed me going with them. Said I didn't have enough experience."

"Well, don't feel too bad, kid. You'd be in worse shape if you'd gone along."

Cody's eyes widened as he realized what Axe meant.

"Are they…"

"Two are, maybe three. Not sure about the others. Come on, mission objectives. What do you know?"

"They were going to grab someone. A woman, I think. They didn't say why and I don't think any of them asked, or cared. But it had to be tonight. That's how I got my… lucky break." He sighed and looked away again.

Don't feel sorry for this guy. He went along with a plan to kidnap a civilian.

"Why tonight?"

"No idea. But they hired me because they couldn't get one of their own crew here. That's what the team leader said." He looked across the floor at the man Haley had shot, laying inside the doorway with his blood spreading in a pool around him. Axe had dragged him in after securing the kid to the beam.

"What was his deal?"

"He was going to interrogate the woman. I heard him and the chief van guy talk about, you know…" Now he looked like he could throw up. "Different ways of making someone talk. A woman, specifically."

He looked imploringly at Axe. "I swear I didn't know this would be the type of thing they did. I would have gotten a job at a gas station instead of this."

I believe him… which presents a dilemma when this is over.

"What else? Anything you overheard. Names, locations, orders."

Cody considered for a second, then spoke. "The guy you shot knew the most. He was the point person and knew how to reach whoever was in charge." The kid glanced at the front door. "The vehicles outside might have cell phones in them. I think the white truck was the dead guy's." He shifted, trying to relieve some pressure on his wrists and legs. "And they had to take the person—her—alive. They wanted to find out how much she knew." He paused, thinking more. "They kept it all on the down low. That's what I got before they decided I couldn't go."

Axe looked at the kid, waiting for him to go on.

"And…" The kid looked uncertain.

"What?"

"It's stupid, but I heard them talk about… I don't know, a place, maybe? I only heard a part of a sentence. I think it was Mount Auck. At first I thought it was in New Zealand, you know, like Auckland? I had a buddy go there on leave. But the way they talked, it seemed like a place they should drive the woman if they couldn't get information out of her. They could be there by morning if they pushed it. Or if questioning her took a while they could go to…" He seemed embarrassed. "Look, I know this isn't right, okay?" He clearly wanted to help, whether because of the potential for Axe to hurt him or because he was actually a good guy, Axe couldn't decide. " But it sounded like…" His brow creased. "What was it? It was like two animals or something." He closed his eyes, concentrating.

"Come on, kid, spit it out."

"Rabbit pig. That's not it, but it's how I remembered it. Like how I pictured it in my mind." He opened his eyes and stared at Axe, a plaintive look on his face. "I wanted to make a good impression, remember what they told me." His eyes closed again.

"You can do it. Let it come."

Damn it, now I'm rooting for the guy.

"Hop hog! That's it! Like a rabbit hopping. And a pig. Hop hog." A smile lit up his face, but it slipped away when he saw Axe's expression.

"What the hell is Hop Hog? A mission name? Come on, what else you got?"

"It's a place," Axe heard Haley say in his ear. "Hop hog. Mount Auk. They're on Long Island, in New York. Also known as Hauppauge and Montauk," she said, pronouncing them correctly.

23

THE STREET

Haley attended college in Connecticut, a two-hour drive from central Long Island, or a short ferry ride. Two of her friends had been from Hauppauge, a medium-size city in the center of Long Island, New York.

A friend of a friend regaled them with tales of summers spent at her parent's beach house in Montauk. Haley had thought nothing of it until she'd seen been invited to a Labor Day party her junior year. The "beach house" sprawled along the shore, displaying their incredible wealth—a vast mansion they used only in July and August.

She returned to her scan of the deserted warehouse district, less worried now. It seemed her earlier shots had gone unheard. Still, her overwatch position demanded constant vigilance. Plus, it kept her mind off what she'd done.

She looked up the street. Then at the entire area around the warehouse. Down the street. All clear.

Cody, the—what? Hostage? Enemy? Kid? He'd been helpful, and clearly sounded so out of his depth she didn't know how to think of him. He had come to the end of his usefulness. She and Axe hadn't discussed what to do with anyone they interrogated once they finished questioning him.

"What are we going to do with him?" she asked Axe over the radio. A second later, she heard Cody ask the same question.

"What are you going to do with me? I've cooperated. Oh, God, please don't kill me!"

She could picture Axe standing over him, pistol drawn.

Or would he go behind the kid, reassure him, even make like he would be let go... then shoot him? A small mercy, dying while thinking freedom was at hand.

"I'm going to shoot you. But—"

"No! No, please, sir, come on—"

"Cody, shut up. I'm going to shoot you in the shoulder."

Haley heard the kid breathing heavily, trying to keep it together, not believing what he'd been told.

"You'll tell them you fought hard. Keep it simple. You and the dead guy went outside because you heard a van and thought the teams had returned. You wanted to help. Instead, a guy jumped out and shot you. You shot back and must have hit me. Your buddy tried to run inside and got hit."

Haley heard Axe moving around, untying Cody.

"You dragged your buddy inside, but he was already dead. You barred the door, bandaged your wound, and waited, not knowing what else to do, but hoping for the return of the other guys."

"But they're not coming back!"

"True. So if no one else comes by morning, you call the main number of AgaDefCo. Say you need to report in because an op has gone to hell and you need medical attention. Then stick to the story. Got it?"

"That could work, I guess. But why all the lying? What if I mess it up?"

"Because if you tell the truth, they'll kill you."

Oh no. More blood on my hands.

Haley was so tired. She'd been through so much in the last few hours. And now, it seemed, Axe would shoot the kid to hopefully save his life. Then they would discuss the next step, which probably meant a drive to Long Island. But how would they find anything there? They didn't have enough.

"We need more," she told Axe, then felt stupid. Of course he understood they needed more. Her nerves were getting the best of her. Abducted, a car chase, killing a man, listening to an interrogation, laying on a roof in the middle of the night providing over watch for a past-his-prime super soldier who seemed to have fun in the midst of this chaos...

I was doing better there for a bit. Now, I think I might be done. This is crazy. I killed someone. I should be home in bed, drive to the office in the morning, sit in a nice, safe cubicle and do what I'm best at: crunch data.

But what else could she do?

I could call in the cavalry.

She had Uncle Jimmy's—the president's—personal number. She could call and tell him what they'd found out. Let the grownups handle it.

No. It would put him at risk. And if he's right, if there is a traitor or someone has discovered a way to monitor his communication, the advantage would shift to the enemy.

What about Gregory? She had an emergency number. If she called, she'd be put directly through to him.

This is far beyond the girl who cried wolf. He'd listen. And act.

But how had the bad guys known about her in the first place? From the president's side? Or hers?

Not Gregory. Never.

Right?

She couldn't believe Gregory would betray his country. She could trust him. But if she was wrong...

More than likely, someone who saw the memo you sent earlier tonight sold you out. You put too many pieces together, shared it with too many people. That's it. That's what got you abducted.

So her group couldn't be trusted? But she couldn't be sure about Gregory, either. Not one hundred percent.

No. She and Axe had to handle it. At least for a while longer, until they had a better sense of who they could rely on and involve.

Even while debating her options, she remained vigilant.

She scanned the street, mostly on autopilot. Clear.

The building. Axe had been adamant about looking over and around the building in case of counter-attack or more guys arriving. No problems. Even the blood stain looked almost innocent as it dried, though the smear trail created by Axe dragging the body made it look less like a puddle of oil and more like the aftermath of a shooting.

She looked to her right just in time to see a car turn slowly onto the road from a side street.

Not just any car, either.

A police car.

24

THE TRUST

Axe had just cut the zip tie holding Cody's hands over his head, around the beam, when Haley's panicked voice rang in his ear, much too loud.

"Police car! Four hundred yards, heading your way!"

Cody heard her voice through the ear bud. His eyes widened. "Is that... It's her, on your radio, isn't it? The one they wanted to..."

Cody knowing about Haley became the least of his problems... but still an issue he'd have to sort out.

Someone must have reported the gun shots after all. The police would see the van's broken windows. The blood—and blood trail from dragging the body—would be obvious to law enforcement. A civilian might have driven by, not knowing what they saw or choosing to mind their own business. But the police would stop.

Axe had a decision to make.

I'm not killing any cops. I'd rather go to jail than harm innocent police doing their jobs.

But he'd prefer to remain free.

Would it be enough to hold them at gunpoint, disarm them, and take off?

What about Cody? Fingerprints? The dead guy?

No, he had to come up with a different plan.

Cody heaved a sigh of relief. "Thank God," he mumbled, still talking about Haley being alive. "I thought they might have... you know." Even as Axe looked around the large, open space, trying to formulate a plan, he noticed an enormous weight seemed to have lifted off the kid's shoulders.

Cody's reaction to overhearing Haley's voice gave him an idea.

Can I actually trust this guy?

"She's an intelligence analyst trying to stop a terrorist plot. Your guys tonight were going to abduct her and torture her to find out how much she knew. I helped her get away, and we traced those guys back to you here." Axe watched his face as he took it in. "Are you ready to switch to the side of the good guys?"

25

THE POLICE

"They're driving slow." Haley's voice over the radio had calmed when Axe assured her they would let nothing happen to the police, but her voice betrayed her concern. "Getting close to you now. Twenty-five yards. Maybe they won't notice the—"

She paused for an instant.

"They're stopping. They noticed the van and the blood."

Axe hid, his body wedged into a storage cabinet near the front door of the warehouse. He reached behind him to turn down the volume of the radio. He didn't need Haley's loud, nervous voice giving away his position.

He could hear Cody's feet as he walked back and forth on the far side of the warehouse.

He'd taken a last look as he closed the cabinet door. Cody had his pistol in hand, occasionally waving it in the air. He mumbled to himself, repeating the same word over and over, looking down and shaking his head. "Stupid, stupid, stupid."

With some coaching from Axe, and the promise that he wouldn't have to harm any police, Cody came on board. True to his word, the kid presented the look of a stressed veteran who had done something unspeakable that he regretted.

"One officer. Out of the car. Door left open. Hand on holstered weapon." Haley's voice whispered, too quiet to hear since he turned the volume down. She must have realized how much her voice could carry in the still night.

He ignored the physical pain of being crouched in a cabinet. The emotional pain was harder to discount. SEALs don't cower in cupboards.

It's the best way to stay on mission while minimizing casualties and collateral damage.

While technically the police should be on their side, he and Haley couldn't involve them yet. They still had no proof of a terrorist plot. And the dead body a few feet away meant they wouldn't be believed, anyway. What a situation.

The only easy day was yesterday.

"He's checked out the van and the blood and is calling it in."

What would he do? It would complicate the escape if he waited for backup, but as long as only two officers were involved, Axe believed the plan could work.

Three or more, though, and he would go to jail.

At least Haley will get away clean. With what she knows now, she can work the problem. Maybe she can find someone to trust and get a replacement for my locked-up ass.

"Gun drawn. Get ready. He's coming in."

He wished he could signal Cody.

Come on, kid. You've got this.

The door opened with a small squeak. Cody's steps changed pace, slowing.

Perfect. Just like we planned.

He could picture the scene. The officer would see the body in the pool of blood. A quick look would confirm the guy DRT: "Dead Right There."

Then he'd sweep the room with his eyes and gun and find...

"Police! Freeze!"

Cody's steps stopped.

"I'm sorry, I'm sorry!" he yelled, then returned to mumbling, louder than earlier for the benefit of the cop. "Stupid, stupid, stupid."

From the direction of his voice, it sounded like Cody had stopped in the perfect spot.

Axe's plan called for the officer advancing into the room, feeling moderately secure of his surroundings given the openness of the warehouse and lack of objects to hide behind. They were counting on the man focusing on the pacing, mumbling kid with the gun.

"Put the weapon on the ground!" The man's voice was tense but in control. He sounded experienced and well trained.

"Okay, I'm putting it down. Don't shoot me! I'm sorry!" Cody sounded scared.

Being held at gunpoint by the police after the night he's had will do that. Now, don't do anything stupid and get yourself shot.

Well, anything more stupid than the next part of the plan.

"Hands on your head and step away from the weapon."

First mistake, and the cop realized it immediately. "Stop!"

Once he had dropped the gun, Cody's orders from Axe were to keep his hands where the officer told him—on his head—then step deliberately through the nearby doorway into the dark office.

"Get back out here! Don't make me shoot you!"

"Don't shoot me," Cody called faintly from inside the office.

The officer's steps sounded like he had changed direction, moving to the side and forward, careful to not stay where he had been standing. His safest move would have been to duck out the door and wait for backup, but with a disarmed suspect running from him, he did as Axe had predicted. He followed the sound of Cody's voice.

The wide-open warehouse clearly held no threats. The danger lay ahead, in the office. He'd clear the back rooms and apprehend the suspect.

In a few seconds, Axe heard his steps halt near the doorway to the offices.

"Homicide suspect in rear offices of warehouse at my location. Potentially armed. Requesting backup."

He heard the dispatcher confirm, then the flick of a light switch.

I hope the kid found a good hiding place.

There hadn't been time to recon the office area, so neither he nor Cody had any idea what options would be available. "You'll adapt and overcome," Axe had reassured him.

"I'm not so good at that. I'm good at following orders. At least it's what my sergeant always said.'"

So Axe had ordered him to find a place to hide. Under a desk, or, ideally, in a closet or another room. "When the lights come on, you start crying. Can you do that?"

"I'm not sure. Like, cry on purpose?"

"Yes. I don't want you to get shot, so you have to hide but give your position away so the guy feels safe. So when you hide, you do this: start thinking of the situation you're in. The whole mess. Think about how unfair it is, how you're going to jail, how screwed you are."

"But you said you'd get me out of jail somehow."

"I will, but don't think about that part. Only think about how badly this night has gone. Then let yourself go."

It would work. It had to, or the kid would get shot.

The officer's quiet footsteps left the concrete floor of the warehouse as he stepped onto the worn, stained commercial carpet of the office.

Axe pushed open the cupboard door and quietly unfolded himself.

"Hands where I can see them! Now!" The cop had found Cody.

"I surrender," Cody sobbed as Axe stepped over the trail of blood and pushed open the door to freedom.

26

THE BACKUP

Axe heard the roar of the powerful engine a half-second before Haley spoke in his ear. "Police backup coming. Three blocks. Maybe 30 seconds."

He slipped along the wall towards the parked vehicles. According to Cody, the white pickup belonged to the leader of the group. Unfortunately, he must have arrived first. It occupied the spot nearest the door, at the edge of the illumination from the dim bulb.

Right where the police were about to converge.

He ducked low and felt along the top of the front driver's side tire and found the keys. *Right where Cody said they would be.*

He caught a break at last. The beat-up, older model pickup didn't have a key fob and electronic locks. It relied on a plain old key. Still crouched, he moved around the front bumper to the passenger side, hoping the dead mercenary had locked his wallet and phone in the glove box as an added level of security in the iffy neighborhood.

The engine noise filled his ears, and he didn't need Haley to tell him he had visitors.

Hurry, or wait?

Would the dome light come on? Could he trust the dead guy's operational security?

He'd seemed on the ball, enough to sense the trap with the duplicate van.

Axe hurried, unlocking the passenger side door and opening it, relieved the dome light either no longer functioned on the old truck or had been switched off prior to the op.

"Five seconds. And I think I hear another car coming behind them, but further out."

He shook his head. *This keeps getting better and better.*

He tried the glove box. Locked, as he'd guessed.

If what he needed was under the driver's seat or hidden somewhere, he'd have to leave it behind. There wasn't time to risk even the fastest searches.

The key slipped into the lock, and he turned. The glove box fell open.

Excellent.

He grabbed a newish leather wallet and a cell phone, took a second to close the glove box, then pushed down the chrome lock knob which stuck up beneath the window. He eased the door shut as the police car squealed to a stop in front of the building's main door on the far side of the truck.

"Down!" He appreciated Haley's warning but didn't need it. He crouched and placed the keyring on the front passenger tire as he heard the police car door open and the second officer run towards the building door.

"Clear, but the next car will be here soon. I don't have a line of sight, but I can hear it. It's close."

Axe made his way behind the truck. The door to the building had swung closed after the second officer had entered. He stood straight and walked casually, without a care in the world, to the van and climbed into the driver's seat.

"Hurry!"

He started the van and threw it into reverse, turning out of the small parking lot, moving backward away from where the police car would come from.

All I need is a few seconds…

Even if the officers in the building weren't focused on appre-hending Cody, they wouldn't have time to get outside before he turned out of sight. The only worry was the other approaching car.

The high beams of a vehicle illuminated the buildings on the corner a short block away. The car would turn towards him any second.

Now!

He cranked the wheel, turning onto the street, driving backwards away from the warehouse. Axe kept his eyes down the block where the lights from the patrol car grew brighter and brighter.

He turned at the first street and sighed with relief as the red brick building on the corner blocked the view and any chance of the officer seeing the van drive backwards up the next street over.

A few seconds later he executed a three-point turn at a normal speed, his lights on, an ordinary delivery van making a course correc-tion in the middle of the night. Over the radio he heard Haley land in the back of his pickup, and the truck start shortly afterward. They both drove slowly from the area, exfilling to a rendezvous where they could stash the van, regroup, and plan their next moves.

Haley's abduction and the plan to torture her revealed she was on to something. An attack was coming, and they were the only ones who could stop it.

27

THE DRIVE

Haley drove the truck away from the warehouse district. Axe drove the van with the smashed windows a few blocks from her, well within range of their radios.

"Any contacts? See any police?" Remarkably, he sounded confident and relaxed, like they'd been out for dinner and a movie instead of a dangerous infiltration op.

Where I killed a man.

"Haley, you with me?"

"Sorry, yes. No contacts. No traffic, though I can hear an ambulance."

"I hear it too. Hope Cody is okay. He's a decent kid. Misguided, but he caught on pretty quick at the end there." He paused, and she knew what came next. He would be worried about her.

I'm worried about me too.

"How are you doing about tonight? You okay?"

The memory of her finger tightening on the trigger. The shots. The man falling.

"Fine."

Liar.

She realized she could be honest with him and admitted the truth. "I can handle it for now. I'll be fine."

I hope.

She could picture him nodding in the van, head tilted to see through the hole in the smashed window. "You saved my life. You did your job. Killing is never easy, especially the first time. But you took out an evil man. You heard what he had planned for you. Torture. Rape. And, eventually, death." She heard his turn signal over the radio as he paused for a moment, and she clicked hers on a second later, turning onto the main road. Ahead of her about a half mile, she saw his van. "Haley, it might sound weird, or wrong, but it's true: you did a good thing. Killing him was justified in the moment and reinforced when we discovered his plans. He was the enemy."

She let his words sink in, percolate through her mind and gut. She took a deep breath and let it out slowly. The words were true. She knew it in her soul.

But I'm still going to have nightmares until I process it fully.

The warehouse neighborhood changed to small, mom-and-pop convenience stores and local restaurants as she drove on the bigger road. Only the occasional gas station and twenty-four-hour diner were open at this hour. It had been years since she'd been out this late.

She told Axe what a part of her mind kept returning to, over and over. "Taking a life is wrong."

"Society tells us it's permissible in certain times. Defending ourselves or others from harm. Protecting our country from aggressors. Killing should never be done lightly, and you're going to relive the moment in dreams. Nightmares. But never forget that by killing him you saved me, saved yourself, and who knows how many other people. Plus, you took an evil man off the face of the earth."

"I'll be okay. Really. And I'm good to go now." This time the words had conviction. She believed them.

"Never out of the fight."

"I'm in it. All the way. Now, what's next?"

"First, we have to ditch the van until this is over and I can return it or report it stolen. I'll figure it out when the mission is complete. Then you can work your tech magic on the leader's phone, which I grabbed from his truck. Hopefully, you can hack your way in and get us intel leading to our next step."

Ahead, she saw his brake lights as he slowed and pulled into the parking lot of a twenty-four-hour mega store. They parked far from the entrance, in a dark area. Axe spent ten minutes with duct tape and trash bags, turning the windows from freshly wrecked to in need of future repair. Then he drove it closer to the entrance. She parked a few rows over, amongst other vehicles, and waited while he wiped down the van for fingerprints. Axe walked to the front of the store, head down, went inside, then came out a minute later, heading directly for her. She slid into the passenger seat, and Axe got in.

"Hopefully, anyone who sees it will assume it's not abandoned. It should buy us a day or two before we have to deal with it."

Seconds later, they were off, back onto the main road for about a mile until Haley saw a familiar sign ahead. "You think it's safe to go in, get some food, and use the bathroom?"

"Good soldiers never pass up a chance to eat. But we'll wear hats and keep our heads down, avoiding security cameras. Not suspiciously, more like we're tired." They pulled into the parking lot of the all night fast-food joint.

Axe retrieved baseball caps from the back seat for them and took her food order. She wasn't usually one to eat her feelings, but desperate times called for desperate measures.

Once in the bathroom, Haley splashed water on her face and examined it in the mirror. She looked the same, but she had changed. For the better, or worse, she hadn't decided yet.

Back in the truck, Axe ate a burger while Haley nibbled on fries and a milkshake. They had sounded great but hit her stomach hard. She fought to keep the food down every time her mind flashed to shooting the man. While Axe gobbled his food like nothing unusual had happened—which, for him, it hadn't—she distracted herself with the man's smart phone.

"This is a very clean phone, most likely used only for the op. I got through the pass code by using his birthday from his driver's license—good call on grabbing the wallet. His name was Jason." On learning the man's name, her stomach had roiled. It made him more real than merely a body in the sights of the M4. She again fought the urge to throw open the truck door and vomit in the parking lot. "There's nothing here to give us a clue of what's going on." She turned the phone screen to show Axe. "See this app?"

Axe looked and nodded while chewing.

"It's a secure messaging and calling app. It deletes all contacts, texts, and call logs." She set the phone down on the truck's center console in frustration. "I'm way out of my depth here. If I had access to my system, I could search for chatter from Long Island and specifically Hauppauge and Montauk. Or look up this guy and see what shakes out. But not while I'm supposedly dead."

"Haley, there's only so much you can do sitting behind a desk, looking at a computer screen."

She growled in dissent. "I can find everything online."

He swallowed the last of his burger and crumpled the wrapper. "So tell me. What's going on? Why did they abduct you, and why tonight, with an under-manned team and a rookie they forced to stay behind? Are you holding back on me?"

"No. I don't know, damn it!"

He needled her with his persistence. "So we need more intel. How did you propose to get it? What online resources can we use?"

She pressed her lips together to keep from taking out her frustrations on him. It pissed her off not having the answers, as did knowing he had a point.

Axe smiled gently at her. "Just because I'm right doesn't mean I'm an asshole. And just because you're stuck doesn't make you bad at what you do."

"It's so frustrating. Something is happening and I don't understand it. I'm used to having the answers… or figuring it out."

He nodded, staring out of the window. "Let me guess. You've never failed before… or at least never hit a wall?"

She shrugged, trying to be casual but surprised he'd nailed it.

"I had that happen. It's why I became a SEAL. I wanted to challenge myself. Until I started hitting walls. Hard. Then it felt much less appealing." He glanced at her with a rueful smile. "But stick with it. Keep pushing. Get used to it. The higher you climb, the harder the problems you go after, the tougher it is. And what gets you to one level usually isn't what you need to get to the next level. But I've seen you in action twice now. You can do it."

Haley kept her face still, practicing her poker face, while inside she fought back tears. Her division wasn't known as an encouraging, feel-good place to work, so the heartfelt encouragement from Axe hit home and felt wonderful.

Without access to her database, she had to trust Axe even more. "So what's the plan? What can we do now?"

"We attack."

28

THE ATTACK

"Attack what?" Haley asked as Axe started the truck.

"AgaDefCo."

She shook her head in disbelief, the lights of the fast-food joint catching her long golden hair. "You want to attack one of the leading US-based military security companies?"

He grinned. "Well, I don't want to, but it makes sense."

"How? No, what makes sense is for me to call the overnight team in my department, report in, and ask for help. Run this guy's name, see what pops."

He weighed the odds. "I can see using your team. It would be a risk, but might be worth it to get more intel. Who knows, your management might finally believe there's a genuine threat now. But I still worry about the mole, leak, or penetration." He steered towards the highway entrance, the world still dark and sleeping peacefully around them. "At this point, you being alive may be no big deal. They tried to hit you, they failed. The element of surprise may not be gone. When were they required to report? With them thinking you are out of the game, we have a slight advantage. Besides, my orders were explicit.

Get proof of a threat. If possible, handle it ourselves. If not, the admiral would be in the same situation we are now of having to figure out who can be trusted."

"Which means giving up our element of surprise."

"Correct. At this moment, they would be torturing you. We still have a window."

"How long?"

Axe pondered it, continuing his sweep of the mirrors, maintaining situational awareness at all times. Most people treated commuting or driving as their alone time, a chance to let their guard down and relax. Listen to music. Chill. In Axe's world, driving alone, without a convoy of protective vehicles, meant being on high alert for danger.

"Hard saying. At least until morning or perhaps mid day, depending on the urgency. My guess is they wanted to find out if you knew more than you had said, but also, who you had told. But perhaps they're more concerned about their comms or methods being compromised. They might also be worried about a mole in their organization they need to handle."

"All we have to go on is what Cody said…"

Axe's mind flashed to the kid in a small, windowless room, handcuffed, being interrogated by police right now.

"AgaDefCo hired him and the other guys, including Jason."

Haley considered it, trying to see the angles, then used Jason's phone to search for AgaDefCo offices nearby. "There's a branch of the company in several major cities, including D.C. That must be where they sent Jason from."

"Yes, but that's not where the order originated."

"How do you know?"

"Abduction and torture of an American are too big for a branch office. Came from higher up."

Haley returned to the phone. "Training centers in Texas and North Dakota." She looked at Axe. "Please tell me we don't have to go to North Dakota."

He laughed. "I hope not. You don't have to look, I know where the HQ is. In fact, I know a few people that work for them. I considered it for a few weeks, too." He steered the truck onto the highway, heading north. "We're going to Brooklyn. If that doesn't work out, Hauppauge, then Montauk. We'll shake the trees until bad guys fall out, then go from there."

Axe looked at Haley and the clock on the dash. "It's about four and a half hours away. If we get lucky, we'll be early enough to miss rush hour. I'm good to drive. I gave up sleeping at night—too many years on ops for my body to adapt, and I slept earlier today. Try to get some rest. We'll need you fresh in the morning when we get more leads."

Haley nodded. The exhaustion hit her as soon as he mentioned sleep. She tipped her seat back. Within seconds, her mouth opened, and she snored softly. He marveled at her beauty and suspected most people saw her for only her looks, never appreciating the incredible mind she also possessed.

Axe set the cruise control at four miles above the speed limit and kept his eyes on the few cars on the road. He felt pleased Haley could sleep for at least a while, but the nightmares would come soon. They were the mind's way of trying to process the stress and trauma. Knowing it never made them easier, though. Talking out the feelings would help, and he'd make sure they took the time once they'd discovered and handled the current threat.

She's done well tonight. She has promise.

He drove through the night on the quiet freeway, northeast, heading towards New York City, brainstorming ways to infiltrate or assault AgaDefCo HQ.

29

THE BEGINNING

The first wave of vehicles left at 1:00 AM. They were newer, American-made mid-sized cars, bought from small dealers across the east coast, often for cash, always using fake driver's licenses.

But operations rely on people, not vehicles. How does one create a criminal organization from scratch?

The entire operation depended on data analytics. Without it, the scheme would have been impossible. Taking the vast amount of data available and supplementing it where needed, the planning team—a small group of high-level computer programmers hand-picked by Todd —had created an artificial intelligence algorithm to find the perfect individuals to approach.

With over a thousand data points on every American, from groceries bought to taste in TV shows, websites visited, news articles read, and social media shares, it was remarkably simple.

By adding data from public records such as local, state, and federal courts, departments of motor vehicles, and others, they created profiles on thousands of potential recruits.

The team in charge also hacked into databases to access arrest reports, prison records, and psychological evaluations, adding valuable information to their database.

Armed with this enormous amount of knowledge, they knew who to approach, the likelihood of interest, and how to appeal to each person; whether to offer money, a sense of belonging, liquor and drugs, or a chance at revenge against whatever group an individual hated—which had also been easy to determine.

The process was revolutionary: data analytics for crime and terror. "Mayhem 2.0," the programmers called it.

The initial test, the proof of concept, had identified small-time criminals, con men who could play a part without showing nerves or arousing suspicion. They had been recruited, well paid, and carefully managed. In short order, they succeeded in their assignment to acquire a fleet of vehicles and deliver them to a large warehouse in Brooklyn.

It had worked like a charm, and the mission proceeded. Delicate negotiations took place, trust was established, and an expert was recruited, paid millions of dollars, and entered the country with his team. Zeno and his men took over much of the operation from the computer and data geeks.

The stolen vehicles were fitted with forged license plates, then modifications were made to the door panels and trunks.

Zeno and his proteges had worked with the data geeks to select a few criminals to teach them the fine art of making car bombs. Each car was filled with steel ball bearings and explosives, engineered to direct the blast outward, creating incredibly destructive car bombs.

Finally, small, idiot-proof wireless remote detonators were left in the cup holders of each car.

All this happened over months. During that time, other teams were also recruited, trained, and managed.

It wouldn't have been possible without Todd's incredible managerial and logistical skills.

Keeping the details from Kelton had proven difficult, but not insurmountable. "Don't worry, I'm handling it. Don't trouble yourself with the details—that's why you have me."

And none of the geeks even thought to question Todd. Why would they? He was Kelton's right-hand man.

Everything was ready on time for the big day.

The final connections were made for the remote detonators, making each car a rolling IED.

Three clean-cut men, dressed in ties and buttoned suit coats that hid their tactical plate carriers and ammunition pouches, sat in a car. The driver nodded to the man in the other car, then pulled in front of the rolling machine of destruction. The cars left the warehouse for their journey across two bridges and down the turnpike. They had three hours to make the seventy-five minute drive to their standby station outside a city in New Jersey. Anyone looking would have seen the ordinary businessmen in the first car and a heavy-set though handsome man in the second. They looked like they were on their way to corporate jobs somewhere.

Three hours later, two fully loaded semi tractors left a warehouse on the outskirts of Perth Amboy, New Jersey, and made their way towards the bridge connecting Staten Island to Brooklyn. The drivers stuck close together, but took care to disguise the fact they were a unit, occasionally passing each other and allowing other vehicles to come between them. They had plenty of time and didn't need to be in formation until the far side of the bridge.

At the same time, from a small car repair shop in Staten Island, men dressed as white-collar office workers drove six passenger vans, complete with bumper stickers with slogans like "Soccer Dad" and "I brake for ice cream." They covered first small roads, then highways, and eventually merged onto the main toll road towards the non-commercial level of the same bridge where the semis were headed.

Other men, also dressed in business attire and sipping from large commuter coffee mugs, duplicated the process from different locations in Brooklyn, following all traffic regulations as they drove to every bridge and tunnel accessing Manhattan and the other boroughs comprising New York City.

Every man had originally bitched about wearing ties, but the suits and carefully practiced full-Windsor knots completed the looks. No one would give them a second glance… until it was too late.

The drivers had all made the trips several times before. They were chosen using the database and algorithm to select the perfect candidates—and well trained. They were excited and looked forward to the day. It was a gig of a lifetime. Where else could they get handsomely paid to create chaos, kill civilians, and have help to get away with it?

With good communication and a little luck, all the bridges and tunnels would be shut down in both directions at the start of rush hour, with exploded cars burning brightly, leaving the gunmen free to wreak havoc on the innocent commuters, then get away clean in the spare cars.

30

THE DAWN

The first strike came as the weak glow of the pre-dawn sun lightened the sky.

A small group of drug-addicted criminals had been identified for an essential task not suitable for the teams on their way to New Jersey, the bridges and tunnels, or the many other destinations in the tri-state area.

Brandon, age 22, rail thin and pale, but clean shaven and sporting an expensive, flattering cut for his dark hair, strolled down the East Village side street, trying to hide his jitters. The cool air kept him from sweating much, but it wouldn't be long until he couldn't hide his need.

He'd arrived at the end of the block fifteen minutes before and hoped his target would show soon. His team leader, Andre, had said the probability was eighty-three percent the man would leave his pricey condo building in this rapidly gentrifying area at 5:30 AM instead of the usual 6:00. An algorithm had sorted the data and predicted it, he was told.

But Brandon would wait as long as needed to get the job done. Failure was not an option.

He fought the desire to slip into a fantasy of the heroin he would receive when he returned to base after killing the man. He wouldn't—couldn't—risk not being one hundred percent aware of his surroundings. If the man unexpectedly took a cab or ride share, or turned left out his building instead of right, Brandon had to be on it.

He had contingency plans for his contingency plans, but if he daydreamed about his upcoming fix and messed up the job... bye-bye dream life.

He thought back to two months before when he'd been paroled, released early into a halfway house after doing a stretch for armed robbery. It hadn't been his fault; he'd only needed to score. His desperation resulted in him assaulting a young gang member foolish enough to think he was untouchable, stealing the little money on him, then using the kid's knife to hold up a tourist couple slumming it on the lower east side of Manhattan at 2 AM. He hadn't counted on the police officers who drove by the small alley at exactly the wrong time.

After the forced detox from his prison stay, the halfway house had sounded perfect. A chance to start over.

He watched the front entrance of the building across the street as he walked—without staring, as they had taught him. He ignored his craving.

It would end soon, as long as he did well.

Within hours of his release, he'd found himself back in the Lower East Side neighborhood of Manhattan, desperate to get money and score the drugs he missed. Which is when he'd been approached by Andre, the man who would become his team leader, who took him to a small, clean apartment nearby and gave him—free—the sweetest, cleanest junk he'd ever experienced. Amazing stuff. Pure. Only a little, though. The man had set up the fix himself, so Brandon didn't OD.

Hours later, when he came out of it, laying on the comfortable futon, the man asked if he wanted more. Not just more. A steady—though controlled—supply, administered under supervision, the amount carefully tailored just to him. He would have sold his mother's soul for it.

All he had to do was join the man's small group of similar addicts. They'd learn some skills, do small jobs well within their capabilities, and in exchange they'd live rent-free in a dorm-type loft in Brooklyn. Clean and safe. A good life without worry about scoring, withdrawals, or sleeping in doorways. A life to be proud of.

Yesterday, Andre had reduced the drug dosage to the bare minimum to function without a terrible detox.

No more perfectly tailored amount twice a day for maintenance, and a larger after-dinner hit for hours of bliss.

He had a job to do, he'd been told. They all had jobs to do. The one they'd been training for with the small but powerful pistols at the indoor gun range in the dorm's basement. The one they knew had been coming, though none of them had discussed, and barely admitted to themselves.

No such thing as a free lunch—or free drugs. Everything has a price.

They'd been ordered to study photographs of men for the past month, without explanation. Yesterday they were told the men in the pictures were cruel and evil. Men who didn't understand drug dependency. Who didn't agree that people with addictions needed help, support, and maintenance doses so they could live happy, productive lives.

No, these men wanted to terminate the program Brandon and the others like him were successfully using. The men wanted to ruin his life. It all seemed far-fetched to Brandon, who, like many addicts, was intelligent and insightful. But it didn't matter. The pure heroin mattered. Nothing else.

This morning their training would pay off. Each of the drug addicts would kill one man. Then they'd receive not only their normal dosage, but a little extra as a bonus.

In the meantime, to ensure one hundred percent focus and motivation, all doses had been greatly reduced.

Brandon's desperation—and motivation—grew by the second.

He tensed as he saw the Asian man with a fashionable black coat and shoes that cost more than Brandon had ever earned. The man hurried out of the building and turned right, as expected. His roundish, dimpled face and square-framed glasses in the latest style matched the updated photo of his target taken yesterday morning and studied all afternoon.

Brandon paced the man from directly across the small side street. He walked leisurely past the many stoops, casually glancing at the lower windows of the basement apartments, staying far from the trash cans chained to the black wrought iron fences at the front of each residential building.

He knew the area like the back of his hand from the years spent as a street junkie, but he wouldn't need the knowledge. He knew the man's potential paths to each of the nearby subway stations.

The man's pattern called for him to turn left, crossing to Brandon's side of the street, with ninety-seven percent probability he would use the crosswalk at the end of the block.

Brandon reached into the pocket of his expensive, lightly padded coat. He gripped the gun, nestled inside a mitten, with a sweaty hand. For a moment he had a flash of conscience. Regret flared. What had his life come to? He'd done stupid things to support his addiction, but he'd never hurt anyone. The knife for the tourists had been for show; if they hadn't handed over the money, he would have turned and run. Now he would kill an innocent man, just for his fix?

As he approached the corner, he slowed, careful to fall behind his target's pace on the opposite sidewalk. He had to time it perfectly.

Andre's face and words flashed in his mind. "These are evil men. Killing is extreme, yes, and not a step we take lightly. But with them out of the way, we can help not only you, but all the still-suffering addicts out there."

Sacrifices must be made. He would be doing the world a favor.

The tiny, self-aware part of him scoffed for an instant. He would do it only for his fix. But if he needed to lie to himself, he would. It wouldn't be the first time.

Ahead, the man cut across the street before the crosswalk, proving that math and algorithms only went so far. A lone car sat at the intersection, and both the man and Brandon had noticed the light would change in a moment, forcing the man to wait to cross. So he jaywalked, cutting left behind the car, heading directly for Brandon, who slowed down to meet him.

A final glance around gave Brandon the last bit of courage he needed. No cops this time. He pulled his hand out of his coat pocket, holding the gun, bringing along with it the thick wool mitten covering it from prying eyes. The spring morning air didn't warrant a mitten, but in New York, people did—and wore—the unusual.

Brandon avoided eye contact, like any good New Yorker, as the man stepped onto the sidewalk three feet in front of him. Before he could think twice, he took one, then a second long step forward, closing quickly on the man. Then he raised his sweaty hand and fired through the mitten until the powerful revolver clicked empty.

The man fell on his face, blood spreading rapidly on the sidewalk, making its way into the patch of brown dirt holding a stick of a tree.

Brandon's hand slid automatically into his pocket, as he had practiced, leaving behind the gun and mitten. He stepped to the man, avoiding the blood, and removed a wallet from the front right pocket where he had been told it would be.

Then he walked a few steps and turned left at the corner. He controlled his pace as best he could. New York streets at 5:30 AM weren't as busy as people around the world thought. The city may never sleep, but most of her residents did.

He didn't think anyone had seen, though the six deafening gunshots would soon bring the police. But with his nice clothes and clean-cut looks, he didn't appear at all to be a junkie heading to his much-needed fix.

By 6:05, nineteen other addicts had killed their targets; a one hundred percent success rate. As predicted.

By 8:00 AM, twenty addicts lay on crisp white sheets on their comfortable bunks in the warehouse converted to a simple yet clean dormitory, ready for their celebratory fix. Light streamed in through the tall windows, flooding the room with warmth. It looked like it would be a beautiful spring day.

By 8:15, all were dead from heroin overdoses administered by their leader, Andre.

31

THE WAR ZONE

In typical fashion for anyone familiar with driving in large metropolitan areas, Axe and Haley hit both construction slowdowns and stop-and-go traffic from a disabled vehicle blocking the middle lane of the turnpike. Haley had woken up in time for a stop at a large, well-appointed rest area for a bathroom break and to fill up the truck with gas. "You never know when we're going to need a full tank," Axe had said. One of them stayed with the truck at all times, so they didn't have to lock up the guns in the toolbox in the back.

On the road, Axe finally sped up again after yet another inexplicable slowdown. There had been no additional accident, but traffic had ground to a maddening twenty miles per hour. "Looks like we won't arrive until after dawn," Axe grumbled, glancing at his phone's GPS app. The next turn remained miles away—a right across Staten Island and on to Brooklyn. If they were lucky, they might still miss the worst of rush hour, if they hit no more random slowdowns.

Haley turned on the radio and switched over to the AM band to listen to traffic and weather. While in college, traveling occasionally to

Manhattan to see Broadway shows, she'd learned the advantages of hearing traffic updates every ten minutes.

"If we can get across the bridge by six, I think we'll be fine," Haley said. It would be close. Cars packed bumper to bumper across all the lanes, sleepy commuters guzzling coffee, few adhering to safe following-distance guidelines. And the traffic only built as they drove north.

Haley turned up the volume as the latest traffic report started. "Breaking news, multiple collisions are being reported on the Verrazano-Narrows Bridge. Best avoid it for now, as the top and bottom spans are blocked. Must have been some kind of spill or something to close it down. In Westchester—"

The phone announced an updated route and much later estimated ETA.

"There go my hopes for a bit of recon before people showed up for work."

Axe braked hard as a small bus signaled left, then immediately moved in front of him, claiming the space he had intentionally left between him and the car ahead. The bus looked like the kind he and a bunch of the guys had taken one night to celebrate a birthday. A party bus for them, but in this case most likely outfitted as a comfortable commuter bus. The driver continued to the far left lane, which moved marginally faster than Axe's middle lane, and sped up, closing the distance to the car in front, practically pushing it to move faster.

Thank God I don't have to commute.

He chuckled softly.

"What?" Haley asked, glancing over at him. She had the phone they'd recovered from Jason, the dead guy, which she used to look for a connection between AgaDefCo, Hauppauge, and Montauk.

"Thinking how much more dangerous my former commute was."

Haley looked at him, not understanding.

"Helicopter. Ninety percent of the time we'd fly in, land several miles away, then patrol to the X. The target. Helicopters seemed to always break down. Might have been the sand, or overuse, whatever. But I had more than my share of close calls and rough landings."

"Do you miss it?"

Every second.

Out loud, he said, "I miss the guys and being part of a team. But working with you helps, so thanks."

"Let's save our thank you's for when this is over."

She didn't mean to sound bitchy, but it came out that way.

She's right. We're on a mission. Have to keep our heads in the game. I should know better. I'm out of practice.

The miles crawled by as they drove well under the full speed limit. Traffic increased. Axe fought his way to the right lane at the same time as seemingly everyone else on the road. The bridge being out of commission left the Holland Tunnel as the best way into Manhattan, where millions of drivers needed to go even at this early hour. From there, they could get to Brooklyn and the AgaDefCo HQ.

The road curved right—east—two lanes forming an exit that, according to his phone, joined with another major road further ahead. Beyond that lay a toll plaza where thousands more cars needed to merge into even fewer lanes, creating more chaos and slowdowns. Just another day on the roads of a vast metropolis.

The truck's height allowed him to see the cause of the most recent slowdown, which was more than the mere merging of too many cars onto too little roadway.

A newer silver car blocked the right lane on the curve ahead. Another four-door sedan had stopped a hundred feet past it to help, or perhaps there had been a collision. Four businessmen stood around the second car, talking and glancing back at the stalled vehicle.

Not another one. How do people live like this, spending so much time trapped in their cars, crawling down the road?

Vehicles in the right lane stopped and tried to merge left—and some to the right, onto the narrow shoulder. The right side had room only for subcompact cars. And unfortunately for the ones trying to merge left, the lane contained drivers unhappy with the idea of their commute taking longer because of someone else's unlucky lane choice.

The commuter bus which had muscled its way past him earlier had made better time than Axe. It had reached the broken-down silver car.

Then it exploded.

32

THE REACTION

Haley gasped, looking up from the phone in time to see the huge fireball. "What happened?"

Axe's eyes narrowed in confusion.

Strange. Like an IED explosion.

The radio emitted an emergency alert tone.

Already? How could they possibly—?

"Multiple reports indicate at least one gunman is active on the Verrazano Bridge. Avoid the area. If you are in the area, authorities advise finding cover. Once again, there is an active shooter on either the upper or lower deck of the Verrazano bridge, or perhaps both."

The bridge. Axe looked closer at the surrounding area. The lanes of traffic, curving east. Hundreds of merging vehicles ahead. The toll plaza and the road narrowing to two lanes through the tunnel. A choke point. Perfect for an IED.

Or an ambush.

Or both.

Axe slammed the truck into park as Haley stared at the burning vehicles ahead, her mouth open in shock. "Haley, switch places. You're driving." He unbuckled his seat belt, then hers, since she hadn't moved. "Slide under me. Haley—focus! Do it now."

His urgent tone got her moving. She slid across as Axe moved away from the steering wheel and bridged himself upward, making space for her. The seat slid forward as she held the electric switch so she could reach the steering wheel and pedals. Axe slid the rest of the way over and leaned into the small backseat of the king cab truck. He grabbed his rifle and plate carrier, the heavy bulk reassuring as he slid it on.

"The truck is insured. So are the other cars. If we get in a situation, you drive into or through vehicles. Don't play nice. Get us where we need to go. Got it?"

"I don't understand. What's going on?"

The crack of semi-automatic rifle fire from several weapons answered the question. Axe saw muzzle flashes near the burning bus, directed at the vehicles near it.

"Put the truck in gear! Turn the wheel to the right. Push between those two cars. Hurry!"

He checked for a chambered round and switched off the safety as Haley followed his directions to the letter. She stomped on the accelerator as she turned the wheel. With a crash of metal, she hit two cars at once, moving the one ahead of them further forward to smash into the minivan in front of it. The one just behind them had the entire front of the car pushed to the right as the heavy-duty truck plowed its way through onto the narrow shoulder.

"Perfect, now, go forward. Fast!"

"We're going towards the shooting?" Haley choked out as the truck's left fender slammed into car after car, pushing them out of the way enough for the truck to get through but also scraping their sides as they passed. "Of course we are," she muttered, answering her own question.

They made it partway to the curve when they ran into trouble. People finally woke to the danger as they saw the gunmen advancing towards them, shooting the occupants of every vehicle while yelling with excitement.

"Stop!"

Haley slammed on the brakes. The first of many drivers turned pedestrians ran towards them on the shoulder.

"Stay here. Get people behind the engine block—it'll stop the bullets. Use the pistol if anyone with a weapon comes near."

"Where—"

He slipped out the door and advanced towards the men shooting, crouched low, using the cars on his left to shield his movements. Depending on the type of bullets, the thin walls of the car wouldn't protect him, but he'd stay out of sight as long as he could.

Then he'd eliminate the threat.

33

THE ATTACK

The lightening sky made it easier for Axe to assess the situation while he ran.

Three shooters. The black balaclavas covering their faces contrasted with the expensive-looking suits and ties they wore. It had to be the men who had stood around looking at the collision.

They were trained, but not experienced.

Killers, but undisciplined.

The closest tango moved fast, running along the far shoulder, two lanes away from Axe. He shot into every car he passed, whooping and hollering, though he didn't take time to aim. It seemed he cared more about shooting than killing, like he was in a competition with the other two to see who could put the most bullets into the cars in the least amount of time.

The others moved methodically, one down the center of the two rows of cars, alternating between firing into the cars to his left—closest to Axe, and the ones on his right that his partner had already unloaded into. He shot to kill.

The third moved slowest and remained the furthest away. He

walked down the median in front of Axe, looking into every car and firing a shot here or there as needed. Mopping up, it looked like. Ensuring no one remained alive.

For several seconds after the explosion, people had sat in their cars, stunned. Now, more and more were getting out to run away. Along both medians and down the middle of the parked cars, men, women, and some children popped out of their vehicles and took off, many of them screaming.

Their flight for safety, though smart, unfortunately meant Axe couldn't risk shooting through them at the killers.

No clear shot. Have to get closer.

Axe darted left, moving to intercept the man moving fastest along the far shoulder. Another few steps and the tango would be level with Axe. He'd have a clean shot between cars with no civilians... since most of the people in the far lane were dead or dying in their cars.

A little more... Now!

Axe fired, hitting the man at least once as he sprinted by the gap area between vehicles. He fell and didn't get up.

Axe's gunfire drew the attention of the remaining two. The different sound his M4 made from their AKs alerted them.

He ducked behind a red sports car as bullets pinged around him from the enemy in the middle of the road.

As the bullets paused for a moment, Axe moved left and forward, through the gap in the lanes of cars, hoping the man had to reload and wasn't merely holding off for Axe to pop out. As no shots followed, Axe raised up, ensured no civilians were in his line of site, and fired twice to keep the man's head down. Then he sprinted forward, crouched low.

Shots rang out, though still aimed at where Axe had been.

Trained, but definitely amateurs.

No experienced combat veteran fires, ducks, then comes up in the same spot to fire again. It's "fire and move," not "fire and pop up in the same place, making a great target for your enemy."

The sound of steady, methodical shooting resumed from the far right shoulder. The third man had returned to his mission—or pleasure —of shooting into cars.

Have to stop them both. Now.

As he ran, he watched to see if the second tango moved forward, back, or held his position. Axe hoped he would be crouched in front of the red truck he'd used as cover while shooting at Axe.

One more car. He'll be right there. Turn and shoot.

The man fired more shots back to where Axe had been, apparently never considering someone would advance on his position. As soon as the several shots stopped, Axe did as planned. He stepped left, facing the middle of the road, and saw the man peering around the truck towards where he'd last seen Axe, cautiously raised up to get a better angle.

He thinks that wild ass shooting hit me. Big mistake.

Axe shot him twice in the body, the bullets entering the man's right side, then once again in the head before he dropped. The blood splatter from the head wound ensured he would cause no more harm.

Two down. One to go.

34

THE TRUCK

Haley's hands trembled. She had frozen for a minute, unable to move from the illusion of safety the truck provided.

It took all her strength to make herself step out, leaving the truck door open for whatever cover it might provide.

She had seen the killer moving along the far median fall when Axe shot him. As she moved to the rear of the truck, she heard Axe's M4 as he engaged the other killer.

What had Axe said? Something about getting people to safety.

People were out of their cars and running away, which seemed like a good idea. But as she looked up, she saw a face in a car behind her of a man frozen in fear, unable to decide what to do.

"Get out of the car! Come here. Hide behind the truck!" She gestured for the Chinese man in the fancy car. He stared at her for a second, then jolted himself into motion and scrambled out of his car, running low the few steps to her position.

A middle-aged woman, dressed well in expensive business clothes and a thick gold necklace, ran past them, then halted as she noticed

Haley and the Chinese man crouched behind the truck. She joined them, bent forward, gasping for breath.

"Stay down." Axe had said to stay behind the engine block, but she'd seen a third shooter moving down the shoulder. The rear would be safest for now.

More gunfire rang out, mostly from the enemy's weapons with their distinctive sound. Two rounds penetrated the window of the car next to them, causing the man to pee his pants.

The business woman, her dark skin glistening with sweat, spoke up. "What's going on?"

"Terrorists," Haley summed up, and both she and the well-dressed man accepted the explanation without question.

"Should we run?" the man asked in lightly accented English.

"We're safe here. My partner is engaging the shooters."

"You're the police?" the man asked, relieved.

"Close enough."

No time to get into it.

She heard Axe's rifle fire three times, controlled shots, and the other rifle fall silent. The third continued firing in short bursts, followed by a few seconds, then more bursts.

He's not engaging Axe. He's killing. Focused.

Then she heard the speed of the shooting change. More shots, faster, on what sounded like full automatic.

He's shooting at Axe. Damn it. What can I do?

35

THE WISH

Axe moved forward two cars, then stopped, trying to see through the windows of the vehicles between him and the man.

His movement must have gotten the man's attention, because several bullets immediately impacted the car near Axe.

That's too close. This guy is better than the others.

The tactical situation sucked. No clear shot, and there were civilians still potentially alive in cars that Axe had to contend with while the enemy didn't. Help might come, but not soon enough to make a difference. At least dozens more would die before any force arrived to help handle the shooter.

Axe on his own. Again. He could go for it, jump onto a car and shoot, hoping for a good clear shot before the guy gunned him down.

Or he could stealth it, take the time to creep forward. If he got lucky, he might catch the guy in the open.

In the meantime, people would continue to die.

What I wouldn't give for the Team right now.

36

THE DISTRACTION

Haley wanted to help, but the man shooting at Axe was too far away for her pistol.

The smart play would be to help the two businesspeople to safety.

She couldn't leave her partner, though.

They could wait here, in relative safety, and she could protect the bystanders if Axe failed.

She would take the gunman on by herself. She would risk her life to save others, even armed only with the small gun.

But could she somehow help Axe?

What would he do if the situation were reversed and a member of his team was in harm's way?

"Stay here and stay low, okay? I'm going to see if I can help my partner."

"Wait! Don't leave us!" the man cried.

Haley glanced at him, then at the woman, torn. The woman looked at her and nodded decisively. "You go. We'll be fine. I'll watch him."

Haley pulled the 9mm from the holster under her sweatshirt,

causing the man to gasp and shy away. Then she got as low as she could and peeked around the rear tire.

She couldn't see anything. Cars hid the man from view.

Then she heard another burst of fire and breaking glass as the man shot into another car.

She sprinted forward the few steps to hide behind the door Axe had left open, hopefully shielded from view.

There! She saw the enemy, face covered by a mask of some sort. Aside from that and the ammo pouches she could see through the gap in his unbuttoned suit coat, he could be a stockbroker or middle manager on the way to the office.

Except, of course, for the rifle he fired into another car as he walked by, before turning and shooting towards where Axe must be pinned down.

She had just seen more people killed, but blocked it from her mind. *Now. While he's shooting at Axe.*

She took a step away from the truck, exposing her entire body on the far side of the open door, steadied herself, and shot, pulling the trigger quickly three times as the man turned towards her.

She didn't hit him. In fact, she didn't know where her rounds landed. But she got his attention. He raised his weapon as she ran away. The *thunk* of bullets against the open door terrified her as she slid to safety behind the truck.

37

THE KILL

He'd know the sound of the small 9mm anywhere. Three shots. Someone firing quickly while still aiming.

Haley!

Axe sprinted forward, staying low. He hoped the man, well-trained though he seemed to be, would take the bait and fire at Haley. An experienced soldier would ignore pistol fire from long range, but would this terrorist be able to?

He heard three shots directed back towards his truck.

It gave Axe the seconds he needed to advance far enough for a clear shot.

As the masked tango finished shooting at Haley, Axe fired, hitting the man with shots to the body. Axe's head shot missed as the man spun and staggered. He didn't go down, but turned towards Axe, bringing his rifle to bear.

Axe fired twice, both shots hitting the man in the head, blowing it apart.

Had it not been for Haley, he never would have gotten the shot. The man had been too alert and too fast. As it was, it had been a close call.

Must be very good body armor to not go down when I hit him.

He didn't need to check on the man. No one could survive the two head shots.

Which made him think.

The first guy…

He turned down the road, scanning the area where he shot the first man, then ran.

He saw movement. Someone crept towards the back of the truck.

Could be a civilian…

His gut told him the truth. His shots hadn't killed the first man.

"Haley! Look out!"

38

THE DEATH

Haley crouched at the rear passenger side of the truck, ready to pop out and shoot again if needed. She heard Axe shoot, then shoot again, followed by silence.

It was over. He had killed them all.

And she had helped, she hoped.

"Haley! Look out!" Axe's bellow made her spin, some part of her knowing the danger wouldn't come from her side of the truck.

In a second, Haley took in the man, balaclava off, face twisted in disbelief, pain… and rage.

His gray suit coat oozed red on his left side. But he crouched on one knee on the far side of the road with a clear shot. He stared at the businessman near Haley, hatred on his face, and weakly raised his gun, struggling to bring it to bear on the man.

Haley's gun barked over and over as she stepped around the two people in front of her, aiming for the gunman's head after guessing he wore a bulletproof vest under his suit coat.

At least three shots hit him. Two in the head knocked him over.

One in his neck spurt blood as he lay staring lifelessly at the morning sky.

She walked forward, numb. She stopped near the remains of the man in front of her, the second life she'd taken in less than twelve hours.

Then she calmly ejected the magazine and replaced it with a fresh one from the holder at her side.

Don't let this get easy. Please, never let this get easy.

39

THE KIT

Axe had heard the pistol fire as he ran. He finally got a line of sight on Haley.

He reached her as she replaced the magazine with a fresh one.

She turned to him, her face inscrutable, before returning her gaze to the dead man in front of them.

Axe felt horrible. He'd left the man alive, and almost gotten his teammate killed.

I've lost my edge. *I got out at the right time.*

"I thought I got him..." he started.

"You did." She tilted her head at the blood still oozing out the man's side. "He could hardly lift the gun. Thank you."

He shook his head. "I should have checked, but the other two..."

"You took them out. I finished this one. Teamwork."

He studied her for a second, worried. Could she hang on, or would she lose it? She looked fine, but was she? "Haley. You've been through so much, but I need you to hold it together a little longer." There wasn't time for shock or tears. "Can you do that? We have people to help."

She nodded once and holstered the pistol, reluctantly pulling her gaze from the man's bloody body. "What next?"

"I'll get my med kit from the truck. You call 911. Tell them our location. Make sure they know three terrorists are down and the situation is under control. Tell them to send ambulances from the north. They'll never get here through the chaos to the south."

They both looked that direction to see hundreds of people fleeing in the distance, vehicles abandoned for at least a mile.

"Haley. You with me? There will be time to process the feelings later. We don't have that luxury now."

She shook her head and blinked. "Got it. Ambulances from the north. Three terrorists down. Under control."

Axe put his hand firmly on her shoulder, the way he would have for any of his former team, then turned and ran to the truck.

A man sat, hyperventilating, while a well-dressed, calm woman tried to reassure him.

Behind him, Axe heard Haley talking to emergency response as he opened the huge silver toolbox in the truck's bed. He removed a large red and gray plastic medical kit that looked like a fishing tackle box, because that's what it was.

He saw the dark-skinned woman stand. "I had a semester of nursing before I switched to a business major. How can I help?"

Axe took in her clothes and jewelry.

"You can handle seeing this? It's bad."

She nodded once. "Yes."

"What about him? Your husband?"

"No, a stranger. He's in shock but not injured."

"Alright, let's go. Start with triage, the cars near us first. But…" He raised his eyebrows at her.

"Jada."

"Jada, I'm Axe. I think we're going to find everyone dead or too far gone to save. But we have to try."

"We have to try," she said as she hurried forward. "I'll take the right, you take the left?"

"Let's go."

They moved forward, opening car doors and checking inside. People on Axe's side were all dead. In Jada's row, there were a bunch of empty cars. People had gotten out and run to safety before the second and third man reached them. But in the cars towards the front of the pileup, no one remained alive.

The former tackle box holding the bandages remained unopened.

They reached the still-smoldering wreckage of the commuter bus and heard the first sirens coming from ahead of them, still far away.

"Jada, I need one more thing."

"Name it."

"I've got to get out of here. I don't want to get shot by police thinking I'm a bad guy, nor do I have time to spend the day in custody answering questions. The woman and I are on the trail of the terrorists. As horrible as this was, it's only part of what's going on, we think."

"Go on then. I'll cover for you."

"Don't lie to them. I don't want you getting into trouble. Tell them what happened. Though not remembering our names for an hour, or forgetting to mention where we were headed, would help us out."

"I've got your back. I owe you both my life. Thank you. You saved so many today."

She stepped forward and hugged him tightly, surprising him. Axe awkwardly hugged her back, keeping his rifle out of the way. For a moment, his control slipped. "Not enough," he whispered. He struggled to hold back his grief, anger, and sense of powerlessness at not being able to do more.

"You did your part, and more. Now go get the rest of those assholes."

40

THE DRIVER

The man who had detonated the car bomb pulled the getaway car back onto the road. Watching his three teammates die shook him much more than the innocent civilians they—and he—had killed.

He was heavyset, out of shape, and no good at shooting, but his skills behind the wheel for a bank robbery crew had earned him the job of driving the car that would take them all to safety.

But only he would escape.

He adjusted the baseball cap featuring a popular local baseball team, pulling the brim lower to cover more of his eyes. There were cameras ahead.

Once he had slowed and stopped the supposedly disabled car at the choke point, he had walked to where the other vehicle, and the three gunmen, waited up the road, to supposedly render assistance.

On the signal that the bus had entered the kill zone, he had pressed the blinking button on the remote, blowing up the car and the bus next to it.

The three men had passed him with their AK-47s to finish the job, shooting at random cars while prioritizing the drivers they'd been assigned, had studied, and whose faces they had memorized.

He had slid into the seat of the getaway car, ready to lead them to safety away when they finished. Watching in the mirror with the occasional glance behind him, he saw a cop of some sort kill his three friends. It was only after he'd seen the third man fall that he left the scene. He was on his own now.

As he drove slowly towards the toll plaza, it sank home what they'd done. Originally, it had all seemed like such an adventure. He'd felt so important. The studying. Driving the route ahead of time to prepare. How they'd treated him like he mattered. Like he was valuable.

His team leader had helped him forward his paycheck money to his wife and kids—well, former wife—all who had disowned him years ago when he'd gone to jail for the third time.

He'd finally started contributing to their lives. Making a difference.

Yes, he'd known people would die, but he didn't think it would be so many, so bloody, so horrible.

He held back the bile that threatened to come up as his mind and body tried to process his actions.

Don't throw up, don't throw up, don't throw up.

The plan called for him and the three others to drive to a rendezvous point in Long Island. He knew the route by heart. Through the tunnel. Across the island of Manhattan. Several choices after that, depending on traffic.

The others were gone, but he had made it. He'd take the bonus money and show up on the doorstep of his ex-wife, give it all to her, and beg her to take him back. He would be a good husband this time. A good father.

He'd gotten lucky when the man approached him about a job. Him, a three-time loser, out after his longest stretch yet in jail. A tough job, he'd been told. But one he would excel at. One he could be proud of.

He smiled. They had given him a second chance.

He slowed through the tunnel's toll plaza, the traffic non-existent. No one in their right mind, even the jaded residents of the New York metro area, had gotten into their cars once they'd heard the first reports of active shooters on the roads.

In less than an hour, he'd exchange the car for a plane ticket and confirmation of the bonus money in his account. Then he'd be on his way, ready for a fresh start.

41

THE ROOF

A man lay on the roof of a building overlooking the toll plaza, wrapped in a thick down coat which had kept him warm for the past hour. A dark blue mid-sized car approached.

He lowered his binoculars and checked the display on his smart phone. The small dot representing his assigned target moved on the map, approaching the toll plaza. He'd known it, had seen the license plate number he'd memorized. But it didn't hurt to be sure. Besides, he had to use the phone to dial.

As the car approached the mouth of the tunnel, he held down the number one on the phone keypad, which dialed the programmed number.

He'd been told he would be far enough away, but he ducked below lip of the building's roof, just in case.

The car blew up as it entered the tunnel, removing another loose end and rendering the tunnel impassable going east, minutes after another car had blown up at the entrance on the other side of the river.

42

THE WINCH

Haley watched with uncertainty as Axe clipped the big silver hook onto the webbing around her waist and legs.

I'm not sure I'm cut out for field work.

Axe offered his hand. "You stand on the edge of the guardrail and let the winch take your weight. That'll be safer when I start to lower you."

She took his hand and used it for balance as she struggled to step onto the guardrail. Axe's heavy duffel bag, slung over her shoulder, made it close to impossible. She felt Axe's hand on her butt, pushing hard, and cried out as she toppled forward. She looked at the potholed street thirty feet below the elevated road where the truck was stuck. They couldn't go forward without disturbing the scene and the many dead people in cars. They would also have to push the smoldering wreckage of the car bomb and bus out of the way.

They couldn't go backwards because of the miles of cars stopped behind them, in the lanes and on the shoulders where people had tried to reverse away from the gunfire before abandoning their vehicles to escape on foot.

Axe's solution made sense. Use the truck's winch to lower them to the street below, carrying as much of Axe's ammo and supplies as possible. Then get a different vehicle and continue the mission.

"Never out of the fight," he'd said.

Holding Axe's hand in a death grip, she turned her back to the drop. Axe extended his arm and the winch cable stopped her after a few inches. She hung over the drop, legs extended, leaning back, at the mercy of the cable.

"Ready?"

She nodded, trying to hold herself together.

"Keep your legs straight! Walk it down."

He jogged to the truck and must have hit a button or switch, because the winch started letting her down. Quickly.

"Wahh!" Startled, she wanted to grab the railing but forced herself to follow Axe's instructions. She stepped backward, her body almost parallel to the ground.

Then the side of the elevated road cut in and she dangled in midair, lowering rapidly. She looked up, trying to see Axe, then down at the ground, approaching fast. How would he know when to stop the winch?

She grunted as the winch stopped suddenly with her feet three feet off the ground.

"How much farther?" Axe yelled.

"Three feet," she called back, successfully keeping the fear out of her voice.

The winch dropped her another two feet, then stopped again.

"One more foot," she yelled, preparing for a hard landing.

Axe let the winch stop two more times until she stood on the ground below the road. She unhooked herself, then slid out of the sling material and hooked it back to the winch. "All clear!"

The hook retracted. The sound of sirens drew closer. Ambulances, she hoped, and not police. They had to get away, or they'd be stuck answering questions.

They'd heard another explosion as they prepared the winch, what sounded like a car bomb a few miles away, near the tunnel. No gunfire followed it. They were too far away to investigate. It sounded like at least some sirens were headed that direction.

She stepped a few feet to the side, taking stock of the area as she lowered the gear bag to the ground. She stood under the elevated road, next to train tracks. A high fence topped with barbed wire ran north to south, parallel to Manhattan, separating the train tracks and overgrown area under the road from an upscale residential building and, to the south, a park with basketball courts.

Axe lowered to the ground, looking at ease as he stopped two feet above the ground.

"A little more, nice and slow!"

He jerked once as Jada threw the switch. He landed softly. "Down! One second."

He unclipped the hook but kept the harness. "Okay, retract."

The clip slid up, clanking on the metal railing of the overpass as Jada recalled it. She would eventually explain what happened. Axe figured it would be an hour or two before anyone made enough sense of the situation to ask questions. In the meantime, Jada would walk south with the businessman she had taken under her wing, who seemed in shock.

Axe unzipped her duffel bag and pulled out a long bolt cutter, then held it for her to slip her arms through the handles like a backpack, making it easier to carry.

She followed Axe to a gate in the fence, securely locked with a thick chain and heavy padlock. With some effort, the bolt cutters sliced through the lock, enabling them to get the gate open and walk through.

"Now what?" She couldn't walk far with this load, and Axe carried an even heavier backpack. They'd cleaned out everything they thought necessary from the toolbox in the back of the truck: the bolt cutters, a crowbar, a tomahawk, the bulletproof vest with metal plates which Axe had slid off, and many extra magazines for the pistol and rifle, along with boxes of ammunition. Her duffel contained the relatively light first aid kit, some MRE food packets, water, clothes for Axe, and much of the ammunition.

"You're not going to like it," Axe said with a wry smile. "I'll tell you in a few minutes. Now we just need to walk. Can you make it to the end of the block?"

She followed his gaze and shrugged. "I've done a lot of things lately I didn't think I could do, so let's see what happens." They walked side by side down the clean sidewalk. A white car came towards them, a dog barking excitedly from inside. It passed them, made a u-turn, then pulled into a parking spot twenty feet down the street at the end of a long row of cars. The dog continued his barking, and she noticed a sign for the dog park ahead.

Axe sped up the pace. "Just follow my lead. Act innocent."

Oh, no. What now?

"Excuse me, is that a Rat Terrier?" Axe's face looked earnest and excited as she glanced between him and the hipster young man, trying to balance his extra-large cup of coffee, get his barking dog under control, and shut the door of his car. He looked tired, but his exactingly trimmed beard, spiked hair, and the pristine bright red down vest showed he had put effort into his appearance.

"What? Oh, yeah." He glanced at them, wary, then must have decided they weren't a threat. "Henry! Calm down! We're almost there. Relax." He shook his head at the barking dog and looked at them. "Too early in the morning for this."

"Do you mind if I pet him? I had a Lab a few years ago and I've been thinking about this breed for my next dog."

"You can try, but he wants to get to the dog park. And he can be territorial, so take it slow."

"Hi Henry, come here, boy." Axe spoke like the sweetest, kindest man in the world, crouching down on one knee and extending his hand, fist closed. "Aren't you the sweetest!" The dog paused in his frantic dancing around to smell Axe's hand, tail wagging and tongue panting happily. Axe scratched the white spot on his chest for a second.

"Thanks. Cute dog." Axe stood. "By the way," he mentioned in an offhand manner, "I'm sorry, but I need your car keys." He smoothly drew the pistol from under his shirt and stepped forward with a smile, letting the man see the gun but not pointing it at him.

The man froze. Axe took the coffee from the stunned man's hand as Henry barked again, stretching the leash as he tried in vain to drag his human to the park.

He passed the coffee to Haley and held out his hand for the keys.

The man wordlessly removed the key fob from his pocket, looking much more awake. "Just don't hurt Henry, okay, man?"

"I'd never hurt a dog." It was the first time she'd seen Axe annoyed, angry at the idea he'd put the animal at risk.

"Phone too." He pocketed the keys and held out his hand. The man's shoulders slumped as slid a phone from his back pocket and handed it to Axe.

"It's brand new."

"Don't worry, I'll leave it in the car."

"How the hell will that help me?"

"You'll have it back by the end of the day."

Henry continued to yap, growing more impatient at the delay. Axe clicked a button on the key fob and the trunk popped open. Haley moved past the man, giving the barking dog a wide berth, and maneuvered the duffel bag into the trunk, then slammed it shut.

Axe walked next to the car, and the man turned to watch. Little Henry grew more excited, thinking they were finally on their way. "Just wake up?" Axe asked him.

The man nodded warily.

"Hear that?" The sound of ambulances, police, and fire trucks came from the roadway above them. "Terrorist attack."

The hipster's eyes widened.

"Not us. We're the good guys."

His eyes narrowed in disbelief as he looked from Haley to Axe and back again

"FBI. Undercover," Haley said. "We took them out." She couldn't tell if the man believed her.

"Take Henry to the park. You can use someone's phone to call 911. But if you could give us a few minutes, we'd appreciate it. The car will be fine. We just need to drive to another vehicle I have staged."

Axe opened the back door and put in his over-sized backpack filled with gear. Haley moved around to the passenger door and Axe signaled for her to get in.

"Sorry, buddy. Cute dog, though. Bye Henry!" he said with his adorable doggy voice. Henry glanced at him, then strained hard in the direction of the park.

"Dude—can you at least leave the coffee?"

Axe laughed as they both climbed into the car. "Sorry brother, I need that most of all."

Then they drove away, leaving the man and his dog standing dejected by the side of the road.

43

THE ASSESSMENT

Axe made a face at the coffee filled with sugar and milk. He preferred his black, but needed the caffeine. It had been a long night, and they had a lot to do before the next chance for sleep.

He handed the cup to Haley, who took a grateful sip and passed it back after Axe made another turn, heading south.

They'd stopped just long enough for Axe to remove the license plates from the stolen car and replace them with others taken from a similar car parked on a side street.

Haley found a news station and turned up the volume. "Our top story: there have been reports of suspected car bombs and several groups of active shooters on many major roadways, bridges, and tunnels in the tri-state area. Stay off the streets unless absolutely necessary. Shelter in place." She turned it down, shaking her head.

Axe nodded at the radio. "You were right. You told them something would happen. What's your assessment?"

"It's starting to make sense. I got the impression those men we killed were Americans, not foreigners. What do you think?"

"I agree. They had training but weren't soldiers. They were flat out killers. The way the first one yelled and hollered? No soldier would do that."

"Could they be criminals? It would explain the lack of crime on the east coast the past year. They could have been recruited and trained for the operation."

"But who's behind it? And can we expect more?"

"I don't know. I should be in the office—I can't help from here."

Axe merged onto the turnpike going south. This road had some traffic in their direction, but almost none north towards Manhattan and the tunnel. "The good news is we're no longer on our own. Every cop in the area is on high alert. By now the FBI is involved and I wouldn't be surprised if the National Guard is mobilizing as we speak. You can go back to work." He glanced at her, his tone serious and supportive. "You did good back there. And last night. I'm happy to work in the field with you any day. But now, let's get you behind a desk, doing what you do best. That they abducted you shows how much they fear your abilities."

"I'm five hours away—assuming they don't lock down the roads to prevent other attacks, which is what I'd do. Instant curfew. Declare a state of emergency. Martial law. Everyone stay home or shelter in place."

"Well, there's no use going to AgaDefCo now. It's not them. They might have been hired to provide training. Someone will have to look into that. But the people who work there aren't indiscriminate killers." He glanced at her. "How about you call your office, tell them about the abduction and report what we did this morning. I'm sure there's a secure facility around here you can work from. I'll hang around to make sure you're safe."

"What about the leak or the mole? We still don't know who can be trusted."

"It doesn't matter now. What you were trying to discover has already happened, right? With the attack, there's no need to hide that you're alive. I suspect the bad guys already know it, anyway, unless they were caught up in the attacks. It's over. Call in. Just pick the person least likely to be a traitor."

She got the dead man's phone from her pocket. Then it rang, a low, ominous rumble. Someone was calling.

44

THE CALL

Haley looked at Axe. He looked like he had an idea.

"Let me talk. Put it on speaker."

She pressed the speaker button.

"I expected a report by now. First stage is complete. What did you find out? How much does she know?"

Axe grabbed the phone from her and slid it face down between his leg and the seat. "Are... there? Can... me?" He mumbled while rubbing the phone along the seat. She got it. The rubbing would create a scratching sound. Combined with the way he spoke, it might fool the man on the other end of the line.

"I can't hear you. What's going on?"

"We..." He paused. "... hours."

Axe looked at Haley and mouthed, "Scream and sob, quietly!"

Haley turned her head towards the window and sobbed, then cried out in anguish, tapping the part of her feelings she'd been holding at bay.

"Database... tough..."

She looked at Axe, hope in both their eyes. This could be a huge score.

The silence stretched for a few seconds, then the man's cold voice returned. "Who is this?"

Axe moved the phone to his face to reply. "Your worst nightmare."

Haley shivered. Axe's tone made her blood run cold.

Thank God he's on my side.

"Who is this?" Axe asked.

"You'll never know."

The call ended.

Axe handed the phone to her. "See if there's any data on where the call originated, a contact name, anything."

She took the phone and examined it. The app automatically erased all data as a security feature, but she tried anyway. "Nothing."

Seconds later, the phone's main screen appeared. She entered the pass code, but the screen flashed. Wrong code. "We've been locked out."

She stared at the screen, frustrated, but a resolve, deeper than any she'd known, grew stronger in her with every second.

'We'll never know?' Think again. I'll know, and sooner than you can imagine.

45

THE SHOCK

The little bitch!

Todd pushed back from his desk after changing the company phone's pass code remotely. He'd have to get one of the special branch IT guys to make sure it couldn't be traced back to them. A huge batch of phones had been ordered and set up for the operation. They should be untraceable, but...

I never planned on the authorities getting one. Let alone falling into the hands of that pain in the ass analyst.

He took a deep breath, calming himself. Then a horrible thought hit him.

What else have I missed?

He stared out the window at the office building across the street, thinking.

Nothing. It doesn't matter. Everything is in place and I've covered my tracks. Besides, they'll have a lot more to worry about in a few minutes.

He smiled wolfishly as his white phone rang. It was finally time.

He could stop pretending and feed Kelton bits and pieces of the big picture. See if he was as smart as he bragged.

Todd entered the pass code and answered. "Relax. All is going according to plan."

"Was this you?" Kelton sounded like his head would explode any second, which made Todd smile even wider.

It's time for you to face the music, my old friend.

"No, it was you. I did exactly as you instructed."

"What the hell are you talking about?"

"You wanted them stopped. I stopped them."

Todd heard a keening moan from the other end of the line. "What have you done?"

"Didn't you want the product launch stopped?"

"Yes, but—"

"Do you remember your exact words?"

"I said, 'Get it done.' But I never thought—"

"You delegated. I executed."

He chucked at the wordplay. While he hadn't pulled the triggers, people had died at his hand. He had executed his grand plan. Well, one third of it. The best was yet to come.

How many people dead—so far?

Lost in thought, he nearly missed Kelton's words. He tuned back in just in time.

"I'm calling the FBI."

"Oh, Kelton, don't do that. If you do, I'll have to release the crumbs leading to evidence implicating you."

The silence was deafening.

"Kelton, we're going to get away with this. Relax. Sit back. Do nothing, and by this time next week you'll have what you always wanted: you'll be the 50th wealthiest man in the world, and Chang will be 51th. Not the other way around, like it is now."

What an idiotic thing to care about. Top 50? Big deal. It pales in comparison to what I'll achieve soon.

"What are you talking about? Not like this. The killing…"

"Don't go soft on me now, Kelton. Think of the all the people you pay far less than they deserve so we can eek out an extra penny of stock share price. Or the overseas child labor we use. We cover it up, but it's there, isn't it? Pennies a day to eight-year-olds. This is no different."

"When I told you about Chang, I wanted a covert hack or cyber attack to disrupt their launch. How the hell did you decide that killing people was the solution?"

"Do you realize how hard an effective cyber attack is these days? Especially against a company like Happastology? Impossible. But you know what no one thinks about any more?" He smiled at his own brilliance. "Forget cyber. Real, physical attacks are the way to go. Hacking computers is difficult. But killing... well, that just takes planning and the right kind of people."

Silence from Kelton. Todd could picture the shocked look on his face while he tried to speak. Finally, Todd heard, "I'm going to—"

"Stop right there. You'll do nothing except sit back. If you do anything I don't like, you go to jail forever, or until they kill you by lethal injection. I may go down, but you'll come with me. No one would believe I'd do this on my own, especially after everything you've said in the press about how," his voice mockingly imitated Kelton's deep baritone, "I'm in charge, it's one hundred percent my effort."

He couldn't help himself. He had to get it out, the issue that started the whole plan. It had been building all this time, bubbling like a volcano. He'd held it down, not mentioning it as it festered inside him. And though the plan revolved around keeping himself in check, he couldn't do it. His voice lowered to an icy whisper. "After all, what did you say about me two years ago on your big feature TV interview?"

"Two years ago? I don't know—"

"You called me your assistant!" he yelled. Spittle flew from his lips. He wiped his mouth with the French cuff of his sleeve, struggling for control. He'd felt himself losing it for months now, had known he wasn't right in the head. But he'd kept it together, waiting. Now he could hold back no longer.

"Todd, you're—"

"A damn assistant!" His voice rose so high it sounded like a shriek. "Like someone who fetches your coffee. Not a manager, not your right-hand man. You didn't mention how I handle everything!" His voice boomed off the walls and for a moment he worried about being over-heard but couldn't help it. He'd be fine; the restaurant wouldn't open for hours. "I am the CEO, not you."

He started pacing to work off some of his bitterness. He shook his head and laughed without humor. "If anything, your role is the entrepreneur. Big picture. I run the company." Todd's voice fell to a mumble as his rage turned to crushing disappointment. "An assistant. You couldn't even call me a vice president."

He looked out the window at the many buildings up and down the block Kelton had bought, fixed up, and leased at a discount to people who wanted to revitalize the small town's business district. All the effort, all the altruism—for strangers. And crumbs for him.

He got himself mostly under control, and his voice returned to normal. "Only do what you would if this tragedy had nothing to do with us. Or it will be the end of you."

He ended the call, still gazing out the window, and took a calming breath.

Losing his cool had been a mistake. Kelton could be a problem.

For all my anger, I shouldn't forget he's a brilliant man.

What could Kelton do, though, holed up at his Montauk compound, guarded by the inner core soldiers of AgaDefCo? Todd had moles throughout the company. Anyone Kelton might turn to would inform Todd. Could Kelton go directly to the press instead of to other managers in the company? Doubtful. His ego wouldn't allow him to admit to being less than totally in charge of his empire. Todd had him checkmated.

Still… he was arrogant, money-hungry, but Todd couldn't think of him as a criminal. Would fear of the death penalty and greed for the money he would make keep him silent?

If he didn't come around, something would have to be done. He presented too much of a loose end.

Todd reviewed the contingencies. He couldn't get to one of the former soldiers in the security detail. Kelton had hand selected them using the algorithm, finding the men with the perfect combination of brutality and corruption whose loyalty could be counted—for a price. He kept them happy with short work hours, a never-ending supply of gourmet food, plus liquor and high-grade pharmaceuticals for their off-duty hours. The visits to a brothel he privately funded—and made Todd manage—were another huge perk.

I'll handle him myself. The plan is in place and it will work if necessary.

He smiled at the surge of desire which spread through him. It wasn't the preferred way to go, but if it had to happen... he already looked forward to the possibility.

I would enjoy getting my hands dirty.

46

THE DEAL

Todd reached the far wall and turned, pacing the other direction as he fantasized about different ways to kill Kelton. The other phone on his desk rang, a distinctive, ominous ring tone he'd set for one specific individual.

He grinned. He'd been looking forward to this call as well. Though he had to hide what he was becoming from this man for a while longer.

The whispered voice was hard to hear with running water in the background.

"Tell me this isn't your doing."

"Are you in the bathroom?"

"Of course I'm in the damn bathroom! Do you think I call you from my office?"

He laughed, picturing it. "No, guess not. Don't worry, all is going according to plan, as agreed."

"I did not agree to the killing of innocent civilians!"

"No one is innocent. And don't worry, they wouldn't have voted for you, anyway. New Yorkers hate you."

The man tried to control his emotions and spoke to Todd like one does to a child. "The plan was for a cyber attack, not—"

"Fireworks?" Todd couldn't resist yanking the man's chain.

The mightier they think they are, the more fun it is to play with them.

"No, not fireworks, you maniac! A travesty."

The word hit him hard. *Maniac? Am I?* He hadn't chosen a label, and now was not the time. *Act rational.*

"You wanted a platform. You've got it. Weak on terror. Can't defend our country. You've been telling him for years he needs to take off the gloves. If he'd only listened to you…"

Todd heard the steadying breath, then the slow, measured voice which had helped the man get as far as he had. "I said something small but impactful. Disruptive. I said nothing about death and destruction. I meant some kind of cyber attack! Disrupting traffic and incapacitating the bridges and tunnels is brilliant. People hate to be inconvenienced. They make noise—and vote. But by messing with the toll plazas, or making stop lights go out. Not bombs and gunmen! We agreed."

"You told me your thoughts. I never agreed. Besides, there's a surprise bonus gift for you."

"What the hell are you talking about now?" Despite the whispering, the exasperation came through loud and clear.

"By the time this is over, you'll have him right where you need him."

"What do you mean, 'By the time this is over'? It's over now!"

"That's cute. No, it's not over. Not by a long shot. Like I said, don't worry." He continued before the man could argue, dangling the carrot he desperately needed. "Which country have you been railing against for years?"

The man paused, then said suspiciously, "Iran, of course. You know this. Everyone does. Why ask?"

"What if I told you that after significant effort and a great deal of digging, it could come to light that Iran had a hand in this attack?"

Todd could tell the man was stunned. He struggled to speak and finally got himself together.

"'Could come to light.' You're a very precise man, so I'm intrigued by your choice of words. They imply that it could possibly not come to light, as well."

"That's what I like about you, Peter, you're perceptive."

"I told you, call me—"

"Of course, my apologies. But yes, you are correct. The information implicating Iran will cost you."

"You bastard, we had a deal! That you broke by killing people, I might add. Why should I trust you? Or give you anything at all you're interested in?"

"Because this information coming to light will ensure you get what you want. Won't it?"

The man hesitated, clearly reluctant to admit the truth. Finally, he whispered, "Yes, it will. It's the coup de gras."

"Exactly."

"What do you want?" he asked, sounding resigned and a little afraid.

"You don't have to pay in advance. All I need is your word." Todd paused, savoring the moment. "I want what you have."

The man thought for a few seconds, trying to decipher the meaning of Todd's demand. "What's that supposed to mean?"

"When you run, and start to beat him in the polls, I want you to select me for your current position, Mr. Vice President."

47

THE SKYLINE

Haley felt Axe's eyes on her as he waited for the light to change. Traffic was heavy near the airport. They'd sat in silence since the call, contemplating the potential horror.

"Stage one complete? Haley, what did he mean? How many stages are there?"

She shrugged, feeling helpless. She needed a computer. Needed to be running searches, reading, putting the pieces together. Solving the puzzle. It felt like an itch she couldn't scratch. At least not until she sat at a desk with full access to the country's intelligence databases. "Obviously, he has more planned. I've got work to do. As soon as you're in the truck, I have to call in."

Axe parked the stolen car in the lot closest to the car rental facility. He left the dog owner's phone on the floor beneath the seat, then retrieved the pack from the back. He helped Haley lift the duffel out of the trunk and strap it on, then locked the car and tossed the key fob into the trunk before closing it.

At the front of the building, the huge rental agency sign was filled with names and parking spot numbers. Haley's name was near the bottom, next to spot number 243.

They walked into the parking garage and down the aisle for the spots labeled 200-250. Near the far end, in their spot, sat the gleaming, black, brand-new pickup, the same model as Axe's old one they'd abandoned on the turnpike… but without the winch.

Axe grinned, then looked at her, his face changing to concern. "You got the full insurance? Everything? With me as a designated second driver?" Putting his name on the record had been a calculated risk. They rented the truck in her name under the assumption that he might be wanted for questioning. Jada had told the story about them by now. Axe's truck would reveal his identity. They didn't need to be slowed down by an investigation into what happened when they were busy figuring out what else was to come.

Haley nodded. "Please, try not to destroy it."

"We'll sort it all out when this is over." They threw the gear into the back seat of the king cab truck, and climbed in, Haley driving.

She navigated through the exit, showing both their driver's licenses to the man at the gate, signed the rental paperwork, then they were off. She pulled into a convenience store parking lot and sighed as she took Axe's phone.

"I don't want to do this."

"You're not in trouble. You predicted it!"

"But they didn't believe me."

He saw her point. People proven wrong rarely enjoyed having to admit their error.

"It'll be fine."

They switched seats so Axe could drive wherever they were sent. She checked her watch. Gregory would be on his way to the office.

She dialed the cell from memory, surprised he answered the unknown number. "Who's this?"

"Haley."

"You better be on your way in, or already there. I'm ten minutes out. What do you have for me?"

"The gunmen and car bombs are only the first stage."

"Any proof?" When Haley didn't speak, Gregory sighed in frustration. "This is another hunch, right? You can't possibly know that. Listen, I'll admit you were right. Both in your first assessment and the one you sent late yesterday. But just figure out who was behind this. Come to my office when you have something."

"First, I already have it. There's more coming. Second, I'm in New Jersey."

"Why are you in New Jersey? I need you here!"

"Men abducted me last night intending to torture me for information about the plot—what else I knew, who I told. I escaped. Long story. They knew about me because there's a leak somewhere. And I sure hope it isn't you."

"What? Abducted? A leak? What the hell have you gotten into?"

It sounded rhetorical, so she remained silent, giving him time to think. When he said nothing either, she chimed in. "Gregory, you there? Did I lose you?"

"I'm here, trying to process what you said. I'm going to need the full story, but what did you mean, you know there's more coming. How?"

"I spoke with a man who's part of the attack."

"What! You…"

Haley opened her mouth to talk, but he interrupted her.

"You're going to tell me everything, but heaven help me, I believe you. I can't imagine how it all fits together, but we'll get to that. First, though, what do you need?"

His quick change of directions—and attitude—floored her.

He is known for being excellent under pressure. You're finally seeing it in action. Now… what do I need?

"I need a secure facility where I can work. Somewhere near Newark. I can figure this out, but I need access."

"Are you mobile?"

"Yes."

"There's an FBI building in Newark. I'll call ahead. Once you get there, call me at the office on a secure phone and take me through it from the beginning. Then find out what else is coming. I'll get the team up to speed." Then he hung up.

She pulled up directions on the phone, and Axe got them moving. They were only five minutes away.

She closed her eyes, remembering the sound of the man's voice when he said the first stage was complete.

I'm on your trail. And I'm coming for you.

It felt great to be back on track. She'd been thrust into field work and done well. She'd saved lives... and killed two men. Someday she'd get back to it once she had more training. But for now, she would focus on what she excelled at. She would hunt. Pull threads. Put the pieces together. She'd be her relentless self, lost in the data. Safe behind a desk.

They were almost to the small FBI building when she heard the muffled sound of explosions in the distance. First one, then a few more, then dozens, one right after another. Some nearby, others way off, sounding like the rumble of distant thunder.

She turned towards Manhattan, where the majority seemed to come from, knowing without question that stage two of the man's plan had started. She could see the iconic skyline.

She watched as, building by building, all the lights of Manhattan winked out.

48

THE SITUATION ROOM

The situation room in the basement of the White House is smaller, and less high-tech, than imagined by most people. It contains a large conference table, speakerphones, and a videoconferencing setup with a large TV along the far wall.

Everyone stood as President James Heringten entered the room. His tan face and muscular body belonged to a man half his age. He'd inspired thousands of other sixty-year-old American men to work out and get back in shape by being the face of fitness for his generation.

His perfectly tailored dark blue suit, paired with a crisp white shirt and subdued red silk tie, made him look more like a politician than a former Navy SEAL. But he radiated power in a way much more like a warrior than any other president in modern times. They had been leaders, thinkers, and charmers, like various breeds of dogs. Labrador Retrievers, Great Danes, a few Pitbulls, plus too many Chihuahuas who were tiny and barked annoyingly, mistakenly believing they were smart, big, and powerful.

Heringten wasn't a dog at all. He was a grizzly bear, a fierce killer —and everyone recognized it.

He took his seat at the head of the table, sitting up with his back straight, dark eyes and heavy eyebrows focused on those closest to him. He waved for everyone to sit. "What the hell is happening? Are we under attack?"

Even as he asked, he wondered who among the people in this room might betray him, leaking both political items and highly classified military secrets to the world.

The FBI director down the table to the president's right spoke first. "Sir, as you heard, gunmen attacked cars on roads throughout the New York and New Jersey area. In addition, there have been car bombs or IEDs detonated on roads, bridges, and tunnels. And just moments ago at least several dozen bombs—car bombs, we believe—hit power substations, major transformers, and transmission lines serving New York City. Manhattan, specifically. Not the boroughs."

"Terrorists? Who's behind this?"

"We're working on it, sir. No one has yet claimed responsibility. However, there are no indications of a foreign attack in progress."

His thoughts turned to the men and women protecting their military bases and embassies. "Any activity overseas?"

"Nothing, sir," the director of the CIA said from the middle of the table on the president's left, her eyes betraying her anger at the domestic attacks. Otherwise, the severe woman in her late 60s, the first female African American CIA director, looked inscrutable, as always. She nodded at her counterpart to her left, the Chairman of the Joint Chiefs of Staff, a pale bald man in his 70s.

"We've issued alerts and have locked down all embassies and bases," he said.

"Next moves?"

"As you instructed from the residence, Mr. President," the Director for Counterterrorism said from further down the table, "we've instituted a no-fly zone for the entire east coast. The governors of New York and New Jersey have already issued shelter in place recommendations and are calling up the National Guard. Further considerations include expanding the no-fly zone to the entire country in case they try to pull something like 9-11." He was the youngest in the group, 44 years old, built like the swimmer he was, and a favorite of Heringten.

"Do it. Force immediate landings for all aircraft. Alaska, Hawaii, the US Virgin Islands, Guam, Puerto Rico, not just the continental US. It may be excessive, but I'd rather inconvenience people than under-react and risk lives." He looked around the table. "And close the stock market for at least today. Anything else?"

No one spoke.

The president stood, the rest of the room standing with him. "I'll be back in thirty minutes. I want an update, a preliminary casualty count, and any recommendations for additional actions we can take to keep this country and her people safe." His voice turned colder. "And I want to know who the hell is behind this… as well as options for how to punish them."

49

THE STORY

Axe dropped Haley off at the FBI building's security checkpoint. The low-level staffer who met her hadn't asked about Axe and the rental pickup. He'd been courteous but stressed. He kept glancing east, the Manhattan skyline visible in the distance. The lovely spring day made it less obvious the power remained out across the island. But knowing what had happened made Haley glance that way as well.

I hope they're okay.

They gave her a tiny conference room with a window. An older desktop computer sat on a small desk in the corner. They left a bottle of water and told her where she could find the cafeteria. She had to ask for a pen and pad of paper for notes, but at least the room had a phone. A videoconferencing monitor and camera dominated the far wall, though no one had explained how to use it.

She figured it out in two minutes and called Gregory. As she waited for an answer, she composed herself. She'd grown in the past twelve hours. Now she had to use what she'd learned.

After a moment, his image appeared, larger than life, in front of her.

"Haley. You look like hell. Tell me everything, but make it quick."

His stress and hurriedness can be an advantage to me. Tell him what he needs to hear. I can always fill him in more later if needed.

With Axe, she had a direct action asset available to her. She didn't want to reveal her ace in the hole. And she definitely didn't want Gregory thinking Uncle Jimmy sent her help. He would think she ran crying to the President of the United States when she didn't get her way.

Which I didn't. Mom went behind my back.

"I know you're busy and I want to dive into the data. Long story short: I got abducted from my apartment last night, escaped, followed the trail of the kidnappers, and got minor information out of a kid they'd left behind to guard their HQ. I was on my way to New York to check out the intel when I got stuck in traffic. A car bomb blew up and gunmen attacked people in the cars. I escaped again. I was about to call you when a cell phone I took from the kidnappers' HQ rang. I answered it. The guy wanted an update. He said, 'First stage is complete,' and wanted to know how my torture and interrogation had gone. How much I knew, what I'd found out."

Gregory stared at her, incredulous. "Why didn't you call in when you escaped the first time?"

"We have a leak, or a mole. They knew to go after me specifically. Is anyone else missing?"

"No."

"I didn't know who I could trust."

"Including me?"

She hesitated, controlling her face, and just shrugged.

"How—"

She didn't want to get into the details. "We don't have time. I told you I wanted to be a field agent. I'm capable. I handled myself. But now I need to get back to my original role. I need to hunt. There's something else coming. Stage two, at least."

"Fine. We'll debrief when this is over. But did you talk to him before the power went out in New York?"

She hadn't thought of that. "Yes, a while before."

"So that could be the second stage. For all we know, it's over."

"What if it's not?"

He paused, assessing the possibility. "Fine. I expect something in an hour. Less, if you're as good as I think you are." The video call ended.

It went better than I hoped.

She turned to the computer and got to work, grateful to be back in her element.

50

THE CLUES

Start at the beginning. Look for common threads.

Haley's fingers flew over the keyboard, entering search parameters. She opened more and more windows, wishing she had a three-monitor setup like at her desk in D.C. Still, this worked.

Why New York? And how did the roads, bridges, and tunnels tie in?

Her search revealed no visiting dignitaries. Nothing important scheduled at the UN, either publicly or behind the scenes. Had there been, her databases would have it.

She hunted.

What were the biggest events scheduled for the day?

A convention for lawyers. Lots of people hated lawyers—until they needed one.

No. Easier to attack the hotel convention area if they were truly the targets.

Two baseball games were scheduled for the evening. Both New York teams.

Most New Yorkers hate one or the other. But enough to blow the power in the morning? No. Besides, they would have hit the stadiums directly, or the roads—more likely, the subways—before or after the games.

Wait. The subway.

Haley's fingers flew as she entered a search string for any unusual activity in or near the subway from late the previous night to the present.

Two robberies. Not unusual. But the victims were murdered. Shot.

That's unusual. The city's gotten so much safer over the past thirty years.

She checked the stats. Last year there were around three hundred murders. Fewer than than one per day. But two near subways this morning. Unusual but not outside of realistic parameters. How many overall today?

Holy shit.

Twenty today. A huge anomaly.

She recalled the businessman telling Jada he was the only survivor of his caravan. The workers in the blown-up bus had been his programmers. Three of the cars behind the bus—in front of him—had contained upper management. All working for the same company.

She dug further. Thirty minutes later, she'd solved a part of the puzzle.

That's it. The piece I needed.

She stood up, ready to take the new information to Gregory. He'd listen now. Wouldn't he? She hesitated. She couldn't be sure.

Do I have enough? Where's the data?

She had data that supported a hunch. It would be generous even to call it a theory.

Not yet.

She picked up the phone. Every number called would be logged. Did they record conversations here? She wasn't sure. If so, it still wouldn't be analyzed in real time. They didn't have the computer power or staffing. At most, the calls would be archived to be listened to in the future if needed. If they were recorded.

That could come in handy to cover your ass with, later.

She hated to think that way, but she had learned. *Trust your gut.*

There's something else planned. Bigger. Much worse.

I can almost… feel it.

She stood and locked the door to the tiny room, then double-checked the video conference line. Muted.

Don't want anyone to overhear. They'd think I'm crazy. More than they already do, I mean.

She dialed Axe's cell.

51

THE HUNCH

"What do you have?" Straight to the point. Haley appreciated that, though Axe sounded like he'd just woken up.

"Where are you?"

"Taking a nap in a hotel parking lot." Haley heard the quiet whine of an electric motor—raising his seat upright, she guessed.

"You awake?"

"I'm ready. Go."

"You have to get to Montauk. Right now."

"You've found something?"

"Well…" Could she admit the thinness of her intel to him? She had to. He deserved to know, and he'd been a good sounding board in the past. "Yes and no."

"Tell me."

She let out an exasperated sigh, letting her frustration show to him. "I don't have it yet. "

"What do you have? A hunch?"

She couldn't contain an exhausted chuckle. "It's not good enough to be called a hunch. Call it a lead."

"Talk it through."

"This morning between 5:30 and 6:15, at least nine employees of a global company called Happastology were murdered in or near subway stations in New York."

"That seems noteworthy."

"And guess who the commuter bus in front of us this morning belonged to?"

"No way."

"Yes. Happastology. They have a corporate housing area in New Jersey and bus a bunch of their people to and from work every day. A perk."

"Not much of one today. But if you're saying the IED took out that particular bus on purpose, why the assholes with AKs we had to kill?"

"Their more senior people—managers—drive themselves. They work late, or leave early. And they don't want to be stuck in a bus with their underlings. But they're all from the same area. They meet up and caravan. They're worried about breakdowns, racial profiling, whatever."

"You think the IED took out the bus but couldn't hit everyone else. Hence the follow-up run and gun?"

"Yes."

"But why?"

"Their company—based in Manhattan—had a world-wide launch planned for today. A huge virtual reality platform combining e-commerce, games, social media, a bunch of stuff. It's revolutionary: the first 3-D, fully virtual world. This company was set to dominate the market—several markets—starting today. It's been planned for over a year. This morning, it looks like all their best programmers and managers were murdered. Disguised to look like random terrorism."

"You said a worldwide launch. With everything in place, they'd go ahead with the launch anyway, I would think. Surely they had backup plans, redundancies? They must have other programmers—thousands of them. And the power went out for Manhattan, but at the very least a company like that had to have its own emergency generator, right?"

"They did. It went offline at 5:55 AM. Shortly before the substations and transformers were hit. The building's engineers are missing. As are their families. Plus, the programmers and managers who died were essential. The cream of the crop. They have other people, but they are nowhere near as good. And who knows what else happened at the company, like a cyber attack? Or a hit on other locations around the world? I haven't taken the time to dive further into those questions."

"This is incredible."

"Axe, I think this is a war against a corporation."

Axe paused, thinking it through. "That seems crazy. Who would do that?"

"I'm still working on it. This launch would have disrupted so many industries, it's hard to pin down who had the most to lose—or gain from their delay."

"Haley, how sure are you? I mean, the theory makes sense. The dead people seem to be more than coincidence. But there are some big holes. Do you have anything else backing it up?"

There. This is what she needed—a skeptical voice. It sounded like something Gregory would say. But more supportive. Wanting her to explain it.

"For a court of law? Nowhere close enough. I'm not even sure I have what I need to go to my boss. Mostly it's just the dead guys, which could be a one-in-a-million, really shitty bad-luck coincidence. But Axe, this is it. The data's there. I feel it. It all fits. The company has not only suffered a personal tragedy of losing employees, and a setback from losing their talents. It's also suffered a PR catastrophe. Not to be callous about the loss of life, obviously. But even if they have backup plans, other programmers, and the ability to launch today, they can't. The news will be rightly focused on the tragedy in New York, not the cool new VR world finally available. If they continued with the launch, every time a consumer thinks of their product, this expansive platform, they'll associate it with death, destruction, failure. Terror. I'm not a business expert, but they'll have to hold off the launch for months, re-brand it, reset everyone's minds."

"The stock will plummet."

"The market will be closed for trading until at least tomorrow. SOP for a crisis or terrorist attack. But that's another area I'll be watching: who profits."

"Haley, I can't get my head around a war against a corporation."

"Come on, Axe. You're not naïve. Get with the times. Corporations make more money than countries, inspire greater loyalty, and often have better leadership. More resources, even. Their leaders are kings."

"What about a board of directors? Share holders?"

"It's the same as in a country. As long as the person in charge keeps things running well, who complains?"

"I guess. I think you need more for your boss, but I'm ready. Who do we go after?"

"It has to be a company that has a lot to lose from the new platform. But run by one person, or a small team. Most employees aren't going along with a war. Cyber, maybe. But not physical violence."

She hesitated, embarrassed at how weak it would sound. "I looked for which people or companies had the most to gain from Happastology missing their launch. I stumbled on some obscure, nerdy gamer forums talking about the company's HappastVR platform. One post this morning referenced how happy Kelton Kellison would be to hear about the postponement of the launch. I searched for why, but couldn't find anything. I went back to the forum to see if anyone had posted a follow up and the whole thread had been deleted. Before I found more, the whole comment section of the site went down. Offline. Poof."

"Who's Kelton Kellison?"

"Who is… are you kidding?"

"I've spent the last decade overseas defending America, so you'll have to forgive me if I'm a bit out of touch."

"I know, sorry. He's one of the top one hundred richest men in the world. In the top fifty, though it fluctuates. He's the CEO of a vast company that has about a hundred smaller companies under its umbrella. He owns so much of the stock he basically controls it. From insurance to social media… and gaming. Cottswoth-Goldentech."

"Wait—this is the guy who owns Cottswoth-Goldentech?"

"How do you know C-G but not the CEO? He's famous."

"Haley, Cottswoth-Goldentech is the parent company of AgaDefCo

—Agasaya Defense Contractor Group. The group behind your abduction."

She drew in her breath, the pieces falling into place. "How—"

"When I left the Teams, a recruiter took me out for dinner. Friend of a friend. He tried to get me to join up, be a trigger puller for them, or a trainer if I wanted out of fieldwork. One of the big perks he dangled included the stock plan. Not AgaDefCo stock—"

"It's not publicly traded."

"Right. He told me I wouldn't get rich on the paycheck he could offer, but the stock options were killer. His word. Stock in Cottswoth-Goldentech."

They shared a silence as they each worked through the problem.

"His HQ is in Montauk?"

"No, his HQ is in Brooklyn, not far from AgaDefCo. But get this. He owns half of downtown Smithtown, NY, which is three miles from Hauppauge."

"Hauppauge. Like Cody said."

"Yes." She felt more pieces fall into place. "And Hauppauge has an industrial park that's the largest on Long Island. Huge. Over a thousand different companies work there, including a branch of C-G. For the higher ups who don't want to live near Brooklyn, or commute from Long Island. And it's had a ton of internet traffic already this morning. Which, to their defense, wouldn't be unusual if a major competitor's launch literally blew up."

"Then why Montauk?"

"Kelton Kellison's personal estate is there, where he has his main office. Twenty acres of his land bordered by a few hundred more acres of forever wild parkland. Well-guarded. And so secluded it has its own dedicated internet line he had installed. It leads to a hub... which we can monitor. Volume of traffic, a few other things—but please, never repeat that to anyone. Right after the car bombs at the power substations, the traffic lit up and has been crazy since then. Perfectly understandable given the attacks on the area and C-G's global reach. But it's another piece of the puzzle."

"Can you get us surveillance on the area? Satellite? A drone, or air support?"

"Are you kidding? I haven't told anyone on my team about this. First, there's the potential mole. Second... Axe, this is all supposition. Guesswork. All I have is a mention on an internet gaming forum that has been deleted, and the name of two towns given up by a guy you threatened to torture."

"But it all fits. Isn't this how you work?"

"It's how I work. Not how the others do it. They would follow the trail, sure, but not act on it."

"Then what's next? I'm up for it, but Montauk is a long way out. If we're wrong, I'm way out of position. And I can't storm the place on your hunch."

"Could you get out there anyway? Despite the shelter in place order? Or at least to Hauppauge?"

She waited while he thought. "I can get out there. I've got an idea. But then what?"

"Get moving. I'll work my end. If you don't have anything by the time you get there, do what you do: shake the trees."

52

THE ANALYSIS

In Haley's tiny conference room, the borrowed computer dinged with an incoming message to everyone logged into her team's secure system. A document containing the team's formal analysis popped up. They had been hard at work as she followed the clues on her own. She reviewed the data the team in D.C. had compiled.

Pretty thin. And... they're wrong. Way off. As long as I'm right, that is.

The videophone behind her rang. She spun on the worn computer chair, hit the answer button on the speaker on the small conference table, and prepared to face Gregory.

How much should I tell him?

"I expected to hear from you already." He sounded disappointed in her and too busy to hide it.

"Sorry, I'm going all out. It's been a rough night."

All true. I haven't lied, but I'd better be careful. I've gotten better at lying since last night, but he could read me like a book last time.

"You read the analysis?"

She nodded.

"I want to hear how it compares to your work. What have you found on the environmental group?"

"I've been looking at other areas."

He looked at her with something in his eyes…

Respect? Admiration?

"You found the Iranian leads already? On your own?"

She fought to keep the surprise off her face. The president had been tough but fair on the Iranians, in her opinion, working piece by piece towards a solution to the ongoing tensions with them. Many thought he moved too slowly and gave them too much compared to what they provided the United States. But knowing Uncle Jimmy, she gave him the benefit of the doubt. If they were behind this, it would be horrible for the United States—and for him politically. Not to mention the Iranians. He couldn't let this stand, not if he wanted to be reelected. Even then, his previous stance suggested he'd face an uphill battle for election to a second term.

Stall for time.

"I'm still digging."

"Fine. I've got to go. Dig deep. Work your magic."

The call ended, and she rushed back to her computer. What had the team found that hadn't made it into the formal analysis?

Could the Iranians be involved, working against Happastology? Perhaps they felt threatened by the HappastVR tech seducing their citizens with the liberal West's online world?

She had work to do. Quickly.

53

THE HELICOPTER

Axe pulled up to the heliport terminal slowly, conscious of how it might look to be come screaming in after this morning's terrorist attacks. He was pleased to see the large, gleaming executive helicopter resting on the nearby pad. The landing area sat next to the water, with the Manhattan skyline on the other side of the Hudson, almost close enough to touch. The city looked abandoned. Every building he could see was dark, there were no cars, and few people outside.

He grabbed the heavy backpack, reorganized to include only his most essential items, and got out of the truck.

I hope this works.

He put on a friendly smile, slung the pack on his left shoulder, and approached the small building housing the office and check-in counter of the flight company.

He opened the glass door and put a relieved smile on his face for the man standing expectantly behind the chest-high counter.

"Hey there, what can I do for you?" the man in his early 50s asked. He looked fit, with a thick chest, bulging biceps, and thick, hairy fore-arms showing from his perfectly smooth white polo shirt with the company logo. Several faded tattoos decorated each arm. Definitely retired military. He wore his light brown hair cropped short. His brown eyes seemed alert, and the pleasant smile on his face didn't extend to them. He looked wary.

"I'm happy you're still here. I'm desperate for a ride. Got to get out of the area and everything that's happening. I need to get to my family on Long Island and I'm hoping we can work something out."

"Sorry, my friend. Everything is grounded. Nobody's flying anywhere."

Axe set down his bag with an exaggerated sigh. "Oh, that's horrible. I was hoping you could make an exception. I've got a credit card here nowhere near its limit. You can name your price."

"No price is high enough to lose my business license, bird, and freedom when they throw me in jail for flying during a no-fly order. Or shoot me down first and ask questions later."

"I understand. I do. By the way, where did you serve?"

The man continued to smile, but his eyes watched Axe like a hawk. "You name it. I've been there and done that."

Axe laughed. "And got the T-shirt."

The man nodded. "What about you?"

"Same thing, brother."

I really hoped it wouldn't come to this.

Axe reached under his shirt to pull his 9mm and make the man see the error of his ways.

The man took a half step back and raised the shotgun he had hidden behind the tall counter, expertly aiming it at Axe's chest. He barked out a small laugh. "You're not fast enough to outrun buckshot, 'brother,'" he said, mocking Axe's attempt at establishing rapport. "You think you're the first one who's ever come in here not ready to take no for an answer?"

Axe brought his hand away from his holster, raising both arms up. "I should have known someone with your experience would be prepared." He dropped the friendly act and got serious. "Listen, warrior to warrior, here's the deal. I have intel that the people behind the terror attacks are in Montauk and they're planning another hit. Bigger. I've got to get out there."

The man faltered for a second, torn, then shook his head. The gun never wavered. "That I almost buy. Not the bullshit about your family. But it could be just another lie. Besides, I need more than some story to give up everything."

"You need more than saving the lives of thousands of people?"

The man's eyes narrowed in anger. "No. But how can I be sure you're not giving me another line of crap? I've been lied to so many times... by the government, by every rich asshole who has ever told me they were on their way and made me wait for hours... and don't get me started on the ex-wife. How can I know what's real and what's a lie?"

"I can get you what you need, I hope. My phone is in my pocket, but it's right by my pistol. So please don't shoot me."

"Just do it slow." The gun held steady. Axe had no doubt the man could—and would—kill him if necessary.

He pulled out his phone, frowning. He didn't enjoy calling for help. *Now is not the time for pride.*

It was time to set his ego aside. Teams are teams for a reason. No one can do everything on his own.

He dialed from memory. This was a number he'd been told not to use except in the worst of emergencies.

The man answered immediately. "You must be in trouble."

"Yes—" He almost added, 'sir' but bit the word back at the last second. Though the man in front of him had been in the military, he didn't need any hint who he was talking to.

"I have to get somewhere in a chopper and—"

"And there's a no fly rule for the entire country right now."

"Yes."

The admiral laughed. "I'm not sure how much you think I can actually do about a nationwide no-fly zone, son."

"I've got a plan. I just need a little assist."

"Tell me."

"I'm standing in front of a retired military helicopter pilot. He has the skill, he has the bird, but he's worried about repercussions."

"And you want me to?"

"He's a patriot. He wants to help."

The shotgun never wavered, but the pilot's eyebrows raised in amusement.

Axe caught the irony of claiming the man wanted to help while holding a shotgun on him.

"With your connections…"

"I could make a phone call. Like what happened in your case a few days ago?"

"Exactly."

"What's this gentleman's name?"

Axe looked at the man. "What's your name?"

The man's eyes narrowed in suspicion, but he answered. "Tucci."

"What unit?"

"Night Stalkers."

Axe paused, reassessing the man. The Night Stalkers is the nickname of the regiment renowned as the Army's best pilots.

"Did you get that?"

"Yes, I heard. Give me five minutes."

He looked at Tucci. "Five minutes. Can I put my hands down?"

Tucci nodded, relaxing his aim but keeping the shotgun pointed enough towards Axe that there was no way to go for his gun without getting blown in half.

Axe regretted not checking his watch when the admiral hung up on him, because he swore only two or three minutes had passed.

Tucci's phone rang, startling Tucci but not Axe.

Thank God he didn't have his finger tighter on the trigger. I would have gotten my head blown off.

"You're going to want to get that, Tucci."

With his hand still on the grip of the shotgun, Tucci reached his other hand down and slapped the phone, putting it on speaker. "Tucci Helicopter Service," he said in a gruff voice.

"Chief Tucci. Do you recognize who this is?" the commanding

voice boomed from the speaker.

Tucci's eyes widened. He looked at the phone, to Axe, and back at the phone. He stood up straighter and squared his shoulders, an involuntary reaction when speaking to brass, even on the phone.

"Yes, sir. How are you, sir?"

"I'd be a damn sight better if assholes weren't blowing up our country."

"Yes, sir."

"I need you to do me a favor, Chief."

"You want me to fly the gentleman standing in front of me wherever he wants to go, don't you, sir?"

"You always were one of the smart ones, Chief. Not only that. I would like you to do whatever the gentleman standing in front of you wants. That includes violating any no-fly order, ignoring any radio communication or threats to shoot down your beloved chopper. Is that clear, son?"

"Sir, well, I—"

"Let me stop you there, Chief."

"Sir?"

"I want you to do it for me. And for your country. We're under attack and it's my understanding you're going to help us fight back. This is time sensitive and probably illegal as hell, but we need to get it done. So, is this something you can do on your own, or do you need me to reactivate your ass?"

"No, sir. I can do it on my own, sir."

"Good man. Get it done. Anything happens, we'll fix it afterward. I've personally got your back. Stay safe and Godspeed."

The man hung up.

Tucci lowered his weapon. "Incredible. That was my former commander. Or rather, my former commander from nine years ago. Do you know who he is now?"

Axe grabbed his go bag. "Nope, but I guess he's pretty high up."

"You could say that." He shook his head, still stunned by the call. "So, Montauk, huh?"

"Montauk. And bring the shotgun."

54

THE FALSE FLAG

This time, Haley called Gregory. She didn't waste time beating around the bush. "The entire explanation is a hoax. There is no United Environmental Front."

Gregory had his tie loosened and top button of his dress shirt unbuttoned. He looked like he'd been up all night, though he'd only been at the office since eight. His graying hair, normally smoothly arranged, stuck out in all directions.

He shook his head. "I've seen the intel, Haley. It's all there."

"That's my point. Intel is never all there."

He smiled, not disagreeing. "And the other crumbs?"

His reaction surprised her. She had expected more push back.

"I've found a few things. Threads I'm pulling... but I don't like what I'm finding."

"I knew you'd find them. But I need you to stand down."

"What? Why?"

He spoke patiently. "Those threads, as you call them, have been unraveled already. I set up an inter-agency task force. They've been focused on getting to the bottom of this. They were told to find who had financed and executed the attacks, no matter where it took them."

Relief rushed over her. He knew. "I agree. But we need more data. You have to get a team to Montauk in case there's more to come."

"Montauk?"

Once again, his reaction caught her off guard. She realized she'd misjudged the situation badly.

Too much stress, too little sleep.

"What the hell are you talking about?"

"It's..." Did she dare divulge her hunch? She had no direct evidence. Again. But it felt right. The data were pointing towards it, though not spelling it out in flashing lights like the United Environmental Front. No. She had to hold back. She'd gotten burned last time. She turned the tables. "What are you talking about?"

"Iran."

"Iran?"

He's still on that? I thought he and the team would see it for what it is: fake.

"No. You're wrong. I saw those threads." The data on the Iranian angle felt like someone extremely clever had made it just obvious enough for dedicated, desperate analysts to find. "They reek of a false flag operation. Can't you see that?"

He shook his head in frustration with her. Again. "Haley, I have ten of my best people on this." He tilted his head in acknowledgment of her abilities. "Not including you, of course. But they're unanimous. The data were extremely well hidden and cleverly disguised, but it's as definitive as it gets in our business. The Iranians are behind this."

"Sir," she started, then tried again. "Gregory, listen—"

"Haley, you were right about this originally and I should have listened to you. I'll admit it. But this time you're wrong. Don't let success make you think you're infallible. You're not."

She did her best to keep her face still, betraying little. But she let the tiniest bit of embarrassment through, coupled with reluctant acceptance. "Yes, sir."

Will he buy it?

"Good, you're learning. In time, you'll be the best. Hell, you might already be. But never forget you're part of a team. And other people are excellent at their jobs, as well."

If he didn't believe her about the Iran situation, she couldn't tell him about Kelton Kellison.

Could she mention her other hunch? She suspected more destruction was on the horizon. Another target. Near the city, but not in it. The threads were there.

Could she let him think the Iranians were involved, so he'd put people on it?

I don't think I can risk it. He already thinks I'm crying wolf. Better to keep digging and, in the meantime, Axe and I will have to handle it.

"Yes, sir," she repeated.

"Find out where the gunmen escaped to. If we can track them down, we can see what they know."

He hung up. Haley turned back to the computer once more, desperate for the smallest shred to prove what she already knew: another attack was coming.

55

THE UPDATE

James Heringten glanced at the man on his right, sitting in the first chair, which had caused the whole group to move down one seat.

Peter—the vice president—had been in the situation room when he returned for an update thirty minutes after the first meeting. He was uninvited, and it was against protocol. In times of crisis like this he should be far from the White House, just in case.

He nodded at the VP and smiled tightly, betraying none of his anger and saying nothing.

What an idiot. I hate having settled for him. I wish I hadn't needed the votes he brought.

The man sat stiffly in his tight-fitting suit, tailored to show off his muscles. He presented himself as the "fit grandpa." The two of them had looked great on the campaign trail together. Peter the statesman, older and with more years in politics. James, eight years younger, taller, the warrior.

Looks were deceiving.

Peter, sixty-eight and balding, had been a hawk and warmonger his entire political career. He made a name for himself—and a livelihood

—by waving the red flag of danger about a variety of overseas threats, depending on which way the political winds blew that election cycle.

He thinks the solution to the Iran problem—any problem, really—is war. He sees glory and doesn't understand violence has to be the last resort.

Many people didn't serve their country. James preferred it that way. But he was the first president in decades to not only serve but to experience combat. He knew war like no other politician. He'd use every trick up his sleeve, including turning the other cheek if it didn't cause any lasting harm, before he'd get this country into another war. Like the ones the vice president seemed desperate to start.

I'd better not die. Now that I know him better, the thought of him running the country is horrifying.

James addressed the group with a skeptical tone. "It's a militant environmental group?"

"Apparently, sir. They haven't been on our radar prior to this." The FBI director looked embarrassed at the miss. "They claim fossil fuels are destroying our planet and see blowing the electrical grid—or at least all the lines serving Manhattan—as a way to draw attention to their cause. Apparently they also believe what they've done will show the grid itself is on its last leg."

"Which it is," the president mumbled under his breath. But the country never had enough money to fix all the infrastructure needing to be addressed. His administration prioritized the aging bridges. That alone cost billions more than they could afford—even before the inevitable delays and cost overruns.

"Sir," Don Samuels, the Director for Counterterrorism, spoke up. "As you know, a small unit of mine has the authority to do analysis spanning the globe, including within the United States."

He knew. It's the unit he'd helped—subtly—Haley get into.

"Yes, Samuels. What have they come up with?" Finally, a group he could trust, especially if Haley helped with the information. Which she must have, since he'd heard nothing about her from his wife, or the admiral. He would have loved an update, but with no one around he could trust one hundred percent, he'd settle for the report from her department.

"Sir, a small team of analysts have found some bread crumbs showing a rather different assessment."

"Samuels, please get to the point." His normally patient demeanor cracked.

"Sorry, sir. Some of the analysts disagree, vehemently, with the assessment that a brand-new environmental group is to blame. They believe a foreign power might be covering its tracks, using the environmental group as pawns. Or they may have made the group up specifically to hide their involvement."

"What's the confidence level?"

"They're frantically looking for more proof, sir. So far they've found clues but no hard evidence." He squirmed as the president stared at him, face set. "Twenty-five percent, sir."

The president didn't care if they saw. He rolled his eyes.

"That's pretty low. Basically, what—conjecture?"

"Yes, sir. They hope to have more for you soon. They're the best. If the trail is there, they'll find it."

"I have no doubt. But while we're on the topic, which foreign power?"

"Sir," Samuels hesitated, uncomfortable. "Given the lack of certainty—"

"Given the leaks in this administration, the reporters will have it before lunch. So at least let me hear it from you instead of seeing it on TV."

He still hesitated.

"Come on, who? Canada? Australia?"

His joke received the requisite smiles and chuckles from the people around the table.

"No, sir. It's Iran, sir."

He'd worried this would come. Iran had ambitions for itself. They'd been a problem for the last four decades, vexing administrations that, he might argue privately, were better and smarter than his.

One of his big worries had always been being presented with thin, so-called evidence suggesting Iran was behind an attack, putting him in an impossible situation. Would he take action when they might or might not have done it? Or be seen as weak at home and abroad, which would be especially dangerous if Iran was truly behind the actions they were accused of.

The United States had gotten into wars on weak grounds before, and he damn sure meant to avoid it during his time leading the country. If doing the right thing for the United States cost him the second term in office he coveted and believed the country needed, then so be it.

"You all see boogie men at every turn. I know you think I'm soft on Iran, but we've made tremendous progress with them. Rest assured, if they are behind this, they'll pay. But you'd better be more than twenty-five percent sure, got it? I'm not risking war in the Middle East over that."

He caught and held the eye of the vice president, who'd long had a hard-on for Iran.

"If we go to war with anyone, it'll be with proof, or as close to it as we can get. We go with allies, and we're all in. We start it, we finish it. No half measures. Got it?"

"Yes, Mr. President," everyone murmured, including, he saw, the VP. Thankfully, Peter appeared smart enough to sit with his mouth shut for the time being.

I wish I knew what Haley thought. She's young, but has one of the best minds I've seen. Smarter than everyone in this room, myself included.

Could he ask Samuels if she was one of the analysts on the team? If so, twenty-five percent would be good enough for him. But Haley had pleaded with him from the start to not interfere in her career. No favors, no pulling strings. She wanted to make it on her own, which he respected and had honored, aside from a few discreet nudges. He'd dropped a hint which had resulted in her job offer to the Central Analysis Group. It had been easy, as she'd already been scouted by the CIA, NSA, and FBI.

He'd also gotten his friend Admiral Nalen to send someone to look after her and help if needed.

I have to get Nalen in here for another beer. Get an update from outside normal channels.

"Any suggestions? Do the governors need help? Is there an action we could take but haven't yet?"

No one spoke up.

"Fine. Get me more. Call me when you have it."

They all stood with him, and he stalked out the door. Even in the midst of this crisis, he had a hundred other details to manage. He put the attacks in a mental box, trusting his people to do their jobs, then turned his focus to the next problem.

56

THE SERIAL KILLERS

Not all the car bombs had been used in the attacks that morning.

Half of the gunmen had been held back as well. They had a more important mission.

But all of them had left before dawn to be in place before the expected shelter-in-place orders. Or—an eighty-two percent chance, the team had predicted—a complete lock-down was issued.

They had to also consider the twelve percent chance that martial law would be declared, along with a curfew ordered and enforced by the police and National Guard.

Only the shelter-in-place directive came to pass, but they had been ready, just in case. Every possibility had been accounted for.

The nice cars filled with well-dressed, well-groomed men had arrived at their assigned locations early in the morning, then drove along pre-planned routes until the first car bombs and firefights.

They were all within a mile or two of their eventual target, spread out near diners, shopping malls, grocery stores, or in commuter parking lots. Each man looked at his phone, the same as thousands of people around them, watching the news and wondering when it would be safe to drive again.

After a few hours, they did what so many others did. They entered the diners, bars, coffee shops, and restaurants nearest them and passed the time. Waiting.

These men had been screened more carefully than any of the other groups. The algorithm had combed through the data and found a small batch of men perfect for the final assignment. Disciplined. Patient. Utterly ruthless.

Their profiles marked each as a potential serial killer. Several, in fact, were, though obviously it hadn't been discussed in their interviews. But the team lead, himself a borderline psychopath, could sense it in them.

Once selected, they all felt surprisingly comfortable around each other, more so than with any other people ever. They never allowed their trainers or handlers to overhear, but at night, in hushed conversations, they hinted at their exploits. They spoke in thinly veiled terms of torture, murder, and the joy they found in causing others pain.

The plan they had trained for would cause agony and destruction on a grand scale. They had all worked harder at the preparations than anything they'd done before, using their incredible focus, discipline, and coldness to practice for hours and hours every day.

They would first get to kill the way each preferred: up close, in person. As they did, they'd soften the defenses of their target, which would allow the next wave to succeed. They would enjoy their part immensely, hopefully surviving to reap the reward by causing the greatest suffering ever experienced in the United States, and perhaps the world. Tens of thousands would die, millions if all went perfectly.

If things didn't go as they hoped, hundreds of thousands would still suffer long, painful deaths.

It thrilled them to the core.

Though each secretly believed he would be one of the survivors, if they personally didn't make it, they would die happy.

So they wore the uncomfortable suits, along with the practiced looks of concern and worry on their faces, mimicking the people around them—those sheep who cared about others, who felt empathy. They were the wolves, but they fit in perfectly. And in a matter of hours, they would destroy the entire area of New York City.

57

THE CHOICE

During Hell Week, the Navy SEAL's final exam of the first phase of training, Axe and his classmates slept four hours in five days.

That had been many years ago.

Aside from an hour nap, he had been up over twenty-four hours. Those hours included a car chase, being choked, threatening to torture a guy, a firefight on an expressway, stealing a car, looking down the barrel of a shotgun, and killing at least six bad guys. Or more, if the tangos in the crashed van didn't make it. He didn't even count the man he'd shot but left for Haley to finish off.

It felt great to be back in the fight. Useful. Granted, getting choked out by the woman he rescued hadn't been fun. And he could have done without Tucci pointing a shotgun at him. But overall, he was doing what he did best.

But at some point, he'd need to sleep. The short nap in the hotel parking lot had helped, but he wasn't a kid anymore.

He couldn't sleep yet. His adrenaline flowed. The helicopter skimmed the waves. The stunning spring day's sun gleamed off the ocean only a few feet below him.

All my time in helicopters and I've never flown up front.

Despite the very real danger, from a potential crash to being shot down by fighter jets patrolling the area, Axe's grin lit up his face.

They flew directly east, the southern coast of Long Island to their left. The chopper's skids were in danger of getting wet, but Tucci expertly timed the ocean swells. They were so low that Axe had to bite his lip to keep from asking the pilot to fly a bit higher. Axe glanced over at him. Tucci had his entire focus locked on flying. Axe didn't dare utter a word for fear of breaking his concentration.

After piling his gear into the back of the luxury helicopter, Axe and Tucci had flown south, skimming over buildings and avoiding the area around the bridge between Staten Island and Brooklyn the terrorists had damaged earlier.

"That'll be the most dangerous area to fly. They'll be looking for potential follow-on attacks," Tucci had explained. "But I can do it."

Axe couldn't decide if he was meant to hear the next part Tucci muttered under his breath. "I hope." They used plenty of dark humor on the Teams to reduce stress and build camaraderie. He hoped Tucci was doing the same.

So far they'd made it without crashing or being detected.

"Radar can't see us this low. At most, we're an intermittent contact. Though I'm surprised they haven't scrambled fighters for a visual yet," Tucci said through the headsets he and Axe wore. His eyes never left the surface of the ocean in front of them.

To their left, they saw a scattering of people lounging on the sand, taking time to enjoy the day, either unaware of the terrorist attacks or unconcerned because they were far from the city, and at the beach. No one attacks a beach.

"You need to decide in the next few minutes where you want me to take you. There's an airport near Hauppauge. Powerful radar. If you want to go there, we have to cut left to avoid it, and go inland, which is dangerous. Buildings, power lines, people calling in about a low-flying chopper. I'll have to land in a park or parking lot. Long Island is crowded. Someone will see you. You'll be on the run without transportation and I'll be out of the game."

"What about Montauk?"

"Much easier. We bear right, go further out to sea to reduce the chance the airport picks us up. Then we angle in. Fewer people would complain about a chopper out there, too. Lots of Richie Riches wishing they could convince their pilots to pick them up and fly them somewhere, or wives hoping it's the husband coming home from Manhattan."

He had a choice to make. He cared less about his safety than Tucci's. But honestly, given the situation, if one or both of them ended up in jail, so be it. The threat to the country warranted the risk, and the punishment, if needed. It might take until the president's last few days in office, but a presidential pardon would be a possibility. Eventually. In the meantime, if he could help stop whatever might be about to happen, he'd take his chances. Tucci would, too.

If Haley's intelligence could be believed, Montauk would be the place to go. Get to the main man. Find out what he had planned. Stop it from happening.

He was about to answer when he had a terrible thought.

The intel is always wrong.

It had long been their half-joking mantra in his Team. Whatever the analysts said could be counted on to be wrong most of the time, it seemed. Intellectually, he realized the intel was right more often than not. The mind didn't latch on to the missions that went well because of good intel. All the ops that went to hell or were a bust stuck in the memory, though.

What if this is another wild goose chase? What if Haley's wrong?

"I need your final answer, Axe."

"Montauk."

Tucci blew out a sigh of relief and banked the bird to the south, gaining a little altitude at the same time. "Any particular place, or dealer's choice?"

Kellison's compound struck him as the logical place to go, but flying near it would be a bad move, especially with all aviation grounded. If he was guilty, they would be sending a message saying, "We know what you're doing and we're coming for you!"

He consulted the map of the area. "What's better for you? Golf course, road, beach, parking lot, or forest?"

"Wow, you're giving me a choice for an LZ? I don't care what anyone says, Axe, you're a wonderful mission planner." Tucci thought it over. "I'll know a good place when I see it. We're looking for off the beaten path enough to not be noticed, but close enough for you to get to your objective. Plus, you need to decide if you want me to risk staying on station. On the ground, not in the air. Or if you're releasing me to fly back and face the music."

These are the type of decisions I avoided by leaving the Teams. I don't want to plan missions. I want to blow shit up and shoot bad guys.

Tucci glanced over at him. "Sucks to be in charge, don't it?"

Axe nodded, thinking it over.

"Let's find an out-of-the-way place to set down. You can stay there and be on standby. Safer than flying back. Let people think we're a member of the one percent who landed at a nearby estate."

"Then you're going to call me in when the shit hits the fan, aren't you?" Tucci grumbled. "Remember, this bird doesn't have missiles or a machine gun."

"There's always your shotgun."

"Brother, if you need me and my shotgun, you've already lost."

58

THE HOUSE

The afternoon sun didn't penetrate the forest canopy where Axe lay, but the pleasant temperature made the overwatch position almost too comfortable. The smell of the earth and trees mixed with the scent of the nearby ocean, making this hide the most pleasant one he'd experienced.

If only they were all like this.

He lay prone, high-powered binoculars held to his eyes, elbows resting comfortably on the soft ground of the small forest bordering Kelton Kellison's estate. The expansive mansion sat before and above him on the highest point around, a half mile away. Its classic seaside architecture surprised Axe. He figured he would find a newer, modern house built with glass and steel. Instead, the house had a wraparound porch with a long white railing. Dark, weathered shingles covered the exterior. It sprawled across impeccably manicured grounds, but it didn't seem ostentatious.

Then again, with as much money as Kellison made, he likely had several other houses to choose from. But none with this scenery, Axe would bet.

The location made the house, not the other way around. Axe had amazing views of the ocean through the trees from where he hid. Standing at the house, the entire area would be visible, from the small, quaint town three miles away to the lighthouse at the far end of the island, four miles to the east. Not to mention the ocean views to the south and bay to the north. The world would be spread out below. Kellison would feel like a king... or a god.

I don't understand how someone with the money for all this decides to kill people, blow up bridges and tunnels, and cut the power to an entire city. Unless he's snapped, it doesn't make sense.

Tucci had set the bird down in a tiny clearing in a state park three miles through the woods to the northeast. Axe had unpacked his bag, taking only the minimal load-out in his smaller assault backpack. Then he'd eaten as much as he could from his store of MREs, sharing the food with Tucci, who agreed to stay behind with the helicopter and pray no one came looking for it. They set up comms using their cell phones, exchanging numbers and discovering the outstanding cell reception, unsurprising given the wealth in the surrounding area. Then he'd hefted his pack, his rifle strapped to the outside but covered with a fleece jacket to hide it from view, and set off to get eyes on his target.

Axe wondered about Haley. He hadn't heard from her since she'd sent him to Montauk and had no way, realistically, to reach her. He could call the Newark FBI office and ask to be put through to her, but it might raise eyebrows. They had agreed she would avoid telling her superiors about him if possible. After all, he was an unsanctioned asset. He didn't want trouble for himself, the admiral, or, ultimately, the president. Better to wait, watch, and gather intel.

He returned to surveying the house and grounds.

Security seemed adequate. He saw roving foot patrols with seemingly random paths. Heavily armed men strolled the beautiful grounds in the springtime sunshine, enjoying the views and the light sea breeze. More guards manned the front gate, and he guessed there would be another outpost close to the water to guard against both an attack and annoying tourists approaching from the beach. There would be more armed men inside, plus a quick reaction force within a few miles, he guessed.

Nice work if you can get it. Maybe I shouldn't have been so quick to turn down the AgaDefCo recruiter.

His blood ran cold when he saw a man round the corner of the house. Next to him panted a focused German Shepard dog.

Damn. Not dogs.

Dogs were difficult to hide from, impossible to run from, and he hated the idea of killing one. If he had to choose between a dog and himself, he'd shoot the dog, but it would be a close decision. Several had been on missions with him during his time in the Teams. He valued and trusted each in the exact way he did the dog's handler and his other human teammates. The dogs could switch from happy to ferocious in a moment. He'd watch men surrender instantly instead of having to face the K9 soldiers.

He sighed. He had no defense against the animal.

I should have said no the moment the admiral started speaking.

The phone in his back pocket vibrated. He tapped his ear bud to answer.

"Go."

"It's me." Haley sounded exhausted and defeated. "Where are you?"

"Overwatch on our target. Where we discussed." No sense broadcasting the specific details to anyone listening. She'd understand. "What do you have for me?"

"The crew there is a separate branch of Aga. All dishonorably discharged for various reasons, mostly to do with excessive force. Now, though, they're pretty disciplined. Happy in their positions. Apparently they worship the ground the man walks on because he takes good care of them. Rumors of excellent pay, plus booze, women, even drugs."

"What have you figured out? Is something else in the works?"

She sighed. "I can't find any hints. Either nothing is planned or everyone has been extremely careful."

Axe considered the options. "Maybe it's over?"

Haley took a second to respond, then came the unconvincing reply. "Maybe."

"So what next?"

"I have a feeling, but I can't nail it down. I'll keep at it, and if the threat is there, I'll find it."

He surveyed the grounds again, wondering if they had any sensors or perimeter security. He couldn't see a fence, but figured there had to be one. The bolt cutters in his pack might come in handy. But cutting locks or fences takes time and makes noise. Any halfway decent security team would be on him in a second.

They'd gotten very lucky during his years in the Teams. Rarely did they battle any force with much training, and never against an enemy with decent weapons or technology.

Had they gone to war with a first world-country, or a second-world one like Iran or North Korea, both the stakes and death toll would have been much higher.

With his old team, going head to head against a highly motivated and well-equipped enemy like the one in front of him would be difficult. Alone, it would be suicidal.

Could he bluff his way in? He could easily work there... aside from the fact that he had integrity and a stellar record. He'd been honorably discharged. If they were looking for renegades, he'd never be selected. No. They'd sniff him out in a second if he tried the old, "Hi, I'm new, where's the boss man?" routine.

"I could try to get in..." he trailed off, hoping Haley wouldn't take him up on the offer.

"Sounds dangerous. Why not hang out until dark? Give me a few more hours to hunt. I might find whatever my mind is telling me is out there."

"Going in at night is less impossible than approaching in the daytime. I'm well hidden and I don't think they patrol this far out. I'll rest. Call the second you need anything."

"Deal. Stay safe."

"You too."

He clicked off and took the ear bud out to hear better if anyone approached. After one last pan of the house and grounds, he set the binoculars down and wedged himself into a spot between two fallen trees, half under one of them.

He'd be very hard to find. Axe closed his eyes and settled into a restful state, almost asleep but alert enough to react instantly if needed.

59

THE IDEA

James walked into the Situation Room in a grim mood, knowing he wouldn't feel any better after the report. Already critics from both political parties were hinting he hadn't done enough to protect the country. Taking political potshots in the middle of a crisis disgusted him. They were hypocrites, too. He'd been criticized often in the past three years when he'd tried to lead the way to better infrastructure security, more money for intelligence, and more robust diplomacy with their friends and enemies. People seemed to want it both ways—or just wanted to bitch without contributing to a solution. It was days like these he longed for his old Team. He would much rather have the simplicity of being in the field with the enemy in his sights and his finger pulling the trigger.

At least the vice president didn't attend the meeting this time.

He remained standing at the head of the long conference table, but impatiently waived for the rest of his crisis team to sit. "What do you have for me?"

"Sir, New York City is in terrible shape," Linwood, the frumpy, middle-aged head of FEMA reported, standing to speak like he was presenting his third-grade class project. What the man lacked in style or grace, though, he made up by being a brilliant logistical manager and leader. "It's a catastrophe in the making."

"What's the problem? Reroute the power. Buy more from the Canadians if you have to." Canada's power plants should be able to supply their needs, at least in the short term, before winter.

"That's not the problem, sir. The terrorists didn't go after the power plants. They hit the power lines and the entire distribution network feeding the area. We have plenty of power. We just can't get it to New York City."

"All the power lines?"

"Not all. But where they couldn't hit the lines, they blew up the infrastructure near them. We can patch some and reroute others, but it will take time. The damage is extensive."

"How did this happen?"

"The plants are well guarded and protected. But not the power distribution. It's too extensive. Power lines are above ground in most places. Substations were protected with chain-link fences which the shrapnel from the car bombs went through or destroyed. Transformers sit exposed. The list goes on, sir. This was a very well planned and coordinated attack. They either did extensive research or had people in the industry advising them. They knew exactly where to hit us, where it would hurt the most."

James figured it would be futile to ask, but he needed to know. "What about generators in Manhattan? Surely some buildings have emergency backup."

"Yes. Many do, but only for emergency power. Exit lights, essential safety services like ventilation. The generators were never designed to run entire buildings."

An idea struck him. "And the generators need fuel. Diesel, which they'll run out of soon, right?"

Linwood nodded, his wrinkled, ill-fitting brown suit looking old enough to have belonged to his father.

The president rubbed his eyes tiredly. "And the bridges and tunnels have all been bombed, so we can't get fuel in."

"Exactly, sir. Many of the bridges and tunnels will be fine. The bombs weren't large enough to destroy them. But each will have to be thoroughly inspected."

Samuels, the Counterterrorism director, spoke up. Thankfully, he didn't stand, though he was younger and in much better shape than Linwood. "However, we can't examine the bridges and tunnels before checking to make sure they haven't been booby-trapped. There is also a concern nearby abandoned vehicles could have been left by the terrorists to explode when moved. And we only have so many bomb disposal units available."

James looked around the table at the expressions of helplessness, anger, and frustration on the faces of his senior staff and smartest advisers. "So we can't get power to Manhattan?"

"No, sir. Not quickly."

"How long?"

"To repair the damage? We're assessing it now."

"Best-case scenario first."

He waited. No one wanted to speak. The president spoke again. "Okay, worst case. Anybody—just give me a guess."

Linwood, still standing, shifted his weight and reluctantly spoke. "Months, sir. Three to six, if we're lucky. They hit us hard."

James sat down heavily upon hearing the bad news. Linwood glanced around the table, saw he was now the only person standing, and lowered himself towards the chair. In mid sit he changed his mind and stood again. "In the meantime, sir, the people on the ground are working hard. There's actually some hope. National Guard helicopters are airlifting portable generators to essential areas like nursing homes and any medical facilities without their own or with ones that are underpowered. Fuel is being delivered to buildings with their own generators. We haven't lost Manhattan. It's just a matter of time until we can install new lines or repair the destroyed connections."

"But for now it's back to the 1800s for them."

"Yes, sir."

"What about looting or civil disorder?"

"Nothing yet. People were coming together, pitching in to help."

For a while, he thought.

"There's also the problem of food, Mr. President. Until we can open the bridges and tunnels, we're using boats to bring in and distribute MREs. We've also set up food tents in dozens of neighborhoods and are providing free hot meals."

"Do we need to evacuate the island?"

"People want to escape the city temporarily. We're already helping by operating twenty-four-hour ferry service across the rivers, then providing transportation to mass transit points." Linwood checked his notes on the yellow legal pad on the polished table in front of him. "We estimate eighty-five thousand people already moved, but there are over one and a half million residents of the island. Many will shelter in place. But realistically, Mr. President, a mass evacuation of Manhattan without the bridges and tunnels is impossible."

"I understand. Anything you need from me?"

"No, sir."

The terrorists, whoever they were, had planned well. Still, he felt proud of his team. They were operating smoothly and efficiently. It was now time for leadership and encouragement.

"Mr. Linwood, you and your team are doing an outstanding job. Please pass along my appreciation for their incredibly hard work."

Linwood, exhausted as he looked, beamed with pride. "I'll tell them, Mr. President."

"Thank you. Now please, sit down," he said with a warm smile. Linwood blushed and sat.

"Any word from the environmentalists—or an update on the potential Iran connection?"

"Nothing new, Mr. President," Samuels, the young Counterterrorism director, said.

James acknowledged the answer with a disappointed frown. So far, no one had leaked the possibility Iran had a hand in the attack, which was a minor miracle as far as he was concerned.

"Anything else?"

"No, sir," echoed from the men and women at the table.

The president stood, and with a resolute nod, turned and left the room.

A short walk up the stairs and through the building gave him a chance to think.

We need to stop playing defense. How can we change the momentum?

Nothing came to him.

Back in the Oval Office, he sat behind his desk, still pondering what he could do. He had a few seconds before his staff would need him for the next item on the day's agenda.

His team had an effective plan to solve the immediate problems. People were working to help the residents of Manhattan, fix blown-up facilities, and keep people safe. He had to think strategically, look at the big picture. What were they missing while focused on the essentials?

There were two quick knocks on the door to his left, and his chief of staff entered without waiting for an invitation.

"Mr. President?"

"Chad, what do you have for me?" Chad David, ten years younger than the president, was a fellow SEAL. He had been with James in the Teams, serving as an excellent junior officer. They had worked well together for years and he had been James' natural choice for the role of adviser and fixer. He was the iron fist in a velvet glove the role of chief of staff required.

"Checking in. How are you holding up?"

"Frustrated and helpless, but fine. The team is doing great. Organized and efficient. But it's going to be months for New York City. And if there's panic, looting, or a fire, they'll be in worse trouble."

Chad nodded at the bad news, but he sounded eager when he said, "I have an outside-the-box idea."

James sat forward. Leave it to a fellow SEAL to come up with an unorthodox plan. "Tell me."

"Solar." He placed the stapled two-page report he'd been holding on the desk. "It would be a massive undertaking, but we could install solar panels on or near seventy-two percent of the buildings in Manhattan. And we could do it much faster and cheaper than bringing in new power lines and repairing much of the destroyed infrastructure."

James sat back and crossed his arms. "Wait a second. You want me to go environmental? Be Jimmy Carter?"

Chad laughed. "That's an image, sir. You on TV wearing a cardigan sweater. No. You'd be JFK. Providing bold leadership. An unusual solution for a horrible situation."

He raised his eyebrows and shook his head. "If you remember, Chad, the environmentalism contributed to Jimmy Carter being only a one-term president. Nor did things end well for Kennedy."

The younger man smiled slightly at the dark humor. "Think of it, sir. You could transform the city along with our domestic solar energy production. In an instant, this country becomes a leader in clean energy."

"You're actually serious about this?"

"Absolutely. Solar panels and battery storage. The technologies are all there, as are much of the inventories we would need. And," he hesitated, then leaned forward excitedly, "New York is only the first step. You make it a national priority to have energy produced closer to the source of consumption. To not rely on our old outdated—and obviously difficult-to-protect—electrical grid network."

This could be what I am looking for.

James had to hand it to him. The idea was way outside the box, but it made sense. If the terrorists, whoever they were, did it once, they could do it again. Maybe not as easily in Chicago, St. Louis, or Los Angeles. But his stomach ached at the thousands of miles of unprotected high-voltage power lines and the rolling brown- and blackouts that could occur if their enemies started hitting them with car bombs.

But there was the political angle. "The other side would have a field day with this. They would say the environmental terrorists are getting their way. That this is what the terrorists want."

"We could control the narrative. It would be bold, decisive leadership. We mention nothing about the environment, greenhouse gas, or global warming. Instead, it's strictly a national security concern. You're protecting Manhattan from any similar attack. Since the vulnerability has been uncovered, you're taking action to protect America."

It made sense. Could he sell it?

Chad pressed harder. "You'd be solving the foreign energy problem, solving the infrastructure issue, and putting forth an economic stimulus and jobs creation package all at the same time. And best of all, sir, you do it without Congressional approval or negotiations."

"How so?"

"You declare a national emergency and tap into billions of dollars available to protect our country."

The president nodded. "And it would be a big F-U to the Middle East. Let them do their happy dance over there. We are out. We wouldn't need them, their oil, or their BS. And, if Iran is behind this, it's the first step at striking back."

"What about the natural gas and fossil-fuel states? The companies based there and the employees?"

"Incentives to those states to retrain their workers. Distributed solar and battery fabrication facilities would be essential for protection, so Texas, North Dakota, and a few others get a sizable piece of it."

"It's a huge risk. Politically, I mean."

"Yes, sir," Chad agreed. Then he shut up and waited for the president to decide.

James didn't have to think hard. He nodded. "One building, done quietly as a trial. Expedited. Make it happen. Let me know if you need me to make calls or sign authorizations. Let's get it done and test it out." Chad nodded and stood, obviously pleased his idea had been well received. "And nice work," the president added.

Time to take control of the situation and strike back.

60

THE BOAT

Axe came to instantly. One second resting, not quite asleep, the next wide awake. While most of him had relaxed, a part remained alert to any changes in his environment. Movement. Unexpected sounds. Every warrior he knew could rest like that. It was one issue they faced when returning to civilization. They spent so much time on high alert, their minds seemed to forget how to stand down.

What felt like a curse in civilian life, however, was a blessing on active duty. Or, in his case, whatever he called this situation he'd volunteered for.

The sun had set while he rested, and the moon rose behind him, already casting a weak glow. He lay still, extending his senses, searching for the noise or movement that had alerted him.

To his left, he faintly heard the steady throb of powerful engines. A boat. A large boat. Closer to shore than a cruise ship or cargo vessel would sail. But too big to be a fishing boat. Sensing nothing else, he raised his head to look around. Nothing.

Then he saw lights on the water. He focused the binoculars on a boat with what seemed like hundreds of lights shining brightly. He saw the bold lines of the mega yacht.

It must be almost as big as a destroyer.

He'd spent more days than he wanted to remember on the Navy's smaller ships and hated every moment. Cramped quarters, poor ventilation, horrible workout rooms. The crew had always welcomed the SEALS, but there was never enough space. For people like him who lived for the woods, ocean, or even the desert, being stuck on the ship had been hell.

He suspected the accommodations on the yacht would be far nicer. Several decks. A helipad on the bow, and one—no, wait—two hot tubs. He got a better view as the ship came closer and seemed to slow as it passed. It looked like it would stop near the base of Kellison's compound. Axe remembered seeing a small private beach there, but no dock. It would be pretty easy to get a large rubber boat up on the sand, though.

The boat slowed more and came to a stop. The sound of the huge anchor dropping carried across the water and through the woods. He looked closer and saw he'd been wrong. The boat had only one hot tub. What he thought was a second one was a swimming pool with a dozen lounge chairs surrounding it.

No need to worry about the lack of amenities in the house when you've got a boat like that.

Axe turned to survey the grounds, then secured the binocular in his pack. Next, he prepared his rifle, checked his plate carrier with ammo pouches, and rubbed more dirt over his face, hands, and wrists. The arrival of the boat would serve as a distraction. He would sneak his way in.

What about the dog?

He'd deal with it.

Adapt and overcome.

61

THE OTHER SHOE

Haley couldn't go on any longer. She allowed her eyes to close. Just for a second.

Images from the previous twenty-four hours assaulted her.

The vision of the man at the warehouse in the sights of the rifle. How he fell when she shot him.

The angry face of the terrorist on the turnpike as he struggled to raise his rifle. His head flying back as her shots hit him. The blood spurting from his neck.

She awoke with a start, lifting her head from the edge of the desk, a long trail of saliva from where she'd drooled in her sleep.

The small window revealed the darkness. In the distance, she should have been able to see the lights of Manhattan, but almost every building was dark.

She'd been at it all day, but had found nothing conclusive. The long day's effort yielded only a hunch, backed by the tiniest fragments of chatter.

If anyone had presented her with a report of the data, she would have laughed them out of the office. Told them to come back when they had more than garbage and guesses.

She'd pulled threads, turned over every stone. Still, despite nearly a complete lack of evidence, she was convinced a third attack was imminent. A big one. Bigger than before.

She had to stop them.

What and when? What are they waiting for? A follow on, a one-two punch? But why?

Could it be the perception of it all—two attacks, not one? The separation of time might make a psychologically bigger impact. Or perhaps the next attack could only be done at a particular time?

She was back to going around in circles. She stared out at the unreal darkness of the Manhattan skyline.

Maybe she could approach it from a different direction. Who would want to do a third hit? The so-called United Environmental Front? No such group existed; it was a complete waste of time.

Kelton Kellison? She couldn't see it. Happastology's launch had been postponed and the company's top talent wiped out. What else could be done to them?

She turned back to her computer but didn't have any new angles to explore.

Don't worry about the data. There's nothing there. They've kept it quiet. All I have now is my mind. Think it through.

What was the motivation for another attack?

Revenge? Greed? Mental illness? Ambition?

Nothing clicked. Looking at it from that angle didn't work, either.

She couldn't think straight. Nothing made sense.

Haley moved closer to the window to look at the dark city. She'd visited enough times to appreciate it for its vibrancy, loving how it brought people together—a giant melting pot of diversity. She'd flirted with the idea of moving there after college, to the extent that she looked at a few terribly small and outrageously expensive apartments before deciding against it. The biggest appeal to her had been the camaraderie. She felt like once she moved there, she'd be a member of the tribe. It didn't seem to matter where one came from or what one did. If you lived in New York, you were a New Yorker. It was like America had been back in the day. Get there, make it work, and you're one of us. We're all in it together.

She fought back tears. They were out of time. Her gut told her the next shoe to drop would come tonight. She felt it in her core, despite the complete lack of proof. It would happen between midnight and four in the morning, when even the magnificent city slept. It would be big enough to wake people up. To make them stumble to their TVs and sit up for hours, watching the horror.

Or make them leave the city. A mass exodus in the middle of the night. Complete darkness because of the lack of electricity. The bridges and tunnels officially closed because of the bombs... until hundreds of thousands of scared people attempted to get through.

Utter chaos.

What would make people flee the city?

A fire? No, too easily contained, though the lack of power made it more difficult.

A plane attack like so many years ago? No, too hard to do now, and limited to one area. It had to impact the entire island of Manhattan. Possibly even all five boroughs. What had that power?

Something people were afraid of deep in their bones.

And could be claimed by the supposed environmentalists.

And where subtle clues could be left blaming the Iranians.

The environment. Iran. Terror.

She had it.

Her eyes flew to the map of the tri-state area on her screen, following the Hudson river thirty-six miles north to the aging nuclear power plant on the bank of the river.

62

THE ONE PERCENT

For anyone else, it wouldn't be enough. But Haley saw the data. No, she felt it, like it moved inside her. Like she and it were one. She had figured it out.

Could she go to Gregory? He'd never buy it, not with what she had now.

Would he believe in her enough to throw the team behind her idea? To seek the rest of the pieces of the puzzle so they'd have the proof they needed to go to the president?

Would he do the bare minimum to cover his ass, but not enough to get the job done in time—or hang himself out to dry if she proved wrong?

Call Axe. Talk it through.

She dialed his number, and it answered immediately again. The line was open, but he had said nothing. Instead, she heard two slight scratches.

He can't talk.

"Can you listen?" she whispered.

One scratch. She realized he must be rubbing the tiny microphone on his ear bud.

"Can you talk?"

Two immediate scratches.

"You want me to call back?"

Nothing for a second, then one scratch, followed by a pause, and five light scratches.

"Five minutes?"

One scratch.

"Will call back in five." She hung up, worried. Was he in trouble? He wouldn't assault the compound without talking to her, would he?

She looked out the window again at the darkness. He may have tired of waiting while she worked… and napped. He would have used the cover of darkness to approach the compound.

I better not get him killed.

Five minutes later, on the dot, she called again.

"Hey, sorry, couldn't talk earlier," Axe said in a whisper. "But I'm good now. Hidden. Huge grounds here. Lovely house. Plus, he has a yacht."

"There's going to be another attack, later tonight. I believe it will be at a nuclear power plant in Westchester county, thirty-six miles north of Manhattan."

"I'm a long way from there."

"You're all I have. Can you get to the chopper?"

"Yes, but what am I going to do alone?"

He's right.

"I hadn't thought it through."

"A nuclear power plant? Why?"

"I haven't figured that part out yet."

"It's an escalation, even for these assholes. How sure are you?"

She couldn't tell him.

"Haley?" he whispered.

"It's a guess," she admitted. "But it's the only logical choice."

"Give me a percentage."

"Ninety-five percent there's another attack coming. Tonight."

"You're holding back. How sure are you it will be the nuclear power plant?"

"Logically? 75%."

"What kind of intel do you have to back this up?"

"Next to nothing, okay?" She sounded too defensive, even to herself. "Maybe… one percent certain from the data."

"One percent!"

"Or a little less."

Silence from Axe. "Less than one percent? Did you take it to your boss?"

"I can't. He doesn't believe me when I have more than I do now."

"Haley, I don't know. Is there anything? I appreciate you telling me the truth, but perhaps you should exaggerate a little to get your boss on board?"

"No. There's nothing to exaggerate. It's hard to explain, but my mind takes in all the data and then I… I sort of… feel it."

Axe didn't reply right away. She waited, thinking it through one more time, trying to figure out a solution.

Finally, Axe spoke. "Always trust your instincts. I didn't do that on one of my last ops, and my team lead nearly died. We walked right into an ambush. I knew it, the guys knew it, but the intel said this bomber guy was there, so—"

"Wait. You were on the op to capture The Boomer?"

"How do you know about it? Hold on." His voice hardened in anger. "You were behind that intel?"

"I told them they were wrong! I told them it would be an ambush. They didn't listen and sent you anyway."

He sighed with relief. "I am so glad to hear you say that. For a second I thought…"

"No. I was right then, I'm right now. So far, I've been right every time. I'm young, so I admit maybe I've just gotten lucky. But I'm not just another analyst. I know it sounds arrogant, but I believe it's true."

"I'll take luck any day. Whatever works."

"From a tactical standpoint, I was wrong earlier. I sent you to Montauk. Now there's no time to stop the attack on the plant."

"I'm not giving up yet. Let's brainstorm. How about we call the plant? Phone in a bomb threat, get them to raise their alert level?"

"It wouldn't work. The alert level isn't the problem. I'm sure they're on high alert already with all that's happened today. The problems are the defenses and manpower. We've seen how well funded the attacks have been. Whatever they have planned won't be a lone guy with a gun. If I'm right, and I admit it's thin, it's going to be huge. Plus, I believe it will be creative, or unusual. Something we don't have a good defense against. It'll overwhelm their normal defenses, even on high alert. So I guess it doesn't matter you're out of position."

Axe contemplated the scenario of terrorists taking over a nuclear power plant less than forty miles from Manhattan, with over twenty million people in the area.

"What if you're wrong?"

She'd considered it. "Then I'll take the fall. But what if I'm right? Axe, we have to do something."

There was a long pause from Axe and she worried she'd lost his faith. "Are you still there?"

"Yes. Just thinking things through. I believe you."

She hadn't realized she had held her breath until she let it out in a sudden sigh of relief.

Axe continued. "I'll make a call."

"Will it be enough?"

"It'll have to be."

63

THE BACK CHANNEL

The admiral answered on the first ring. "Go ahead." Right to the point.

"I have a tip." Axe lay in a slight dip in the ground, fifty feet outside the high-security black fencing designed to be attractive and decorative instead of intimidating. He hated talking so near the roving patrols—and dog—but it would be riskier to sneak away, then come back. So he lay with his face pressed into the dirt, his pack over his head, and spoke as quietly as he could and still be heard.

"Go on."

"The nuclear plant north of Manhattan. Midnight to four AM is the intelligence." The time for code words and subterfuge had passed. Let the NSA listen. Maybe they'd call in the cavalry and help out.

"How do you know this?"

"Our friend." He didn't say her name. If people were listening, it might protect her if it turned out she was wrong.

"Why doesn't our friend take it up the chain of command?"

"Lack of support."

"This is too big to not believe. He'd have to act on it to at least cover his own ass."

"Unless he's the mole. But the big problem is…" He hesitated. He didn't want to spell it out.

"What?"

"I'm going to put it all on the line here, sir. Our friend is remarkable and, I'm sure, a top-notch analyst. But they do things their own way. Maybe it's a type of synesthesia, or they're so brilliant they see what others can't. Either way, they know it's going to happen, but they don't have any proof. They explained it to me and I think it's thin, too. But I have faith, sir. They've been right all along, and no one's listened. They're too young, smart, and don't have the political skills to finesse their way. And finally, as you said when we first met: what if? What if they're right and we do nothing?"

"What the hell do you expect me to do about it? I can't take this to anyone either. Just my friend," the admiral mused out loud, meaning the president. "But what could he or I do?"

"Back channel it. Like you did with me yesterday and with the chopper pilot this morning. You must know someone on the Department of Energy's Special Response Teams. Tell them. Unofficially. Have them order a surprise security inspection. A sweep, or a drill."

"You're asking an awful lot for someone with no credible proof. And who, I might remind you, is supposed to be handling this on his own."

"I'm at the source, working on a way to get it called off. I can't be in two places at once."

Axe held his tongue while the admiral thought. He heard footsteps and figured he would be pacing, weighing the odds of calling in this big of a favor, whether an ask of this magnitude should even be brought through back channels. Would he take it to the president? And if he tried, who else would find out about it in the process? Would a warning be sent out to the terrorists and their time line moved up?

I hate this spy bullshit. Give me clear orders and a target any day.

The admiral spoke, his voice firm. "Try to stop it in case my end doesn't work out. I'm going way out on a limb and not sure I can pull it off, but I'll do what I can."

"From you, sir, that's very reassuring. Look for car bombs like earlier today. And something else. Our friend isn't sure what, but it's more than bombs and guns. Something they haven't seen yet. Something... creative. Their term."

"God help us all."

64

THE INVISIBLE MAN

The key points of weakness for the compound were the beach, the cliffs, and the main entrance. All three would be better watched and defended.

The main entrance had a guard shack, and what looked like cleverly concealed fortified positions inside the gate. The beach would most likely have a permanent post, protected from the elements. It would be difficult to adequately patrol the cliffs and woods surrounding the property—hence Axe's ability to get close to the grounds. But with virtually unlimited funds, every surveillance technology available would monitor the area.

Axe had noticed the disguised security cameras as he left the woods owned by the state. He'd already been on his stomach, moving painstakingly slowly, and had gotten lucky when he stopped to survey every tree he could see. A few tiny, unnatural-looking lumps caught his eyes, even in the dark, right where he would have placed them had he been in charge.

He had threaded a path through a narrow slot caused by recent erosion that he hoped would allow him to avoid any infrared or night vision technology. Only after fifteen minutes, when no one came searching for him, did he breathe a sigh of relief.

Either he had avoided the cameras or human nature let them down. Technology only went so far, and sitting in a comfortable chair, staring at a view that never changed for months on end gave way to complacency, even in the most well-trained men.

I'd have monthly test infiltration drills and surprise inspections to keep people sharp. Guess it's not done here. Lucky someone's not as thorough as I am.

He spent another hour crawling forward. A turtle would have passed him. He'd move a few inches at most, in super slow motion, then freeze for thirty to ninety seconds. Never the same amount of time twice, and every few minutes he'd stop and lay still for a while.

Overkill, but better slow than dead.

There wasn't much of a plan. He would get close to the building, possibly even inside, depending on how tight the inner ring of security seemed. Perhaps he could listen in on a conversation, or find an isolated goon to have a chat with.

He preferred having a detailed plan of attack, but in the absence of one, he could wing it with the best of them. Step one would be getting in. After that, the path would become clear, he was sure.

He had found a narrow game trail leading in the general direction of the back of the house. In the increasing moonlight, he'd followed it under a series of bushes into what must have been a spectacular flower, tree, and shrub garden in the daylight. Rabbits used the path, he guessed, or groundhogs. He also caught the lingering smell of a skunk that had passed through recently.

A flagstone walkway off to his right side gave him pause. Though he crept under various bushes and around trees, hidden from above, he was only three feet from the pathway.

All the more reason to take it slow. But it's about time to move again.

Axe moved forward but froze. He hadn't seen anything, but some instinctive part of him knew to stop.

Two seconds later he heard the tiniest sound, perhaps a scuff of a shoe sole on the flagstone. Someone was nearby.

In sniper training, Axe had been near the top of his class in shooting, but what made him stand out from the rest of the equally motivated and skilled classmates had been his ability to simply disappear. For a while, they'd nicknamed him the Invisible Man. Most of the other students seemed to radiate an energy to varying degrees. An unconscious aura allowed their instructors, who had trained class after class and knew the practice ranges like the backs of their hands, to stop and point at them, despite being perfectly hidden to the eye.

Once Axe found a position, however, he could fade into the earth, the trees, or brush. He vanished. One fabled instructor had believed he'd spotted Axe. When he stalked the twenty-five yards to where he was convinced Axe lay in the brown, knee-high grass, he couldn't find a trace. He stomped around the immediate area for twenty minutes, cursing up a storm and drawing the attention of the other instructors, plus every student as, one by one, they were spotted and called out.

Trying without success to hide his frustration and his respect for Axe's ability, he reluctantly admitted defeat. Silently, Axe stood, four feet behind the man, much to the delight of Axe's watching classmates. The instructor had scowled in confusion at the laughter directed his way, then literally jumped in surprise when Axe gently tapped him on the shoulder.

They'd all had to run an extra five miles before dinner as punishment for laughing, but it had been worth it.

The instructor had found Axe and several of his buddies in a bar after graduation, shaken Axe's hand, and bought him beer all night long.

Axe used the same trick now with the unknown tango nearby. He relaxed, stilled his mind, and vanished.

65

THE COMPETITION

The tango had training and his own excellent instincts. He stood silently, only a few feet from Axe.

Impressive. He can sense me. Wonder if it's anyone I know.

The upper level of the warrior community is tight knit. Any fighter reaching a certain level becomes known, whether they serve their time in Delta, Recon, the SEALS, or any of the other highly trained units. While warriors from different branches might not have met in person, their names and reputations will proceed them.

Axe heard the man walk away, up the path towards the house, then stop for another full minute, listening. Then he sensed the man move silently away from the house, back towards where Axe lay motionless in his invisibility mode. The man stopped closer to where Axe lay than he'd stood before, then disappeared himself. Axe knew where he stood, but couldn't detect him.

Definitely a master sniper.

As in most sniper battles, it became a test of patience and wills. The man on the path had the advantage of being away from the bugs. Axe lay so still they decided it would be safe to crawl over him and into his clothes, seeking warmth as the spring night cooled. While he disliked it, he never moved.

Axe had two advantages. He had no set time frame. And he could rest horizontally. While it wasn't relaxing, laying motionless to avoid detection took less effort than standing still to remain hidden.

Fifteen minutes later, Axe finally felt the man. Then a small sound. Two brief noises.

He's responding to a check-in call. The others I saw earlier all had ear pieces and radios on their chest rigs. I bet he just clicked twice, indicating all is well.

Did SOP call for verbal responses on this unit? Would the click check show something amiss and draw attention? Or was a click check SOP, in order to maintain silence and preserve the stealth of each patrol?

The tango may have given up the silent hunt, but he apparently still had his concerns. He stepped once on the path, not attempting stealth, then his shoe landed on the manicured mulch of the area just off the flagstone.

He doesn't know I'm here, but he's suspicious... and coming to investigate.

He took his time, walking completely around the bush hiding Axe, peering down at the ground but not using a flashlight.

Doesn't want to ruin his night vision if there's nothing here. He's mostly given up, but it bothers him.

Axe stared at the heels of the man's performance combat boots, ten inches in front of his face. The man's legs pushed against the bush branches. If he moved back any more, he'd step on Axe's head.

This guy's good.

He didn't want to kill an American, especially one who might have medals and commendations to go along with his incredible skill. Then he remembered the brief from Haley: "All dishonorably discharged, mostly for excessive force."

In times of conflict or war, force was expected and encouraged. To be dishonorably discharged for excessive force meant this guy—all the guys here—would be bad men. Axe had to think of them as the enemy.

The man shut down, going silent again, apparently not quite ready to give up. Would he be able to feel Axe now that he stood almost on top of him?

As a minute stretched into two, Axe began to worry. While he didn't have a timeline, it wouldn't do Haley or the nuclear power plant any good for him to lie in a garden all night. He had the skill to do it, but not the will.

He's too much of a threat. I have to take him out. When—if—he moves.

Seconds later, Axe sensed it. The man had given up. One moment after that, he let out a quiet sigh and took a step forward.

Axe sprung up, drawing his knife as he rose, the branches of the bush scraping his pack and clothes noisily. To his credit, the man reacted instantly, turning towards the sudden threat. But like the sniper-school instructor, Axe's nearness after so much time, after he'd given up on the hunt, must have startled him. Instead of calling out, reaching for his slung weapon, or even putting up his hands in defense, he turned to see what had remained hidden from him.

His body moved as Axe expected. Axe plunged his knife into the man's throat, silencing him instantly except for the gargling of blood from the wound and his mouth. The man's face showed fear, surprise, and shock for only moments while he clawed at the knife buried in him. Then the shine went out of the eyes and he was dead.

Axe caught him in his arm and lowered him to the ground, pulling the knife from the throat and wiping it on the man's pant leg.

Rest easy, brother.

66

THE SRT

The men and women of the Department of Energy's Special Response Teams—SRT—are a serious, dedicated group. They defend America's nuclear sites, along with being tasked to recover nuclear material, neutralize threats, and more. If it's dangerous and involves keeping America's stockpile of nuclear material safe, they're involved.

The seven teams are composed of intelligent, highly trained contractors, recruited from Delta, SEALS, top police forces, and other elite units.

And while some regular military units might bitch and moan about an unexpected call up, especially for a surprise drill, not one of this group of twenty men and four women did. They lived for their jobs. And after the events of the day, they understood the importance of drills. They would gladly drop everything to go to the nuclear plant and augment the security officers who protect the facility on a normal day.

Because the day had been anything but normal.

And though none mentioned it, they all wondered about the timing of what many, in their minds, dubbed "the so-called drill." They understood better than anyone the sensitivity of their missions. A drill would be a simple way to get them involved in a situation without panicking people.

No matter how careful, word might get out. Hence, a normal, everyday training "drill."

Their suspicions were further confirmed when they were told to mount up not in their lightly armored Peacekeeper vehicles, but to pair up and drive their own cars and trucks to the site.

Loaded with their personal kits, including M4s, pistols, shotguns, sniper rifles, machine guns, and grenade launchers, they formed up in the parking lot of their HQ.

It raised more eyebrows when crates of Stinger surface-to-air missiles were loaded into the two pickup trucks.

Heads were counted as badges were issued. They were instructed to arrive at the plant—which they knew well from previous training exercises—ten to twenty minutes prior to the 11 PM shift change. To not convoy, but make their own way. To drive naturally: just reporting for another night at the plant.

They didn't have to ask. This would be no drill.

67

THE NAPS

The serial killers took turns napping throughout the afternoon, using car window shade covers to hide the fact they were sleeping in parking lots of various establishments. One would nap with the other on watch in the driver's seat. After a time, they would switch. If approached, they could have driven away or mentioned how their sleeping friend wasn't coping well with the stress from the attacks of the morning.

When each pair had slept, they exited and casually switched with another team, who drove to a different area of the parking lot and repeated the process.

They all needed to be well rested for what they had started calling, between themselves, "The evening's festivities."

None of them found it odd they slept easily in cars filled with hundreds of pounds of high explosives. They didn't even think of why they could nap when they were due to murder hundreds of thousands of people—or perhaps millions in less that twelve hours.

They had merely tilted their seats back, closed their eyes, and slept, most with happy little smiles on their faces.

68

THE REPORT

Axe stashed his backpack ten yards away under a bush, hoping he'd be able to retrieve it at the end of the mission. Assuming he lived through it. Then he stood on the flagstone walkway, quiet and still.

He had swapped his M4 for the guard's, casually slung as the man had worn it. He'd also commandeered the man's ammo rig, radio, and finally his pistol and holster, which he strapped on to his upper thigh as the guard had. As backup, his own 9mm rested in the inside-the-pants holster where he'd been carrying it lately. In the dark, he looked enough like the dead guy to pass as him. Similar build, same moves, same gear.

Any minute now.

"One, report," the bored man's voice came through the bud lodged in Axe's ear and attached via a curly cord to the radio at his chest. Axe glanced at his watch.

Every quarter hour.

"No contacts."

"Two, report."

"All quiet."

"Three, report."

"Ares just took a dump on the lawn and I don't have a bag. Remind me to pick it up on the next pass."

"Three, get your shit together. Literally."

"Let it go. I'll pick it up."

"If you don't, you're going on report."

"Yeah, yeah. Stop your bitching. He goes when he goes."

"Four, report."

Silence.

"Four, you asshole, stop your games. You find something or not? Check in."

Axe double clicked the transmit button as he'd heard the guard —"Four," apparently—do fifteen minutes ago. The same as he'd done with Haley earlier.

"Fine, be that way, asshole. Shape up too, or you'll go on report with Three. You know what that means."

"No nookie for us," Three chimed in, chuckling.

"Shut it. Heads up out there. The chief is going to the yacht soon. Don't let me—or especially him—catch you out of position or screwing around."

Axe felt a flood of relief as all three other units responded with a double click of their comms. He joined in at his prescribed turn.

He walked forward at a medium pace, towards the rear of the house, just another warrior guarding his sector. He was home free. Unless he ran into one of the other three units.

69

THE PREPARATION

"As you may have guessed, this isn't a drill." Robinson, the SRT commander, bellowed, his deep voice booming in the large repair facility where they gathered.

"We have been put on alert to augment the capable defenses the facility already has. We will be a final inner perimeter. The snipers will serve in their usual long-range, reach-out-and-touch-someone manner."

He paused, eying his team. "In addition, they have tasked us with being on the lookout for, and I quote, 'something creative.'"

The assembled defenders looked at each other with raised eyebrows and skeptical looks.

The commander continued. "I've also been told, straight up, the intel is thin on this one, which is why tonight is technically a readiness drill. But you know the events of the day. We're not taking chances, even though this facility will be decommissioned in a year or two. There are still a lot of things we don't want broken or taken here."

He looked at them again, meeting their eyes. "You know your jobs. Keep your heads on straight. The intel, such as it is, indicated midnight to four AM, but you never know. Stay alert. You're weapons free.

Anything that seems like a threat, we take care of. Try to let the main defense force engage first; it's their house. But if you see something they don't, announce it and engage. Cover your sectors. Stay sharp. Break up into your assigned groups and get yourselves situated. No one gets to this facility tonight."

They hoisted their weapons, extra ammunition, and dispersed.

Eight three-person teams took up preassigned, elevated positions. The machine gunners set up first, in communication with the teams on either side to ensure overlapping fields of fire where possible. Since they didn't need to cover the entire perimeter, they had extra teams assigned to the most likely approaches: the river and the roads. It left the north and south flanks with only one team each, with no overlapping fields of fire. They would most likely be out of any fight that came, which annoyed them.

The snipers lay prone near the machine gunners, on elevated platforms previously constructed where good natural positions weren't available. Their spotters, also excellent marksmen, acted as assault leaders and managed the comms.

Robinson strolled the grounds, giving his people time to set up. All seemed fine, though he felt the sense of warning he had while on active duty as a member of Delta. Back before he aged out of running and gunning.

Satisfied he had given the teams the time they needed, he stopped at the rear of the building nearest the river. Behind him loomed the three reactor buildings, though only one still produced electricity. The others had been decommissioned already.

Nearby, in the middle of the complex, lay another building which housed the spent fuel pool. As its name indicated, the pools had storage racks to hold fuel rods from the reactors. The deep water, constantly cooled and circulated, contained the incredible heat and radiation from the fuel rods which had been used in the nuclear reactors.

The entire place had been built well. The permanent security force was top notch. At most, he and his people would be a reassuring presence tonight while giving his team some good training on the day of the terrorists attacks forty miles south. Give all of them a reminder of why they worked so hard.

But his gut didn't agree. His gut told him there would be action tonight.

He called for check in. "River One?"

"In place, ready."

"River Two?"

"In place, ready."

This continued through River Three, Front One, Two, and Three, and Flank One and Two. The teams were experienced pros. Eyes were on binoculars, guns were loaded.

If the assholes want this facility, they have to go through us first.

70

THE BREACH

Axe didn't like imitating the dead guard.

In all his years, prior to the van at the warehouse the night before, Axe had never bluffed his way to a target. Other agencies excelled at it, but normally the SEALs stalked to a target, moving silently through the night. At times they'd fast rope onto a roof, parachute in, swim, or insert via boat.

He hated the secret spy shit.

Still, he'd do whatever it took to achieve the mission.

I'm on guard duty. All I have to do is act like it.

He walked up the winding flagstone pathway towards the back of the house and soon came to the secure, but classy looking, black fence. Axe kept his head down, happy his shorter hair somewhat matched the dead guard's, certain there would be a camera on the gate he approached. He took the key card attached by a clip to his waist, where the man he had killed had worn it. He pulled, and the retractable cord extended, allowing him to place it against the silver card reader next to the gate handle.

The lock clicked. He released the card to snap back to his waist, and he smoothly opened the gate and stepped into the inner perimeter. He caught the self-closing gate before it clanged shut, and thought about the next steps.

He first had to decide how far to take the bluff. Could he walk to the front door and enter the house? Find Kellison and interrogate him without being seen or caught?

The similarity to the dead guard might pass in this less-lit area at the edge of the enormous lawn, but in the brightness near the house, no one seeing him in person would be fooled. On camera, with his head down, he had a chance, if he got lucky. But not in the light. Not if the group was as tight as he suspected.

He looked at the back of the house. Two double garage doors, closed. He'd seen a side door around the corner to the right and had scoped out the front and far side of the house from the woods. The guards would be headquartered in the basement or a section of the garage. With the principal in residence, they wouldn't be encouraged to use the front door or relax on the porch.

They'd said the chief would be headed for the yacht soon. In his experience, "soon" from a principal meant "whenever I'm damn well ready." It could be from thirty seconds to hours later, depending on how truly busy they were and how much they liked to dominate their protection detail. Some principals got off on keeping everyone on their toes, standing by for hours while they dawdled. Would Kellison be a busy executive, an arrogant jerk, or neither?

Axe could make his way straight to the beach and handle any security there. Then he could set up an ambush. Kellison would likely have one or more guards escort him the several hundred yards down the paved pathway to the beach. Axe hadn't seen a dock earlier from the woods, but the angle had been bad, so there might be one.

The more he thought about it, the better it sounded. He'd get ahead of them, away from the house and any quick backup. The only problem might come if Number Four, the role he played now in place of the dead guard, had escort duty as well as patrol duty, but it didn't seem likely. More guards would be assigned to the interior of the house, and at least two should be body men, stationed near the principal. In the hallway outside an office or bedroom, at least. They would be part of the escort.

People worth fourteen billion dollars took their security seriously, even at their secluded, well-defended country homes.

Axe froze when he first sensed, then heard, and finally saw the guard with the dog—Ares, he remembered—approaching from the semi-darkness to his right, along the fence where it curved further away from the house.

Turn towards the house. Turn towards the house.

Then he shut down, going further within himself. With any luck, the man would angle towards the house. If he didn't stay close to the fence, he might walk within feet of Axe and not see him because of the area being half in darkness. His eyes would have a harder time picking Axe out, especially in sniper stealth mode.

But what about the dog?

The dog would be the problem.

They moved closer, neither noticing Axe standing in shadow with his back to the closed gate.

Fifty feet. Twenty-five.

They weren't hugging the fence. They'd pass right in front of him, six feet away, if they kept on their current trajectory.

Twenty.

Fifteen.

Ares turned his head in Axe's general direction, possibly catching his scent.

Ten feet.

Ares let out a quiet growl.

The guard's pace slowed.

"What is it, boy?" he whispered, stopping.

Ares turned full towards Axe and growled, louder. He had Axe's scent.

Axe watched out of his peripheral vision, but didn't look directly at Ares. Dogs like that don't take kindly to anyone staring them down.

The guard looked in Axe's direction, searching.

"You better not have found another skunk, Ares," he chided the dog, but his voice revealed his concern.

Then the man jolted. "Damn it!" He let out a frustrated sigh tinged with embarrassment. "How many times have I told you not to do that? You freak out the dog."

Axe raised his arm in a small wave at the man and relaxed his posture.

"Ares, calm down." The dog stopped growling but didn't relax. He knew what his handler didn't: Axe wasn't a friend. He was a threat.

Shaking his head, the man approached, holding Ares on a tight lead. The dog, a German Shepard, had his hackles up. His front lips curled back, baring his teeth without the accompanying growl.

Four feet.

"You're an asshole, you know that?"

They were the last words he said.

Axe stepped towards him casually, then quickly reached up. His hands took hold of the startled man's head and twisted sharply, breaking his neck with a solid cracking noise. He died instantly.

"Ares, calm down" Axe said in his command voice, imitating the handler. The dog looked at him, not liking the order, clearly torn.

Holding the second dead guard under his arms to keep him upright, he tried the tone and German phrase used with the dogs during missions. "Ares! *Daun*!"

The dog sat, then slowly lay down, his eyes locked on Axe and teeth still bared.

Axe hated the idea of lowering the man to the ground, uncertain what the dog would do. He didn't want his face to be anywhere near the dog's huge white teeth that seemed to glow in the low light near the fence. But he couldn't hold the man up forever. He shifted his grip, moving so the body would block the dog should he decide to attack, then gently lowered the man to the grass.

Ares looked from the dead man to Axe and growled. Then he rose from his crouch.

"Ares. *Nein*." Axe changed his tone slightly. Though he still spoke commandingly, he added a soft tone, attempting to communicate that he understood how confusing the situation seemed. But Axe was in charge.

The dog lowered to the ground again, eyes still on Axe, plainly unsure about his duty.

With slow deliberation, Axe unclipped the man's radio from his belt and removed his earpiece, putting it into his right ear and clipping the radio onto his own belt. Then he reached into the man's pocket, hoping for the best. Military training emphasizes uniformity. Carry your med kit in this pocket. Your tourniquet here. And for the K-9 handlers Axe worked with, the dog treats were carried in the front left pocket.

Right where they're supposed to be. Now for the true test.

He already understood the dog and handler hadn't served overseas together. Axe's attempt to take command wouldn't have worked for a moment in that type of relationship. He guessed the dog had served, retired, then been put back into service in the civilian world. Either way, the dead man wasn't Ares' first and only handler. There might even be other handlers who worked with him on the dead guy's days off. A dog like this should have a single handler who cared for it, fed it, and rewarded it. No other member of the guard unit would be allowed to give him affection. But they had broken the rules, leading to Ares' confusion and stress, which Axe hated. But he had to take advantage. Millions of lives were at stake.

Axe picked up the leash, still clenched in the guard's hand, and stood tall.

"Ares. *Braver hund.* Eat."

He held his hand out, holding the treat for the dog.

Ares hesitated, looking at Axe, then at treat. Then he opened his mouth and delicately took the snack from Axe's hand before chomping happily.

Axe looked down at the body of the man. He would prefer to drag it closer to the darkness at the base of the fence, but he didn't think Ares would tolerate it.

Sorry, brother. It was me, you, or you and the dog. And I like dogs.

He drew the lead tight and gave one of the other commands he remembered—heel. "Ares, *fuss*." The dog stood, ready to go. They walked forward, parallel to the fence, in the direction of the beach.

This works. I'll give him some reassurance that he just switched handlers. And a guard dog might come in handy for the ambush.

He'd seen men quake, cry, and pee their pants while begging for the snarling dog to not be sicced on them. Axe doubted he had enough bonding with Ares to order him to attack. But if he remembered the proper command, he might scare Kellison into coughing up the details of the plans for the power plant.

Axe thought back to his time on the Teams and the verbal commands the handlers used. Unfortunately, he'd been in different areas when the dogs were let off leash. He'd have to wing it and hope for the best.

They'd only made it fifty feet towards the beach when one of the garage doors opened at the house behind him. He veered closer to the darker area near the fence, at the edge of the effective range of the house lights.

"The man's on the move. Front door, one mike," came the voice over the radio, no longer sounding bored.

Axe waited, hearing guards one and two respond with clicks on their microphones, doing the same with first guard number three's radio, then switching to guard number four's.

A luxury golf cart, complete with large, off-road style tires and two extra bench seats, zoomed out of the garage. It sped to the front of the house, its bright lights briefly catching Axe and Ares as they stood watching along the fence. It completed a tight circle and came to a smooth stop at the foot of the front steps, facing the correct direction to start down the cart path to the beach. Seconds later, a tall, wiry man with perfectly styled, wavy black hair, dressed in a white polo shirt and jeans, pushed open the house's front door and stomped down the stairs. He slid onto the seat directly behind the cart's driver while two burly men, obviously his personal security guards, hustled through the door and down the stairs after him.

They first had gotten onto the third row bench seat, with the other right on his heels, when Axe heard the man bark, "Go, go!"

The driver immediately hit the gas, leaving the second body guard to grab the cart's canopy support bar and clumsily drag himself on board as the cart sprang away.

Once again Axe and Ares were lit by the headlights as the cart turned onto the path and sped down the hill towards the beach. It took a curve to the right and moved out of sight.

"Three, why the hell are you so far out of position? And four, you'd better not be on another one of your wild goose chases. I swear, people, you are slipping. Three, you're on no cat house visits for two weeks."

While watching the golf cart and Kellison disappear from view, out of the corner of his eye Axe caught another man emerge from the house. Turning, he saw a short, burly man standing stiff and straight on the porch, his head turned toward the microphone at his shoulder.

Axe nodded and let himself slump at the rebuke.

"Four, report. Where the—"

The boss had turned his head to the left to survey the grounds near the garden gate, but his head snapped back towards Axe. They stared at each other across the expanse of lawn.

Busted. I'm heavier than Three by fifty pounds. Taller, too. I could pass as Four, but not with the dog.

He reached up and held the microphone button down on Three's radio, effectively preventing the man in charge from alerting anyone of the situation. He leaned down to Ares to whisper fiercely in his ear.

"Ares, attack!"

The dog looked at Axe, his head tilted in confusion.

Nope. Wrong word. What was "attack" in German?

"Ares, come on!"

He didn't know if it would work, but with Kellison on his way to the yacht, he had no reason to hang around a house filled with the enemy. But he would take the dog with him.

He started running for the beach, holding the mic down with one hand and the leash with the other. Ares joined him, keeping pace.

The path had small solar-powered lights every few feet, so Axe angled away from it, building up speed as the man on the porch started yelling.

"Breach! Breach!" He kept yelling, but it sounded like he'd stepped back inside the house.

Then the grounds lit up like the middle of a football stadium during a night game, destroying what little night vision Axe had developed. It seemed like the sun had risen instantly. He kept running, Ares at his side.

Just have to get to the bluff, then angle to the path, then the beach, then the dock, then the water. No problem.

The officer's voice boomed out, louder than before.

"Ares. *Fass!*"

To Axe, it sounded like 'fast,' without the last letter.

His brain clicked. *That's the word to attack.*

He had a second when Ares remained confused, maybe torn between running with the man he assumed was his new handler and the other voice he recognized as the alpha of the pack.

The bluff lay ahead, seconds away.

"Ares, no."

He shouldn't have spoken. Instead of the commanding tone he'd meant, it sounded like a request. Worse, a request laced with fear. Ares dropped a pace back, then two, no longer interested in running next to Axe.

"Ares, *fass!*" the man yelled again.

Axe didn't dare look back. The dog was close.

Then sharp teeth clamped onto his calf.

Axe fell to the ground in agony.

"Ares, leave it!"

The command seemed to make the dog angrier, and he started shaking his head, yanking Axe's leg back and forth.

Axe screamed. The white hot pain radiated through him. Without thinking, he used his left heel to kick at the dog.

He must have hit him in the perfect spot because Ares let go with a snarl, then lunged back at Axe. He ignored Axe's bloody leg, though, and went straight for Axe's crotch.

Once again, Axe's reflexes and years of training paid off. He caught the dog's head in his hands and pushed with all his strength. Ares only went backwards a foot or so, but it was enough. Axe rolled sideways once, then again, feeling Ares closing in.

Then he tumbled over the edge of the bluff, leaving the dog snapping at the air where he'd been an instant before.

71

THE FALL

The bluff's angle was steep enough for Axe to fly often on the way down, but not steep enough to keep him from hitting the mixture of clay and stone that made up the bluff. Each fall lasted just long enough for him to build up momentum, which made the contact with the earth more jarring and painful.

The first impact knocked the breath out of him. Then he fell a few more feet and his head hit a rock, stunning him.

After that, he fell, bounced, and tumbled with little awareness or pain.

He landed with a heavy thud at the bottom of the hundred-foot cliff and lay still, face down in the sand. He weakly tilted his head enough to breathe, sucking in grains of sand with every breath.

He forced himself awake. He had a mission, though for several seconds he couldn't remember what he had to do.

The crashing waves reminded him.

A boat. I have to get to a boat.

Navy SEALs differ from other special forces in their extensive water training. At BUD/S, the instructors drilled into their heads: the water is your friend. Your ally. It can be used to approach, to hide, to escape. For most people, especially the enemy, the water is not understood and consequently feared. To SEALs, it's home.

Without being fully aware of his surroundings or his mission, he crawled towards the sound of the water.

72

THE BEACH

Axe pulled his head together as he crawled.

The boat. The nuclear power plant. Kelton Kellison.

Halfway to the water, he got to his feet. He swayed but stayed upright.

Possible concussion. And a few cracked ribs.

He gingerly touched his lower left chest and pain thundered through him.

Maybe not just cracked. Broken.

The pain matched the throbbing in his right calf. He looked at it in the moonlight. There seemed to be a lot of blood on his pant leg.

No matter. He put the pain in a box to deal with later. If it became too intense, he'd welcome the agony and use it as motivation.

He continued forward, moving faster on his feet than he'd been able to crawl.

He remembered his mission, but couldn't recall other important details.

It came back to him in a rush, and he quickened his pace. Of course. The enemy. The bluff. The dog.

Dogs like that don't give up. Without orders to the contrary, they'll continue the attack. They're like SEALs: they find a way.

He looked to the right. The light of the moon and the object's dark body on the light-colored sand made it easy to see. Ares ran full tilt straight at him, like a missile locked on to its target.

Axe ran. Or tried to. His right leg didn't want to move correctly, and the soft, deep sand pulled at him.

Muscle memory kicked in from the hundreds of miles he'd run in the sand. On the beaches of Coronado during training, and in countless desert countries for the last fifteen years. He could do this.

If he hurried, he would make it to the surf before Ares made it to him. And even injured, he could out swim the dog. He was sure of it.

He pushed his legs hard. A distant, rational part of him realized what he considered a fast run amounted to no more than a slow walk, but he ignored it. Nothing mattered but getting to the safety of the water, no matter how fast—or slow—he moved.

Almost there.

He felt the fire of the bullet before he heard the shot. His right side, low, below the bullet-proof plate.

He kept running.

Then he fell, the impact of the second bullet hitting the center of his back, caught by the ceramic plate, pushing him forward. He landed in wet sand.

From the bluff? That's an excellent shot.

The front edge of a tiny wave hit his face. He had arrived at the water's edge.

He crawled forward. The next wave covered his head, but he wasn't far enough for the water to cover his body.

He pulled at the wet sand with his hands, arms, and elbows while pushing with his feet.

Another bullet slammed into his back and ricocheted. He felt a slash of pain across the back of his head.

The next wave of icy water covered him from head to toe, though as the water receded he remained on the sand instead of escaping to the shallows.

One more push. The next wave will carry you out.

He howled in pain as Ares sank his teeth into his right ankle. A wave filled his mouth, nose, and throat with salt water.

73

THE SURF

In training, Axe had gotten smacked in the face by countless waves and swallowed gallons of water.

For Ares, it was an unfamiliar experience.

He let go of Axe's ankle and snorted, shaking his head to clear his mouth and nose.

The wave's force dragged Axe along with it as it retreated off the beach.

In water so shallow his knees hit sand and rocks, Axe swam, his arms moving in a breast stroke and his legs kicking, partly in the water, partly off the bottom.

He heard another shot. A miss.

He ducked under the next wave, swimming harder, the heavy bulletproof plate and gear making it easy. When he surfaced, Ares barked madly behind him, unwilling to follow him into the water.

More shots whipped by as he swam, diving under water as much as his injured body allowed, but none hit him.

As he got into deeper water, he unslung the M4 and let it sink, then did the same with the radios. Finally, he shrugged out of his plate carrier that had been dragging him down. He kept his small backup knife in its black sheath suspended horizontally on his hip, along with his personal pistol under his shirt at his right side. He unstrapped Three's gun and let it join the rest of the gear on the ocean floor.

The cold water brought him fully back to his senses, and the pain came along. He welcomed it. He would use it to fuel him. Or, at least until he went numb, which wouldn't be long.

He surfaced, oriented himself towards the boat, and swam below the surface.

Were there sharks in the area? He visualized a map of the east coast. Cape Cod, to the northeast, had them in the summer. Was the surrounding ocean filled with migrating sharks at the moment?

He surfaced again and saw how far he had to swim for the boat. Looking back, he noted he was out of range of anyone on the bluff unless they had a sniper rifle. And he didn't see anyone on the beach. There also wasn't a dock or other boats. Apparently even one of the richest men in the world couldn't get permission to build a pier to make getting to his yacht more convenient.

He switched to the combat swimmer stroke, his ribs, back, side, head, calf, and ankle all hurting like hell despite the cold water and encroaching numbness. He could swim for miles like this. Or at least until he got attacked by a shark or passed out from the pain, cold, or loss of blood.

He swam, stroking and kicking, over and over.

Axe had never been the best shooter, fastest swimmer, or strongest tactician. But he could he stick with a task.

He swam on.

He used all his stubbornness, all the tenacity at his disposal.

He fought the current and lost himself in the task.

The pain faded with his body's heat.

No sharks attacked.

There was only the water, the moonlight, and the boat.

He could admit to himself he was in bad shape. Always in the fight didn't mean avoiding reality.

His wounds weren't bleeding much due to the cold water and his body shutting down to protect itself. But he'd lost a lot of blood. He suspected he had internal bleeding, as well. But he wouldn't give up.

Go until you can't. Giving up right at the moment isn't a good idea, anyway. Make it to the boat, then reassess the mission.

He surfaced from the latest swim stroke and took a bead on the boat. It seemed closer. He would make it.

Then he passed out, his body sinking below the surface.

74

THE WATER

Axe came to consciousness, floating underwater, and clawed his way to the surface, gasping for air.

Not good. One bullet might have nicked something important.

He had a small trauma kit in his pants pocket. He would deal with it on the boat.

Axe looked back at the distant shore. He had no idea how long he'd been swimming and didn't have the strength to check his watch. It didn't matter, anyway. Getting on the boat was the next step. But that depended on the security and how alert they were. Would the shore detail claim they'd killed him with their shots to save face for being infiltrated? Or would they be honest and admit he could still be alive?

Who would believe he'd be able to swim so far, potentially injured, through such cold water?

He felt himself slipping again. He latched onto an idea to keep him going. Without getting to Kellison and forcing him to call off whatever attack he had planned, millions of people would die.

The importance of the mission invigorated him, and he swam better.

He finally neared the boat and treaded water. The mega yacht's lights lit up the night and the water surrounding it. He took in its length from the dark water just out of range of the lights. In his condition, without a rope or other gear, he had only one option: the platform at the boat's stern. Fortunately, the ship had swung at anchor with the current, so he faced the rear. He'd have to fight the current, but he could do it.

He saw a small powerboat tied up to the right side of the huge docking area, and a smaller craft that looked like a tiny jet airplane suspended from a short crane.

Wow. The man has his own mini submarine.

He couldn't risk approaching on the surface of the brightly lit water.

Axe took several breaths, deeper each time, letting the air out fully after each. Finally prepared, he took the deepest one he could, gulped even more air in two times, then dove under the water and swam with everything he had left.

He flashed back to BUD/S. He had been one of the slower swimmers at first. Of course it earned him extra attention, which meant extra swimming. It helped him improve, but tired him out more than his classmates.

They had to swim fifty meters underwater in the pool without pushing off or surfacing. Exhausted, he passed out under water and had technically drowned. The instructors pulled him out and brought him back to life.

He had died before giving up.

The next morning he had to repeat the swim.

He'd made it without drowning again—barely.

Failure hadn't been an option back then, and it wasn't now. But back then he had been younger, the pool had been warmer, and he hadn't been bleeding from several wounds.

75

THE DOCK

The salt water stung his eyes, but Axe saw fairly well because of the bright lights from the yacht.

Besides, it would be impossible to miss a boat this large, even approaching it under water, against the current, from the rear. And even as he fought to keep from losing consciousness again.

He had to make it. There were no instructors to fish him out and revive him.

This is why the instructors pushed them all so hard at training. They learned what their bodies could do if they stayed in control and kept their minds right.

My body is a liar. Don't believe it. I can keep going.

His hand found the bottom step of the swim ladder he'd aimed for. He resisted surfacing to take a gasp of air. Instead, he stayed underwater, moving right, guiding himself around the speedboat tied to the docking platform.

Partly hidden by the bulk of the small craft, he silently surfaced. Instead of loudly sucking in air, he forced himself to take in just enough to keep himself going for another few seconds, then instantly sunk back down, waiting and listening for a shot or shout.

Nothing.

He surfaced again and relaxed for a few seconds, treading water. He'd made it to the objective. Suddenly, the pain and exhaustion crashed down on him.

Take care of the wounds. Rest for a minute if you can find a safe, hidden spot. Then continue the mission.

If he was honest with himself, the dog bites, and especially the fall, had taken a toll. He would check in a minute, but either one of the bullets had hit something vital or he had internal bleeding from rolling over the bluff and hitting every rock on the way down.

He knew his capabilities. The dog bites, long fall, and bullets weren't a walk in the park, but he wouldn't feel as bad as he did unless he had lost a lot of blood.

He peeked around the bow of the speedboat and saw no one on the dock, so he sank low in the water and eased his way over to the platform. He'd meant to avoid the swim ladder, but realized he wouldn't have the strength. Instead, he grabbed the gleaming chrome bars, put his foot on the steps, and climbed aboard the boat.

He hated being in the glare of the lights, but he had to rest for a second. He lay back, praying no one would come.

"If you're not a SEAL, you should have been."

Axe's head snapped up, locking onto the source of the voice. A man, about ten years older than him, stood in the speedboat's bow, pointing a shotgun at him.

76

THE SHOWDOWN

This is the second time today I've looked down the wrong end of a shotgun.

The hard-looking man seemed familiar, but Axe couldn't quite place him.

He recognized the two huge goons standing next to him, though. Kellison's personal bodyguards. They climbed carefully out of the speedboat, rocking it with their bulk. Axe tensed, hoping for an opening, but the older man moved expertly as the boat swayed, the shotgun staying squarely on Axe's body.

The goons stood on the platform next to the small boat, focused on him with angry expressions. Their similarities convinced Axe they were brothers. Two fleshy, middle-America white guys who might have been sumo wrestlers had they been born in Japan. Small, beady eyes, short black hair, weak chins.

"Boy, do you look like shit. Pale. Blood loss and hypothermia, my guess. But I told them you'd make it."

His eyes flicked briefly to the two men. "You both owe me a

hundred bucks." They didn't acknowledge him. They only stood, waiting for orders.

"Take him alive."

77

THE GOONS

Axe had no moves left. He lay on his back. There was nothing nearby for cover. The knife at his side and the wet pistol under his shirt could help, but he'd be shot before getting to either. It was over.

He lowered his head to the deck in defeat and closed his eyes.

When he opened them a few seconds later, he saw goon number one's large, fleshy face, filled with an evil grin, staring down at him from near his feet.

As he hoped, the man had assumed the wounds, the cold, and his posture of defeat meant he would be easy prey. And if Axe hadn't been a SEAL, he would have been.

The man went straight for Axe's pistol, obvious through the tightness of his wet shirt. He leaned over Axe's prone body, his short arm reaching for Axe's waist. He stretched out, leaning across Axe's body from the left on short, stubby legs as thick as tree trunks.

As soon as Axe sensed the stubby fingers take hold of his gun, he grabbed the idiot's wrist with both hands and rolled to his right, away from the man... towards the edge of the dock.

An experienced grappler would have let go instead of being pulled off balance.

A warrior would have let go and kicked Axe in the back to pacify him.

But a huge bodyguard who, because of his intimidating size had likely rarely fought—and never grappled—couldn't grasp the idea of letting go to win. He pulled the gun out of the holster at the expense of his balance.

Axe's sudden sideways yank pulled the man forward, causing him to stumble and fight for his footing. Axe pulled a second time, ignoring the searing pain all over his body. The man's short legs kept churning under him, trying not to fall...

With a grunt from Axe and a surprised sound from the man, he tripped over Axe's body. Still struggling to regain his balance, he tumbled off the platform, hitting the water with a sharp smacking sound as he landing on his face and chest in the cold ocean.

Axe groaned loudly and raised his hands in surrender, waiting for the shotgun blast, but it didn't come.

They really want me alive. Big mistake.

He glanced back at the speedboat and the older man's tight lips and angry expression, but turned his attention to goon number two who had started towards him in a rush.

"He can't swim!" the man cried, switching his gaze from Axe to his partner and back again.

He then made a fatal mistake, moving towards the edge of the dock to help his partner... and directly between Axe and the man with the shotgun.

Axe pulled the small fixed-blade knife from its horizontal sheath, hoping his body would hide his movement if the man's bulk didn't.

The goon's rush made it easy. As he hurried past, Axe sat up. He thrust the four-inch knife straight into the man's exposed family jewels, then yanked upwards, the knife cutting through flesh like butter.

78

THE BODYGUARD

The bodyguard's anguish came out in a barely audible squeak. He stood over Axe, having come to an abrupt stop as the knife entered his body.

His bulk had screened the entire action from the man with the gun.

"Stop screwing around and get him up!" the older man barked.

Axe pushed himself up to a crouch, pulling out the knife.

The goon stood, stooped forward, using both hands to cup himself, trying to both stop the flow of blood and hold his most essential anatomy together.

"Please," the man whispered, his eyes wide with pain and terror. "Please!" Axe didn't know whether he was begging for help or to be finished off.

Axe didn't have the strength or time for either. But he did the next best thing. He grabbed the man by the head and used him as a shield. He stepped backwards and to the side, pulling the bodyguard along with him to hide his body from the gunman, heading to the open doorway near him that separated the docking area from the rest of the ship.

"Where are you—"

Axe pushed the man backwards and dove through the open doorway as the shotgun blast rang out. The goon cried in pain again as Axe pushed on the heavy metal door, trying to stay out of the angle of fire. The stabbed and now shot man reached weakly for the door, more in a desperate grab for help or protection than an attempt at stopping Axe. As the door slammed shut, another blast rang out, peppering the door with shot. Blood and brain matter covered the door's round window as the goon's agonized cries abruptly stopped.

Axe spun the wheel in the middle of the door to secure it as another blast hit it, then flipped down the locking bar, buying himself some time.

79

THE ROOM

Axe staggered down the hallway, weaving from one side to the other, leaving a trail of blood on the floor and the walls. The wound on his side bled freely.

Would the master suite be on top, with the best view? Or lower, where the motion of the boat would be lessened?

On top, he decided. Views and ego would win out over comfort for someone with this much wealth. Or perhaps the ship had dampeners to minimize excess motion.

He held his hand to his right side, gritting at the pain but needing the pressure to control the flow of blood. He needed time to take care of himself, and he wouldn't get it with Mr. Shotgun hunting him.

Especially leaving an obvious blood trail as he went.

He came to a larger hallway, which he took, leaning against the left wall, forcing himself along.

After ten feet, the hall ended in a massive open area. Fresh flowers filled vases on every available surface.

Must be a few thousand dollars' worth of flowers. Imagine being able to spend so much money on perishable decorations every week.

A grand staircase curved upwards, looking straight out of a magnificent mansion. Axe marveled at the opulence.

He dragged himself painfully up each step using the polished gold railing. He climbed one level, then another, wondering the entire time how long it would take Mr. Shotgun to get through the locked door or find another way around. At each moment he feared a blast blowing him off his feet. He hated to do it, but his best bet for the moment was to hide.

He wasn't proud of the decision. But to stay in the fight, he had to survive. He was man enough to admit he wouldn't make it much longer if he didn't stop the bleeding.

So he pulled himself up the stairs as fast as his taxed body would go.

He reached the top landing and paused, noting the ornately carved wooden door in front of him. He looked behind him, taking in the expensive carpet, the priceless artwork on the walls, the windows offering what must be an amazing view in the daytime.

The only thing on this level was the opening to the staircase and the small landing. The master suite took up the entire floor.

He heard a sound on the floor below him and moved as quietly as his injured state allowed over the carpeted floor to the door. The knob turned easily when he tried it.

If you're wrong about this, you're dead.

He heard hurried footsteps on the staircase behind him, coming on fast, and stepped through the door, closing and locking the deadbolt. Mr. Shotgun wasn't far behind.

The door looked solid and could stop the buckshot in the weapon. Unless the man had keys...

Axe hurriedly looked around. What he hoped to find would be near the bed or bathroom.

The master suite lay before him. A seating area directly in front, centered around an honest-to-goodness fireplace in the middle of the room, its chimney rising to the ceiling fourteen feet above.

To the far left, a fancy exercise bike faced the stern of the ship, just inside closed sliding glass windows that opened onto the deck with the hot tub he'd seen earlier in the day.

The entire right side of the ship—to forward—was taken up by the actual bedroom. A four-post bed covered much of the floor space. It had to be two king-sized beds joined together, draped with a majestic canopy of dark red silk. The gold comforter looked plush and comfortable. He wanted to lie down and sleep for days.

If you lay down, you die.

The bed faced the port side of the ship, set against a wall that ran down the middle of the boat. Another wall ran at a right angle to it, with two doorways. Axe figured the first would be an enormous closet. The second would be a bathroom. Both doors were closed.

He started towards them and sensed the door behind him opening. He ran, hoping the man wouldn't shoot up the billionaire's master bedroom.

Two doors. He had to get it right.

The carpet was so thick and plush he couldn't hear the footsteps of the man behind him, but he felt him there. He pushed his body to the max, knowing it would soon be over, one way or the other. Either he guessed correctly, and he'd have some time, or he'd be captured. Or dead.

He flung the left door open and kept moving, looking… looking…

He saw a narrow doorway on the right, between two wooden closet organizers. He flung himself at it as he heard the howl of anger from the man behind him, just starting through the closet doorway.

As he stepped inside the small room, his bloody hand slapped the large red button on the wall just inside.

The pocket door slammed shut, pushed by powerful hydraulics, and instantly locked.

Axe slumped to the ground as the pounding started. He let himself relax for a second as he surveyed the well-stocked panic room.

80

THE BLOOD

The pounding finally stopped, which Axe preferred. It had been getting on his nerves.

"You can't stay in there forever, you know." The man had to be yelling, but Axe could barely hear him through the thick walls.

Reinforced. Secure. No expense spared.

He'd gambled and won. Again. He'd figured a man whose net worth dwarfed many small countries would have a safe, secure facility to use in an emergency. He'd been right.

Axe reached for his small trauma kit, then shook his head. He could save that for the next emergency. Along the back wall sat a white cabinet. It looked straight out of a medical facility. He forced himself up, swayed and nearly collapsed, but stumbled forward.

His hands smeared blood everywhere he touched, but he found what he needed.

Without regard for neatness, he grabbed the essentials and pulled a small stool from the wall next to the cabinet, sitting down gingerly.

He used the safety shears on his shirt and pants, still dripping from his swim. In his black boxer briefs, he shivered uncontrollably, so he tore open the packet containing a mylar emergency blanket, unfolded it, and draped it over his shoulders. He unwrapped two chemical heat packets and shook them a few seconds, then put one between his knees and the other under his arm.

Next, he chugged a full litre bottle of expensive spring water. Then he got to work.

What he found didn't thrill him.

His calf had deep punctures from Ares' teeth. They oozed fresh blood as his body warmed. His ankle bled too, with more bite marks. At least they were less deep.

The hole in his side worried him. He gritted his teeth and dumped quick clot granules into it before gently adding gauze, then large bandages to cover it. He suspected the bullet had nicked an artery. With luck, the clotting agent would help and he'd be fine for a few hours.

He'd forgotten about the back of his head until the blood started dripping loudly onto the chair. When he reached back, his hand came away covered in red.

Lots of blood vessels up there. Maybe that's how I lost so much blood.

He sprinkled more clotting grains there, then slapped a bandage on it as well.

He touched his ribs with his fingers and almost passed out from the pain. Warming up was a double-edge sword. He would soon no longer be hypothermic, but the numbness from the cold had already started to fade.

If he had internal bleeding from broken ribs, he had to get to a hospital sooner even than he'd planned.

Satisfied he had done everything possible for the moment, Axe found a variety of men's clothing stored neatly in drawers. He got dressed in a black long sleeve shirt, thick, dark blue wool sweater, and thin black workout pants with a white stripe up the side. They probably cost several hundred dollars, but he hated the lack of extra pockets. Still, he transferred the essentials from the pants to the sweats.

Next up: fuel. Axe found the food stores. He drank more water, slammed down a candy bar for the quick sugar, and cracked a container of cashews.

His body taken care of for the time being, he sat down on the small stool. All he had to do now was to figure out how to escape, survive, and continue the mission.

81

THE RECOGNITION

A tablet computer sat in a narrow wire basket on the wall near the doorway, plugged in to a charger.

Axe lifted it up, unplugged it, and tapped the round button on the front. It required a password.

He searched nearby, finally finding a small index card hidden in the toe of an expensive leather shoe. The password was printed on in careful handwriting.

Perfect.

He poked around, exploring the device.

It looked like he had full control of the security system and video surveillance.

First things first.

He followed the user friendly design, clicking on 'Video Monitors,' 'Penthouse Level,' and finally 'Closet.' He found himself looking down at the man with the shotgun, pacing back and forth in front of the door.

Axe clicked on the small microphone icon below the photo.

"Just you and the two goons? Don't tell me you designed this shitty security."

The man stopped pacing and turned to look directly at Axe. Or at least the security camera Axe figured had to be mounted above the door.

He played it cool. "The man wanted privacy. Has something planned." He shrugged. "What are you gonna do?"

"Seriously, it's just you and me?"

"Looks like it." He smiled, but his eyes were cold and calculating. "Except for the captain and a few crew. But they're civilians. Can I count on you to leave them alone? They'll stay out of the way."

"Sure, if I get out of here. What about Goons One and Two?"

"One sank like a stone. Serves him right."

Axe listened while searching the food cupboard, where he found a stash of energy gels and started sucking them down.

"Two is gone. That was cold-blooded, man, sticking him like that. Of course it didn't help he blocked me from shooting you, I guess. Still, better to be out of his misery than with a wound like that."

The pieces clicked for Axe as the man spoke.

"You'd know all about cold-blooded, wouldn't you, Devlin?"

The man froze. His face betrayed nothing, but the sudden stillness said everything. Axe had guessed right.

Axe knew only one part of what surely must be an incredible story, which happened a few years before his time in the Teams.

An experienced SEAL named Devlin had been a loose cannon, violent and uncontrollable. The brass loved him because he got the job done, but his men hated him.

No one ever said what things he did. Only that they had been excessive and illegal. The implication in the stories was that he killed innocent civilians with abandon. It wasn't every op, though. Most nights would be fine, but once in a while Devlin would go nuts. No one on his unit had been able to put a stop to it internally.

Finally, the men had enough.

There had been a night with a busted op. Bad intel. No one had been at the compound they raided. So on the hike out, his men had taken the action they'd long debated. They shot Devlin in the knee from behind and called it a sniper casualty. They gave him a choice: go along with their story, receive the purple heart for bravery and being wounded in action. Retire a hero.

The other option had been plain, as each of his men aimed their weapon at him. He'd die, shot multiple times in a firefight, another brave, tragic victim of the conflict.

While in BUD/S, Axe had seen a newspaper article about the so-called hero. On the dock earlier, he had recognized the man's face, and finally put it together when he saw the slight limp in the right leg as he paced in the closet.

"By the way, how's the knee? I wouldn't have made it in here if you didn't have the limp."

Devlin finally spoke, his voice low and controlled. "I guessed it. Fellow frogman. No one else could have snuck onto the grounds, killed two of my top guys, and commandeered our K9 unit. Let alone fought off the dog and survived falling off the cliff. My chief told me he shot you at least twice. He said he watched you drown, you know that?" He shook his head in disgust. "Asshole."

"He got me twice, but I had a vest on, which I ditched. That's when he saw me drown. I sunk while I took it off."

"Well, I'm impressed. You think a Ranger could have done what you did? Delta? Please." He rolled his eyes. "By the way, have we met?"

"No. You were before my time."

Devlin nodded. "You made it this far, but it's the end of the line. You realize that, right? You're safe in there, but you're also trapped. Whatever your plan, you're screwed now. Can't stay in there forever," he repeated. "Especially wounded. You've lost a lot of blood. House-keeping is going to throw a fit when they see it."

"Yeah, your guys worked me over. And that dog... I'm pretty messed up. But as you said, since I'm safe here, if you don't mind, I think I'm just going to pass out for a while. So... yeah. See ya."

Axe closed the connection. Passing out for a bit sounded like a wonderful idea.

82

THE UNSANCTIONED ASSET

"Report." Haley had never heard Gregory sound like he did now, so many hours into what had been a long day—with no end in sight. On the video conference screen, he looked haggard and spent, but his voice still sounded forceful. The word snapped at Haley as the video connected sounded both angry and disappointed.

I can't read all that into a single word.

She understood the pressure on him—on all the upper level of America's intelligence services—had to be incredible. The president and the country needed answers.

And as always, the shit rolled down hill. When the upper level got yelled at and called to task, they would share with their underlings, all the way down, until it landed on Haley with one forcefully barked command. She couldn't stall any longer. It was time to come clean.

"Sir, I've looked at all the data from the inter-agency team. I've sifted and sorted, and I've concluded that…" Could she say it? She had to. "Well, sir, they're wrong. It's not the Iranians."

Gregory closed his eyes and shook his head in exasperation, letting out an enormous sigh.

"Haley, I can't go through this with you again. If you have nothing useful to add—"

She couldn't take any more. Why wouldn't he believe her? She'd been right over and over. Was it her looks? Her youth? Would she be listened to if she were a handsome young man instead?

No way of knowing.

"I have a lot to add," she said impulsively. "I've figured it all out and have been right the whole time. But you don't want to hear it."

Gregory looked like he was counting to five to keep from blowing up at her.

"Proof, Haley. Anything. At this point, I'd take a tidbit. What do you have?"

Absolutely nothing. The data just sort of... fit.

"Nothing concrete."

"Hunches?" He shook his head and rolled his eyes. "Fine, just to humor you, tell me your hunches."

"It's not the Iranians, that's for sure. The clues are well hidden, clever even, but too neat."

"What then?"

Play the game. Avoid the questions you don't want to answer.

"Another attack is coming."

"Not this again. What, where, and most importantly, how do you know?"

"Tonight. The nuclear power plant north of Manhattan."

Gregory's posture changed at the revelation. He sat up straighter. The look on his face showed he was finally taking her seriously. "Continue."

"Possibly between midnight and four AM."

"Not what I meant. How do you know?"

She tried not to, but she caught herself biting her lip and realized it was one of her tells.

"I see. No proof." His posture sagged, and he leaned back tiredly in his chair. "Haley, what if each of my analysts came to me like you are? 'They're going to hit Grand Central Station.' 'No, they're going to hit the Statue of Liberty tomorrow morning.' 'Well, I think they're going to spray nerve gas from crop dusters flying over Central Park!' If everyone on the team made a best-guess prediction, and terrorists do strike again, one of them might be right. But it's like high school math, Haley: you've got to show your work, not guess at the answer."

She couldn't help herself. Now she was pissed.

Don't say it.

"I'm working on getting you something. Actual proof. Or stopping it on my own. Either way."

"Working on? Stopping it? How?"

Ooops.

"I, um…"

Gregory no longer looked exhausted and frustrated. Now he looked pissed.

"What the hell are you up to?"

"I have an asset—"

"You what? You're an analyst. You don't run assets!"

Interestingly, the angrier Gregory became, the calmer she got.

"Remember, I told you I got abducted? A… friend…"

Let him think what he wants.

"Was coming over to my place. He helped me escape. When I got a lead about what I believe is actually going on," she couldn't resist the dig, "I asked him to help. Gather intel on the ground."

Gregory stared at her, speechless. Finally, he mustered the words and his tone made Haley cold. "Your connections to the president notwithstanding, when you're back in the office, you and I are going to have a long, serious discussion about your future. And when we're finished, you're going to tell me you'd like a transfer. Understood?"

She only nodded… but she stared straight at the lens of the teleconference camera in fierce defiance.

They sat silent for what seemed like hours, but was only several seconds. Then Gregory spoke again. "And has your unsanctioned asset uncovered any intelligence of value?"

"I've tried to reach him for the past two hours. The last I heard, he had begun to infiltrate the target location to gather intel by eavesdropping or…"

"Or what?"

"Interrogation."

"Oh my God," Gregory muttered under his breath. "An unsanctioned asset interrogating… Who?"

"The man I believe is the mastermind of the operation."

He stared at her. "I need the name, Haley. Even more so since you're obviously reluctant to tell me."

Don't squirm!

She held herself still. "Kelton Kellison."

If the situation had been any less intense, the day's events less deadly, she would have laughed out loud. Gregory gasped like a shocked old woman.

"One of the richest men in the world? That Kelton Kellison."

"Yes, sir. That Kelton Kellison."

Once again, the silence seemed to last for years.

"You are in so much trouble. Please tell me your 'friend' is an ordinary, everyday person who has no real chance of ever getting close to Kelton Kellison. Please." He sounded like he was begging for his life.

"Sorry. He's exceptional, and I have no doubt he'll succeed."

83

THE OLD FRIENDS

Kelton stared, horrified, at his right-hand man. Todd turned the phone so Kelton could see the headline: *Rumors: Iran Behind Morning's Terrorist Attacks.*

"See, it's going according to plan. Nothing at all can be traced back to us. You never give me enough credit," he added with a sad frown.

Todd relaxed in Kelton's office, which took up the full bow of the ship's main level. The front and both sides had windows looking over the dark water and the lights of his understated mansion on top of the bluff. He sat behind Kelton's desk in the exquisitely comfortable chair, facing the view, his back to the locked door.

Kelton glared at Todd from the guest chair in front of his desk. It had been custom designed to be uncomfortable, with subtle ridges, lumps, and unusual angles forcing the body to tilt uncomfortably. Countless business associates had struggled to sit in the impossible chair.

Now Kelton regretted his previous actions. With his ankles and wrists zip-tied, he couldn't move. His arms and legs screamed from being bound so long, his back ached from being forced into a twisted position by the chair, and his butt hurt from the horrible seat.

He couldn't resist engaging Todd. He'd been a salesman all his life, convincing others to believe in him, back his dreams, or buy his products. He had to make Todd stop his horrible plan.

He'd arrived on board the yacht, his greatest pleasure. His sanctuary. When the small powerboat docked, he had been so caught up in getting to his office and finding some way out of this mess—to either stop or report Todd—he hadn't noticed the lack of his normal security contingent. Before he stepped into the office, he had told his two huge personal guards to wait outside the door.

Todd had been laying in wait, sucker punching him, then tied him to the chair. With the soundproof door closed, the two guards hadn't any idea of his situation. It was then Todd explained the full extent of the plan.

Kelton had quickly concluded his long-time friend had gone off the deep end. He had no idea what happened, but the man was certifiably crazy… and he hadn't noticed any signs.

He would try a different approach. He filled his voice with regret and sorrow. "You're right. I'll admit it. I've underestimated you and haven't given you the credit you deserve."

Todd looked up, taken aback. "What did you say?"

"You've run the entire company for years. You've given me the freedom to live this life," he looked around his gorgeous office, "without having to worry about any of the mundane daily operations." He warmed to the task and put more into it. "Hell, forget day to day. Year to year operations."

He saw the look on Todd's face go from pleased to skeptical. He'd overdone it. Todd had been buying it for a second, but the last part had made him suspicious.

"Nice try. You're not talking your way out of this one."

Kelton's eyes narrowed, sudden rage blooming in his heart. Not concern for himself, strangely enough. He felt for the people who had been harmed and killed already, and worried there would be more death and destruction. An interesting feeling, unusual for him. "I may have taken you for granted, Todd, but I know you well. You have more planned, don't you? Listen, I'm not worried about me. Shoot me and dump my body overboard, if it would make you feel better. But stop whatever else is coming. Would you do that? For old time's sake?"

Todd just laughed. "You're right on several accounts. One, you have taken me for granted. Two, your body will be dumped overboard at some point. But not until later. After the other activity I have planned." He smiled coldly. "But don't worry, we're safe here."

"What is it? What's going to happen?"

Todd grinned, happy to be asked. "It's beautiful. Brilliant, even. Had you not been such a baby about this morning, you would have benefited as much as I." He checked his watch, "In just a bit, there will be an attack—"

Todd's phone rang, a distinctive, ominous ring tone. His eyes lit up, and he glanced at Kelton. "Promise to be quiet and I'll let you listen in?"

Kelton nodded, not knowing what else to do.

Todd entered a code on the keypad and hit a button, putting the encrypted call on speaker. "Go ahead."

"You've got problems," the voice said.

Kelton recognized the voice from somewhere. Then he had it. "Mr. Vice President?"

"Who the hell is that, Todd?"

Todd hurried around the desk, glaring at Kelton.

"Mr. Vice President, it's Kelton—"

The savage punch to his exposed stomach took his breath away. The second punch to his head rocked him backwards and he almost blacked out. If not for the sturdiness of the uncomfortable chair, he would have also fallen over backwards.

"You have me on speaker? You idiot. I can't believe—"

"Do not call me an idiot," Todd hissed in a voice so cold the Vice President of the United States fell silent—and stayed that way.

After a pause, Todd continued in a friendlier voice as Kelton listened, struggling to get control of his breath and his focus.

"First, don't worry about Mr. Kellison. He's not long for this world.

He's going to have an unfortunate accident, fall off his mega yacht, and drown." Kelton stared at Todd's face, a foot in front of him, wondering at the coldness he saw in the expression of his oldest friend. "Next, what did you mean, I have problems?"

"An analyst has seen through your lies. They've put an asset into place to infiltrate Kellison's operation."

Todd paused, thinking. "Is that what they said? Kellison's operation?"

"Yes. It sounded like they were working under the assumption that Kellison had a hand in things and they were looking to interrogate him. They also believe something else is planned for tonight."

"And their proof?"

"My source admitted they had nothing. A hunch."

"I think I know who is behind this. Not to worry. I doubt there are any clues for them to find, but they would all point to our friend Mr. Kellison, here. As for the supposed asset, I'm safe and well protected. We had some commotion earlier, but they have reassured me they have handled it. And tonight's activities are still on."

"About that—"

"No. I told you. You don't need to know. But it'll be exactly what we need."

Kelton's breath had partly returned, and he opened his mouth to speak, only to receive a vicious punch below the belt this time, which doubled him over, took his breath away again, and made tears stream down his face.

"I said be quiet and listen," Todd whispered in his ear. "Listen to this, and marvel."

"Mr. Vice President, I think the time has come. I would very much like to hear you agree to the terms I mentioned during our last call."

"What? Oh." There was a long pause. "Fine. If you provide what you have promised, I'll do it."

Todd chuckled. "Excellent. But I need to hear the words, sir. Tell me what I get out of it."

He excitedly nudged Kelton, gesturing towards the phone. Kelton focused his attention, desperate to avoid another strike... and wondered again about Todd's sanity.

A long, defeated sigh came through the line. "When I win, you'll be my vice president."

84

THE SHOCK

Axe lowered the screen, not believing what he'd seen and heard.

The Vice President of the United States involved in a terrorist attack?

And Kellison's right-hand man Todd behind it, all so he could be vice president himself.

The VP going along with it all.

His thoughts swirled at the possibilities.

He also confirmed the other attack, starting soon.

He wouldn't have believed it if he hadn't seen and heard it himself via the tablet, which showed an overhead view of the ship's lavish office.

The president had been correct—he had a traitor in his inner circle.

And there must be at least one other mole, someone from whom the vice president received his information. A person Haley had informed about Axe and his attempt to gain entry to Kellison's compound.

He leaned back against the wall of the safe room. He was weak from the blood loss, and the wound in his side still oozed despite his efforts to stop it.

Not moving helped, but he no longer had that luxury.

He had to get to Todd and make him call off the attack.

85

THE ATTACK

The planning for the nuclear plant assault had been extensive. The serial killers had seen the maps and charts. They showed locations of fixed defenses, the workforce at the plant on a normal night shift, and the differences when on high alert, like tonight.

There were meticulous details of what would happen and when. Contingencies for the most likely scenarios.

Their training had been rigorous. Weeks of discipline had gone into the preparations for the night.

They were assured of success.

The time to attack had finally come.

The group of killers from B Team had pushed the plane to the end of the private airport's dark runway. Once they'd gotten it rolling, it hadn't been so bad, but their gear stashed inside the plane made it hard to get moving.

They wouldn't risk the engine noise or lights until the last possible moment, though the nationwide no-fly rule had been suspended hours earlier. The sleepy upstate New York airstrip along the freeway an hour north of the city wasn't set up for nighttime operations, and a plane taking off would raise the eyebrows of the other flying enthusiasts who lived nearby.

After a full flight check—minus starting the engine—their pilot, also a die-hard criminal, fired up the engines and immediately started down the runway. The eight men crammed into the back of the plane smiled at each other in anticipation. In a half hour, they would jump into the darkness as they had trained, silently approach the nuclear plant from the sky, land on the roof of the security building, and begin their evening of killing.

The eight men of C Team walked through the woods, carrying their heavy, precious cargo in large backpacks. Straps cut into their shoulders from the loads, but they didn't complain. Their task would be the kill stroke. The rest of the teams served only as a distraction for the real assault.

They had been a part of the original group at the start of training. In ones and twos, individuals had been selected for specific assignments based on skill, attitude, and aptitude. Each of them had been chosen for their focus, dexterity, and complete lack of empathy. Out of a group of suspected serial killers, they were the worst of the worst.

Once recruited to the unit, they had been segregated from the others and moved to their own facility on a farm in the far eastern end of Long Island. Surrounded by a few hundred acres of cropland, they had learned their specialized skill, all while being continually assured of their uniqueness and the essential aspect of their assignment.

The entire operation had been planned for and around them.

After two hours of walking through the dark on a path they'd traveled dozens of times in training, they turned off the trail at a small cairn of rocks dabbed with glow-in-the-dark paint. They cut down a small side trail only traveled by themselves to an opening in the woods originally identified by their handlers on a satellite map.

They set up on a small rock outcropping and unpacked their gear.

First came the bulky hard-sided cases which were coaxed gingerly from the packs, then opened reverently. Each man eyed the drone they'd worked so hard to master.

Once assembled, they each attached the next items pulled from the packs. The thirteen-pound bombs went on the underside of the drones as payload.

Then they sat on the edge of the rock jutting out over the soft forest floor five feet below, their heads slightly above the nearby trees, with a direct line of sight to the nuclear power plant across the river.

At the nuclear power plant, the dedicated men and women in the security bunker picked up the plane on radar ten minutes after it took off. They designated it as a potential threat, though its current flight path would take it well to the south of the plant.

Following standard procedure, they alerted the security detail, as well as their "special guests," as they referred to the SRT team.

"Flank 1, break out the Stingers," Robinson told the team on the south side of the complex.

They struggled to contain their enthusiasm while they cracked open the cases carrying the powerful—and expensive—weapons. Two were removed and prepped. They had never fired the missile during a mission, and had only test fired one per team, though they had no doubt their skills were up to the task.

If a plane needed to be shot down, they would be happy to do it.

86

THE DOOR

Axe manipulated the tablet to show the view outside the safe room door. There had been muffled thuds from time to time. He watched now as Devlin struggled in vain to open the door with a long crowbar.

Trapped.

There had to be a solution.

Work the problem. Think it through like a rich guy.

Or like the rich guy's security-conscious boat designer.

Got it.

He pushed aside the white medical cabinet and knelt, feeling along the wall.

There. Seams.

He looked around for a button or switch, finally finding it at the back of a nearby shelf, covered in sweaters.

The sweaters also hid a short barrel 12-gauge shotgun and two boxes of ammunition. He filled his pockets with the shells after making sure the gun was fully loaded.

Axe took one last check of the tablet and saw Devlin prepare to swing the crowbar in frustration, then heard the thump on the door. He switched to the view of Kellison's office and saw Todd with a knife, kneeling in front of Kellison. He was about to kill him, torture the man, or cut the zip from Kellison's wrists and ankles. No matter which, Axe had to hurry.

He slid the tablet into his rear waistband, then reached to the back of the shelf and pressed the release button. The lower half of the wall swung out silently. He pushed gently, opening the small hidden door fully, then ducked through the opening.

He emerged in the bathroom, standing at the far end of the large shower enclosure.

Man, a hot shower would be great right about now.

He pushed the panel back into place, hearing the quiet click as the lock reengaged. Standing in front of the secret door, knowing where to look, he still couldn't see the seam.

Quality workmanship. No expense spared.

He stalked quietly through large walk-in shower opening, moving slowly but surely towards the bathroom door.

The sound of the metal bar hitting the safe room door came from the closet, along with angry cursing from Devlin.

"Open the door, you asshole! You coward. Come out here and fight like a man. You're no SEAL, you chickenshit!"

A few steps on the thick carpet brought him to the open closet door. "Surprise, Devlin."

The man's head spun to the door, eyes wide in surprise. Axe pulled the trigger, blowing Devlin's blood and guts all over the closet full of fancy designer clothes.

87

THE PILOT

The timing had to be perfect. The pilot increased his airspeed for a few minutes to get on schedule. He'd slow down again before the men jumped.

He adjusted his heading, steering further away from the plant. The plan called for the plane to not be perceived as a threat, and occasional small course corrections away would ensure it.

He checked his watch yet again, which he'd been doing every few seconds for the last half hour, then throttled back to the optimum jump speed.

"One minute," he called to the men in back. Not that they needed it. Every one had been following the time on their own watches and had already risen to their knees in the cramped rear of the plane. The leader slid the side door open and the chilly spring night's wind whipped around. Luck would be on their side with the breeze blowing towards the plant, making their long-range glide easier than they had trained for.

They checked their stubby automatic rifles, secured tightly to their chests, and superstitiously ran their hands over ammo pouches containing an excessive amount of extra magazines. They'd need much less, if the intel could be believed, but the extra bullets would allow them to have even more fun once they neutralized their primary targets.

This would be the night of their lives.

88

THE FIRST STRIKE

A man named Eric had the honor of striking the plant first.

He checked his watch as he turned the corner from the main highway to the plant's winding access road.

He was right on time.

He slowed and the three men on his team jumped out of the mid-size car without a word. They'd already thanked him for his sacrifice. "See you in hell," their team lead joked. They had all laughed, but knew in their hearts the truth of the statement. They would see him there. Very soon, they guessed. But he'd get there first and pave the way.

His foot pushed the accelerator pedal gently, attempting to continue the charade as long as possible, but aware he'd been under surveillance from the turn.

Humans, however, are imperfect. Despite the attacks of the morning and the expected high-alert at the plant, you never knew. Maybe whoever should have been monitoring the cameras along the approach road had gone to the restroom, or was caught up in a book.

He sped up and continued down the long, curving road towards the guard gate.

Eric marveled at his situation. He'd been approached shortly after his diagnosis for stage four cancer in his lungs, brain, and stomach. He'd been offered a special assignment, one last gig. And while he might be dying, he was still a killer. He'd done time for crimes he committed, but had gotten away with many others, including murder.

He still lived—or would have, for another few weeks—for death and destruction. Tonight, his face beamed with pleasure. Because of the offer, he would cheat death. No waiting around to die. He'd go in a blaze of glory, taking many people with him, and paving the way for the other men in the D Team assault group.

Behind him, as the men moved smoothly forward to their positions, a second car turned onto the main approach road.

Behind that, coming from both directions, were other cars filled with armed men who had to work hard to contain their excitement.

89

THE START

"Sir," a security technician called to the shift supervisor inside the fortified security room. "I have thermals exiting the plane."

"Copy." The supervisor, a retired Marine named Williams, walked over to the tech's station and joined him looking at the screen.

"The plane is continuing on course away from the facility."

"Fine. Alert the authorities to have them meet it wherever he lands."

"On it."

"South teams, alert. Incoming bogeys by air. Look for parachutes in your sectors. Clear to engage when in range."

"Sir, what if they're protesters or something?" one of the younger, newer techs asked.

"Son, tonight anyone approaching this facility is a threat. I'm fine with people carrying banners, banging drums, and marching on the place to call attention to how bad nuclear energy is. I say, 'Bring 'em on.' Everyone's entitled to their opinion, no matter how wrong." The dozen men and women in the room chuckled at their leader's words. "But at three AM on the morning after two different terrorist attacks less than thirty miles from us, any peaceful protester better be home safe in bed. Handcuffing yourself to our gate is one thing. You do that, fine, we cut you lose after you get your face on the TV. You parachute in, though, your ass is mine."

A few minutes later, another tech called out "Sir, it's starting." His monitor displayed four views of the front approach to the main gate. The top left showed a nice, newer car illuminated in the lights along the roadway. The top right window revealed a second car that had turned onto the approach road.

In the bottom left, a thermal view showed blobs of red: men, crouched in the grass—apparently thinking themselves unseen. Their rifles glowed red on the screen.

"Look at the guns. They should have at least turned off the heater in the car," the tech mumbled, shaking his head.

Williams took it all in with one glance.

"All stations, stand by for attack. Front gate, lock it up and put your heads down."

They had defenses specifically hardened against car bombs. Additionally, with the touch of a button, a huge metal car barrier rose from the road, twenty-five yards from the gate, which was itself fortified.

They watched as the car accelerated around one last curve, having yet to see the hidden—secret—barrier.

"Sir, secondary road has three cars approaching fast."

"Sir, north side has tangos cutting through the fence."

"Impressive. They're all going to hit at the same time. This is no protest, ladies and gentleman, this is the real deal. All stations: engage once targets are in range. Lethal methods authorized. I say again, lethal methods authorized. SRT: welcome to the show. We appreciate your backup. Engage as needed."

Robinson, laying on the roof of the building at the rear of the facility, facing the river, repeated the order for his men and women. "You heard the chief, people. Back up the main team as needed. Looks like plenty of targets to go around."

90

THE ALERT

Robinson released the button on his mic and turned to the team he lay close to, his three best people.

"Got anything?"

"Nothing—wait. Sir, yes. I switched to thermals. A target. Across the river, in the woods. Hard to see, but it looks like a bunch of live bodies, sir, in a line."

"What are they doing?"

"Just sitting there, sir."

His machine gunner, an Army veteran named Whiting who didn't take shit from anyone, spoke up. "They might be filming it, sir. Like to show on TV? Propaganda or whatever?"

"Possibly. But—"

"Sir, I've got something." Dellis, his best sniper, a former policewoman who had scored the highest marks he'd ever seen on the range, called to him in her quiet, controlled voice.

"What is it?"

"Movement. From near the clearing containing the targets. There for a second, then gone."

"Best guess?"

"Drones, sir. Gotta be."

"Damn."

They had defenses, some of which worked better than others. But at night, flying low and moving fast, drones would be difficult to hit.

"All teams, all teams. Possible sighting of drones, originally from the west. Be on the lookout, call out targets, engage when in range."

91

THE TARGET

The drones flew fast and low, skimming the treetops. The operators sat on the rock outcropping, their feet dangling over the edge like little kids as they used their phones to see what the drones' cameras saw. They flew the drones confidently, jinking left and right at random intervals, though they believed the drones were both too far out and too difficult to be engaged by the expected weapons at the plant.

Each pilot had his own general path laid out, though he could deviate as necessary. They needed to avoid being too close together until right over their target. Then, by necessity, they would land on the roof of the building covering the spent fuel pools.

The first two drones would blow a hole in the building's roof. Then three would fly in and damage the interior cooling systems, including the backup, redundant systems.

The other three would target the heat exchangers and water supply lines leading into the building.

With the systems damaged or destroyed, the water temperature in the pools would quickly rise. Under water, the fuel rods from the reactors would continue to release incredible heat and radiation previously used in the nuclear reactors. Radiation levels would rise, and hydrogen gas would accumulate. Eventually, the building would explode, releasing radiation into the atmosphere and the Hudson river.

The men had been told the explosion would set up off a chain of other explosions, culminating in yet more radiation released.

Millions would die.

92

THE ASSAULT

Eric floored the car, his blood pounding as he picked up speed. Dying this way would be so much better than wasting away in a hospice bed.

As he swung wide around the road's final curve, fenced in by guard rails, his lights picked up the thick raised barrier across the road. Disappointment flooded him. He wouldn't take any people with him. Still, he'd do his part. He would blow the barrier, which would allow the follow cars to advance to the gate.

The rest of them would get through.

Then the people of the city would pay.

He grinned madly and pushed the button on his detonator a second before the speeding car slammed into the barrier, blowing himself and the car sky high, lighting the night with a fireball seen for miles. The car flipped end over end as it exploded, coming to rest on its hood, fifteen yards from the main gate, blazing.

Ten yards behind it, the barrier stood, scorched but unharmed.

On top of the building a hundred yards behind the front gate, Jamison, Front 1's sniper, called to his team leader. "Permission to light up the guys in the grass, sir?" With the burning car, the men who had believed themselves hidden by the dark were now easily seen if one knew where to look.

The team lead called to his counterpart at the front gate, who confirmed the men would be at the outer limit of his men's weapons.

"Light them up, Jamison."

He took a breath, let it out, and fired once, striking the first assaulter in the head. Two more shots resulted in two more kills.

"Targets eliminated."

"Nice work, Jamison."

The second car accelerated towards them, speeding up as much as possible with the windy road. "Think you can take out the driver of the car?"

"No problem."

"Do it."

He took a few extra seconds, tracking the vehicle, preparing for the next curve, then fired. A half second later, the car slowed and turned lazily to the side. It eventually crashed into the guardrail. Three men jumped out, carrying weapons and running forward, leaping over the railing lining the road, heading towards the gate.

"Stand down. Let the main guards take them."

As he finished speaking, several automatic weapons fired, mowing the three men down.

They repeated this five more times, with Jamison taking out the driver before the car could come close, and the guards handling the passengers.

The machine gunner on Jamison's team grumbled. "Snipers have all the fun." But he said it with admiration. "Good shooting, Jaim."

On the north flank, the SRT team stood by, letting the everyday security crew take care of the foot-mobile assaulters who had cut through the tall fence. The tangos got the occasional wild shot off as they closed, but they didn't connect, and died far from their objective.

To the south, the sniper, machine gunner, and team lead shot the skydivers, disappointed the plane had turned away and they didn't get to fire the missiles.

To the west, at the river, things were not going as smoothly. The machine gunners on all three teams attempted to engage the drones as they started flying over the river in front of them, coming close to hitting one. But the potential collateral damage stopped them. There were vehicles on the road along the shore behind the fast-moving, zig-zagging targets, and no one wanted shot-up civilians.

The snipers didn't have shots either.

The drones were going to make it through.

93

THE 50

"Deploy drone nets," Robinson said on the open network.

Near him on the roof, Dellis and Whiting groaned. They called the drone guns 'One Shot Wonders' because they could only be fired once and weren't successful in the long-term. They didn't work half as well as advertised. The drone had to be flying relatively slowly, straight, and nearby for the shotgun-like weapon's netting to fly true, snagging the drone and taking it to the ground.

Every one of them preferred their chances with a gun, despite the difficulty of hitting the small drones with a bullet.

The facility had geofencing around it, preventing any drones with working software from approaching. But given the sophistication of the attack so far, Robinson suspected the enemy had hacked the software to ignore the automatic exclusion zone.

"Sir, I need you to range for me," Dellis said in her calm, serious voice.

He glanced over at her. She lay behind the dangerous-looking 50-cal sniper rifle. She'd gotten permission to acquire and train with the long-range weapon, the team's only one. The other snipers had been envious, but figured she'd never get a chance to use it. Their shorter-range weapons were more versatile and just as accurate, though didn't have the far reach the 50 did.

She'd worked her ass off on the range, kicking in her own money to buy ammo for training when she rapidly ran through her portion of the team's budget. This was the first chance to field the weapon that was comically taller and—they joked—heavier than she was. She'd allowed one day's worth of remarks about it, then put a stop to it with a demonstration of the range and power of the weapon, followed by hard, long stares into the eyes of the men who had been joshing about her new 'boyfriend.'

"Dellis, it's gotta be a mile plus. Across a river, with a breeze, and you can hardly see them through the trees."

"I can see their heads, sir," she said. Her lips were the only part of her body moving as she lay glued to the scope, her finger already on the trigger.

He admired her cockiness.

"We have local police on their way to the area now."

"They won't make it, you know that. What, they're going to park at the trailhead and yell at them? Or walk the miles in to the clearing in time to make a difference?"

She had a point.

"You think you can actually hit anything, or you just want to live fire your 50?"

"Give me a range, sir."

Her breathing slowed. She was preparing for the shots, waiting for his spotting and permission.

He had to call it in.

"River 3 to Base."

"Go River 3."

"We won't get all the drones. The success rate of the net guns on fast moving targets is low. Permission to engage targets across the river who appear to be drone operators?"

"How sure are you?"

She answered on the radio for him. "It's Dellis, sir. One hundred percent. Eight tangos and we've seen approximately eight drones. They're sitting there in a line, looking at their phones, occasionally glancing up at the facility. I can see their faces lit up in the glow, sir, and their hands are holding joystick controllers. It's them."

The response came immediately. "Permission granted. Engage at will."

"Sir?" Dellis said, her voice signaling the urgency.

He got to work with his spotting scope.

"Elevation: plus one hundred. Winds from the south at five, gusting up to ten." He knew she would be making adjustments as he spoke.

He narrowed his focus, in tune with Dellis. They'd done this enough times on the range for their breathing to slow and sync up.

"Twenty-two hundred yards. Eight targets. Start left to right: south to north."

"Shooter ready."

"Send it."

He heard the crack of the weapon.

Normally they would wait to see where the shot landed, but they didn't have that luxury. He kept his spotting scope on the first target while calling out the next, a formality, since she already knew where he sat. "Next target, two feet to the right, north."

Dellis answered without hesitation.

"Shooter ready."

"Send it."

As the rifle cracked again, he saw the first shot impact the tango on the left, blowing his head apart. The timing gave the illusion the second shot had covered the distance instantly and killed him.

"Head shot. Target one eliminated."

"Shooter ready." She wasn't even waiting for his spotting now.

"Send it."

Another shot rang out, and again it seemed like shot number three blew up target number two. But due to the several second flight time of the bullet, they were one behind.

"Two down." He adjusted his view to the right to see the next tango jump off the cliff. He lowered the scope to see through the many branches and panned right.

"Shot three missed. Down five, over one. Lots of trees and branches."

Dellis worked to reacquire.

"Think it's worth it? Lots of trees."

"Shooter ready," came her response, though he heard the frustration and concern in the two words.

"Send it."

Seconds later, he saw tango three collapse, dropping his drone controller and clutching his leg. With the power and size of the bullet, he would bleed out in a minute. The damage the 50-cal slug did at that range was devastating. "Target hit, leg."

The other men had also jumped off the ledge. "Target four, two feet right."

"Shooter ready."

"Send it."

"Shit," Dellis mumbled, then immediately fired again.

"Target down." The woman's abilities were amazing.

The rest of the tangos finally got smart and hid.

"I have no clear targets."

"Harassing fire?"

"Great idea. Send at will."

She fired. He saw the bullet impact the edge of a medium-sized tree one tango hid behind, then miraculously a body tumbled to the side, clutching his elbow.

"Hit! Must have ricocheted or gone through the tree."

She fired again, then ejected the magazine and inserted a new one. The man in his scope scrambled on the ground, then jolted as Dellis' kill shot struck true. "Target eliminated."

Five men were down, but the rest of the pilots had learned their lessons and stayed still behind cover.

Dellis kept up steady shots to the area, hoping to throw the men off their focus.

They had evened the odds: five pilots could no longer zig and zag their drones.

But they suspected the drones had been programmed to fly to their targets automatically.

94

THE CLEARING

As they hid behind thick trees, making themselves as small as possible, the remaining three serial killers realized their mission would fail. They'd been told five drones were needed to damage the facility enough to release radiation.

The five drones without living pilots would fly their pre-programmed routes, level and straight... and likely be picked off.

While jinking their craft on final approach, they discussed the situation.

"There are more defenders than we were told to expect," one said bitterly.

"Even in the worst-case scenario," another mumbled. He watched on his phone as tracers from a machine gun flew towards his drone. He angled to the side in time, then adjusted his altitude, diving lower towards the river.

"What do we do?" the first asked.

The third man, who considered himself in command since both their leader and his sergeant had gotten their heads blown off, argued for continuing. "It's the best chance at mass casualties. We don't know —the other drones might get through. We have to stick with the plan."

There was a brief silence from the other two. Then they each agreed, reluctantly. They were almost done. Success was no longer assured, but it would be spectacular if they pulled it off.

The first speaker, bitter about the extra defenders, set his controller down on the pine needles of the forest floor, angling the glow from the phone away from him so he would remain in darkness. He took three quick steps to the nearby tree where their new so-called leader crouched. His knife flashed in the glow from the surprised leader's phone, but the man didn't release his drone controller until a few seconds later when he died, his throat cut so deeply his head tilted back grotesquely.

The killer grinned, watching the blood spurt from the wound.

His joy at his latest kill—the tenth of his young life—was short-lived. He felt a stabbing pain in the middle of his back. He believed for a moment that the second speaker, the mumbler, had punched him. Then the terrible reality dawned on him.

He tried to turn. The knife in his back, which remained sunk in him to the hilt, twisted, slicing his aorta. He saw the excitement in the eyes of his teammate, a man he'd trained with for months. They'd laughed together, celebrated minor achievements, and looked forward to watching the TV news in the morning, relishing their deed.

Instead, his life left him as his heart pumped blood out of the wound. For a moment he grasped the irony of being betrayed by a killer seconds after doing the same himself.

Then he collapsed, dead, landing on his side, his lifeless eyes facing the man he'd murdered seconds before.

95

THE GOLD

Todd stood in front of Kelton, holding a gleaming knife. "I'm going to cut you loose. You're coming with me. Time for your big finale. I can see the headlines now: *Young Billionaire Dies Tragically on Mega Yacht.* Too bad, too. If you hadn't been so squeamish, I had planned on having you step down as CEO. You could have pursued some sort of side project. Space exploration or using your billions to cure diseases. But no, suddenly Mr. In-It-For-Himself is all about the little man."

"I'm not going anywhere with you. You want to kill me, kill me." Kelton put on his best salesman voice. "But how about a deal? I go with you, willingly. Or I'll write a suicide letter. How about that? Then you push me off the ship and sail away. I swim well, but I doubt I could make it to shore. *Young Billionaire Commits Suicide, Leaves Everything to Company Co-Founder.*"

He saw the gleam in Todd's eyes as he pondered the idea. "I like it."

"But in exchange, call off whatever you have planned."

Todd hesitated, then glanced at his watch. "Can't do it. One, it's already started. I couldn't call if off if I wanted. Two, as gratifying as it would be to assist you with the note, and hear you call me the company co-founder, it wouldn't work. I'm sure your will is ironclad, and I doubt it mentions me at all. Am I right?"

Kelton nodded. He'd never even considered putting Todd in his will. Why would he? They'd been college roommates, then Todd had helped him run the company. He could admit to himself that Todd had been the hands-on manager, but everything had still been his idea... and his seed capital. Without those, where would Todd be? Nowhere.

But he had to play along. He might be able to break free and get information to the authorities. His cell phone was still tucked into his front pocket. He'd dial 911. They were close enough to shore for cell coverage. They'd track the signal and send help, wouldn't they?

"What is starting? Will you at least tell me?"

Todd nodded, looking proud of himself and happy to brag. "Happy to. You know the nuclear power plant north of the city?"

"Nuclear... Todd, what have you done? You're insane!"

"I'm not crazy."

Kelton's face betrayed his skepticism.

"I'm. Not. Crazy!" Todd screeched out the sentence. For an instant, he looked like he didn't believe his own words.

Todd took a deep breath. "Don't worry. I am not insane. But I'm very good at what I do... not that you've ever recognized it." He stood and grinned maliciously. "I set them up to come close. Very close. The attack might succeed if they're extremely lucky. But they'll fail. Well... probably. There's little chance the bombs will damage the containment pools enough to release much radiation. But the attack will be explosive and the talk of the world."

He chuckled, seeming to enjoy Kelton's shocked expression. "And it will be discovered the Iranians are behind it, giving the VP what he needs to run and win next year. Giving me his old job..." Todd's eyes gleamed with a calculating look. "And should our friend have an unfortunate accident, I would end up in the Oval Office. To serve my country, of course, and finally have people realize my abilities."

Kelton tried to move to a more comfortable position in the chair and decided. "I won't go with you."

Todd picked up a two-pound gold bar from Kelton's desk, worth over sixty thousand dollars… and used as a paperweight. He hefted it, then knelt, setting it on the floor while he methodically removed Kelton's expensive leather shoe.

"There are worse things than dying, Kelton."

He pulled off Kelton's sock, which cost more than most people made in a day, then picked up the shiny bar. "I'm going to enjoy this," he breathed. As Kelton struggled to move his foot, Todd gripped it, then slammed the corner of the bar onto the pinky toe. The crunching sound came an instant before Kelton's scream.

Without hesitating, Todd brought the bar down on the next toe, and Kelton's screams rang off the walls of the room.

"Let it out. Make as much noise as you need," he yelled over the cries. "One, you've bragged on countless occasions about how much extra you paid to have the room sound proofed. Two, by now my man will have taken care of your two guards, and the only other people on the ship—the crew—have been confined to their stations on your orders, supposedly." He snorted. "You gave me so much power, and so little recognition. It's all coming back on you now, though."

Todd reached forward to the middle toe. "Now, what do you say? Ready to come along nicely, or do we finish this foot, and the other, then start with my knife?"

"Why, Todd?" Kelton gasped through the tears of pain.

"You called me your assistant!" He slammed the bar down on the third toe, then the other two in quick succession.

"Stop, please! I'm sorry, really, I am," Kelton panted. "I've been a jerk. No excuse. Just please, stop."

"Ready to go, or do you want the next foot?"

Kelton hung his head sadly, defeated. He couldn't take any more pain. And maybe there would be a chance to get away as they moved beyond the office. "I'm ready to go."

96

THE SHOTS

"Movement!" Robinson called, seeing motion in the clearing through the trees.

"I have it. Sending." Dellis didn't wait for the command. She fired, then fired again, then a third time, her first clear shots in two minutes. Though 'clear shots' was a stretch, given the tree limbs and branches between her and the man holding a knife in the green glow of her night-vision scope.

"Body shot," Robinson called. "Target down."

She heard machine guns open up near her, but kept her eyes on the clearing. She saw no movement.

"Splash one drone," came the excited call over their radio. A machine gunner from the next team sounded very pleased with himself.

"Two," the same gunner called. Robinson looked around at the three guns firing at the drones racing over the water. He couldn't see the drones, but trusted they had actual targets.

"Three!"

"Four!"

The gunners had an easier time with the drones as they flew straight and low, skimming the surface of the river. Since they were so close, the downward angle ensured no collateral damage. Except for the fish, and the machine gunners could live with those deaths.

"Five!"

"Don't shoot up the facility," Robinson called out, hoping it went without saying. Still, better to make it clear so the machine gunners would stop before destroying anything important along the edge of the river. "Switch to the net guns when the drones are feet dry."

"Switching. Here they come!"

The three remaining drones rose fast, then flew level and steady directly at the gunners spread out on the roof, apparently heading for a target further inland.

He heard the pops of the net guns.

The shriek of three small engines trying to spin rotors ensnared in netting sounded like angry, wounded animals. Three drones fell onto the ground at the base of the building.

Everyone dropped to the roof, heads down, waiting for explosions, but all they heard were the engines whining until they sputtered and stopped, ruined.

The men and women glanced at each other, making sure they were all intact and safe. Then they returned to scanning their sectors.

On the north flank, as well as at the front gate, the gunfire sputtered to a stop.

Still, they scanned the ground, the sky, and the river. Waiting, watching.

They saw no threats, but the night wasn't over yet. Until told to stand down, they would protect the facility. But in their guts, they sensed the truth.

They had won.

97

THE ATRIUM

Devlin had said there were no other security personnel, and the crew were confined to their stations, but Axe took every precaution he could. He glanced around the corner before he moved from the bedroom suite to the hallway.

Then he poked his head over the railing, looking down into the luxurious atrium at the flowers three decks below. Almost directly under him would be the office he had seen on the tablet security monitor. If he hurried, he might ambush the man holding Kellison hostage as they left the room.

As he crept down the stairs, shotgun at the ready, he couldn't help but notice the blood seeping from the gunshot wound on his side, soaking the expensive shirt and sweater he'd liberated from the safe room.

Not good.

His chest hurt from what he believed to be the several broken ribs. He wondered if his breathing had changed.

I bet the lung is punctured, or close to it.

He ignored the pain as best he could. The mission came first. If he could stop the attack on the nuclear plant, it would all be worth it.

He'd made it down less than half a level on the grand staircase when he heard a grunt from below, followed by a heavy door closing.

"Move. To the stern."

He recognized the voice as the man holding Kellison hostage: Todd.

He had nowhere to hide, but he moved to the far wall and crouched low. He'd be out of sight as they walked across the vast atrium to the wide hallway, then the narrower hallway leading to the speedboat at the back of the yacht.

He froze and tried to go into stealth mode, shutting down his body's energy, not entirely sure he could do it while in so much pain.

Todd pushed Kellison ahead of him, one hand gripping the taller man's neck, the other holding a pistol to his back. Todd didn't even look around as he marched a limping Kellison forward.

The shotgun would be ineffective: not enough range, and it would be dangerous to use so near a hostage, anyway.

But he still had the knife. He could creep silently behind them while Todd had his attention on his hostage, then—

"Help!" Kellison cried out, having noticed Axe out of the corner of his eye. "Help me!"

Idiot!

Axe dove to the left as the pistol went off, bullets dinging the wall where he'd been crouching. Then he slid on his stomach down the stairs, the edge of each one slamming agonizingly into his broken ribs as the bullets came closer and closer.

The next level was just ahead and would offer protection—if he could get there before a shot landed.

I'm not going to make it.

"No! Not my ship!" Kellison's anguished cry distracted Todd for the second Axe needed.

He slid to the small landing and rolled sideways over and over to safety. The pistol continued to shoot... but the bullets weren't near him any more. He recognized the sound of bullets striking flesh. A body hit the floor, followed by a long moan.

Axe brought the shotgun to bear as footsteps raced across the marble floor of the atrium below him. He fired at Todd just as he disappeared into the safety of the wide hallway.

Axe hadn't been fast enough. Sudden anger threatened to overwhelm him.

Five years ago I would have nailed him.

He had himself under control as quickly as he'd lost it.

Not now. Deal with the feeling later.

He kept the shotgun aimed at the corner, ready to fire if Todd stuck his head around to take a shot.

Standing, wincing in more pain than he'd felt in his life, he moved gingerly down the stairs until he reached the atrium.

The heady scent of the flower bouquets couldn't hide the smells of gunpowder and the blood coming from Kellison who lay on the cold white marble floor.

"I'm sorry. I'm an ass. 'Not my ship.'" He shook his head and rolled his eyes as looked at Axe, his hands on his bloody stomach. "What have I become?"

"Don't worry about it now." Axe knelt over the man, his eyes still looking at the hallway in anticipation of Todd coming to finish them off. "How do I stop the attack at the nuclear plant?"

"What? You can't. I tried. I offered to trade my life for it. He said it had already started and he couldn't stop it if he wanted to." Kellison looked down at his bloody stomach. "Go get him. Take the bastard out. I don't care about me."

Can I do it? Leave a man to die?

"Did you believe him when he said it was too late to stop it? Did he tell the truth?"

"Yes. Definitely."

"Then my priority is taking care of you." He reached into the back pocket of the pants he'd taken from the closet. He had not only his original trauma kit, but various additional pieces from the white medical cabinet.

"You keep your eyes on that hallway and yell the second you see Todd or anyone else. If you get distracted or close your eyes, we die. Understand?"

"I understand. But... are you wearing my clothes?"

"Yes, thanks. Nice safe room, by the way. Now, focus on the hallway."

Axe gently removed the man's hands from his stomach and ripped the shirt, revealing three entrance wounds. He felt under the man's back. No exit wounds.

He went to it, efficiently working to stop the bleeding. He glanced at Kellison's eyes to make sure he was following directions, and also looked at the hallway every few seconds, just in case.

In a few minutes, he'd done as much as he could. "You have a cell phone?"

"Front pocket."

Axe retrieved it and grabbed Kellison's finger to unlock it, then dialed Tucci.

"Still alive?" Tucci sounded surprised.

"Barely. Need a medivac. Me plus one. Three gunshots to the stomach. ASAP." He heard switches being flicked and the sound of the helicopter's engine turning over before he finished speaking.

"Just tell me where."

"Off the coast of the estate, south shore of the island. Look for the enormous yacht. Helipad on the bow."

"You're on a yacht?"

"Hurry. Neither one of us is in good shape."

"On the way. Hang in there."

He ended the call—Tucci wouldn't be able to hear much with the engine starting anyway—and handed the phone back to Kellison. "Help is on the way. Will your crew come out to help?"

"I'm not sure. They were told to stay at their stations."

"Okay, well, try. Either way, when you hear the helicopter land, get to it. If I'm not there in a few minutes, you can leave without me."

"What do you mean, 'get to it?' I'm shot!"

"Welcome to the club."

He stood and had to grab a spindly antique table for balance and support, knocking over a large vase and bouquet of flowers, which crashed to the floor.

"Sorry."

"Wait! Where are you going?"

"I'm going to get Todd."

98

THE DOOR

Axe felt drunk. Light-headed, unfocused, and unsteady on his feet. He looked at the blood dripping from his side.

No worries. Medevac is on the way.

After reloading the shotgun with shells from his pocket, he cleared the big hallway, then hurried to the small one. He didn't see Todd.

There were several doorways. Had he been with his teammates, they would have cleared them before moving forward. Alone, he didn't have time for it. If Todd was smart, which he must be, he would make his escape.

Then Axe had a thought that made him pause, hesitating exposed in the middle of the narrower hallway leading to the stern of the ship. Todd could be waiting behind a door for Axe to pass, ready to jump out and shoot him, removing the only person who knew about his involvement in the attacks.

Is he the type of person to stay and fight? Or run and hide?

He regretted not asking Kellison.

He's no operator. But he's smart. So why choose one when you can have both?

The lightweight buckshot in the shotgun was designed for home defense. It wouldn't penetrate walls or do damage from a distance. But it was all he had. He wished he had his M4 or pistol, but the shotgun would have to do. Might be more suitable, in fact, if Todd had chosen the strategy Axe figured.

Remember, he's younger and faster. Plus, I'm not moving well. Do it right.

Axe kept low as he approached the closed door to the swim and docking platform, remembering its heaviness from earlier. Definitely a disadvantage in that it would be slow to open. On the other hand, it offered protection from bullets.

He tried to get an angle on the view and partly succeeded. He should have been able to see part of the mini submarine through the window in the door, even with the splattered blood of body guard number two. Since he couldn't, someone had moved it.

I'd go for the sub, too, depending on its range. Harder to track.

He rehearsed the plan in his head. Open the door, check the right side of the docking platform for the submarine. Shoot, then back. The door closes, providing protection. If nothing happens, repeat and shoot towards the speedboat.

He might be already gone.

He had a feeling. No, he would try his luck. Go for the win.

Axe prepared himself, opened the door, and fired once, then again, the short barrel shotgun loud in the narrow corridor. Then he pulled back and swung the door shut, just as three bullets pinged off it. If he'd stayed exposed a second longer, he'd be dead.

Axe hadn't seen him, but he guessed Todd was standing in the submarine hatch, like a tank commander in his turret.

He repeated the procedure, sticking only the gun around the corner, firing again, hoping for a lucky shot.

Once again, bullets slammed into the door.

He's an excellent shot.

They were at an impasse, at least until Tucci came with the bird. Then Todd would either be distracted, gone, or shooting at the medevac.

It was time to finish it. He reloaded the shotgun, then took a deep breath, psyching himself up for the maneuver.

Here's hoping he's almost out of ammo. Or nervous under fire.

He lunged through the door, shooting as he went, heading for the speedboat, hoping to use it for cover. But he skidded to a stop as he watched the submarine sliding below the surface.

Change of plan.

He closed on it, emptying the shotgun at it, doing no noticeable damage to the expensive craft.

Instead, the water closed over it.

Axe heard a helicopter in the distance as, without thinking, he dropped the gun, ran forward, and dove into the water after the sub.

99

THE DIVE

The cold water took away both his breath and his pain. He couldn't see it, but he could sense the submarine below him. It couldn't be far.

He kicked, reached, and felt the smooth skin of the exterior. Then it slipped away.

He kicked and pulled himself down, refusing to stop. He reached again and felt the sub. His hand slid once more along the top of it, then...

Got it!

He had a hold of the stern cleat used to moor it to the dock.

He was being dragged deeper into the cold, dark sea.

It had seemed like a good idea at the time. But now what?

He felt like a dog chasing a car who didn't know what to do once he caught it.

He tried to pull himself closer to the submarine, hoping to find another handhold, and another, until he could get to the hatch near the bow.

He wasn't thinking straight.

There's not going to be any way to open it from the outside, espe-cially under water. No one would design it that way.

He felt his lung go. If it hadn't collapsed from the broken rib earlier, it was now.

He'd been trained to never give up.

He'd made it through Hell Week. Been in impossible situations and found ways to live.

But he didn't have an exit strategy for this.

He equalized the pressure in his ears, hating the situation.

Then he reluctantly let go of the submarine and swam for the surface.

100

THE SUB

Todd leveled out the submersible and seethed. He resisted the nearly overwhelming urge to pound on the control panel, afraid he'd damage the expensive equipment and ruin his escape.

He would not become Vice President of the United States and finally have his talents recognized.

All his planning and effort... for nothing.

No. There is much more than nothing.

He'd make millions of dollars from his bets on the stock market.

And Kelton was likely laying dead in a pool of blood, ruining the tile floor of his precious yacht.

He smiled at the memory of shooting the man. It had been cathartic.

Todd adjusted his course slightly, angling closer to the coastline. He didn't have far to go. A yacht, much smaller than Kelton's but still extravagant, sat in a private marina several miles to the west.

No paper trail connected it to him.

He had never visited it, though he knew it inside and out.

A service kept it tuned, fueled, stocked, and ready to go at a moment's notice, just like several of the other nearby boats. The men and women who maintained the yachts for the supremely wealthy no longer marveled at the cost of keeping boats ready for owners who rarely—if ever—used them.

He would approach the coast and surface the sub. Then he'd swim to shore, letting the sub drift away or, if he could figure out how to override the safety measures, he'd sink it.

Either way, in a few hours he'd safely motor into the Atlantic, just another boat heading out at dawn for a beautiful spring day on the water.

Then he'd begin to plot his next step… and his revenge.

At the top of his list: the analyst and her fighter who had ruined everything.

His heart pounded faster and he smiled coldly. He would enjoy killing them.

101

THE BIRD

Axe swam on autopilot, moving slowly back to the yacht. He used the trick from BUD/S training, setting tiny goals. Part of him understood he had to make it to the docking platform if he wanted to survive, but he couldn't conceive of achieving it. Instead, he focused on what he could handle.

Three more strokes.

He accomplished it and relaxed for a second until the water dragged him under. Then he started another three. And another.

It surprised him when his arm touched the platform. In his pain and stupor he wondered if he had run into a whale, then realized he'd made it to the yacht.

Just get to the swim ladder. That's it.

He pulled himself hand over hand to the ladder and grabbed it, wondering if he had what it took.

Part of him, a larger part than ever before, told him to quit. To let go, float backwards, become one with the water. The pain would stop. The exhaustion, the frustration, and, most of all, the sense of failure.

He tried to force his mind away from it, but he couldn't. He'd failed Haley. He hadn't stopped the attack, hadn't interrogated the subject or gained any intel. And he had let the perpetrator, the madman, escape. All because he gave up.

Why not give up completely?

Perhaps it was his imagination, perhaps the ocean carried the ringing from a far-off buoy, but he distinctly heard a bell. It took him back to the days in the cold water at the edge of the beach on Coronado Island, linked arm and arm with his fellow students, suffering in the water. The instructors always had the bell nearby. They made it easy for anyone who wanted to quit. All they had to do was walk a few yards, shivering, exhausted, and miserable, and ring the bell. Then they could be comfortable.

I could be comfortable. All I have to do is give up, ring the—

His entire being rebelled.

No.

He pulled himself up, painstakingly, one rung at a time.

He flopped on the deck where he'd been earlier when Devlin held him at gunpoint. He had been spent then, but a SEAL saying claimed when you believed you were entirely spent, you still had forty percent left to give.

He'd given that amount, if not more. He was at zero.

His eyes closed for a moment. When he opened them, he wondered if he was reliving the night all over again. A face loomed above him.

He struggled for his knife, realizing how slowly he moved.

Then he recognized the face. Tucci.

"You don't look so good, brother," he said. "Can you walk, or do you need Army to carry your sorry ass?"

Axe held out his arm and Tucci heaved him up, then carried most of his weight as they walked to the helicopter waiting at the front of the ship.

He wasn't sure he would make it, and the word had to get out. "Call Haley Graves at the FBI building in Newark, NJ. But only her. Tell her everything. Got that?"

"Got it."

"Say it back."

He did and Axe nodded, satisfied.

"Just in case I don't make it, this is the important part. Tell her it was Todd, Kellison's number two. He got away on a mini sub."

He stumbled. Tucci took all his weight before he could get his feet back under him.

"Could you go get her? In Newark?"

"Yes, the no-fly rule ended earlier tonight."

They stopped next to the helicopter. Tucci tried to get him positioned near the rear door, but Axe grabbed him tight.

"If I don't make it, tell her this, but only in person: the vice president is in on it."

Tucci's eyes locked on his. "The VP? Of the United States?"

Axe nodded. "Don't tell anyone else, though. Let her handle it."

Tucci's face showed him fighting through the shock, but he finally nodded. Then he helped Axe sit in the open rear doorway of the bird and lay back.

"Hang on, this will hurt," Tucci said, then lifted Axe's feet as gently as possible and pushed him backwards along the floor.

Kellison lay next to him. He spoke, but Axe couldn't hold on any longer. The darkness took him.

102

THE ANGEL

Axe came to, confused. Someone was yelling at him.

"What the hell are you doing, Frogman? Who said you could pass out on me?"

He opened his eyes. A person leaned over him, the face indistinct, her dark hair lit from behind by the helicopter's interior light. An angel.

The angel's hand poked his side, peeling off the sodden gauze, making Axe cry out.

Not an angel. A devil.

She kept hurting him, pulling the dressing from the wound. When he started to black out again, she yelled at him over the noise of the helicopter. "'I will never quit.' Say it."

The words from the SEAL ethos meant everything to him.

He tried. His lips moved soundlessly. But the mere act of trying to speak made part of his soul stir. The part that made it through Hell Week. The part that had carried Ron through a running firefight.

"'I persevere...' Come on, let's hear it."

He whispered the words, not sure she could hear, but his mind latched onto the paragraph. "I persevere..." His eyes closed, but he forced them open to focus on the concerned face of the woman working on him, her hands covered in blood. His blood.

"And?"

"... and thrive on adversity. My Nation..."

He wasn't sure how long his eyes were closed this time, but some part of him wouldn't quit. He opened them and watched the angel above him move with practiced efficiency. "... expects me to be physically harder..." His eyes fluttered again and he let them close, a concession which allowed him to continue speaking. "... and mentally stronger than my enemies."

"Keep going. I can save you, but you have to fight for it."

"If knocked down, I will get back up, every time." He got the full sentence out. The helicopter sounds confused him, and he hoped they were flying away from action and not towards it. Either way, though, he had to get up. He got back up every time. He put his hand flat on the vibrating deck of the chopper and attempted to push himself upward.

The woman held him down. "You don't have to actually get up. Tonight, take it as a metaphor. Getting back up right now means staying conscious. Keep going. What's the rest of it?"

He settled down. He could do this. Especially if he didn't have to stand. He felt stronger, whether from whatever the woman was doing to his wounded body or the power of his mind and will, he didn't know. "I will draw on every remaining ounce of strength to protect my teammates and—"

His teammates.

Haley.

He had to find and protect Haley. He opened his eyes and struggled to push himself up again. "My team. Haley."

The angel held him down. He felt a tiny twinge of pride at the effort she put into it. "She's safe. And Tucci's up front, flying us to the hospital. Your team is fine."

He stopped struggling, relieved.

"Go on, finish it. Just the rest of this part," she encouraged gently. "You can do it."

"I will draw on every remaining ounce of strength," he repeated, "to protect my teammates and to accomplish our mission." He looked at her and she nodded, seeming less stressed about his condition. He noted the IV bag hanging from the seat above him. When had she put that there? Maybe that's why he felt better.

He felt the chopper slow and descend. "Hospital?"

She nodded.

He looked to his right. On the other side of the angel, in the narrow space next to him between the helicopter's front and back seats, lay Kellison, his pale face contrasting with his dark unkempt hair as he lay on his back, eyes closed. "What about him?"

"He'll be fine, thanks to you. Nice job treating the wounds. You saved his life."

His eyes caught hers and he once again believed she was an angel. "Thank you for saving mine."

She only nodded. "You're not getting out of this bird until you tell me the rest."

He felt the chopper land as he lost himself in her dark eyes. "I am never out of the fight."

"You're damn right you're not."

Then the doors slid open, and they took him away from her.

103

THE HOSPITAL

Axe came to slowly, drifting peacefully on the water, the sun warming his body. He kept his eyes closed, enjoying the feeling. He had no idea where he was, but guessed he rested on some sort of air mattress, near the shore but beyond the breaking waves. The ocean cradled him. He was safe.

He didn't want the moment to end, but he felt a flicker inside him. He had something to do. Were people waiting for him on the shore? Who would wait for him? He smiled. A woman, perhaps. An angel with dark eyes and dark hair. Strong, steady. Not prone to panic. Beautiful and capable.

He could almost picture her leaning over him…

With a jolt, he came fully awake. The yacht. The helicopter.

The angel.

Is she here?

He opened his eyes, then closed them again as the bright sun streaming through the hospital window blinded him.

"Hey, Axe. Take it slow."

It didn't sound like the angel.

"Haley?"

He cracked his eyes, squinting, as a strong yet delicate hand took his.

"I'm here."

He finally coaxed his eyes fully open and looked around. He lay on a bed in a spacious, single-patient hospital room. An enormous bouquet of flowers sat on the table under the TV mounted to the wall.

It touched him. "You brought flowers?"

She laughed. "No, sorry. Those are from Kellison, as is the private room and all your medical bills. You've made a friend."

He rolled his eyes tiredly. "Saving a guy's life tends to make people grateful. But what about—"

"Hold that thought. Someone's coming. By the way, I'm your daughter."

"Wait, what?"

"Excellent, you're awake." A nurse, mid-20s with short red hair, bustled in and checked on him. After a few minutes, she left, saying, "I'll get the doctor. She's excited to see her star patient."

As she left, Axe turned to Haley, his eyebrows raised. "Daughter?" *Am I actually old enough to be her father? Damn.*

"They wouldn't have let me in otherwise." She chuckled. With the sun streaming in, her blond hair shone, and he saw for the first time how smooth her face was, unravaged, as yet, by time. "And they'd never buy me as your girlfriend."

"Okay, I guess." He never realized how ancient the younger guys on the Team—and now Haley—must have considered him. "What's this about her star patient?"

"You took four units of blood, were hypothermic, had three broken ribs, a collapsed lung, internal bleeding, a bullet in your side, a bullet in the back of your head, two separate dog bites, plus—"

"Hold on. A bullet in my head?"

"Yes. I'm still working on a story to explain it, so play dumb. No memory of what happened. Got it?"

He nodded, trying to grasp the extent of his damages and how he'd gotten a bullet in his head. The ricochet?

He smiled at her tiredly. "Haley. You did good. We make an excellent team. I'm happy to work with you again... if it ever comes up."

She grinned, then hushed him. "Here she comes. She might pressure you into letting her use you as a case study or something. Just say you'll think about it."

A case study would bring more unwelcome attention, which he wouldn't allow. Too many questions.

The doctor entered, mid-fifties, carrying a metal chart holder, her blond hair flowing to her shoulders with streaks of gray throughout, all smiles. "Mr. Southmark, I'm sure you don't remember me, but I worked on you earlier this morning when you came in. I'm Doctor Abbey. How are you feeling?"

How am I feeling?

"Surprisingly well, based on what my... daughter," he managed to croak out the word, "says are my injuries."

"Well, that feeling is the drugs, but we'll be weaning you off those pretty quickly." She poked and prodded at him more extensively than the nurse had, but seemed satisfied with his status. "I never would have believed you could survive your ordeal, and frankly, thought you would die on the table last night. Want to tell me about what happened?"

"It's all a blur, actually."

She raised her eyebrows and he could tell she didn't believe him.

"I remember a helicopter..."

"Mr. Southmark, you don't have to be modest with me. I just spoke with Mr. Kellison, and he regaled me with the whole story. You're a hero, defending him from the men who attempted to take over his yacht, then saving his life after they shot him."

His eyes must have betrayed his shock at the audacious lie, which the doctor misunderstood. "Mr. Kellison said you'd be humble." She spoke quietly with her eyebrows raised. "Maybe now he'll be able to remember your name!"

Axe covered. "Yes, well, he's so wealthy, and I'm just one of many in his security detail."

Her eyes dropped, and she frowned. "Of course, I'm sorry about your colleagues who died. A tragedy."

He felt bad for the two personal bodyguards who had been misled by Devlin and Todd. But they'd more than likely also been bad guys, dishonorably discharged from the military, and there had been too much at stake to allow himself to be captured.

"The police will want to speak with you, of course, but Mr. Kellison has already made it clear he doesn't want any publicity for himself or his security team. He assumed you'd feel the same." She left it as a question.

"Honestly, I don't remember much about last night. A few flashes: a helicopter, as I said, and…"

"And?"

He hesitated again. He knew how it would sound. "An angel?"

Both women looked at him strangely.

Dr. Abbey shared a quick look with Haley, then addressed Axe. "You didn't code when I had you, so I don't know about angels. But on the medivac chopper…" She hesitated, then asked, "Did you see a bright light, or a tunnel of light, anything like that?"

They had it wrong… or did they? Had he died? "In the helicopter," he started, looking at Haley, then back at the doctor. "I saw… a woman." There had to be a logical explanation. "A nurse or doctor?"

Both women shook their heads. "I didn't see the helicopter, sorry."

She checked her chart, made a note, then addressed Haley more than Axe. "Anything you and your father need, don't hesitate to ask. Mr. Kellison has made it clear. Whatever you need."

"Thank you, doctor, we appreciate it."

The doctor turned to Axe. "Rest now, Mr. Southmark. The pain medication will wear off shortly. You'll start to hurt. I'd like to get you off the good stuff as soon as possible, but if you need one more dose, we can discuss it. Just ring your call button when you start to feel pain. I'm just down the hall."

Haley handled the pleasantries as the doctor left.

"I should get with Kellison and hear what crazy story he's come up with. You okay for a bit?"

"No!" His vehemence took her back. "What happened at the nuclear power plant? What's going on?"

"You don't know? I'm sorry, of course you haven't heard. The attack failed. A Special Resources Team showed up around 11 PM to augment security. They made the difference."

He didn't realize how tense he'd been until he relaxed upon hearing her words.

"I'm relieved. Nice job."

"Me? You're the one who called in the cavalry."

"Your intel."

She shrugged modestly. "We got lucky. Relax, Axe," she said, attempting to reassure him. "We won."

He looked around the room, suddenly wondering how much they should be discussing. The large room had all kinds of equipment, but he didn't see a security camera. Did the nurses monitor the rooms via video and audio these days? "But what about what I had Tucci tell you?" he whispered.

Haley realized the situation as well, and leaned close, whispering. "I couldn't do anything about Todd. A submarine? I was way out on a limb already, and though I was correct about the power plant, I never brought it up officially, so suddenly announcing we had to pursue an undersea craft off the coast of Long Island wouldn't have gone over at all."

"So he's in the wind?"

"Or the water, but yes. Don't worry, though. I'll find him."

The look in her eyes left him with no doubt.

"Any sign of more attacks coming?"

"Nothing. So I came here when Tucci showed up with the helicopter. Lovely way to travel."

Why is she so chipper? What about the rest of it?

He struggled to lean closer to her but gave up. She leaned down when he beckoned, putting her ear next to his mouth. "What about the vice president?"

She pulled back and looked at him in confusion. She whispered, "What about him?"

"Didn't Tucci…?"

"He said he had more for me if you didn't make it." Her expression changed as pieces she'd previously considered started falling into place. She looked at Axe, then around the hospital room, looking again for security cameras, before finally turning back to him. "The vice president?" she mouthed soundlessly.

He gestured for her to come close again. He pressed his lips to her ear and told her the entire story.

Haley sat back, stunned, her face pale. "What now?"

"What now? I figured you would handle the spy stuff. Especially given…" He gestured at the chest tube for his lung and the IV in his vein.

She looked at him, eyes wide. "I don't know what to do with this!"

Axe closed his eyes, thinking.

"We can't do much ourselves, but you can pass along the intel. Can you get me a pen and a pad of paper? We have to go low tech."

104

THE ARMY

Axe wrote for a total of three hours. He had to rest twice and take a break for the police interview, entrusting the legal pad with his debrief to Haley while he claimed complete amnesia about the events on the yacht. He felt bad about it, but knew Kellison would supply all the needed details. Later, if necessary—and after a long conversation with Kellison—he could 'remember' important details to collaborate the account.

Tucci had remained on standby for Axe. He arrived in the hospital room less than fifteen minutes after Axe called him.

"Looking better. You scared me for a minute there."

Haley had swept the room and didn't see any monitoring devices, so they decided talking about the events of the night would be fine—at least in general terms.

"I wouldn't have made it without you. You saved my life." He extended his hand and Tucci came closer to the bed to take it. "Thank you, brother."

"Army is always saving asses. It's what we do."

He let the interdepartmental rivalry go. He was the best of the best, like Axe and his former Team. Tucci had earned his bragging rights.

"Besides, all I did was carry your half-dead body across the whole damn boat, then fly you to the hospital. It was Connie who saved you."

The angel. I knew it!

"Connie?"

"I know warriors, and I saw the look in your eye when we first landed in Montauk. Figured you'd more than likely need a medivac before the night was out. I called my ex-wife, who's a nurse in New Jersey, and begged for a favor. She put out the word on her network that I needed a nurse on standby to help a patriot who had a line on the terrorists. Long story short, a friend of a friend from Long Island volunteered. She drove out. I met her at the state park trail head and walked her to the clearing where I landed the bird. Spent a lovely day with her, showing her the helicopter, chatting. Cute, huh?" He whispered, "I hoped she liked me," he frowned, "but then I saw her face after she treated your sorry ass." He shook his head in mock annoyance. "SEALs." Tucci rolled his eyes. "She thought you were a goner when she started on you. Was very impressed you didn't give up."

"Is she here?"

"No, she had to get back to work at a hospital near the city. But I got her number. I was going to ask her out, but I could tell she wasn't interested. In me, at least."

He shrugged with regret and took his business card out of his wallet and stuck it in Axe's hand. It had the woman's name in perfect penmanship—Connie—and her phone number.

"She asked if I'd give this to you."

He took it gratefully and decided to press his luck. "You got one more favor for me?"

"Are you kidding? Mr. Kellison deposited a ton of money into my account, to be on standby for him, or you. I'll fly you wherever you want to go."

"Not me. Haley."

"Whoever. Where are we going?"

105

THE JAIL

"He won't talk to you," the muscular guard said, pulling at the key ring attached to his belt. His bald head, shaped like a bullet, gleamed in the bright fluorescent light of the worn prison hallway. "He hasn't said a word, except his name. Not one word. Can you believe it?"

"Unheard of," Timothy Jarsdel joked. He was one of the hottest up-and-coming defense lawyers in the D.C. area. His suit cost more than the guard earned in a month, but he was friendly with the man and treated him with respect. It paid to have friends, whether they were guards, police, or criminals. People hated lawyers... until they needed a good one.

"But no trouble, right? I mean, aside from not being talkative?"

The guard used his linebacker build to push open the heavy door to the attorney-client meeting room and smiled, the slight gap in his front teeth revealed. "Nope. Nice to have, for a change. Didn't even cuss at me." He gestured for the attorney to enter. "Bang on the door when you're done, counselor."

Next to the guard's solid build, the muscles Timothy worked so hard for paled in comparison. "Thanks..."

"Boone," the guard said, "Yes, like Daniel, but no relation. I don't think."

"Thanks, Boone. I'll be taking him off your hands soon. Glad he didn't bother you."

Boone closed the door and locked it. Jarsdel turned to look at his latest client, already seated with his hands cuffed in front of him, the chain running through a ring bolted to the table which itself was bolted to the floor.

Cody, the kid's name was, he recalled.

He slid into the seat across from him. "Hello, Cody. I'm Timothy Jarsdel. I'm your attorney. Your bail has been posted and you're getting out of here. Additionally, you have nothing to be concerned with. It may take a while, but I'll either get the charges dismissed or a not guilty verdict if the case goes to trial."

The red-haired kid, thin and lanky, sat stoically, staring at him without expression.

Jarsdel admired the kid's discipline.

When he had gotten to the office three hours ago, early as usual, one of the firm's partners had been waiting impatiently outside Timothy's office. "Come with me. Now," he'd said. Timothy had followed him to the large conference room at the end of the hall.

The seven other partners had been seated around the immense table, furiously writing on legal pads or typing on their laptops. It stopped him in his tracks. Rarely did the partners do legal work themselves. They had a dozen other young men and women like him, along with twice as many paralegals, to do the detail work. The partners met with clients and prospects to keep the business coming their way. They were the rainmakers.

"All right, finish up and get the file together," directed the founder of the company as Timothy entered. The partners sprang into action, tearing off pages from notepads and hitting the print button on their laptops. Soon the high-speed printer tucked discretely in the corner of the room hummed and spit out page after page.

"You will go to the prison," the company founder said. The man had to be in his eighties but showed up earlier than anyone else every morning. His sharp mind was an encyclopedia not only of the law but of all the power players in D.C.—and half the world.

"There, you will post bail for our client. He has been falsely accused of murder. You will escort him to a hotel—details in the file—where you will check him in. Make sure he has a complete understanding of how to order spa services to his room, delivery from nearby eateries, and the hotel's room service features. You will stay with him for the rest of the day, making sure he's comfortable, while reviewing his file and planning your defense of his case. Clear so far?"

Timothy had nodded, amazed. What—or who—had made these titans of the legal world jump like this? It had to be someone powerful or extremely wealthy to have this effect on the upper echelon of his firm.

"At no point will you interview our client about the events in question. You will use the police report, along with the information you will find in the file, to prepare. Should you need any assistance, you may call me at my cell number day or night and I will see to it. The number is in the file, along with the direct cell of every partner in the room."

Timothy's eyes widened. The phone numbers were well-guarded secrets. And the idea of calling the founder for help, day or night, made his stomach tighten. What had he gotten pulled into?

"There is case law, precedents, and more in the file. You will get this man off, preferably by having the charges dropped. There will be no discussion of a plea bargain. Our client is innocent and will be freed." The elderly man walked to Timothy, still standing near the door to the conference room, as he hadn't been invited to sit. The partners stared at him, silent and serious.

"If you feel you cannot get this man off, you will tell us immediately and provide us with specific reasons, along with your letter of resignation. Understood?"

"Yes, sir." He felt a trickle of sweat run down the small of his back despite the pleasant temperature of the room.

"Off the record," the man said, leaning in so close his well-styled white hair brushed Timothy's face as he whispered in his ear, "you are authorized to play hardball. Beg, threaten, or bribe if you have to.

Unlimited funds are available, though if caught, of course, it's your ass."

He stood straight again and grabbed Timothy's hand in a firm shake. "Make us proud, son. We're counting on you."

Sitting across from his new client, Timothy opened the thick folder in front of him, flicking through the papers, looking for the phrase he'd been provided to prove he was there as a trusted resource. He found it and looked up at Cody, who remained staring at him, expressionless. "I have a message for you to prove I'm here to help. I was told to tell you…" he looked at the page to be sure he didn't mess it up. "The only easy day was yesterday."

A relieved smile spread across the kid's face. His posture relaxed as he nodded in gratitude.

Timothy waited for the reply: one phrase if everything was fine, and another if the kid was in trouble. He replied with the phrase for all okay. "It pays to be a winner."

106

THE KITCHEN

The president sat across from his wife at the kitchen table of the residence at the White House.

The events of the previous few days had taken a toll on James. He looked exhausted, but despite the death and destruction, they had gotten lucky.

While the devastation on the bridges and tunnels had been horrible, the nuclear power plant attack had shaken him to the core. What might have been filled his mind the last two nights. After much debate with his top advisers, he had finally given the go-ahead to implement a crash solar and battery backup program for Manhattan, as per his chief of staff's suggestion. He would catch hell from some, and more than one adviser delicately suggested it might cost him a second term, but he saw it as a necessity for the safety and security of the city.

Through it all, the residents of New York City had stayed calm. The Oval Office speech, broadcast the night of the attacks live on TV and the internet, helped reassure them their government had a plan and had already begun working around the clock to provide them with food, water, and shelter. Ferries, helicopters and ships from all branches of the armed services were used to help anyone who wanted off the island. Private citizens had pitched in from up and down the coast, sailing their personal vessels to assist those in need.

Miraculously, the city came together. Crime was virtually non-existent, though when it happened, the local neighborhoods took it upon themselves to handle it, often harshly. And as much as he opposed the vigilantism, he and his advisers agreed it was better than lawlessness and rioting, at least until they had National Guard units on most blocks.

Brenda stood and turned on the fancy radio mounted under the kitchen cabinet, tuning it to a mellow jazz station and turning the volume up.

"Can you turn that down, please? It's been a long day."

"Dance with me."

"Honey—"

"James. Dance with me." The voice stopped him. Low, serious, and insistent.

He put down his glass of wine and stood, moving to her. One arm circled her waist while he extended the other to dance properly, but she pulled him close, holding onto his shoulders with both hands. He wrapped his other arm around her and they swayed.

"I went out this afternoon," she whispered in his ear.

"What? Where?" The country had been under attack earlier in the week. He couldn't believe she'd left the White House and was surprised he hadn't been told.

"Not so loud. Just to Sarah's house." Her best friend from grade school. Haley's mom. "Well vetted, well protected, and I told the Secret Service they could have all the time they needed, as long as it happened today."

It sounded suspicious. "Why?"

"Four years ago, when you declared your intent to run for office, Sarah and I made a pact. If either of us ever needed the other, for any reason, we would call. She's been my best friend forever, and I knew it would be good to have a friend not involved in the craziness of the campaign, or when you won, the White House."

"Go on."

"We chat every few days anyway, you know that. But this morning she called and used a code word we'd worked out back then. She needed me, no questions asked, so I went."

"And we're standing in our kitchen with the jazz station playing loud, whispering in each other's ears, because—" He closed his eyes, figuring out the situation. It had taken him longer than it should have. He was exhausted. They were whispering just in case he wasn't paranoid and people had succeeded in eavesdropping on him in the residence. "Haley."

"Yes. A back channel."

"What is it?"

"I don't know, but it's serious and extremely sensitive. Sarah didn't know either, but she looked terrified. Haley has apparently never asked for help before—you know how independent she can be—but yesterday Haley appeared next to Sarah in the grocery store line, to avoid anyone seeing them together, begging for help. She asked her mom to call me and get me to come over."

He felt her hand between them slide what felt like an envelope filled with pages of folded paper into the pocket of his slacks.

"Haley said for you to read it. It's the only copy, and she'll never speak of it, but if you needed to hear it one on one, she could arrange it. If you thought it would be safe, whatever that means."

"Thank you, my darling." He kissed her deeply, then said in a louder voice. "Time for bed?"

"Yes, I think so. Thanks for the dance."

107

THE FORT

James walked through the residence with the weight of the envelope heavy in his front pocket. He felt foolish, wandering around looking for a safe place to read the letter. His first idea had been to hide under the covers in the bedroom, but he discounted it as too suspicious looking. He doubted there could actually be surveillance of him in the residence, but just in case, he wanted to look normal.

He ended up back at the kitchen table, where the light was good.

If I am being watched, maybe they would skip a camera in the kitchen. No one would think of me doing important work here.

He removed the thick business-size envelope from his pocket. It had no writing on the front. The back flap was sealed normally and also had a small blob of what appeared to be candle wax on it. Haley, either being cute or cautious, though he suspected the latter.

Dear Uncle Jimmy, it began. It was one of the few sentences that didn't stun him.

First came the background. The entire story of Haley's abduction, the events at the warehouse. Her ordeal on the turnpike. The search for answers and the lack of evidence.

Then she started on the conclusions she'd reached… and how she'd been right so far. She did it without malice or blame, merely stating the facts. The presentation was logical, clear, and better than most of the briefings he received. All written in her neat cursive penmanship.

The kid missed her calling. She should have been a lawyer.

She described her asset that Admiral Nalen had sent her. A former SEAL, like himself, though James had never heard the name. He unfortunately had too many other details on his plate to learn the names of the generations of SEALS who followed him. He sounded extremely capable in Haley's description, though more cautious than he would expect. But, he supposed, it might be because of his age. Older and wiser.

It concluded with a word of warning. "Uncle Jimmy, what you're about to read is unverified by myself. I have little to no hope of confirming it via other sources. But you trusted Admiral Nalen, and he trusted Axe, as do I. He saved my life twice and nearly died getting this information. I believe him completely. I'll return after his report to add my final thoughts."

James had to pause. Reading Haley's report, which differed so greatly from the intelligence he'd received from other agencies, made him question so much.

She's brilliant… but none of the facts can be substantiated. Still, her intelligence had been correct all along. But how does it fit with what I've worried about—being under surveillance or having a traitor in my inner circle?

He reached for the last few sips in the wineglass he'd left on the table a short while ago, then stopped. He hefted the thick pages remaining to read. No more alcohol. He needed his focus. Instead, he rose and poured himself some orange juice, then started on the second letter.

108

THE LETTER

James put down the papers and reached for the glass of wine.

Screw it. I need this.

He downed it like he had just finished a marathon and needed a sports drink to replenish. The yellow papers, jagged at the top from being torn off the pad, lay in front of him on the homey wooden kitchen table, brought specially from their home in rural Virginia as a reminder of their roots.

It made complete sense. Between what he knew and what Axe had reported in the letter, the puzzle came together.

The vice president is a traitor.

He held himself in check, resisting both cursing and dropping his head in despair.

Work the problem.

He had inadvertently painted himself into a corner. Axe's actions were unsanctioned. If called to testify in front of Congress or in a courtroom, some would believe him, but others wouldn't. Many others.

In an investigation, the entire story would come out. His own actions enlisting the admiral's help would be revealed, along with Haley and Axe's roles. And yes, what Axe supposedly heard… while he sat, injured and bleeding, on a billionaire's yacht, hiding in a safe room and eavesdropping via a high-tech security system.

The vice president would have a cloud of suspicion, but there wasn't a shred of proof besides Axe's word.

Meanwhile, as president, his judgment would be called into question. There would be ample proof of his own misdeeds.

Peter would run against him in the primary and possibly win. If James beat him, he would then have to face the candidate from the other side, who would beat him up with the inappropriateness—or illegality—of his actions. James respected one or two of his challengers, but a few were idiots he dreaded running the country.

Of course, there is the possibility that Congress doesn't believe Axe and impeaches me for my misdeeds… leaving Peter in charge.

He wouldn't let the maniac win.

He considered his options, skipping for now the two that seemed smartest… and most extreme.

Leaking stories to the press was an option, hinting at the vice president's involvement in the terrorist attacks. But who would believe it? Would the sophisticated technology of today's reporters and their thirst for scandal uncover what Haley couldn't?

There were no guarantees.

Could he give Haley her own department and top secret mandate to find proof of the VP's treachery? No, she didn't think she could find any solid evidence, and the digging would eventually come to light.

And he still didn't know how deep the conspiracy went. Who fed Peter his information? Were they doing it out of loyalty? Duty? Had they been ordered to?

Every idea had immediate impracticalities or downsides.

He looked at the clock, surprised to see it after midnight. He had to be up in less than five hours for another day of managing this great country. Gathering up the papers, he returned them to the envelope and used tape from the kitchen's junk drawer to seal it closed. He'd sleep with it under his pillow and carry it on him until he'd read it a few more times, then burn it.

James leaned against the kitchen counter, absently turning the envelope over and over, searching his mind for any way to avoid doing what made the most strategic and tactical sense.

109

THE DATE

Axe's body had always healed quickly.

After writing the report for the president, and with Haley gone to handle the next steps, he gave himself permission to rest and recover.

He dreamed of his angel leaning over him and speaking his name. It wasn't the first time it had happened. Every time he'd slept in the past few days, he'd dreamed of her.

He opened his eyes, hoping this time would be different.

She wasn't there. Again.

But the nurse opened the door and poked her head in. "Mr. South-mark, you up for a visitor?"

Not if it's the police again

But he smiled politely. "Of course, thank you."

He waited, expecting yet another police interview. Apparently professing to have little memory of the events on the yacht bothered them, and they kept popping by for, "a few more questions." Earlier in the day, Kellison's lawyer had stopped by for a few quiet words, assuring Axe that all was in control and to stick to his lack of memory story. He was happy to. The police questioning bored him, but couldn't compare to the interrogation training courses he'd taken.

Instead of the detectives, in walked his angel. She was much more beautiful in person than in his memory.

She stood in the open doorway, a shy smile on her face.

"You up for some company?"

"Yes, please."

She didn't move. The skin around her gorgeous eyes crinkled as she chuckled. "You should see the look on your face."

He blushed. "Well, for a while I thought you were—"

Shut up, you fool.

She walked in, letting the door swing shut. Her face had little makeup, allowing her natural beauty to show. As she walked, the dark hair tied in a ponytail bounced. She wore a tight black long-sleeve shirt with dark pants, and her stylish black boots clicked on the floor as she walked to the side of his bed and sat in the guest chair facing him.

"Thought I was what?"

He tried to think but found himself tongue-tied, a first for him. He'd never been a smooth-talking ladies' man, but he had also never been a bumbling imbecile like he felt now.

"I've never seen a SEAL blush before. It's cute." Her sweet voice swept him away as much as her eyes did.

"I thought you were an angel," he blurted out. "I even asked the doctor and my friend about you. They were convinced I died and went to Heaven or something." He shook his head at the story and grinned at her. She smiled back.

"Well, I know your name is Alex, and I'm Connie."

"Yes, Tucci mentioned. But only after I made a fool of myself with the doctor and my friend."

"Your… friend?"

"Well, the staff knows her as my daughter, but she's not. More like work colleagues."

Connie seemed relieved. "Sounds like there's a story there."

He nodded. "You wouldn't believe it, trust me."

They sat looking at each other for a second until Axe spoke.

"Thank you for saving my life. I didn't think I would make it. The doctor and Tucci both said if it hadn't been for you…"

"You're welcome," Connie answered sincerely. "Just doing my job. Same as you. And don't worry, I don't expect you to tell me any part of what happened. I know how it goes."

He could see on her face she had experience in the secrets department.

"How did you know the SEAL ethos?"

"I dated a SEAL for a time. Quite a while, actually."

"Uh oh. Sorry. We can be a little… much."

"No, not a problem. I didn't mind the deployments—I value my alone time, and I am as dedicated to what I do as he was. It worked out great, actually. Some people look at long-distance relationships as a burden, all the bad with little of the good. But I loved it. Plenty of free time followed by a few weeks or months of fun when he came home from deployment. Right about when things were getting a little stale, he'd be off again."

"So what was the problem? If you don't mind me prying? Did he…"

"Oh, no, he's still out there. Though don't ask—I won't tell you his name. But let's just say monogamy wasn't his strong suit."

"Ah."

Risk little, win little.

"And now? Are you single?"

"Yes. Are you?"

"Yes."

They grinned at each other like teenagers.

"Well then," Connie said, "should we count this as our first date, or wait until you're back on your feet?"

110

THE CONFRONTATION

James planned the op as he had other dangerous missions he'd conducted.

The objective. Constraints. Resources. He considered previous mission lessons and how they could be applied here.

A list of all the actions needed to be taken.

Potential holes in the plan.

Contingencies.

Understandably, he committed nothing to paper. The plan lived solely in his head. He never considered asking Chad, his exceptional chief of staff, for input. It would have been helpful to talk it out, and Chad's advice would have been tremendous, he had no doubt. He would have kept his mouth shut, too. But James wouldn't put his old friend in a potentially difficult situation.

No. For this mission, he was a team of one.

After finalizing the plan, James gave himself two days to ponder it, looking for problems… and alternative solutions.

When he had the best plan possible and had ruled out all other possibilities, he put it into motion.

He invited the vice president to the Oval Office to discuss ways to proceed with the ongoing efforts to restore power to Manhattan.

It took an incredible amount of will to hide his revulsion for the man.

James put off the serious discussion for some time, asking Peter first about his workout regime, then about his children and grandchildren. He shared a long, drawn out story about his own family, and finished by saying, "But enough of the chitchat, Peter. We have a serious issue to discuss, don't we?"

They chatted for an hour. Not all of Peter's ideas were terrible. But eventually, James nicely escorted him from the office. After the door closed behind him, James returned to his desk and stopped the recording app on his secure tablet.

The mission continued when he later asked his chief of staff and a few of his closest advisers if the VP had been acting strangely. "He seemed... I don't know. Distracted. A little down."

Plant the seeds.

James ordered salads with fat-free dressing every day for lunch, and made a point of joking about his weight a few times around various people, from the Secret Service to his secretaries. He started taking an afternoon walk in the building, saying hello to staffers and walking up and down flights of stairs.

"Have to get in better shape before the campaign starts," he joked.

The final step came two weeks later when, fortuitously, a staffer mentioned the vice president's wife would be out of town for a few days.

Perfect.

Towards the end of the day, he asked his secretary to call the vice president's office and see if he was still in, and if he had a few minutes. "Tell him I need some exercise and I'd like to come to him. And I need some workout tips." Then he confided to her, "I hear he's been feeling not himself lately. A drop in might cheer him up."

A minute later, she poked her head in. "He's happy to come to you, sir."

James stood, picked up a pad of paper and his tablet, and hurried to the door. "No, no. I'll come over. The walk will do me good."

Since the journey remained in the building and it had become a habit for him to walk around towards the end of the day, it wasn't a big deal. He had his normal afternoon Secret Service detail leading and trailing him discretely along the way as he greeted the staffers he came upon.

He arrived at the vice president's outer office and greeted his staff with a few pleasantries. The VP stood in the doorway, looking pleasantly surprised at the visit. In the halls of power, who visited whose office made a difference. The president making the trip over showed respect.

"Mr. President, welcome."

"Mr. Vice President, thank you for seeing me," he joked. There were a few quiet, polite chuckles from the nearby office staff. Even the Secret Service agents waiting by the door to the hallway twitched their lips in tiny smiles. It never hurt to laugh at the boss's jokes.

"This is a rare treat, James," Peter said as he closed the door to his finely decorated office. While smaller than the Oval Office, the walls were painted a striking, rich blue, and the space seemed both more intimate and conducive to quiet conversation.

"I won't stay long," he said, moving to the windows and closing the heavy curtains after setting his pad of paper and tablet down on the coffee table by the couch. Peter would take it as a power move, like he owned the room and the VP only occupied it. But he needed the curtains closed. He couldn't risk anyone seeing what came next. "I just had a few questions for you."

"Sure, what's on your mind?"

"Well, a few things, but first, could you show me those fancy resistance bands you mentioned a few weeks ago? I'm trying to get into better shape and the old body doesn't respond well to heavy weight lifting these days."

Peter stepped behind his desk and opened the large lower drawer, pulling out three different brightly colored bands with a set of handles on the ends of the yellow band.

"Which is the hardest one?"

Peter handed him the yellow one. James put the middle under his feet and pulled as if doing a curl move with dumbbells. He nodded, impressed with the difficulty.

Peter seemed pleased with his approval. "I encourage you to get a set. You can carry them in a briefcase. Great for the campaign trail coming up, right?"

He hid it well, but James guessed Peter enjoyed the game, knowing he would soon declare his intention to run for president himself. He would revel in the publicity and chaos caused by a sitting vice president running for president against his own 'boss.'

"Can we talk, Peter?" James asked, holding the band and moving towards the couch.

"Of course, James." His voice had the smallest tinge of concern, impossible for most to detect. But James knew the man well.

Peter joined James in the small seating area in the middle of the room, directly under the grand chandelier, blazing brightly.

Here goes. This better work.

His tone turned somber, and he leveled his gaze at the man—the traitor—sitting in the comfortable straight-back chair next to him. "I've had my suspicions a while now, but I didn't want to believe it."

"Iran?"

James smiled. The man could play the game. Instead of sitting back and playing defense, he brought the fight.

This could be more difficult than I thought.

"I've always had concerns about them, but they aren't what I'm talking about."

The vice president wore a serious, encouraging look and waited for him to continue.

"I'm talking about your betrayal of our country, of course." He watched Peter closely, but the man reacted perfectly. His brows furrowed and head pulled back in surprise, which quickly turned to indignation.

"Excuse me?"

James waited. Silence can be a deadly weapon in experienced hands.

Peter turned angry. "I love this country, and I would never—"

James spoke coldly, interrupting him. "Stop. You're only insulting me and embarrassing yourself."

An innocent man would have protested and refused to stop. Peter shut up and glared.

Now I'm getting somewhere.

James continued, locking eyes with the man. "I kept the probe off the books by using Haley, my adopted niece. I know you've heard of her."

Peter sat still, his face showing nothing, but his silence revealing the awful truth of the situation.

It wouldn't hold up in a court of law, but this is all the confirmation I need. He's guilty, the bastard.

"I also enlisted a former SEAL. I guess you could call it my own mini CIA."

The VP must have seen the opening James dangled, because he jumped in with faked indignation. "That sounds illegal as—"

"As what you've been up to?"

The two men stared at each other, no longer bothering to hide their hatred.

Peter leaned back, ready to try a different approach. "James, I really don't understand where you're coming from."

"Cut the bullshit. Haley and the SEAL tracked down and caught your buddy Todd Burkley. They've been interrogating him for two days now. He's singing like the whole damn choir."

James caught a flash of fear in the man's eyes, gone an instant later. He sat in silence, but his body language betrayed him when he crossed first his legs, then his arms, moving into a subconscious protective posture.

"He's told a pretty interesting story." He stared at the man who dared betray the country. "About how you gave him the idea for the attack on Manhattan's electrical grid. You must have gotten the idea from the infrastructure report last year. He said you pointed him in the right direction to get started."

"That's a lie!"

James continued, ignoring the interruption. "All so the two of you could frame Iran and run against me for being soft. How could you?"

The vice president was losing it. His body tightened, and he shook his head emphatically as James spoke.

"None of that is true. The man is insane. All of it came from him. His idea, his—"

Gotcha.

Peter must have seen a look on James' face, because he halted, realizing he'd just been trapped into confirming his involvement.

You've got him on the ropes. Don't let up. Attack.

James gave him a concessionary nod, as if agreeing with him that what Burkley said might not be one hundred percent accurate. "But you went along with it, at the very least. You could have put a stop to it. Saved lives!"

Peter sat for a second, thinking, then visibly relaxed. He shifted in his seat, uncrossing his arms and resting his elbows on the ornate wooden arms of the chair. He looked like he realized the truth had come out, but wasn't at all close to conceding. "None of what he says is admissible in court."

James let out an angry laugh. "Court? You're smooth, Peter. I'll give you that." He shook his head with regret and looked at the floor, fuming. "You've boxed me in. There's not a thing I can do with this information, and you know it, you bastard."

He glanced up at the VP, who smiled smugly and seemed to sit up straighter.

Time to wipe that grin off his face and see how horrible he truly is.

"But the nuclear power plant," he said softly, aghast. "How could you put millions of lives at risk like that?"

"I had no idea about it!" Peter leaned forward, trying to convince James. "He sprang it on me, like everything else. All I agreed to was a small event. He's in technology. What we discussed led me to believe it would be a cyber attack on the electrical grid. A warning about our vulnerabilities. That's all!"

Whether it's with guns or other weapons, SEALs are trained to not only attack, but attack hard, with overwhelming force. To bring to their enemies more firepower and aggressiveness than expected. James did as he'd been taught so many years ago, this time with words. "He says it was all your idea. He wanted a cyber attack, but you said no, it had to be bigger and more explosive."

"A lie, James, you have to believe me."

And now the attack on the flank to achieve the true objective.

"When did you know about the nuclear plant? Early enough to stop it?"

James caught him unaware, not in control of his emotions. Not prepared to lie. His face told it all: he could have prevented it.

Belatedly, Peter must have realized what his face showed. He started to shut down, then stopped, his eyes locked on James. His look revealed he understood how much he'd given away. He sat back, crossing his arms again, reverting to his former position. "Sorry, James. Nothing you can do about it."

James sat back himself, realizing he'd leaned forward in his verbal attack. He sighed. "You're right. I can't say a word about this without dragging myself down. Some wouldn't believe it no matter what I said. Others would think I planned it and you were being sacrificed, taking the fall for me. Either way, I'd have to admit to selecting a traitorous vice president, illegally running an intelligence operation, torture, and more. Your political career would be over, but so would mine. We'd both be lucky if we were only impeached, but I suspect jail time would be a real possibility. More importantly to me, however, would be the damage done to our country."

"You have choices, James."

Here comes the sales pitch. This ought to be good.

James displayed little interest and tried to look defeated, gazing dejectedly at his feet.

"We pretend it never happened."

He looked up, raising his eyebrows.

Peter continued, leaning forward to persuade him. "No one knows but Burkley. Just Haley, but she's family, right? The SEAL will keep his mouth shut if you order him to. And Burkley swore the only traces left would point to Iran."

This time James held his tongue. He wanted to see how corrupt the man had actually become.

"We continue on as usual."

James paused for a moment, as if considering the idea. "Todd Burkley says you planned to declare your intention to run against me for president."

He shrugged an apology. "I could let that go."

James nodded.

Wait for it...

"But I'd need a few concessions from you."

There it is. The bastard. I wasn't sure before, but now I know. I have to do it.

"Concessions?"

"We'd have to strike Iran."

"They're innocent!"

"They're not innocent, James, they are merely not guilty of this particular offense we'll blame on them."

James held his tongue for a moment, then asked, "What else?"

"You'd put me in charge of foreign policy and prosecuting the attacks."

His voice dripped sarcasm. "So, just attack a foreign country because you hate them, and let you have full rein. Nothing else?"

"I didn't say that. Only one other thing."

"I'm waiting."

"You announce you're not running for re-election, and pass the torch to me."

111

THE BLUFF

Peter sat back in his chair. He locked his hands behind his head and stretched out his legs in the classic pose of someone who thinks they have won. His bald head gleamed in the light of the chandelier.

James took a deep breath and let it out slowly, preparing himself for what came next.

"Hand over the presidency to a traitor?"

"Not a traitor, James, a patriot. Iran is a threat which needs to be dealt with, decisively. You've proven you're not up to the task."

He nodded, which Peter mistook as acceptance.

"Well. I'm glad we had this discussion, James."

"Me too." He looked up at the smug grin on Peter's face, hating the man with his entire being, but controlling the rage that threatened to spill out.

He'd reluctantly selected the man solely for the votes he brought to the ticket, and had never guessed the choice would be so disastrous.

Part of him wanted to confess it had all been a ploy, that Todd hadn't been found, let alone captured. That when he walked into the room, he'd been suspicious but had doubts about what Haley and Alex had presented him. That Peter had fallen for it hook, line, and sinker, and wasn't half as smart or capable as he believed.

Instead, he played his second-to-last card. "I can't accept those terms, Peter."

The vice president looked surprised but unworried. "They are non-negotiable. I'm not willing to wait four more years for your endorsement."

"My endorsement will never come. In fact, we need to go the opposite direction."

Now Peter looked worried. "What direction would that be?"

"I need your resignation."

The VP looked stunned.

"Why in hell would I resign?"

"Let's leave out the fact you're a traitor and focus on the carrot... and the stick. You resign, effective tomorrow at noon. I'm sure you have plans in place to announce you're running for president. Instead of waiting a few more months, you can do it tomorrow at 12:00 PM. You resign under protest to my handling of the recent crisis. You can even hint at Iran being behind it, if you choose." He shook his head. "Hell, say whatever you want to say. But you'll say it as the former VP. Then, we run against each other." He narrowed his eyes and stared Peter down. "And let the best man win."

"A few problems. One, why would I possibly speed up my timeline for you?"

"Because of the stick."

"Which is?"

"I go public with everything. First, I'll go to Congress and tell all. I'll request a special prosecutor. Turn over Todd Burkley, Haley, and the SEAL. Instruct them to answer fully and honestly. Then, I'll answer every question put to me by the prosecutor... and the press."

He leaned forward with such ferocity it caused Peter to quickly press back into his chair.

"I will risk my own political future and reputation. If necessary, I'll burn us both to the ground."

He wasn't bluffing. He could see on Peter's face he understood the truth behind the words.

"So why let me resign and run against you? What dirty trick do you have up your sleeve?"

"No dirty tricks. I'm doing it because I believe I can beat you."

Peter laughed. "After allowing the greatest terrorist attack in years? Then not punishing the people responsible? Or," he conceded with another smug grin, "the people I will say are responsible?"

"If you're so sure, you have nothing to lose, do you?"

Peter sat, lost in thought for a full minute as James waited.

James saw on his face he'd reached a decision. "You give me until tomorrow at noon before mentioning my resignation to anyone."

One more concession. He shook his head in wonder.

Some people have to feel like they beat the other person. What ever happened to win-win?

"Fine. Noon for both of us."

Peter eyed him suspiciously. "How do I know you won't go to the press immediately?"

James stood and straightened his suit coat. "Would you say I'm an honorable man?"

Peter stood as well and nodded reluctantly. "Yes, I would." They stared at each other, the younger, heavier man with full, dark hair and the older, balding vice president, slightly shorter, both fit and strong.

"Then take me at my word. I will not mention it until noon." He looked at the VP with suspicion of his own. "Or until you do. I won't wait if the press has it when I wake up. You wait until noon as well. Do we have a deal?" James extended his hand.

They stared at each other, grim faced. Finally, Peter extended his as well. "We have a deal." They shook briefly.

"But, I need the letter now." He turned and walked to the vice president's desk and stood behind the chair, pulling it out and offering it for the VP to sit. "I'll dictate it, you write."

"Fine." Peter walked to the desk and sat down. He pulled a piece of paper from his top right-hand drawer and picked up a fancy pen laying on the desk. "But short and sweet. I won't thank you for the opportunity. Nothing like that."

"How about, 'I regret to inform you I am resigning my position as Vice President of the United States of America, effective at 12 noon on tomorrow's date.'"

James stood next to and partly behind the seated VP, controlling his breathing. Ready.

Peter moved the paper closer to him. "I can live with that," he muttered, and started writing.

James watched him carefully. As he finished the second word, he exclaimed, "Wait!"

Peter stopped writing with an exasperated sigh and started to turn to look at the president. "What now?"

James clamped his right hand over the man's mouth as he snaked his left hand around his neck. Then he held firm, applying pressure against Peter's cardioid arteries feeding blood to the brain.

112

THE LIGHTS

Peter's surprise wasted a full second before he made a sound, but James had planned for it.

"And then," James said loudly, laughing, "he fell over backwards, right into the water! Can you believe that?"

The office was by necessity resistant to eavesdropping, but James couldn't take any chances. So he continued his made-up story, laughing and carrying on as Peter struggled, trying to cry for help while using his considerable strength to free himself from James' experienced hold.

It takes less than ten seconds without blood to the brain to choke someone out. Sixty seconds would have killed him, which wasn't the plan.

Yet.

As soon as the vice president's head slumped, James released him. He hurried to the couch, grabbed the yellow workout strap and threaded one handle through the other as he returned to the limp form in the chair.

He slid the makeshift noose around Peter's neck and pulled

upward. The strap applied pressure on the arteries and cut off airflow at the windpipe.

He completed the process just as the man started to regain consciousness.

Peter, disoriented, reached for the strap digging into his neck before blacking out again.

James held on tight for another few seconds, making sure the man stayed unconscious, then spun the desk chair towards him. With a heave, he pitched the muscular body onto his shoulder in a firefighter's carry. He walked Peter to the chair where the man had smugly sat a few minutes earlier. He nudged it into place with his foot, he lowered Peter onto it.

Once again James held the strap high, cutting off the blood flow and oxygen, making sure Peter didn't regain consciousness. After a few more seconds, he stepped between the vice president's legs and stood on the edge of the chair, draping the end of the band around the sturdy main support of the chandelier.

He quietly stepped down, took the still-limp body in a bear hug, and hefted him up. Then, using muscles he hadn't worked this hard in years, he stepped up onto the chair and pushed hard, carrying them both upwards, his muscles screaming.

Clinging to Peter with one arm, he used his other hand to twirl the band around the chandelier several times before cautiously letting go of the body, letting the band stretch, tightening on itself and locking into place. The light fixture took the man's weight without breaking or dropping from the ceiling in a cloud of plaster and dust, which had been one of James' big concerns.

He stood, pressed against Peter to keep him from swinging, and waited.

Eventually, he used his handkerchief to wipe down the band where he could reach, doing what he could to minimize the fingerprints, just in case.

James stepped down, dusted the chair off, then pushed it backward so Peter's now-lifeless body dangled a few feet off the floor.

He retrieved his tablet and opened the recording he'd made of the

VP and him talking in the Oval Office days before, set the tablet on an antique table near the office door, and pressed play. He adjusted the volume, guessing at the correct level to be heard as a slight murmur outside the office.

He wiped the desk chair where he may have touched it, then used his handkerchief to move the vice president's pen to a more natural position, as if he had set it on the desk when he stopped writing suddenly. Then he angled the chair properly for someone who had abruptly stood up.

He looked at the paper on the desk. In his distinctive handwriting, Peter had written the date on the top right of the page. On the left were the words, "I regret" followed by the vast emptiness of the off-white paper.

People will ponder his regrets for years. If I get away with it.

Then he moved to the door, his back to it, listening to the recorded conversation between him and Peter. He took out his own pen and started making notes about the brand name of the resistance bands, their cost, and the workouts the vice president had suggested earlier. Then he turned a page and brainstormed solutions to the situation in Manhattan, adding suggestions the vice president had mentioned earlier.

From time to time, he glanced without regret at the body hanging from the light fixture.

James had done what was necessary for the country. A man like that couldn't be allowed to run for president. Couldn't be allowed out of office with the secrets he had learned as vice president. He'd proven his willingness to betray the people of his country for his own gain. This had been the only way.

Time for exfil.

James stopped the recording at the end of their casual discussion. He picked up the tablet, holding it behind the pad of paper. Then he put on his game face and opened the door a crack.

"Thank you for your suggestions, Peter. I appreciate it—and you," he said, standing in the doorway and looking back. "See you tomorrow. Have a good night."

He stepped through the door, shielding the scene behind him with his bulk, then smiled at the vice president's secretary. "Sheila, he said he wanted about an hour to do some thinking about this Manhattan issue we discussed." He waved the pad of paper with his notes.

"Yes, sir." She was in her late thirties and rarely saw the president. Though she was the gatekeeper for the second most powerful man in the free world, having earned the position as Peter's long-time aide, it still awed her to be speaking to the President of the United States.

"And can I ask you something in confidence?" James asked, leaning close so the Secret Service agents stationed near the door couldn't hear.

"Of course, sir." She looked eager to help.

"I understand if you're reluctant to discuss this, of course, but…"

"What is it, sir?"

"Has the vice president seemed… I don't know, I guess I've felt he hasn't been himself lately."

Sheila looked away for an instant, then back. It seemed to James like she either had noticed, or was uncomfortable speaking about her long-time boss.

"Never mind. I'm sorry I asked. But if he—or you, for that matter —ever needs me, please don't hesitate to reach out. Understand? The responsibilities we bear can be overwhelming at times."

The young aid looked relieved she didn't have to divulge anything. "Yes, Mr. President."

"Thank you, Sheila," James said in full voice. "Have a good evening."

"You too, Mr. President."

He walked through the west wing to his office, and called to his secretary through the open doorway.

"Mary Beth, would you please find me some exercise bands? The VP has just shown me his, and I liked them. They are…" he checked his notes and told her the brand name. "And would you find out from the chef what the vice president's favorite dessert is and have some prepared for tomorrow as a surprise? He seemed a bit down tonight."

"Of course, Mr. President."

"Thank you. I'm done for the day. Good night."

"Good night, Mr. President. See you tomorrow."

He took a second to delete the earlier conversation from his tablet, empty the device's trash, and leave it and his pad of notes on the desk.

Then he left through the side door, heading to the residence, where he would wait for the chaos to start.

Would there be questions, rumors, and conspiracy theories? No doubt.

Would he get away with it?

Definitely.

113

THE MOLE

Haley waited patiently outside Gregory's office, feeling confident and in control. The tables were turned. She would now confront Gregory, instead of the other way around.

While keeping her focus on the hunt for Todd Burkley and those who had worked with him, she made time each day for hours of snooping into Gregory's life. Bank accounts, investments, lifestyle, travel, all the big things. Plus the tiny details that could give away a mole.

She found nothing unusual. No financial irregularities, no family drama, and absolutely no strange behavior. He worked, he enjoyed dinner with his wife, a glass of wine while watching a series of streaming shows Haley suspected his wife picked for her enjoyment more than his, and retired for bed most evenings by 9:30. Then he woke around five, ran on a treadmill in their tiny spare bedroom while watching the news, and came to work to do it all over again.

She kept digging, expanding her search, eventually concluding that Gregory either wasn't a mole or was better at hiding his tracks than she was at uncovering them.

Finally, with the president's quiet approval, communicated through Haley's mom, then the first lady, to the president and back again, it had come to this.

She would confront him and, as Axe would say, "Shake the tree to see what falls out."

His footsteps echoed down the hall, giving her a chance to stand tall and prepare her recently discovered game face.

"Haley." Gregory didn't seem at all surprised to see her waiting without notice outside his office this early in the morning.

Did that mean he knew what she meant to do? He had been at this profession decades longer than she. Did it reveal his guilt... or his innocence?

He unlocked the solid door to his office and flipped the light switch as he entered, gesturing for Haley to follow. Gregory didn't seem to be in a hurry or reluctant. To Haley, it seemed like he treated it as another day at the office.

When he sat down behind his desk, blank except for a computer, which he didn't bother to boot up yet, she knew he understood this would not be a typical meeting involving updates on her various assignments or a warning of another upcoming attack.

He removed his glasses, sprayed them with cleaner he took from his top right drawer, then dried them with a cloth. When he replaced the round frames on his face, he stared at her appraisingly, waiting for her to make the first move.

Two could play that game.

Haley sat back in the comfortable leather guest chair across the desk from him, leg crossed over knee, wearing one of her several plain black pantsuits that mostly hid her figure, and waited.

After what she guessed was a solid sixty seconds of them staring at each other, Gregory slowly nodded. "I'm impressed, Haley. You've grown from the experiences you had a few weeks ago. Whether for the better or worse, however, remains to be seen."

She kept her face impassive, betraying nothing, though his analysis was accurate. Killing a man from a sniper position on top of a roof and a second man with a pistol—up close and personal—had changed her.

So had making tough choices as an analyst and as a case officer running a dangerous, highly competent asset willing to do her bidding.

She had grown up.

Gregory chuckled. "I would have gladly played poker with you last month. Now? Not so much."

Haley smiled slightly, though she doubted her eyes showed the same appreciation for the attempt at levity.

"Let's talk about you and the vice president."

Axe had taught her about attacking, though she had a lot to learn. She doubted she could get a man like Gregory to confess or give much anyway, but their discussion would be a good step one.

And it was a safer—and permitted—tactic, unlike Axe's plan, which had involved much more drastic measures of questioning... or at least the threat of them.

"What do you want to know?" Gregory looked unsurprised by the question—and open to answering.

"What were you feeding him, and why?"

At this he paused, narrowed his eyes, and appraised her again, even more closely. "Who is this coming from? You, or..." His head gestured in the general direction of the White House.

She stared at him, letting him wonder. He knew she loathed pulling strings or relying on her connections.

His face showed he had decided. He sat up straight in his chair and clasped his hands together, resting them on the desk. "I told the vice president everything, kept him frequently in the loop. The reason? He called me a few months ago and said he didn't feel confident the daily updates he received were unfiltered enough. He wanted a clearer, more direct snapshot, and he asked if he could talk to me directly should the country ever experience a threat or crisis." Gregory shrugged. "He hinted at wanting to look good in front of the president. To provide reassurances—if ever needed—straight from the horse's mouth, as he said."

"You told him specifically about my analysis."

"Yes." He had the decency to look uncomfortable, perhaps chagrined. "I..." he faltered. "Fine. I mentioned you by name several times. I wanted…" He stopped. Haley had seen him at a loss for words. "I played the game," he admitted in a rush. "Brown-nosing. Bringing your name to the vice president was a way to presidential favor. I always spoke highly of you, shared your outrageous hunches—"

She must have let her face betray her because he stopped and nodded a concession. "Which, yes, turned out to be entirely accurate. But Haley, to return to the school analogy, you don't show your work. You're doing calculations in your head the rest of us have to use scratch paper for. Until this crisis, you had no real track record, aside from the Boomer not being in that stupid village. How was I to know you're so brilliant?"

Was this the truth? Or a tactic to distract her with flattery?

"The vice president?"

"It was an unusual request, but entirely legal. I did what I did." He ran a hand through his long, gray hair, sat back, and crossed his arms. He looked finished.

Did she believe him? She checked her gut, which had never let her down.

Yes. He had bypassed channels, but legally and morally did nothing wrong. He'd tried to butter up the president via the vice president, demonstrating he was looking after her and touting her brilliance, hoping to move up in the world. Perhaps even his lofty position felt beneath him after a while.

Haley stood. "I'm only a junior analyst. You're the director. Thank you for indulging my questions."

Am I going to do this? It's an enormous step.

"You've given me some excellent advice and I know how much more I have to learn." She leaned forward, putting her hands flat on Gregory's desk and staring him down. He drew back in his chair. "But let me give you some advice, if you don't mind?"

Gregory nodded.

"Watch your step. If you're dirty, come clean. Or it will end badly for you." It was her turn to tilt her head toward the White House, where the country's former vice president had been found dead, having committed suicide by hanging himself from his office chandelier. "I'll see to it personally."

She held his eyes, her face set in stone, and watched his thought process play out. Wondering, like many, about the 'suicide.' And searching Haley's face to ascertain both the seriousness of the threat and her ability to carry it out.

His face paled as he realized the truth—it would happen as she said, if she decided it was needed.

Gregory nodded his understanding. She nodded back, straightened, and left without another word.

114

THE TEAM

Three Months Later

It took Haley and the intel team time to track him down, but they'd done it.

Axe had used the months to heal, get into great shape, and spend an excessive amount of time on the range. He had requested one favor from a grateful Admiral Nalen: when and if Haley found the bastard, he wanted to go on the assault to capture or kill him.

The strings that needed pulling had seemed insurmountable, but the grateful president, himself a former SEAL, made it happen.

"Welcome back, brother!" Red greeted him with a smile and a handshake after escorting him through the gate at the Naval base, a gate he had been welcomed through without waiting so many times before.

In some ways it seemed ages ago. In others, the time had flown by.

"Feels great to be back." Axe climbed into the passenger seat of the

Humvee as more memories flooded in. The base, the waiting, and of course the fifteen years of ops all over the world.

"I don't know how you pulled the strings, but I'm impressed. You must have some friends in high places."

He was fishing without making it obvious, giving Axe a chance to tell him the story if he wanted, or could.

Axe shrugged and shook his head.

The drive to the Team compound took only a few minutes. Along the way, Red explained the situation. "Not everybody's going to be happy to see you. A couple new guys aren't thrilled about an old man tagging along. And honestly, you know how it goes: once you're out, you're out. To a few, you're dead weight." He raised his hand as Axe protested. "Look, everybody knows you're capable and can handle yourself, but you haven't been training with us the last year. You haven't been on ops. Axe, you're not part of the team."

Axe nodded. "I know I'm along for the ride. I don't want to step on toes, and I appreciate the chance to tag along. Don't worry, I won't hold anybody back. And while I haven't trained as hard as you guys, I can hold my own."

"Glad we're on the same page. One more thing I'll tell you now, instead of in front of the men. I tried to get you stationed in a situation room far from the action. But, honestly, I didn't have the clout. I put my foot down, though. You're not in the lead element."

"Understood. I wasn't expecting to be."

Axe was disappointed, but had he been in their shoes, he wouldn't want a has-been disrupting the group dynamic, either.

"Where are you sticking me?"

"Towards the rear, with the Explosive Ordnance Disposal tech. For the assault, you'll be a nice, safe 800 yards away on overwatch."

A half mile from the action. He didn't like it, but he would live with it.

"Are you at least going to let me have a weapon?"

"Of course, no SEAL of mine goes into the field without a weapon. You'll have an M4 and a sniper rifle. We'll be happy to have you backing us up."

They pulled up at the building, and Red turned off the vehicle. "Remember, play it cool. Don't be too upset about the men's reaction. You're going and you're valued, even if you will be a little far from the action."

Axe didn't know what to expect as he walked in. At first no one paid any attention to him, but the room felt strange. He felt like everyone knew he had arrived, but no one wanted to be the first to welcome him.

After a few minutes, a few men looked up.

"Oh, hey, Axe," one of his old teammates called out casually.

"Hey guys."

Strange. The vibe the last time he stood in this room had been farewell handshakes and promises to keep in touch. Now, no one wanted him there.

Red waved him over to the wall of lockers where he stood next to a man in his late twenties. "I want you to meet Conrad. The 'Con Man' took your old spot."

The kid was young, younger than Axe had been when he joined the team. But he looked focused and extremely fit. The man wouldn't be here if he wasn't extremely capable.

He felt old.

It's a good thing I got out when I did.

"Nice to meet you, Axe. Heard a lot of good things. By the way, when we heard you were joining us, we pitched in and got a few things for the op. Hope you don't mind." He turned to his locker and reached into the lower part, pulling out a small box of adult diapers. With all seriousness, he handed them ceremonially to Axe. "Here you go, man. I know once you reach a certain age..." He looked sympathetically at Axe, not showing even a hint of a smile.

Axe took the box solemnly, nodding. "Thanks, Con Man. Very thoughtful."

"Axe," one of his other former teammates called to him from several lockers down the row. The entire Team had gathered around now, watching to see Axe's reaction.

"Listen, it's gonna be a long hike in to the X." He paused, considering. "The X is what we call the target."

They were laying it on thick now, treating him like both an old man and a new guy.

"You can use this. Just in from R and D. It's a mobile insertion device designed just for you." He nodded to a few other Teammates standing shoulder to shoulder. They stepped to the side, showing what they'd been hiding.

They revealed a walker designed for the elderly or those having difficulty with their balance.

It had four brand-new tennis balls, one on each leg.

He stepped closer to see they had covered it entirely with camouflage duct tape, making it ready for the op.

He looked at the men he had fought with. Ronbo, Hector, and Link, his old Team, were nearby now, trying to keep their faces straight and mostly failing.

There were giggles behind him, like children unable to keep the prank going any longer.

He fought for control of his expression. He let out a small chuckle to cover how touched he felt. The teasing was a sign of inclusion. He loved it. They accepted him, at least temporarily, back into the Team.

"That'll help tremendously, thank you all." He couldn't hold back a huge grin.

"All right, briefing in fifteen."

In small groups, everyone came over to shake his hand and ask what he'd been up to.

Link asked the question Axe suspected was on everyone's mind. "The only 'observers' we ever get on our ops are spies. Is that what you are, now?"

"More like 'spry,' than spy," Thor mumbled, to much laughter.

"Yeah, he's a real double oh seventy-seven!"

After slapping his back and welcoming him, they drifted towards the briefing room.

Ron held back to the end. He showed no sign of a limp from the blast that tore up his leg more than a year before. "Welcome back, brother. You were gone by the time I got fixed up. I never got a chance to thank you." He grabbed him in a tight bear hug and whispered in his ear. "You saved my life. Hell, you saved all our lives that night. Thank you."

It sounded to Axe like he fought back tears.

"I'm happy to have you along for this op… even if you are an old man."

115

THE VILLAGE

The tiny village has no cars because there are no actual roads. None of the small lanes are named, at least officially, though the locals surely had some way to discuss the location of various places. There are no maps—or there weren't until the intel geeks went to work and created one.

There is a yacht club in the small town. The expat community hangs out there, which is how Haley found the first clue of where their target had landed.

One of the younger expats, a self-made millionaire who sold his company and retired early, has a recently divorced sister back in the states. He mentioned in an email that she could come visit, jokingly adding he had met a reserved but pleasant man he wanted to introduce her to. She would love him, he wrote, as he has the most striking blue eyes he'd ever seen.

His sister works for the FBI. She had read a bulletin a few months before to be on the lookout for a man wanted as part of the Manhattan bombings. Their only proper description of him: he had penetrating, beautiful, "striking" blue eyes.

She reported the vague intel. From there, things took off quickly.

A pair of agents in their fifties visited, supposedly to research retiring to the area. Instead of visiting like the rest of the day trippers from the nearby popular tourist resorts up the coast, they stayed several days in the village's one tiny hotel, overlooking the beach. Of course they visited the yacht club twice to speak with the mostly American and Canadian expats to discuss the realities of living in another country. They balanced their questions about settling in the area with keeping to themselves, holding hands and enjoying a romantic vacation. The wife, a tan, attractive bottle-blond with an easy smile and friendly eyes, enjoyed walking along the beach and chatting up the locals with excellent Spanish.

Her husband, with his beer belly and pale skin, preferred to stay near the hotel with his binoculars, watching for wildlife such as the many bird species in the trees inland, or the whales that migrated offshore.

He caught sight of a tall, muscular man shortly after dawn one morning, exiting the local bakery with bread and a steaming coffee. Even from a distance, with his binoculars, it was easy to see the beautiful blue eyes, eyes that, as he put it later in his report, "could take your breath away."

Satellites had been tasked, and the man was tracked 24/7 as the mission planning began.

Axe and the rest of the larger-than-usual team inserted via a Combatant Craft Assault boat. It would wait on standby for them to return to their insertion point—a sandy beach leading to a small trail which wound its way through a lush jungle, eventually ending at the north end of the village—or come straight into the bay.

Some of the group hoped for the latter, as it would mean they were able to capture their target alive for interrogation.

Others hoped to enjoy the long walk through the trees to the beach, because the target would be dead.

The night was warm and humid. The sound of gently lapping waves fought with the quiet noise of insects in the trees as the men walked through the dark jungle. Axe brought up the rear, save for two men who kept watch behind them. He carried a long sniper rifle on his back, as well as the smaller M4. Not his original one from the previous year. Who knew what had happened to it—reissued to someone else or scrapped, as it had seen a lot of use. He had spent a few days of training on the range with the men to make sure it fired true.

More importantly, the men had a few days on and off the range with him to see he could still handle himself, and not pose a risk to them.

The narrow, four-story hotel lay on the north side of the village, almost directly across the small bay from the target's three-story apartment on a hill with what must have been a spectacular view of sunsets over the ocean.

The roof of the hotel would allow a great field of fire across the entire front of the apartment, including all the windows and one door. It would also serve as a perfect location to provide cover fire during exfil, though none of the SEALS figured they would need it. The locals didn't seem to be the type who would take up arms to protect an expat, no matter how much money he threw around.

Ronbo gave Axe a nod from his place further up the line of silently moving men, and Axe peeled off from the group. This was his stop.

The hotel made it easy. An outdoor staircase led past all the rooms, two to a floor, and ended at the roof, which served as a place for the laundry to dry during the day. He set up the sniper rifle, unfolding the bipod, then stretched out behind it, looking across the village. He could see the apartment perfectly through his high-power night vision scope.

As the team silently approached the target, weaving down the narrow lanes, Axe swept his focus on the apartment's third-story covered patio, the second-story windows, which the analysts believed looked into the bedroom, and the first-floor window and door. With a quick glance at the dirt walkway in front of the home, he returned to his observation of the building. He would continue his vigilance until the target was dead or in custody and he was called to meet the team for exfil.

At 2:30 AM, nothing stirred, until a dog barked from inside a home near Axe, quieting down after a few seconds, more than likely hushed by its owner.

Axe saw the team approach the building. They broke into smaller groups to cover the back and the pathways to and from the home.

The assault team stacked up, pressing themselves close to the building's exterior.

The time had finally come.

A man who moved differently than the rest, not as smoothly, stepped around the two men in front of him and approached the door. The bomb tech had worked with the team before. They considered him the best of a highly trained group. There had never been any doubt about him coming along. They had all read the after-action report from the last time Axe and the men had gone after the bomber. The tech would make sure the entrance had no trip wires, then be third through the door, immediately searching for wires, bombs, and any sort of trap.

They would do everything in their power to avoid the situation they found themselves in last time.

Axe's scan continued. The porch, then the windows below it. Down to the ground-floor window and door. Finally, the path, noting the tech's progress. Then he began again at the top of the building.

He saw a flicker of movement in the second-floor window. The gauzy curtains had moved. It could have been the light evening breeze off the water, but Axe had a bad feeling. He glued his focus on the window and saw the curtains move again. This time he saw a man part them with his finger and look out furtively, glancing first up the narrow lane that passed as a road, then the other direction, searching.

The curtains closed, but the man's peek had moved them enough to allow Axe the narrowest view into the room.

The man's side could be seen. It appeared to Axe that he was getting dressed, sliding his arms into a shirt, or jacket, or a—

"Hold!"

He'd been told to stay off the radio unless he had an emergency.

Watching the man slip on a suicide vest constituted an emergency in Axe's mind.

"Target at second floor east window just slipped on a suicide vest."

Axe waited, his focus on the window, willing the man back into view.

A second later, the man parted the curtain again and looked out. Axe could see concern, but also doubt, on his face. Perhaps the bark of the dog earlier had woken him. The visiting CIA couple may have aroused his suspicions, and he'd taken to sitting up, awake and alert, from one in the morning until dawn, knowing it would be the most likely time for an attack.

Or perhaps he just got up to pee and the energy of the village felt wrong.

Axe didn't care. He only hoped his teammates were pressed flat against the wall of the building below the man, unable to be seen, and the men up and down the lane were hidden.

The man surveyed the homes nearby and the tiny streets, then turned his focus further away. In a few seconds, his attention turned towards the roof of the hotel.

Axe stared through the scope into eyes that seemed, impossibly, to lock onto his.

Even through the night vision scope, Axe had no doubt. Between the piercing gaze and the suicide vest, Axe was sure. The man was the bomber who had trained the terrorists, built the car bombs, and worked for Todd Burkley on the attacks.

And he was reaching for a small square box near his shoulder that had a blinking light on the top.

Axe didn't think about how little time he'd spent on the range with the sniper rifle.

He didn't worry about the long distance or the breeze off the water.

He wasn't concerned he wouldn't be fast enough.

He exhaled and did what he'd been trained to do.

He took the shot.

116

THE SHOT

Axe gently squeezed the trigger and watched the man's head explode in the green glow of the night vision scope.

"Tango eliminated," he said into the radio. "He had on a suicide vest and was reaching for the detonator. No other view inside."

"EOD up," Ron said on the radio. Axe continued his scan of the building, noting the bomb tech checking the door again.

As risky as it would be, they still had to go in. With the bomber dead, their only hope would be any intel they could find.

The tech earned his salary, and all the beer he could drink whenever one of the Team was around to buy. He found tripwires, traps, and even land mines in the home, all armed and ready to explode, killing anyone wandering into the home. All were also primed to detonate if the blinking light of the detonator, found on the dead bomber's vest, had been pushed.

Standing in the second-floor window, Ron nodded to Axe across the bay, then pulled open the thin curtains so Axe could see in better. "Nice shooting, Papa," Ron said, using the new call sign Axe had been given as a joking reminder of his age and place. He wasn't quite old enough to be a dad to any of the team members, but that hadn't stopped them choosing it.

Two nights later, in a bar near their base, they spoke in low voices, reliving the success of the mission. The EOD tech was feeling no pain after the continuous supply of free beer from the Team. He commented about the explosives, shaking his head at the complexity he had found with the wiring and staging. "He had enough to take out half the town. We all would have been dead."

"Well, except for Papa here. He might have been far enough away," Hector the funnyman said, slapping his older friend on the back.

"Good thing it wasn't his nap time," Red added. "Laying down behind the rifle like that? And being up so late?"

"No," Link said seriously, leaning his large body forward. "I heard old people don't need as much sleep. They go to bed at eight, sure, but they're up at two in the morning. We planned the op around his sleep schedule. Why we had dinner at 4pm, too. Old man's special. Perfect."

Axe sat back and sipped his beer with a smile, reveling in the camaraderie of a job well done.

And payback delivered.

117

THE GUARD DOG

One Month Later

Axe stood in the small room towards the back of the art gallery in downtown D.C. He'd approved the final staging of his photos for his first gallery show. Dozens lined the walls, hung with care by his art-dealer friend and her staff, who went on endlessly about his art.

He turned his mind to the photo in front of him as he sensed Connie hurrying over. "The doors open in thirty minutes, but Kate says people are going to show up outside soon," she said as her hand slid into his. "If you want to get out of here, now's the time to make our escape."

He didn't want to stand around and have people ask him questions about his environmental views, the meaning behind his so-called art, or what lens he used.

He squeezed her hand and kept looking at the photo, debating.

Connie had talked him into displaying it. "It's spectacular. People should see it, even if it's not for sale."

He couldn't bear the thought of it hanging on the wall of someone who wouldn't understand.

He had been coming back from a nearby river where he'd spent two weeks trying for a shot. He was proud of the five-foot square print which hung near the entrance of the gallery as the showpiece. In it, a bald eagle's wings flared and its talons extended, snatching a fish out of the water. The eagle had looked directly at him as he clicked the shutter. Lit by the rising sun, the eagle had a challenging look in its eyes as it stared, mouth partly open, proud and unafraid.

A killer.

In its grip, the eagle's talons piercing its flesh, the fish looked as if it knew its fate... but couldn't believe it.

The photograph was magical, but it was not a pretty picture. There was a rawness to it. Predator and prey, caught in the moment of confrontation as the eagle won and the fish lost.

On the way home after nailing the shot, he'd stumbled into the right place at the right time. Several miles down the road from his cabin, he had stopped to grab a few photos of his neighbor's sheep. They stood around munching grass without a care in the world.

He wasn't sure why he stopped. Sheep weren't the wild animals he worked hard to capture. But something about the idyllic scene spoke to him, so he pulled off the gravel road, grabbed his camera, and approached the barbed wire fence to see if he could find a shot.

The sheep were unafraid and mostly ignored him, aside from glancing his way from time to time. But as soon as he kneeled down to get a shot through the fence, he felt a presence nearby. An immense white Great Pyrenees dog stalked towards him, stopping directly between him and the sheep. He stared at Axe. The challenge and warning in his eyes were clear. "Stay back... or else," he seemed to say.

Axe slowly raised his camera, adjusted the aperture, and shot away, getting the dog in focus in the foreground and the sheep slightly out of focus behind him, along with another guard dog further away.

It wasn't until he got home and saw the shots on his big computer monitor that he realized the specialness of the pictures. He saw the content, well-fed sheep who felt protected. And in the foreground, he saw faded crimson blood on the pure white fur around the dog's mouth. It was hard to see, but there if you looked. The dog had recently killed to protect his flock.

Connie had understood the specialness of the print the first time she saw it in his cabin, hanging in an out-of-the-way spot by the back door. He didn't need it displayed prominently, but wanted it out as a reminder of how he saw his role in the world. He protected the flock from predators.

The small sign next to it said, "Sold" in neatly printed letters where the other photos listed the exorbitant prices Kate had recommended.

Axe couldn't see the typical buyer of his pictures—wealthy women redecorating their homes, looking to add nature to a hallway or bedroom—choosing this one. And besides, he would hate himself for selling it to someone like that. Let them enjoy the idyllic photographs of wildflowers, the warmth of the mama bear and her cubs in the forest clearing, or even the majestic eagle and defeated fish. But not this one.

"How much for the one of the dog?" a woman's voice came from behind them.

Damn.

He'd dawdled too long, trying to decide about pulling the photograph. Now he'd have to deal with a potential buyer.

"Sorry, it's not for sale," Connie and he said simultaneously. He squeezed her hand and felt his heart swell with gratitude as she turned to deal with the woman so he wouldn't have to.

"Oh!" Connie sound startled. "Alex?"

He turned and found himself face to face with the First Lady of the United States.

He recovered quickly from the shock. "Mrs. Heringten, I'm Alex Southmark. It's a pleasure to meet you."

Who says SEALS can't be smooth?

"Mr. Southmark, the pleasure is all mine," she said, extending her hand for him to shake. "I've heard great things about your... photography... from my niece."

He nodded, unsure what to say.

"I understand it's not for sale. Pity. My husband would..." she paused, searching for the correct words. "Greatly appreciate it."

Axe didn't hesitate. The president would understand the meaning in the photograph. He removed the picture from the wall and motioned to Kate, who was hovering as close as she could without intruding. "It would be my honor for your husband to have it. No charge. I'll have Kate box it up for you."

"That's very kind. Would you mind if I made a donation in your name to a charity supporting wounded veterans?"

He was touched. "Not at all. That would be very considerate of you."

Her eyes held his, and he wondered how many details she knew from either her husband, her best friend, or her niece. She offered her hand once more. "Thank you, Mr. Southmark. For everything."

They gave the first lady a few minutes to leave out the back door, then they slipped out the same way.

118

THE OFFER

Haley fired smoothly, then reloaded before the *clangs* from the bullets hitting the targets faded.

"Nice shooting," Axe said, stepping forward.

"What could I have done better, coach?" She wore her blond hair scrunched up in a messy ponytail, black noise-reduction ear muffs, and amber-tinted shooting glasses.

Axe shook his head. "Nothing. You're a natural." He'd been meeting Haley at the range twice a week for the camaraderie... and to prepare her for a transition to the field some day.

At his suggestion, she carried a pistol full-time now. She'd also bought a small house—in the name of a shell company, to avoid a paper trail. Axe helped her add a security system, reinforced doors, the works.

Todd Burkley remained at large. He'd been rich before the terror attacks. Not as rich as Kellison, but still a millionaire. Haley and the analysts guessed he might have made millions more betting the stock market would crash and, specifically, the share price of Happastology would collapse.

He had the means and motivation to stay hidden.

Haley would keep searching.

He had no doubt she'd find him, no matter how long it took.

Axe got ready to do his own shooting.

Show the kid how it's done.

He'd been training hard, keeping up the skills, and was as good as ever. He'd also gotten faster.

Before he could start, he heard a voice he recognized from a shooting lane to their left.

"Impressive shooting."

Axe shook his head with a grin. The sneaky bastard had done it to him again.

"Admiral, come on over. I'd like to introduce you to someone."

He introduced Haley to Admiral Nalen.

"I'm glad I ran into you two," the admiral said, his eyes glinting. He again wore blue jeans and a pressed white t-shirt.

"Yes, quite the coincidence," Axe said dryly.

Nalen looked around and saw no one nearby. "The president has decided he needs a team dedicated to him. People he can trust, without layers upon layers of bureaucracy."

Haley shifted uneasily. "Bureaucracy insulates the president. Plausible deniability."

"Doesn't want it, doesn't need it. He'll win the election, and he wants a team in place. People who can get things done."

"Isn't that illegal?" Axe asked.

"Not if you're part of a newly created clandestine organization. Ultra secure. Elite. Small."

"How small?"

"Only two people. For now."

Axe saw Haley's excited look, then turned back at the admiral. "Let me guess. Haley and me?"

He nodded. "Are you interested?"

Hell yes.

"Maybe. Who's the boss?"

Nalen grinned, strange to see on his normally serious face.

"You?"

He nodded. Axe stuck out his hand. Admiral Nalen gripped it, then turned to Haley and shook hers, too.

Haley's smile lit up her face.

"Welcome aboard."

119

THE DAWN

Connie's kiss was full of promise. "Come to bed soon."

She went inside the cabin, leaving him to watch another few minutes of the sunrise. They made the drive to see each other every few weeks to spend a long weekend together. It worked out well for them, especially since she had switched to the night shift.

During his time off with Connie, they would relax, hike, and have fun. He didn't bother to take his camera out with them because, despite what the helpers at Kate's gallery had said, he wasn't an artist.

He would continue taking pictures as a career. He loved being in nature. Enjoyed the challenge of the hunt. And didn't mind sharing the beauty of the photographs with others who couldn't—or wouldn't—seek it out themselves.

But the mission that brought Connie and him together had reminded him what he was, deep down.

He was a warrior. A hunter. And, when necessary, a killer.

The world needed men and women like him. On ships and flying jets, grunts on the ground and analysts behind computer screens, they all worked together to keep the country safe.

But the world also needed him, specifically. Not on his former Team, as much as he wished it were possible. No, he was a few years too old, a half-second too slow for front-line direct action. There were others better suited for it.

He could be useful, though. With Haley and the admiral, they would do good work if—when—they were needed.

He was unique. Young enough to kick ass, but old enough to hold back when necessary. The mind of a strategist and a tactician. A sense of when to follow the rules, and when to break them.

And the dedication to never, ever quit.

The first three words of a line in the Navy SEAL ethos had always meant the most to him. He had lived it for fifteen years of active duty. Now he would continue to make them the cornerstone of his life. With one last look at the sunrise, the words came to his mind again.

I stand ready.

Author's Note

Thank you so much for reading. I really appreciate you taking a chance on the book and hope you enjoyed it.

I write a short story every month and send it exclusively to my newsletter subscribers as a way of saying thanks for your support.

First, you get the free short story about Axe's first combat operation as a SEAL, when the goat stepped on the landmine.

After that, each month (ish) you'll get a new (free) short story delivered to your email. For more details, go to: www.authorbradlee. com/shortstoryclub

Read more of Axe and Haley's thrilling ops in *A Team of Two, A Team of Three*, and *A Team of Four.* Visit www.authorbradlee.com for more or find them on Amazon.

Also, if you liked the book, please leave a five-star or written review. It helps new readers discover the book and makes it possible for me to continue bringing you stories.

I'm pretty active on social media, sharing photos (like Axe would take!) and writing progress updates.

I also occasionally ask for input on character names, plot points, or reader preferences as I'm writing the next book or story, so follow me and help out. (I'd also love to hear if you found any typos!)

I'm most active on Facebook but also post the occasional update on Twitter and IG.

Find me here:

Facebook: https://www.facebook.com/AuthorBradLee

Twitter: https://twitter.com/AuthorBradlee

Instagram: https://www.instagram.com/bradleeauthor/

License was taken in describing places, units, tactics, and military capabilities. Where technical issues and the story conflicted, I made the story paramount. I may also have made mistakes. I'm far from perfect. But I hope you enjoyed the story, characters, and plot despite any issues.

Made in the USA
Las Vegas, NV
30 September 2022